A new paper was being published. Its leading topic was the Queen's relationship with John Brown. There was a cartoon entitled "A Brown Study" which showed John Brown sprawling against the throne with his back to it and a glass in his hand, while the British Lion roared at his feet.

When Bertie saw it he was secretly amused. He had suffered so much criticism regarding his own conduct, but what was that compared with this?

Bertie arrived one day, uninvited, at the Queen's apartments and found the way barred by John Brown.

"Ye canna see the Queen now," said John Brown. "The woman's resting."

"I think the Queen will not be pleased to hear that the Prince of Wales has been denied admittance."

The Queen, hearing voices, called out: "Brown, who is that?"

"It's your eldest," answered Brown. "I've told him ye'll see him in the morning. Ye're too tired to be bothered the night."

"Thank you, Brown," said the Queen.

And what could Bertie do after that but go away fuming? Brown would have to go.

THE WIDOW
OF WINDSOR

by

Jean Plaidy

FAWCETT CREST • NEW YORK

THE WIDOW OF WINDSOR

THIS BOOK CONTAINS THE COMPLETE TEXT OF THE
ORIGINAL HARDCOVER EDITION.

Published by Fawcett Crest Books, a unit of CBS Publications,
the Consumer Publishing Division of CBS Inc., by arrangement
with G. P. Putnam's Sons

Copyright © 1974 by Jean Plaidy
ALL RIGHTS RESERVED

ISBN: 0-449-24151-3

First Fawcett printing: October 1979

Printed in the United States of America

10 9 8 7 6 5 4 3 2 1

Ceremony at Windsor

Mourning hung heavily over Windsor. The Queen was stunned; now and then her tears would cease and she would ask in a bewildered voice: "It's not true? Tell me it's not true. This time last year he was with us. Oh God, how could this be? I always believed we should go together."

But he was gone; and she would never see his dear face again, never chide him for not sitting long enough over his meals, scold him for going out without a warm coat or getting his feet wet; never again would they sing their duets together, sketch, walk, ride; never again would her temper flare up and force her to say hurtful things to him which he with his calm, loving kindness always forgave. Never, never again.

"Dearest Mama," pleaded Alice, "you must try to stop brooding."

"Do you think I shall ever forget him?"

"No, Mama, never. None of us will ever forget dear Papa."

"To you he was the best father in the world, the wisest, most tender parent a child ever had, but he was my life. Now that he . . . has gone, part of me has gone with him."

"Dearest Mama, you still have us . . . your children who love you."

Always demonstrative, the Queen embraced her daughter, but she thought: Nothing . . . no one can ever be to me what he was. But he has gone and life is over for me. I shall never be happy again.

5

She had made a terrible discovery. She had gone over everything that had happened during those days before the Beloved Being's death. He had been ill for some time. She should have heeded the warning; she should have been more insistent that he take care of himself. His colds, his fevers, his rheumatisms had plagued him for years and although she had never taken them exactly for granted she had not thought they could be fatal. And . . . feeling sick and ill he had gone to Cambridge to see Bertie. This was terrible. If he had not gone to Cambridge in that dreadful weather, if he had stayed at home to be nursed by his loving wife, the Queen, he would be here today.

But he had said: "I must go to Cambridge. It is imperative." And he had gone and he came back ill with that dreaded fever. And so he had passed away.

To be angry gave a little comfort; and she was angry. Bertie was wicked, for Bertie was responsible for his father's death. How could Bertie have behaved so? The Queen said to herself: The Prince of Wales, my eldest son, has killed his father, the Prince Consort.

Bertie knew. She saw from his face that this was so. He was shamefaced—only that! He should have been heartbroken. She could not understand Bertie. He was the only one of her children who seemed destined to plague her. The others were good children. Bertie was . . . well not so much bad (perhaps he was too young for that and it would come later) as careless, thoughtless, frivolous and, she feared, rapidly rushing along the road to ruin. He needed the firm hand of his father and that hand had been removed. The tragedy was that Bertie was the eldest son, Prince of Wales and heir to the throne, and he was responsible for his father's death.

Darling, beloved, most wonderful Albert had not told her why he must go to Cambridge. If he had not died and she had not seen the letter from Baron Stockmar among those not yet put away on his desk she would not have known that Bertie had been involved in a disgraceful affair with an actress when he was in Ireland at the Curragh Camp. This affair had gone as far as it was possible for such an affair to go—the Queen shuddered at the implication—and according to the Baron was one of the scandals being discussed all over Europe. How sad Albert must have been when he read of his son's conduct and how noble of him to try to keep this from her knowledge in order to save her pain. Instead he had gone out when already ill in dreadful weather to remonstrate with his frivolous son, his fever had progressed and he had come home to his deathbed.

I shall never, never forgive Bertie, she told herself vehemently.

Dear Alice was a comfort. She had grown up in a few days, changing from a child to a woman. Only a short time ago she had become betrothed to Prince Louis of Hesse with Albert's consent. What a delightful day that had been when dear Louis, so much in love, had been unable to hide his feelings any more and had proposed to Alice. Dear child, she was young—nearly eighteen—but then Vicky had been married at seventeen and was now a mother.

The Queen's tears spurted forth afresh. How Albert had loved his eldest daughter! In fact there were times which she believed she had been a little jealous of Vicky. She had disliked anything that took his mind from her, his wife—even his devotion to their eldest daughter. How wrong of her and how good Albert had always been. Now she was back to the eternal question. What was she going to do without Albert?

She thought of the others, Alfred who was nearly seventeen; Helena whom Albert had called Lenchen and who was fifteen; Louise, thirteen; Arthur, eleven; Leopold, eight and Baby Beatrice, four. Nine children and now she was remembering how she had dreaded their arrivals and the dreary months of pregnancy, how she had complained, been irritable and lost her temper—and that dear saint had always been there to guide her.

And now he was gone; everything brought her back to that dreadful truth.

There should be a mausoleum for him; she would superintend its erection herself. It would help to keep her sane, for when the enormity of her grief forced itself upon her she felt as though she were going mad. Life without Albert, going on and on for years alone! She realized with a pang that she was only forty-two, which was not really old.

But I cannot live long without him, she reassured herself. It will be a mausoleum for us both. Soon I shall be lying beside him.

Alice came to her and she told her of her plan.

"It shall be at Frogmore," she said. "I shall choose the spot and Bertie must be there with me when I do so." She shivered. But she could not speak of Bertie's behaviour to an unmarried girl. It would have been different if Vicky had been there.

"Yes, Mama," said Alice. "It will be something for us to do."

Alice was competent and cool, although grief-stricken herself but Alice had been her mother's daughter. It was Vicky who had been her father's.

Bertie was waiting at Frogmore to receive her—eyes averted, reading her thoughts.

His father's murderer! Our own son! Oh, what a price he has paid for his wickedness.

Bertie tried hard to show her that he intended to be a good son but she could not bear to look at him. She took Alice's arm and she and her daughter led the procession round the garden.

"This would be a good spot," she decided. "We shall lie here together."

The Queen's Uncle Leopold, King of the Belgians, who had been the father-figure of her childhood and the most important man in her life until her accession, when Lord Melbourne, her now dead Prime Minister, had stepped into his shoes, wrote from Brussels that she must not stay at Windsor.

He understood as no one else could, he insisted. He had lost two beloved wives himself; he was well aware of the Queen's affectionate nature; it would be disastrous if she stayed at Windsor. She must leave at once for Osborne. He understood the intensity of her grief and he knew that she needed the peace of her island home. There she would mourn silently. She must not attend Albert's state funeral. The experience would be unendurable. Bertie should be chief mourner and he must beg of her, as she trusted him, to leave at once for Osborne.

"Osborne!" she said to Alice. "Perhaps Uncle Leopold is right."

"But, Mama, you would not wish to leave yet. You will want to see dear Papa laid to rest."

"I don't think I could bear it, my child."

"But . . ."

The Queen silenced her by laying a hand on her arm. Yes, she would leave Windsor. Uncle Leopold was right. She would die or go mad if she stayed here. She did not wish to tell Alice that she had before her marriage sometimes thought of going mad. It was due to the fact that her grandfather,

George III, had lived out the last years of his life in that clouded state and there had been rumours that some of the uncles had taken after their father in this respect. Albert's guiding hand had led her into a calmer state of mind; but now that was no longer there and the fear returned.

Yes, she would go to Osborne.

Osborne in December was grey and gloomy. What place on earth would not be grey and gloomy in *that* December? There were memories everywhere. Together they had come to the old Osborne and his genius had created the charming place it was today. Here he had played his games with the children; making sure that there was always a lesson to be learned from play. What a wonderful father he had been—an example to all as both father and husband!

Why had Uncle Leopold thought she could feel better at Osborne than anywhere else? As if she could feel better *anywhere*!

And in the room at Osborne, *their* room, she must go to bed all alone. How cold, how dreary! She smiled fleetingly, thinking of how he was often asleep when she came up because she had stayed up for some reason. He had always been so ready to sleep. They should have taken greater care of him; but because his mind was so great they had forgotten his physical weakness.

She took a portrait of him and laid it on the pillow where his head used to be.

"Darling Albert," she whispered, "I could almost believe now that you are near me."

She crowned it with a laurel wreath and sat by the bed looking down at it and weeping.

"I have wept so much, dearest Albert," she said, "that I would seem to have no tears left."

She could not sleep; she put out her hand and touched the portrait; then she rose, and finding one of his nightshirts in the drawer, she took it to bed with her and holding it in her arms was comforted.

It was midnight at Osborne, with the wild sea shrieking as though it knew what a tragedy had taken place. The Queen liked to hear it. She could not have borne it if it had been calm, blue and smiling. But she was shivering; she could not keep warm, which was strange really for in the past she had been so eager for fresh air and had enjoyed the cool keen winds. Her attendants had, she knew, continually complained of draughts from the windows she had insisted should remain open. Albert had been so much better in the spring and autumn than in the heat of summer; although he had so many colds in the winter.

How the days dragged! Could it really be only a week since that terrible day?

There was a commotion without, indicating that someone had arrived. She rose and went to the top of the stairs. Her brother-in-law Ernest, Duke of Saxe-Coburg-Gotha, was below. He and his servants were dishevelled; they had just landed and the night was wild.

He saw her standing there and ran up the stairs to embrace her. They wept together.

"Oh, Ernest," she cried. "He has gone. We have lost him!"

Ernest could only murmur brokenly. But it helped her a little to see that the visitors were well received and looked after. She became for a moment the ordinary little housewife she had sometimes told Albert she would have liked to be; and when living in small houses like Osborne she had been able to play at being.

Ernest sat with her, talking. He was a year older than Albert and he might so easily have been her husband. She shuddered at the thought. How different he was from that incomparable angel. One could hardly believe they were brothers. Ernest so dark and saturnine—Albert fair and angelic. Ernest resembled his father the late Duke, not only in looks but in his ways. There had been a horrible rumour about Albert's birth and malicious people had tried to spread the story that he was not his father's son, because his mother had been involved in a scandal with a member of her husband's household, had been divorced and Albert had not seen her after he was four years old. What wicked stories people concocted about *good* people of whom they could only be envious. Albert certainly was different from his father and brother; she had become aware how different at the time of her marriage when Ernest had stayed with them and confessed that he was suffering from a horrible disease which was a result of his conduct in Berlin.

Dear Albert, how shocked he had been! He loved his brother though and had done everything to help him. That was years ago and now Ernest was married and had stepped into his father's shoes and become Duke of Saxe-Coburg-Gotha; he had no children. Albert had told her that this was sometimes a result of this terrible disease which she reminded herself severely he had brought on himself. She very much doubted that Ernest had mended his ways. In any case this childlessness raised a problem because if he had no heir one of Albert's sons would inherit the Dukedom—Alfred possibly. This was hardly a matter to be discussed at this time though.

They sat up late talking of Albert. Victoria told Ernest of the happiness she had known with him, of the thousands of joys now lost to her, Ernest talked of the old days when they had been boys together, fencing, riding, hunting, roaming the forests and finding specimens for their museum. "The Ernest and Albert Museum, we called it. We were as one. We had never been separated in our lives until the time came for Albert to prepare for his marriage."

They wept together and talked of lovely Rosenau where the boys had spent so many happy days and where Albert had delighted in showing Victoria the room he and Ernest had shared, the fencing marks in the wall, the trophies of their childhood, the mountains, rivers and pine forests.

When Ernest left for Windsor where he would attend the funeral she remained at a window waving until he could no longer be seen; and she shuddered to think how fortunate she had been to have chosen Albert.

That brought her back to the recriminations. I should have taken greater care of him. I should never have allowed him to go to Cambridge.

Oh, Bertie, Bertie, what have you done!

The Prince of Wales was dreading the ordeal. He was relieved though that his mother was not present. He knew what those reproachful looks implied. Papa should never have come to Cambridge on that wet and blustery day. Of what use had it been? The affair was over and he had promised not to behave in such a way again; but Papa need not have come tearing down to Cambridge on such a day to extract the promise.

Bertie was full of remorse naturally, but he could not help feeling that life might be a good deal more tolerable without his father's supervision. Everything he had ever done had been criticized; even his recent success in Canada and the United States had been attributed by his parents to General Bruce, his governor.

But life had become easier in the last year or so and this was entirely due to the fact that he was growing up. They could not treat him as a child for ever—much as they would like to. And Bertie knew that he had some quality which that dead saint had lacked. The people saw it—those in the streets, those he had met on his tour. They warmed to him. He smiled readily; he could not remember seeing his father smile. Bertie had a way of saying something to people which amused them or endeared him to them in some way. He had a sneaking feeling that those who knew of the Curragh Camp escapade thought it "only natural" and liked him none the less for it—perhaps a bit more. Lord Palmerston, the Prime Minister, for instance, had refused to give General Bruce the honour Bertie's parents had asked for him to have. "It was the success of the Prince of Wales," Palmerston had replied "not that of General Bruce, and Your Majesty's Government would never agree to give honours where it did not consider them due." Good old Palmerston! He had winked once at Bertie when he was leaving the Queen's presence after, Bertie was sure, having heard a diatribe on the reprehensible behaviour of the Prince of Wales. Palmerston had been a rake himself in his youth—and later. He understood that a young man had to break out sometimes.

Bertie was, of course, sorry that his father's fever had increased through his journey up to Cambridge in foul weather, but it was self-imposed and unnecessary—and Bertie refused to blame himself.

There was muffled bustle throughout the castle appropriate to the occasion. He would be glad when it was over.

The Guard of Honour of the Grenadier Guards, of which Prince Albert had been Colonel, was at the entrance of the State Apartments and members of the royal family and the heads of foreign states were assembled in the Chapter Room of St George's Chapel, waiting to be taken to their places in the procession.

It was time to set out.

Behind the coffin walked Bertie, chief mourner with his eleven-year-old brother Arthur and Uncle Ernest; members of the royal houses of Europe followed and the solemn procession began.

Bertie's features were serious; he was trying to think of the goodness of his father and he could only see that stern face which had also been so cold when turned towards him. He had been different with Vicky and the Queen and some of the younger children. But always he was the mentor, critical of others' weaknesses because he was so good himself. He had rarely smiled; he had frowned often at Bertie's laughter which had overflowed far too frequently according to his father.

"It was all for my own good," Bertie told himself. It was the best he could think of.

The choir were singing the opening sentences of the burial service. Outside in the Long Walk minute guns were firing.

The ceremony progressed.

At last they had placed the coffin at the entrance of the royal vault where it would remain until the mausoleum at Frogmore was ready to receive it. The funeral of the Prince Consort was over.

Bertie Must Marry

The Queen had decided that Albert's wishes should be carried out as though he were still with them; his rooms naturally should remain as though he occupied them; his clothes should be laid out every evening; she was determined to keep his memory fresh.

His greatest concern before he had died had been for the welfare of his son and he had thought that a visit to the Holy Land might have a sobering effect on Bertie. The Queen had agreed. Did she not agree wholeheartedly with all Albert's plans for the children? And never before, in spite of his very difficult childhood, had Bertie shown such need for guidance and care as he did at this time.

Alice was with her constantly. What a dear devoted daughter! So pretty too. Albert had said she was the beauty of the family. Her marriage should take place as arranged, which would be later in the year, though what a travesty it would be without her father's presence!

Alice was sympathetic and gentle—far more so than Vicky had ever been; but Vicky was now a woman of the world; and it was only to Vicky, of all her children, to whom she could talk of Bertie's deficiencies. Vicky, alas, was far away in Berlin, with problems of her own; but she did not shirk her duty and wrote constantly to her sorrowful mother. Perhaps Vicky more than any understood her grief and shared it to some extent, for Vicky had loved her father more than any of the others, as he had her. But Vicky now had her Fritz, who was kind and gentle, and her children Wilhelm and Charlotte. Darling little Wilhelm with his poor sad arm! His shoulder had been dislocated at his birth and he would carry that deformity through life, she feared. Not that it affected the dear child, who was bright and clever and as Vicky said, so full of his own importance. Vicky also had to contend with a certain amount of hostility at the German Court. She was the foreigner there just as her precious father had been when he came to England. How many times had the Queen been hurt and angered by the constant references to him in the Press as "The German". So Vicky was her confidante at this time and to her she wrote of her distress over Bertie.

Vicky replied that while she was horrified by Bertie's misdemeanour, she believed that he should not be judged too harshly. He would know that dearest Papa had died and that one of the last things he had done was to visit him, his eldest son, to remonstrate with him over his disgraceful behaviour in Ireland. Bertie must feel heartbroken because of this.

Heartbroken! thought the Queen. Bertie's feelings were too facile for heartbreak. He was not like the rest of the family. He was far more inclined to enjoy life than take it seriously.

Vicky believed that Bertie should continue with the tour of the Holy Land which Papa had mapped out for him, and while he was away the Queen would not be tormented by thoughts of his wicked conduct and travel could have a good influence on Bertie. One thing that had occurred to Vicky was that Bertie needed to be married.

Vicky spoke from the experience of her married status. Bertie, she said, was clearly not capable of great *restraint* and it might well be that if he remained unmarried there would be other escapades. The influence of a good wife could work miracles; and Mama would remember that dearest Papa had been considering this before he died.

He had, it was true. He had compiled a list of suitable Princesses—not that there were many, for they must be worthy and Protestant, and preferably German of course. He had so relied on Vicky's judgment that he had asked her to keep her eyes open for a suitable bride for Bertie; and Vicky, good daughter that she was, had taken a journey through Europe visiting different capitals and had carried out her father's instructions. None of the Princesses was entirely suitable for Bertie who would, in Vicky's opinion, need a beautiful and charming wife if he were going to be kept on a straight moral course.

Did Mama remember Countess Walburga von Hohenthal—but of course Mama remembered dear Wally. She was Vicky's very favourite lady-in-waiting because she was so gay and witty, fun to be with, and more English than anyone at the Prussian Court. As a matter of fact she had married Augustus Paget, the Minister to Denmark, and was now English by marriage. When she had gone to Denmark to marry him she had seen the family of Prince Christian, and Alexandra, his eldest daughter, was the most delightful Princess Wally had ever seen. Wally had thought at once what a good wife Alexandra would be for Bertie.

And, emphasized Vicky, it was imperative to get Bertie married.

So, thought the Queen, first a visit to the Holy Land and then marriage for Bertie.

Alice was peeping round the door, holding Baby Beatrice by the hand.

Four-year-old Beatrice was the only one who could comfort the Queen—although she would not admit to being comforted at all, which seemed sacrilege to Albert's memory—but Alice had seen her eyes light up at the sight of the child.

Beatrice ran forward and climbed on to her mother's lap.

"Oh, Mama," she cried, "you are still wearing your sad sad cap."

"Yes, my love," said the Queen.

"Take it off, Mama," said Beatrice.

"Mama cannot do that."

"But it is a *sad* cap."

"Mama *is* sad."

"Why?"

"Because Papa has gone away."

"Perhaps he'll come back."

The Queen's eyes filled with tears.

"He will if Baby wants him to," said Beatrice confidently.

"Oh, my love, and Baby wants her dear papa."

Beatrice was thoughtful. "Baby wants Mama to take off her sad cap," she announced.

"Mama, would you like me to take her away?" asked Alice.

But the Queen shook her head.

Bertie was delighted to leave England and escape the sombre atmosphere which the Queen created about her. How could he endure the reproachful looks which came his way?

Why couldn't his mother understand that he had only acted as thousands of young men did; in fact what he had done was taken as a matter of course by worldly people. A young man had to sow his wild oats; and how ever much he was restrained was certain sooner or later to find a way of breaking out.

He was going to be married fairly soon and he was not displeased by the idea. They were considering Alexandra of Denmark and if she passed the stringent test his mother would insist on, it was almost certain that she would be his bride.

She was unusually pretty. Vicky had arranged a meeting. Trust Vicky. She had always liked to command him and in the days of their childhood had had plenty of opportunities of doing so. He might have been Prince of Wales but Vicky had been Queen of the Nursery. She had always been so much brighter and cleverer than he was; and because she was his father's favourite had been his mother's also. He thought Alice much more charming than Vicky really, and clever too, but not in such a flamboyant way. Alice was always reading—he himself hardly ever read anything unless he was forced to; she knew quite a bit about painting and architecture, and what Bertie thought of as "things like that"; but because she was quiet and didn't call attention to herself they tended to overlook her type of cleverness.

Now Vicky was planning and plotting with Mama and the two of them wrote at great length to each other. Mama had always been a great letter writer. There was her Journal too; she was happiest now with a pen in her hands.

So matchmaking Vicky had arranged that he and Alexandra should meet "by accident". Last September she had invited him to visit her. What a contrived meeting!

Vicky had said he must see some of the German cathedrals which were very grand.

"Not too many," he had wailed. "In fact none at all."

"Bertie, don't be so unintellectual," Vicky had scolded. "In any case there is one you simply must see. Speier. It's magnificent."

Bertie grumbled but he could see by Vicky's conspiratorial air that something was afoot, so in spite of the fact that he was heartily sick of being led this way and that and was, as he had confided to some of the few friends he had managed to know at Cambridge, "in a straitjacket", he decided that there might be something more in this visit to Speier Cathedral than he had at first imagined.

He was right. There was. They drove out to Speier; and as Vicky led her brother in by the south door and was pointing out the intricate elegance of the moulding, at the north door the Princess of Denmark entered with two girls.

They greeted each other with just too great a show of surprise so that Bertie knew clever Vicky had arranged this; one of the girls was Princess Dagmar and the other Princess Alexandra. There was no doubt about it, they were two extremely pretty girls, which was surprising, for the beauty of Princesses was often exaggerated, disastrously so from the point of view of the Princes who had no choice but to marry them.

Alexandra? Yes, he could be quite interested in her; for what was almost as pleasant as her good looks was a certain sense of fun which to fun-starved Bertie was a great asset indeed.

It was quite clear that they took an immediate liking to each other, which would most certainly be reported back home by the vigilant Vicky.

So, in the not far distant future, marriage; and in the meantime, the Holy Land.

Of course he could not expect too much pleasure. He would have to be very solemn—or try to be. But his recent visit to Canada and America had given him a taste for travel and meeting people. It was something he was rather good at. He had an air of jollity which the people seemed to like as certainly as his parents had disliked it. He had what he had heard called "the royal gift". He could remember people whom he had met some time before, and could usually call them by their right names too. Although in his parents' presence he had been tongue-tied and inclined. to stammer, when he was meeting the people he was affable and voluble. The fact was though Bertie in private family life might be a dismal failure, in public life he was a success, and he could not help being thoroughly delighted that this was so. Now with his father it had been the opposite. The saintly Albert, revered by the Queen and the master of his family, had been definitely disliked by the people. Bertie would not have been human if he had not been gratified on those occasions when they had appeared together to notice how the people cheered him, the Prince of Wales, and ignored his father—and sometimes made hostile comment—wickedly gratifying but unavoidably so.

He had to be accompanied by a set of guardians naturally, and, before his death, his father had arranged that the Rev. Arthur Penrhyn Stanley should be of the party. Therefore nothing would satisfy the Queen than that this gentleman should be included.

The Prince groaned. The Rev. Arthur would no doubt be puritanical, otherwise his father would not have chosen him. Also in the party would be General Bruce, that martinet who had had charge of him for some time, Major Teesdale, and Captain Keppel. It was not a large party considering the way royalty usually travelled and that was hopeful.

The journey was exciting. The Rev. Arthur turned out to be a warm and sympathetic character, and General Bruce was no longer the stern governor he had once been.

After all, thought Bertie, I am almost of age. The Queen was always talking of lying beside his father in the mausoleum which was being erected at Frogmore and when she did, Bertie would be King of England, so naturally those about him must remember this.

How pleasant to visit the Pyramids, to stand close to the Sphinx, to ride on camels over the sand and later to journey on to Palestine.

The Rev. Arthur said that it was an important occasion because it was the first time since the fourteenth century that an English heir to the throne had visited Jerusalem. Here, Richard Cœur de Lion and Edward I had come to fight their crusades.

"Most inspiring," said Bertie; he would tell the Queen about it on his return.

He felt quite drawn towards Stanley, perhaps because he

had turned out so much better than he had expected, and when news reached them that Stanley's mother had died Bertie was very sympathetic. His easy manner of getting along with people was a great comfort to his new friend and Stanley was deeply touched when Bertie passed on to him a copy of *East Lynne* by Mrs Henry Wood which Bertie thought so entertaining that it would take his mind from his trouble. It was scarcely the type of literature with which Dr Stanley was in the habit of passing his leisure hours, but he appreciated the thought behind the offer.

They spent Easter Sunday at Lake Tiberius and from there journeyed to Damascus, Beirut, Tripoli, Constantinople and Athens. It was exciting travelling through these exotic places; and the more he travelled the more apparent became the Prince's flair for behaving in a manner which was acceptable to the people. He had a natural charm; the stammering Bertie whom his parents had deplored had become the garrulous, charming young man, invariably affable and with a very natural interest in beautiful women. Bertie began to realize that this failure to please his parents had in fact been his complete difference from his father.

He thought affectionately of the family at home—the sisters and brothers—and whenever he could find exotic articles, the sort of things they wouldn't have seen before, he bought them to take back to them. Vicky was interested in flowers; these he collected for her and dried them so that she would have some sort of idea of the kind of flowers that grew in far-off places.

During the tour poor General Bruce fell ill and it soon became clear that he was suffering from a fever which he had contracted in some foreign place.

The Queen was most concerned because Albert had chosen him to be Bertie's mentor and therefore she regarded him as the best possible choice for the role.

Bertie was less concerned; he remembered what life had been like under General Bruce, not always very pleasant, and although the General had changed his attitude towards him a little as he was growing older, Bertie had very much resented the restraint he had put on him.

He was finding that little had changed while he had been away. His mother was as mournful as ever. He had hoped that a lapse of time would have lessened her grief. But not so; it was as fresh as ever and her presence in her black mourning garment and widow's cap made gaiety impossible.

The children were delighted with the gifts he had brought. They shrieked with delight as they dressed up in the strange garments he had brought for them. Alice smiled quietly and when their mirth grew too noisy she reproved them gently.

"Don't let Mama hear you laughing so much."

So it was rather a grim home-coming.

Alice was a little unhappy because Prince Louis could not provide her with a home just at first. There was some wrangling going on about finding a palace for the pair which, considering he was heir to the Grand Duke of Hesse-Darmstadt, was, said the Queen, remarkable. However, it did mean that Alice would not have to leave her immediately; but she would be a wife and that would change her a little. With a husband beside her she would have less time to devote to her stricken Mama.

"Lenchen will do all for you that I have done," Alice consoled her. "She is growing up fast."

"Dear child! She tries hard. But there is no consolation for me, Alice. It lifts my spirits a little, though, to realize what satisfaction it must be to you to know how much dear Papa enjoyed your reading to him only a little while before he was taken from us. Do you remember the day when nothing would please him . . . not even Sir Walter Scott?"

Oh dear, thought Alice, she will go on talking about scenes from the past and work herself into such a state of misery that she will be ill.

"I remember, Mama," she said; and began to talk about the possibility of Bertie's marrying.

But it was so easy for the Queen to lead the conversation back to the happy days of her married life and the terrible loss and the certain knowledge that there could never again be any joy in her life.

Then there was more sorrow when General Bruce died.

The Queen felt this to be a terrible blow.

"Poor Bertie. What will he do now? Where will he turn? He has lost the dearest of fathers and now that good and honest man who was chosen to care for him and advise him has gone. He has sacrificed himself for Bertie for if he had not accompanied him on his travels he would never have caught that dreadful fever. Another death! Another valued life gone!

"Now," she confided to Alice, "there will be the task of finding a new Governor for Bertie. Oh, if your dear father were here how easy it would be. What a burden he took from my poor shoulders. Every day I realize more and more the tragic depth of my loss."

Alice's wedding day was approaching.

"Is it a funeral or a wedding?" the Prince of Wales asked his favourite sister.

"Poor Mama," said Alice. "She cannot forget Papa's death even on my wedding day."

"The people won't like it . . . a private wedding with no processions and no rejoicing!"

"Bertie, how could we have rejoiced so soon after dearest Papa's death?"

Bertie smiled at her affectionately. Poor Alice! She had borne the brunt of looking after the Queen while he had been enjoying life in the Middle East.

"It's no use living in the past," said Bertie. "Once you get away you'll feel better."

Alice gave him her quizzical smile. "It'll be your turn next, Bertie," she said.

He agreed.

The dining-room at Osborne had been turned into a chapel. The Queen sat near the altar under the Winterhalter picture of the family. She had made no concessions to the occasion and was wearing her widow's black with the cap which Princess Beatrice did not care for.

The Archbishop of York read the service and the Queen felt drawn to him because he was so clearly moved. She knew that his wife had died about three years previously and he was still mourning her. Before the ceremony they had talked of their dead and wept together.

The Queen sat forlornly thinking of how different it should have been. A fine wedding in London, with dear Albert, splendid in uniform, leading Alice to the altar.

This, she thought, is like plunging a dagger into my already bleeding heart.

When the married couple left for their honeymoon, which was to be spent at Ryde, she would send for Lenchen and tell her about her own wedding all those years ago and how nervous she had been, how young and inexperienced, how their father had looked as handsome as a god and even then she had not known what a blessing was being conferred on her.

My only consolation now is to do what he would have wished, she told herself.

So now she must concern herself with Bertie, for Albert had constantly said during that last year they had had together: "Bertie must marry. His nature is too ardent for him to remain a virtuous bachelor. His only hope is a good woman."

A good woman. Princess Alexandra? There must be no delay. But she must make sure first that Princess Alexandra was the *right* wife for Bertie.

Bertie himself was thinking: What a wedding! More like a funeral. Poor Alice. She'll be better off though with a husband and a life of her own. Poor Lenchen. It's her turn now to look after Mama. And my turn for marriage! What will it be like to have a wife? He was quite eager to find out.

He kissed his sister after the ceremony. "Bless you," he said.

"Oh, Bertie . . . dearest Bertie."

Her eyes smiled into his.

Your turn next, they said.

The Family at the Yellow Palace

Seventeen years before the death of the Prince Consort, there was great expectation in the Yellow Palace on the Amaliegade Street in Copenhagen where Prince Christian and his wife Louise were expecting their second child. Their son Frederick, known as Fredy, was just a year old.

Christian and Louise were poor; the Yellow Palace did not belong to them and it was only by the grace of King Christian that they were allowed to occupy it; but they were in love and happy. Christian was not ambitious; Louise was more so; but in these early days of marriage her great desire was to have a family and live for them. So, in spite of the expense of a new baby the child would be warmly welcomed into the household.

Louise stood at the window, with little Fredy beside her, watching Christian leave for the barracks. He was tall and handsome and if he were poor she did not care, for besides being extremely good looking he was kind, gentle and as anxious as she was to bring up their family in a proper manner. They had often talked about the children they would have. Theirs should be a happy family, although of course the children would be reprimanded when necessary, even punished—but only in a manner which would be good for them.

Oh yes, they had often made plans for the family, and now Fredy was to be joined by a little brother or sister.

Christian turned to wave; his groom, whose livery, she noticed, should have been replaced some months ago, helped him on to his horse, bowed, and Christian waving to his wife at the window rode off.

She smiled, thinking of her tall blue-eyed husband, Prince Christian of Schleswig-Holstein-Sonderburg-Glücksburg—a very magnificent-sounding title for a penniless Prince. But they were fortunate because of the kindness of the King, which was good of him really for they had no claim on him. Christian was merely the fourth son of Duke Frederick of Schleswig-Holstein; and even the eldest son had inherited a bankrupt kingdom because the Napoleonic Wars had ruined them; but since there was a family connection, King Christian VIII had befriended his young namesake, had given him a commission in the Royal Guard and the Yellow Palace for his home.

They were lucky. The palace was not unlike a French château of the smaller type. One stepped into it straight from the street, entering by big gates which opened on to a courtyard. It was an exciting house, even though some of the rooms were small; there were odd winding staircases and passages and nooks and crannies in unexpected places. It was, in any case, a home, and they were grateful for it.

King Christian lived near by in the Royal Palace and Prince Christian and Louise were often invited to pay an informal visit; close by in an imposing mansion lived Louise's parents—the Landgrave and Landgravine of Hesse-Cassel. The Landgravine had been Princess Charlotte, and was King Christian's sister.

It was all rather cosy and informal for Charlotte was good to the family at the Yellow Palace and was constantly sending gifts and between the King and the Landgravine they just managed on Christian's pay which was only ten pounds a month. Not very much to sustain life in a palace—even one such as the Yellow Palace—and maintain some semblance of royalty. But Prince Christian was happy; he was proud of his position in the Army; he had a wife whom he admired as well as loved, a son and another child on the way; he asked only to be able to keep them in comparative comfort.

Louise turned from the window. There were the servants to receive their orders—not many of them, only those whom her mother said she must have. Louise could manage very well. What a difference there had been in the Yellow Palace since she had taken over! Now all the cobwebs were swept away and the furniture shining; meals were served hot and promptly. She was a wonderful housewife.

The Landgravine tut-tutted and reminded her that she was the niece of the King, to which Louise replied gravely that she had reason to remember that with gratitude for to the King they owed their home and Christian's post in the Guards so she was not likely to forget.

The Landgravine was impatient. "With your looks and your talents you should not be an ordinary *hausfrau*. And when I think of Frederick . . . the only heir to the throne, what will become of Denmark I can't imagine!"

Frederick, the King's only son, was a trial to everyone except himself of course and his cronies—and there were many of them. They consisted of the artists and writers with whom he liked to sit and drink, and his mistresses with whom he walked arm in arm through the streets; or if they were shopping he would carry their parcels for them like any bourgeois husband. Frederick was a scandal in the royal family.

But she and her little family were aloof from royalty in a way. They rarely went to Court functions simply because they wouldn't have the suitable clothes and jewels. Even in the regiment Christian was poor. But who cared? Certainly they did not.

Life in Copenhagen was full of interest. She had enjoyed taking Fredy down to the harbour and showing him the big ships—Danish some of them, others coming in from all over the world. She would walk along the Sund pushing her son in his baby carriage like any matron of the town.

And now there would be another child.

She turned away from the window, shivering a little for it was very cold. Soon it would be Christmas. The baby should arrive a few weeks before the festival, she hoped. How wonderful that would be. Little Fredy would have his first Christmas tree and a little brother or sister as well.

The next day, which was the first of December, her child was born. It was a girl.

There was a great deal of discussion about the child's name, between her parents that was. She was not considered to be of sufficient significance for the King or the Landgravine and her husband to think it mattered what she was called.

Louise, however, suggested that it would be a pleasant gesture to name her Alexandra after the sister of Alexander of Russia who had been married to her brother and had recently died.

Christian said this was a capital idea; he usually thought Louise's ideas were capital. So the name was decided on. It was to be Alexandra Caroline Marie Charlotte Louise Julie.

"Now," said Christian, "everybody can be satisfied."

The King was kind and professed to be very interested in the child's birth. He said she must have the silver gilt font for her baptism which was always used by members of the royal family.

Young Christian and Louise expressed their gratitude, the font was sent to the Yellow Palace and Alexandra was baptized.

How pleasant to have another child. Little Fredy was delighted. He couldn't say Alexandra but he managed Alix and from then on the baby was known by that name.

Louise wheeled her round to the grandparents' palace which was only a short distance away. The Landgravine was delighted with her granddaughter and had presents waiting for her and some extra money for her daughter which she presented with the comment, "How you manage, my dear, I do not know."

But Louise smiled serenely and assured her mother that she managed adequately and repeated that the generosity of the King and herself made life quite easy for them.

The old Landgrave was less amiable but he loved his daughter. He was quick-tempered and somewhat eccentric; he spent hours in his enormous library reading the books in the order of which they had been acquired and placed on the shelves.

He peered at the baby and declared that she was unattractive.

"Take it away," he said. "I don't want to look at that ugly little thing."

The Landgravine smiled at her daughter. "Don't take any notice of Papa," she said.

"But ugly, Mama!" cried Louise indignantly. "Alix is beautiful."

"What a good thing all babies are to their mamas. Never mind, my dear, the plain babies often turn out to be the prettiest women in the long run."

Louise was astonished. She and Christian had thought their daughter the most wonderful child on earth . . . as wonderful as Fredy of course.

She would not bring Alix to see the Landgrave again in a hurry.

Alix's first memories of Rumpenheim were of the time when she was three years old. Rumpenheim was a beautiful castle on the banks of the River Main, not very far from the town of Frankfurt; the gardens were beautifully laid out, the rooms much larger than those of the Yellow Palace. Rumpenheim was like something out of a fairy tale.

Nor was it only the house and the gardens which were so entrancing. There were so many people staying at the castle and they all knew each other and at reunions they greeted each other with demonstrations of great affection. When Alix was introduced to them, they kissed her, gave her presents and talked to her about Copenhagen and the Yellow Palace and the Sund.

Who were these people? she asked her mother.

Louise, who liked her children to ask intelligent questions, replied that they were all members of her family and the reason they came to Rumpenheim in the summer was that Louise's grandfather, the Landgrave of Hesse, had left the castle to his family on the condition that, during the summer months, some members of the family were always at the castle.

What a wonderful grandfather he must have been! commented Alix.

Her own family had grown in the last few years and she had a little brother William (called Willy) and there was a new baby girl, Dagmar. She loved them all dearly and it was a wonderful cosy feeling to belong to such a family.

At Rumpenheim was her cousin Princess Mary of Cambridge, who lived in England and was very attractive in Alix's eyes. She seemed quite old, being thirteen, and she and Alix took to each other from the start. Mary asked permission to wheel the baby Dagmar in her carriage about the grounds and this was given; so while Mary wheeled Dagmar, Alix would trot along beside her and sometimes Mary would lift up Alix and set her in the carriage opposite Dagmar and push them both.

Because Mary was that wonderful being, not quite an adult and certainly not a child, Alix could feel less restricted in her company than she did in that of grown-ups and at the same time draw on that inexhaustible fund of knowledge which seemed to be Mary's.

Mary explained the complicated ties which made them related. Her ancestor King George III of England had had fifteen children, nine sons and six daughters; one of these sons was Adolphus, Duke of Cambridge. He married Princess Augusta, who was the daughter of Frederick, Landgrave of Hesse-Cassel. It was this Frederick who had given Rumpenheim to his family. Frederick's eldest son had married Alix's mother's mother. So Alix would see the family connection between herself and Mary.

It was very complicated for the little girl to understand but it gave her such a nice warm rich feeling to know that Mary Adelaide was a kind of cousin and that there would be many more summers spent at delightful Rumpenheim.

Dagmar sat solemnly in her carriage. Poor Dagmar, thought Alix, who could not join in this fascinating conversation.

Every day, after lessons, for Louise insisted that there should be lessons even at Rumpenheim, and it was one of her maxims that children were never too young to learn, Alix would seek out Mary and this wonderful thirteen-year-old cousin seemed to find greater pleasure in the company of the child than in that of relations nearer her own age.

While the children played, their elders discussed serious

matters and the affairs of Denmark at this time were giving some cause for alarm.

The Landgravine Charlotte in her apartments at the palace talked of this with her daughter Louise, for she said they were of greater concern to them than to any of the other members of the family who were at Rumpenheim at this time.

"King Christian cannot live much longer," said Charlotte. "And then . . . Frederick."

"It is alarming to think of it," agreed Louise.

"And trouble is brewing all over Europe. There are revolutionary pamphlets being distributed everywhere. They are particularly virulent in France, but I don't think for one moment that Denmark can escape."

"The King, unfortunately, is not popular," said Louise. "And he won't be until he gives the people the constitution they want."

"Which he feels, with some reason, would put his crown in jeopardy if he granted it."

"It may well be a question of granting it or losing his crown."

Charlotte looked with approval at her daughter. She was talented and intelligent; if she were heir to the throne, how much happier for Denmark. But Frederick, with his loose living and his immoral friends, was the heir and Louise was nothing more than a housewife.

"What will happen when Frederick comes to the throne I tremble to think," said Charlotte. "I have tried to talk of these matters with your father but his temper is so quick and all he thinks of is his library, so that it is quite impossible to discuss them with him."

"There is one thing that has struck me, Mother," said Louise. "If the King dies, what will become of Christian's position in the Army? What if we should be turned out of the Yellow Palace!"

"That would be most unpleasant," said the Landgravine Charlotte. "You could of course come to us but I don't know what your father would say to noisy children playing in the gardens."

"We can only wait and see what happens," said Louise philosophically, "for there is nothing we can do about it."

But she was uneasy and so those summer days at Rumpenheim were not so idyllic to her as they were to her little daughter.

* * *

When the King asked his sister Charlotte to call on him at the Royal Palace she sensed his anxiety immediately.

"You look well," he told her. "Rumpenheim has done you good."

"It always does," she told him. "I was glad that Louise and the children were able to stay. It's so good for them to get away from the Yellow Palace."

The King nodded. "Louise is a clever girl. You must be proud of her." He spoke wistfully and Charlotte knew he was thinking of the unsatisfactory Frederick.

The King was a good man, but it was a pity his personality was not one to please the people. He was so reserved that he appeared to be unfriendly. It didn't matter that he was ready to sacrifice a good deal for the benefit of Denmark, and the reason he did not wish to grant the country a Constitution was because he knew it was not prepared for it yet. He had not that natural bonhomie which people demanded in their rulers and it seemed they would prefer a rogue with it, than an idealist without it.

"It's a pity," said Charlotte, "that they find it so difficult to make ends meet. But she is an excellent manager and I think Christian realizes his good fortune in marrying her."

"How I wish Frederick could have been as fortunate."

"Perhaps he would not have realized the worth of such a wife."

"He seems to be keeping with this new woman."

"And indulging in adventures meanwhile."

"Frederick calls himself the cosmopolitan bohemian."

"And this Louise Rasmussen. I hear she was a Parisian midinette. Is that true?"

"She has also had a post as governess, and she has been a ballet dancer, so she is a woman of many parts. She is well known because they are seen strolling together arm in arm or he waits patiently while she shops and then carries the parcels home for her."

"Quite domesticated. I should hardly have thought Frederick was that."

"Frederick is anything that is not usual. I do wonder what will happen, Charlotte, when I'm dead."

"Frederick will come to the throne."

"But what will become of Denmark under such a king?"

"Denmark has had some unworthy kings and managed to survive."

"The great point is that he has no heir and he never will have one."

"Is that quite out of the question?"

"My dear sister, he has been divorced three times. Each of his wives was selected for her suitability and what was the result—no heirs, no marriage—for each one of them has ended. He cannot marry this woman he is now living with. Even Frederick must see that we cannot have a French midinette for Queen of Denmark. So when I die and Frederick comes to the throne there will be no heir to follow him. There could not be a more disastrous state of affairs. Schleswig-Holstein is always ready to give us trouble. What would happen, do you think, if Frederick died and there was no one to follow him? I can tell you, sister, that I have spent some sleepless nights over this matter."

"Do you think Frederick should marry again?"

The King shook his head. "Even so, I don't think there would be a child. We were talking about Louise. She is astute; she is clever."

"Louise! How could Louise come into this?"

"You are forgetting that as my sister you are in the line of succession. If Frederick should produce no heirs you could be the Queen of Denmark."

"I! Oh no, impossible! I should not be fitted for the task."

"I knew you would say that, Charlotte, and that is why I asked you to come here to discuss this plan of mine. I want you to claim the throne. I want you to be recognized as the heir provided Frederick does not produce a son; then I suggest that you pass your claim to Louise. Louise has a husband. He is not exactly brilliant but he is adequate. He is honest, good looking and capable. With Louise to guide him he would be a good King."

"Louise and Christian, Queen and King of Denmark!"

"Why not? I should feel much happier if they were next in succession than I do now with Frederick in that position."

Charlotte was thoughtful. She had always said that she did not wish her daughter to degenerate into an ordinary *hausfrau*; as Queen of Denmark she would hardly do that. One might say she would be ruler of Denmark, because it was certain that she would be the one who guided her husband.

"I see," said her brother, "that you are not displeased with my idea. Good. I will put it before my ministers."

Prince Christian rode into the courtyard. It was noon; he

always came in at precisely the same time. Louise often said that he was obsessed by time. "Punctuality is high on the list of good manners," he was fond of declaring. "One should never be even one minute late."

His custom was to take off his uniform, put on a loose jerkin and go to a room which was called the gymnasium. There at precisely twenty minutes past twelve the children must assemble. He would then conduct physical jerks, which he said must be performed every day and were very necessary to good health.

Louise, who had been waiting for him, saw him arrive and hurried into the bedroom where he was changing his uniform.

"Christian," she said, "I must speak to you."

He looked at his watch. "After the exercises," he said. "There is no time now."

"This is more important than the exercises, Christian. My mother called this morning. I have had a very serious talk with her. It concerns our future."

Christian paused as he was taking off his coat to look at her and an anxious frown furrowed his brow. He was always afraid that they were going to be turned out of the Yellow Palace and such news could very likely come through Louise's mother.

Her next words made him feel that there was some foundation for his misgivings. "She came from the King, who is convinced that Frederick cannot produce an heir. On his death the throne will go to my mother and she will renounce it in favour of me."

"Good God!"

"Yes, Christian, and I am to renounce it in favour of you."

"Me! King of Denmark!"

"That's what it would appear."

"Impossible!"

"No, Christian, quite possible."

"A penniless, obscure member of the family!"

"You would be neither if you were King."

"I couldn't do it."

"Yes, you could, Christian, because I should be there."

He looked at her and smiled slowly. "I believe you would be capable of anything."

"Do you think you would be a worse king than Frederick will be?"

"He's the King's son. I'm not."

"There would be wonderful opportunities for the children."

"The children." Christian looked at his watch.

"It's all right," said Louise calmly. "You have ten minutes yet. We have four children—two boys and two girls. What do you think their prospects are going to be in our present circumstances?"

"If they are happy that's all I shall ask."

"There is no reason why they shouldn't be happy and well placed. The two can go together and although in some cases poverty doesn't prevent happiness, everybody is the better for not having to wonder whether they are going to have the roof over their heads suddenly removed."

It was a sobering thought. But King! He was not suited for the role. He didn't want it. He wanted to go on living quietly with his pleasant little family and his clever Louise.

His spirits lifted. It was a crazy notion. It would never come to pass. Frederick wouldn't agree. He would marry and produce an heir. There was no need to worry unduly.

He looked again at his watch.

"You will get there just in time," said Louise with a smile, and as he hastily slipped into his spring clothes she couldn't help marvelling at his lack of ambition. But it was gratifying in one way. It showed clearly that he had not married her because of her relationship to the King but because he had fallen in love with her. Wasn't that better than ambition?

The children were waiting for him—with one exception. Alix.

He looked at his watch. It was exactly twenty minutes past twelve.

"Where is your sister?" he asked.

Willy said she was coming, she really was. Poor Willy, he always made excuses for Alix. But almost immediately Alix was there, breathless and so pretty that her father's heart lifted with pride at the sight of her.

He forced himself to look stern. "You are one minute late."

"Yes, Papa."

"Why should you be one minute late?"

"Well, Papa, I was playing with my doll and I had to put her away and . . ."

Christian shook his head sadly. "You must learn to be punctual, my child. It's not the first time this has happened. If it happens again I shall have to punish you."

All the children looked suitably horrified, except Alix who

could not believe that dear kind Papa could really punish anybody. Mama could be much more stern.

"Well," said Christian, "we must waste no more time. Take your place."

So Alix stood in line and the children lifted their arms, touched the floor, swung this way and that, skipped and jumped; and it was all very exciting. Even Baby Dagmar did her best to follow them.

Then Christian stood on his hands and turned a somersault. Let them all try and do that. They did. Alix was best at it.

She stood on her hands, her skirts fallen over her face, her legs in their long pantaloons waving in the air.

"Bravo, Alix!" cried Christian. "Now, you boys, you're not going to let your sister beat you, are you?"

So the boys turned their somersaults and it was all very exhilarating.

"Stand at ease," commanded Christian, and there they stood, little Dagmar imitating the others, a fine little family.

What did he want with a crown and the anxieties of government which went with it? This was his little world and he loved it.

No cause for anxiety, he assured himself. It was a crazy notion which would come to nothing. He thought he was right for when the King put his idea of the succession to his ministers it was shrugged aside and the matter rested there.

There was a new King in Denmark. When King Christian had felt that his end was near he had been right. His son Frederick now ruled Denmark.

"What will become of us now?" said Louise to her husband. "Frederick may well turn us out of the Yellow Palace. Where shall we go? We can of course take refuge in my parents' home, but I do hope, Christian, that it won't come to that."

The country was in a state of great unrest—nor was it the only one. Revolution was sweeping across Europe. The French monarch was deposed; there was trouble in England where the Chartists were in revolt and there had been an occasion when it was thought they were marching on Buckingham Palace.

Frederick—not the most attractive of monarchs—arrived in Copenhagen. He was no blond Scandinavian giant, but short, plump, hook-nosed and swarthy. His father had divorced his mother and there were rumors that Frederick was not in fact Christian's son—and it seemed not unlikely for Frederick was the complete antithesis of King Christian. Christian had cared passionately for Denmark; Frederick was indifferent. Christian had refused to grant the country the constitution which all countries were seeking from their kings. What of Frederick?

At his first council meeting he was blànd and careless. The people wanted a constitution? Then certainly they must have a constitution. He would not stand in their way. If by any chance they, like the rest of Europe, were tired of kings they had only to say so. He would retire to his estates in the country; he was quite ready to take on the life of an ordinary nobleman which he assured them was far more comfortable than that of a king.

Would he marry? they wanted to know. No, he would not marry. Would he give up his mistress? No, he would not do that either. If they wished for a conventional king who would give them their constitution and an heir they had only to say so and he would happily abdicate.

The people were nonplussed. They had been ready to plunge into revolution, to drive the new King from his newly acquired throne, but how could they when he had no desire to retain it and was ready to save them the trouble of revolution by immediate abdication?

They were amused. He had promised them their constitution. Let them accept it and with it their new King, who was colourful and made them laugh. They quickly discovered that they were content with their King.

So, much to the surprise of all those who had feared that Frederick's accession might precipitate the country into revolution, he became in a few days more popular than his father had ever been.

The people of Denmark wanted no revolution. They had their new constitution and they wanted Frederick as the King, for it was quite clear that he was going to be a very free and easy monarch with the gift of amusing them by his unconventional behaviour.

Frederick showed no surprise at their attitude. He settled into the Royal Palace with his ex-midinette and they were often seen strolling about the streets of Copenhagen much to the amusement of the people.

He quickly realized the anxiety of the family at the Yellow Palace and one day in his unceremonious manner he called.

Christian was in the middle of giving the gymnastic lesson and the King, having told the servant not to announce him, stood at the door watching them.

"I wish I could do that!" he cried.

Christian stood to attention; the children were very still.

"No need to stand on ceremony," said Frederick.

But Christian signed to them to bow and curtsey.

"His Majesty has honoured us with a visit," he said.

"You'd better call me Uncle Frederick," replied the King.

Louise came hurrying in.

"Your Majesty . . ."

Frederick smiled. "I wanted to have a talk with you," he explained.

"Then if you will come into the drawing-room . . . They should not have let you come in unannounced."

"Oh, don't worry. I'm not used yet to being treated like a king."

Christian dismissed the children. Alix took Dagmar by the hand and led her away, the boys following.

"Nice little family," said the King. "Pretty little girls."

Christian and Louise exchanged glances. They couldn't help wondering whether this visit meant they were going to be told they could no longer have the Yellow Palace. But surely if this had been the case someone else would have told them? But how could they be sure with a king as unconventional as Frederick.

In the drawing-room Frederick sprawled on the sofa as he spoke, pulling at the place there which Louise herself had darned.

"Don't imagine," he said, "that my coming to the throne makes any difference as far as this place is concerned. It's yours while you want it."

The relief was too intense to hide.

"My place in the Guards . . ." began Christian.

"You don't think I want to disband my army and lose my best men," said Frederick with a grin. "There's a possibility that you will be heir to the throne, you know."

"Oh no, Your Majesty will have sons."

"I think that's hardly likely. I'd have to find a wife first, wouldn't I? As a matter of fact I'm going to marry Countess Danner." He laughed. "You look surprised. Perhaps you know her better as Mademoiselle Louise Rasmussen. I've just made her a Countess. But of course they'd call that a morganatic marriage, wouldn't they, and even if we had children they wouldn't be allowed to inherit." He pointed gleefully at Christian. "You may well be for it, my boy. So enjoy your freedom from the affairs of state while you can."

A very undignified monarch, thought Louise. When her Christian was King—which he might well be—it would be a very different matter. She was secretly elated because her eldest son Frederick could very likely in due course follow his father and be the King of Denmark.

In the meantime there was nothing to worry about. The country was no longer on the edge of revolution and the new King was even more benevolent than the old.

There was tension throughout the Yellow Palace. Fredy knew why. It was war. He whispered it to Alix in the little room which she shared with Dagmar. Funny Uncle Frederick would put on his beautiful coat with all the gold braid and buttons and the medals and march to war. Papa would go with him because he was a soldier.

"Bang, bang," said Fredy. "Then Uncle Frederick and Papa will come home and all the bands will play and we'll stand on the balcony and watch."

Alix listened wide-eyed to Fredy's account of what war meant.

In the privacy of their room Louise tried to conceal her anxiety even from her husband. Christian, with his particular buoyancy and innocent outlook on life, believed that the war would soon be over. Louise, more realistic, was not so sure.

She tried to assess what would happen to her family if Frederick was defeated. Also she feared for her husband. Christian, good soldier that he was, had no desire to go to war because it meant leaving his family. His idea of being a soldier was to report to the barracks daily and come home to teach gymnastics and bring his children up with the aid of their clever mother. To leave them now was a tragedy. His great consolation was that they would be in the capable hands of their mother.

"It was bound to come sooner or later," said Louise. "Schleswig-Holstein has always been a source of anxiety to Denmark. It has been boiling up for years."

"And now, of course, with Frederick's accession, the Holsteiners have used this as an opportunity."

Louise nodded. The position of Schleswig-Holstein, lying to the south of Denmark as a border to the German states, was in itself provocative. The trouble was that while Schleswig was content to be under Danish rule, Holstein was not. The Holsteiners preferred to consider themselves Germans, so there was friction and the Holsteiners were constantly attempting to persuade the people of Schleswig to their way of thinking.

One member of the royal family of Oldenburg, a branch of the royal family, was the Duke of Augustenburg, who had in fact a claim to the Danish throne. With German support he decided to make a bid for it. Hence the war which had broken out.

"If the people of Holstein should win . . ." began Louise.

"That's impossible," declared Christian.

"It's all very well for you to be loyal to your country," said Louise rather impatiently, "but what if they get help from some of the German states? Could Denmark stand up against that? And what sort of commander is Frederick going to be?"

Louise could not bear to think of the defeat of the Danish armies. If Duke Christian of Augustenburg defeated Frederick he would most certainly become at least heir to the Danish throne which would mean that Louise's husband and her son would be passed over. She realized how dear that project had become to her since it had been suggested to her by her mother through the last King. There was a more immediate problem. If the war were lost what would become of her family? They would most certainly be turned out of the Yellow Palace and Christian would no longer have a post in the Army.

It was a gloomy prospect.

"Let us pray," she said, "that this war will soon be over."

The children assembled in the music room while Louise sat at the piano and they all sang hymns. The "God help us" kind of hymns, said Alix to Fredy, which meant that people were frightened because they always asked God's help then in a special sort of way.

Their father read to them from the Bible and that too was all about God's helping them in their battles.

Fredy had made war sound rather glorious but Alix sensed that her parents' attitude was rather different.

Shortly afterwards their father left with the Army.

"I'll soon be back," he told them.

But the war dragged on, and it was three years before it was over.

A Dazzling Prospect

Life had gone on much as before in the Yellow Palace. Alix and Dagmar shared an attic room which contained two narrow beds, a chest of drawers and very little room for anything else. There were lessons every day with their mother. Music played a very big part in their lives. Louise played her pianoforte with skill and feeling and she was anxious that the children should do the same. Alix was taught to make her own clothes for they were much too expensive to buy; and as soon as Dagmar was old enough she would learn too. In the meantime she was allowed to watch. Alix had developed a skill in dressmaking which was a pleasure to her mother; she could choose the most becoming colours with ease and had a natural artistic bent. She enjoyed making clothes and when they were completed would like to parade up and down before her brothers and little sister while they applauded.

When she walked out with her mother wearing the new dress or jacket which she had helped to make she would be very conscious of its cut and would compare it with clothes worn by others; on her return she would, on her mother's orders, take it off, put on something less precious, and hang it up in her wardrobe so that it should be fresh when next required. There were the visits to Rumpenheim which still went on in spite of the war. There Alix became aware that her clothes were very simple compared with those of her female relations.

"Never mind," said her mother. "You *wear* yours so much better that they look as good."

This impressed Alix. It was true. Some of them slouched or did not stand up straight. She must remember that.

They continued with their physical exercises.

"Papa will expect it when he comes home," said Louise.

And at last Papa did come home.

What rejoicing there was! It was just as Fredy had said all those years ago—it seemed an age—when the war had started. The bands played; there were marches through the streets; uniforms and general rejoicing. Uncle Frederick had won his war against the rebels of Schleswig-Holstein. Denmark was safe and the King was a hero. So was Prince Christian.

How proud they all were and how delighted the Prince was to be home with his family!

Mama played the piano and they all sang Danish songs. Songs of triumph now. No need to ask for God's help. They had won the war. They were safe.

Papa explained it all to them and they listened eagerly.

Schleswig-Holstein had "come to its senses"; it was content now to be a part of Denmark; and the wicked ogre of the story, who oddly had the same name as Papa, Prince Christian, though of Augustenburg, had gone to Germany.

Papa was jubilant; he had conducted himself with honour in the war and had worked closely with King Frederick so that they had become good friends.

It was all wonderful.

Louise, however, was not so optimistic; she had qualms about the future and she often discussed these when she was alone with her husband.

"It's a temporary peace," she said. "A truce really."

"Why, my dear," remonstrated Christian, "we well and truly trounced them."

"What about Prussia? There are plots brewing there, I'm sure."

"You worry too much."

But dear Christian was a little naïve and none knew it better than his wife. The European powers shared Louise's fears of the growing ambitions of Prussia and realized that a strong Denmark was essential to curb those ambitions. And as Frederick was without a son to follow him, the succession was still unsettled. A conference of the powers took place in London and one of the items discussed was a possible heir to the throne of Denmark, and now that Prince Christian of Augustenburg was in disgrace, it was decided that, in accordance with an earlier suggestion of the late King, it should be settled on Prince Christian through his wife Louise.

There was an immediate agreement to this.

Prince Christian heard the news with some misgivings, Louise with secret elation.

All would be well. When the time came she would be beside her husband to guide him.

She had made an important discovery. She was to have another child.

Uncle Frederick called at the Yellow Palace with his morganatic wife, Countess Danner. Frederick was bluff and hearty and very friendly; Countess Danner was less so. She could scarcely feel pleased that Christian and Louise should be the heirs to the throne when it was not impossible that she might have a child. Large—she and Frederick were both very fat—she sprawled on a sofa and assessed the contents of the room: very clean but also shabby. She looked at the glittering rings on her fingers and then gazed somewhat contemptuously at the bare hands of Louise crossed in her lap. It was clear that she would have liked to snub the whole family but that was more than even she dared to do. Frederick was easy-going but after all these people had become important. This was the future King and Queen while she must remain the morganatic wife to whom many people referred as the mistress.

All the children were brought in to pay their respects to the King. Dagmar stared round-eyed at the enormously fat, rather short man with the hooked nose and beaming smile.

"What a pleasant family, eh?" he cried. "You're a lucky man, Christian."

"Yes, sir," agreed Christian. "I know it well."

"What I've come to say is this. The Yellow Palace should not be your sole residence now you're heir to the throne. What would you say to Bernstorff Castle as another residence, eh?"

"Bernstorff!" cried Christian very loudly so that Louise would know she had not been mistaken. Louise had grown a little deaf in the last years and did not like to admit it. "But that would be wonderful."

"Why yes," agreed Louise. "It would be most useful to have Bernstorff as an alternative residence."

"Well, it's yours."

They overwhelmed him with gratitude.

"Don't forget," he said with a grin. "You're the heir to the throne now."

It was not to be thought, Louise explained to the children, that now they had two residences they were rich. Far from it. A palace and a castle needed a big outlay to keep them going, and although Papa would one day be the King of Denmark they were still the poor relations. They must continue to live simply, make their own dresses and not expect luxuries.

It didn't matter. There was so much to make life exciting. Bernstorff was wonderful and it was always an adventure to be there. It was some ten miles from Copenhagen and set in a beautiful park. Here they could ride every day, and Alix loved being in the saddle; they could play all sorts of games and the entire family were very good at inventing them. There were lessons every day; Papa continued with the physical exercises and it was no unusual sight to see him with the children—including Dagmar—turning somersaults on the lawns of Bernstorff.

A new sister had arrived. She was called Thyra and for a while the whole family could talk of nothing else but this wonderful child; then Thyra ceased to be a baby and in due course she was there in the schoolroom and in the gymnasium. And the happy life continued.

There were the trips to Rumpenheim to be enjoyed each year and best of all was the reunion with aunts and cousins, and relatives of all kinds.

There were picnics and dancing, riding and endless conversation; there were games of all kinds; and there was Cousin Mary of Cambridge. Each year they met and their friendship had grown. It was true that Mary was ten years older than Alix but as the years passed the difference seemed less.

As they walked through the avenues of trees and sometimes planned the next day's excursion, Mary would talk about her home in England. She lived in Kew Lodge on Kew Green, that part of the world which was made famous by King George III, the mad King of England, and his severe wife Queen Charlotte from whom Mary was directly descended. Mary occasionally saw Queen Victoria, who was really very kind but could be a little forbidding; she sometimes met the Queen's children. The eldest, Vicky, was *much* younger than Mary, being only four years older than Alix, and a year younger was Bertie who was reputed to be rather naughty and was the Prince of Wales. They weren't allowed to mix with other children very much and, it was said in the family, Prince Albert was very severe. The family really did not like Prince Albert very much because he was German, but the Queen thought he was perfect, which was right really since she was his wife.

There was so much to talk about. For one thing how the Queen had been shot at on Constitution Hill, which was near Buckingham Palace, and the Great Exhibition which had been set up in Hyde Park. A great Crystal Palace, said Mary. It had to be seen to be believed. And they had removed it all and set it up in a place called Sydenham.

Alix could not hear enough about England.

Then one day Mary said: "I don't see why you shouldn't pay us a visit. I'll ask Mama to invite you."

Alix was very excited and Mary was true to her word. There came an invitation for Alix to visit the Duchess of Cambridge at Kew.

Alix had become a very important person. Her brothers and sisters were envious of her since she had been selected for a great adventure; and it was all due to the interest Cousin Mary had shown in her. She was to go and stay with them at Cambridge Lodge.

Louise said that she must have some new clothes; they would not be elaborate and she would probably meet people who were very splendidly dressed, but if she carried herself well and continued with the exercises Papa had taught her, she could make the plainest of dresses seem elegant. Alix was well aware of this. She delighted in clothes and this was obvious as soon as she put on any garment. So it was a challenge that she should have so few clothes and that none was elaborate.

The great day came when she left Denmark in the company of the Cambridges and how exciting it was to travel! The Channel was far from smooth but what seemed to cause discomfort to some people delighted Alix; and it was wonderful to stand beside Mary while she pointed out the land which was the coastline of England.

Cambridge Lodge was grand by Danish standards, but there was more splendour to come.

She and Mary rode out together in the Cambridge carriage through the village of Kew—"Dear little Kew" as the family often referred to it, quoting George III and Queen Charlotte who had talked of it thus long ago. They went to London and it was all so much bigger than Copenhagen, everything seemed so grand and on a larger scale; but there was another side to it. There were more beggars than in Copenhagen; there were more street vendors, more poor people, more everything.

One day Mary was very excited because she had arranged a party and the Queen had given her permission for the Princess Royal and the Prince of Wales, Prince Alfred and Princess Alice to visit Cambridge Lodge.

Mary told her they were about her age . . . at least Alfred was exactly the same, Alice a year older, the Prince of Wales a little more than a year older than Alice, and Vicky, the Princess Royal, a year older than he was.

Alix felt a little nervous.

"Oh, you needn't be," said Mary. "They are only children, and they haven't played half the games that you have!" Alix wore a white muslin dress which her mother had said would be the right thing for a special party. She supposed it was special since she was to meet these important people even if they were only children.

She reminded herself that she herself was a Princess and her father was heir to the throne; so her rank was as high as these children's.

Mary introduced them.

The Princess Royal was the important one. She came first and said in German with a very assured manner: "Hello, Alix. How do you like England?"

Vicky was a little terrifying; she seemed to know everything, and what was worse was fully aware that she did.

"This is Bertie, Alice and Alfred," said Vicky.

Alix bowed her head; she couldn't very well curtsey to children of her own age, although she fancied Vicky expected it.

Bertie eyed her with slight interest and Alice smiled in a friendly way. She warmed to Alice immediately. Alfred was friendly too.

"We could play some games," said Mary in her role of elder cousin eager to have the children amuse themselves.

"What games do you play in Denmark?" asked Vicky.

"We play hoops and with tops and letting rooms."

"What's letting rooms?" asked Vicky.

"Well, some people have a house and others come and look for rooms."

"How odd!" said Vicky. "Why should they come to look for rooms?"

"People do," put in Mary helpfully, "when they haven't a house and want somewhere to live."

"Oh, the poor," said Vicky.

"Sometimes we play guessing games. We are rivers going through the country and we say all the towns through which we pass. If you miss one there's a forfeit."

Vicky felt that she might score at that and was interested.

"We do music too," said Alix; "and we do gymnastics. We turn somersaults."

"You mean over and over?"

Alix nodded.

All the children were interested now, and Alix was about to show them when Mary said: "Not in the drawing-room, Alix."

Vicky said, very well, they would play the river game and she would choose the river which was the Thames and she was very soon reeling off the list of towns and winning the game.

Bertie was not interested and strolled off with Alfred who seemed like his shadow. Alice remained and said very quietly that perhaps they should have a Danish river because that would be more fair for Alix.

But by that time Vicky was tired of the river game and it was tea-time.

So those were the royal children.

Mary told her about them afterwards.

"Vicky is the favourite," she said. "Poor Bertie is always in trouble. Of course Prince Albert is very strict and the Queen agrees with him about everything, so I'm afraid poor Bertie doesn't have a very good time. And, Alix dear, don't turn somersaults here because if the Prince Consort heard of it he would be very shocked and that would mean that the Queen was too and you would never be invited to Buckingham Palace."

"Why?" asked Alix. "My father says it is good for people. You should see him go over and over. I can do three turn-overs without stopping."

"Yes, I expect it is good for you, but the Prince wouldn't think it right. The Prince is just a little prim."

"Oh," said Alix solemnly; and forgot all about the royal family until Mary told her that the Queen had sent her an invitation to go to Buckingham Palace.

She was a little alarmed, partly because everyone was telling her that she must do this and not do that and she felt quite bewildered.

The Queen turned out to be small and plump and had kind blue eyes. At the same time there was something rather terrifying about her; Alix feared all the time that she would do something which was wrong. But perhaps that was because she had been warned so frequently.

The Queen asked questions about her mother and father; and whether she was enjoying England. And then she was tapped on the shoulder and understood that she was to stand aside while someone else spoke to Her Majesty.

Afterwards the children went into the gardens and she met Lenchen, who was really Helena and was two years younger than herself which was a comfort, and Louise who was two years younger than that.

They were sweet and as Vicky wasn't there and Bertie and Alfred didn't want to play with girls she had a very pleasant time with Alice, Lenchen and Louise. She told them about the Yellow Palace and Rumpenheim and Bernstorff; their eyes glowed with excitement and they kept asking questions.

"Of course," she said, "there is nothing so grand as this."

Lenchen grimaced and said: "But your palaces sound so much more fun." Then she added: "And you should see Windsor. It's worse than this."

"Osborne and Balmoral are lovely," said Alice.

"Oh, what a pity Alix can't go to Osborne and Balmoral," cried Louise.

Then they told her about Osborne in the Isle of Wight and how they could see the sea from the windows; and how they played on the sands and went sea bathing. And Balmoral . . . Balmoral was the best of the lot although there was no sea. They rode out on their ponies and Papa would take them for long walks and they collected stones and grasses and flowers and Papa knew *all* about flowers.

Alix questioned this as she would have done at home. Her father said that only God knew all about everything.

"Only God and our papa," said Lenchen.

"Who said your papa did?" Alix wanted to know.

"Our mama," replied Lenchen. "And she must be right because she is the Queen."

That settled it.

So it was a very happy afternoon at Buckingham Palace in spite of the grandeur and the terrifying aspect of the Queen.

Riding back to Cambridge Lodge in the carriage Mary asked Alix how she had enjoyed visiting the Queen.

"Very much," replied Alix. "Well, not exactly the Queen but the Princesses."

"You will be able to tell them at home that the Queen of England spoke to you."

Alix agreed though she doubted that Fredy, Willy and Dagmar would be very impressed. Uncle Frederick was a king and nobody was very excited when he spoke to them.

At last it was time to go home and there was the excitement of reunion with the family. They all wanted to hear what had happened and see what presents she had brought for them.

But after a while the excitement was forgotten and the visit seemed to have happened long, long ago.

But the Cambridges did not forget.

"What a charming child Alix is!" said the Duchess to Mary. "I'm not surprised you're taken with her. One day the Prince of Wales will need a wife."

"That's years away."

"You'd be surprised how time flies. And when he does I don't see why your Alix shouldn't be in the running."

Mary was very pleased with the idea. She would bear it in mind.

One of the loveliest days of the year at the Yellow Palace was Christmas Eve, when the old traditional feast of Jul took place. For weeks before they had all been unbearably excited, making their presents for each other which must be kept a secret, and how difficult that was with children running in and out of the schoolroom at any time of the day. Alix was good with her needle—far better than she was at mathematics, geography or history; although she was moderately good at languages and better still at music; she excelled most at sport and riding which pleased her father; her mother was gratified by her aptitude with the needle, particularly her flair for clothes as, she confided to Christian, if she made a brilliant marriage and was able to employ the best dressmakers in the world, she would be outstanding by her individual way of wearing her clothes. This was a feminine angle which Christian shrugged aside; all he knew was that Alix, secretly his favourite daughter, was a delight to look at, and to see her turning somersaults on the lawns of Bernstorff or in the gardens of the Yellow Palace filled him with admiration and pride.

It was cold and the snow was piling in the streets.

"Just what Christmas ought to be!" said Alix.

Little Dagmar, three years younger than Alix, regarded her sister as an oracle and Alix reminded her of other Christmases at the Yellow Palace when the poor people had come in and been given cake and wine by the family.

"I remember Mama's watching how much they ate and drank because she was afraid there wouldn't be enough to go round."

"I wish we didn't have to be so poor," said Dagmar.

Alix considered this and decided that it would be better if they had more money and didn't have to wonder whether they could afford things—although they were richer now that Papa was Crown Prince. Then she thought of the grandeur of Buckingham Palace and launched into a description of that imposing building, the grand staircase and the drawing-room where she had seen the Queen.

"But the Yellow Palace is really nicer," she added, "and our mama and papa are really much more . . ." she paused for a word . . . "cosy than theirs. Poor Alice! Poor Lenchen! They had to be very careful, because their papa is very easily shocked and the Queen their mama says everything he does is right."

"Everything our papa does is not right," pointed out Dagmar. "Mama is always telling him . . ."

Alix smiled. "I'd hate to have a father who is always right. No papa is as nice as ours even if he is wrong sometimes."

Dagmar was prepared to agree with Alix as always.

So they talked as they stitched at their presents, with that wonderful sense of excitement because at any moment they might have to be slipped into a drawer if the intended recipient came into the room.

Christmas Eve came at last, with all the Christmas trees—one for each member of the family. The children tiptoed in with awe and wonder to examine them. Their names were on each table—Fredy, Alix, Willy, Dagmar, Thyra. They squealed with pleasure for each had their candles which would look beautiful when it grew dark—and in the centre of the room was the big tree laden with gifts in brightly coloured packages for everybody.

It was so exciting. Alix dressing for dinner—a very special occasion—tried on a red sash with her white muslin dress. Oh no, she thought, the blue would be best; and there was the blue sash with the little white flowers on it embroidered by Dagmar for her birthday. She must wear the blue sash—Dagmar would be so pleased. She put it on and studied the effect. How gracefully the skirt fell. The dress was as good as anything she had seen in the expensive shops. It was as good as anything she had seen worn at Cambridge Lodge and Buckingham Palace.

The red sash was more suitable for Christmas, because red was a Christmas colour. She changed the sash. Yes, definitely the red. But Dagmar would like the blue.

The blue . . . the red . . . She changed half a dozen times and then decided that it was better to please Dagmar than wear the Christmas colour.

The bell had gone. Oh dear, she should be down now and it was difficult to tie the sash exactly right, which she must of course do.

The family were at the table when she arrived. Papa gave her a reproachful look, but as it was Christmas Eve she would not be punished by standing up to drink her coffee and not be given second helpings, or perhaps go without her sweet. But she was contrite because dear Papa cared so much that people were where they should be at precisely the appointed minute.

The children were chattering about the trees. They were bigger than last year, there were more candles and hadn't the big tree looked wonderful? Little Thyra speculated on what the odd-shaped parcel in blue paper contained and wondered whether it was for her.

Louise and Christian exchanged glances. They were very happy with their little family. Christian hoped that they could go on enjoying these simple pleasures for a long time to come; Louise, more ambitious, was a little sad thinking that soon the children would be grown up and it would be necessary for them to marry and go away, for what could there be for any of them in Denmark—except Fredy, of course, who would follow his father to the throne.

After the meal it was present-giving time—the highlight of Christmas when the family assembled round the big tree and there were squeals of delight as paper crunched and gifts emerged and arms were flung round necks and the giver assured that it was just what the receiver had always wanted.

And when the excitement had died down they clustered round the grand piano and Louise played Christmas carols and hymns and they all sang together; then the older children took it in turns to play and Alix and Dagmar performed a duet which their parents loudly applauded.

Alix sat by her father afterwards who said very gently that he wanted to speak to her seriously.

"You know, my dear, you are a good child but you have one distressing fault. You are constantly unpunctual."

"Yes, Papa, I'm *so* sorry."

"But, my darling child, it is no use being sorry only—although sorry you should be. You must try to rectify the fault."

"I do, Papa."

A look of affectionate exasperation crossed Prince Christian's face.

"But, Alix, if you really tried how could you fail to succeed? It is so easy. You have to be at a certain spot at a certain time. What but your own carelessness can prevent you?"

"It's true, I know, Papa. But somehow I don't *think* until I hear the gong and then I am in a fluster."

"But, my child, you must think. You must remember what time the gong goes—it is always precisely on the minute so you know it's coming. You must be ready before it strikes and then . . . there you are at your place like the rest of us."

"But, Papa, is it so important?"

"My dear child, it is of the utmost importance. It is something you will have to remember when you are older, for to keep people waiting is most impolite, giving an impression as it does of being in no haste to see them since you cannot make the effort to be there on time."

"Oh, Papa, I will try . . . I really will."

He nodded. "I hope you were never late when you were in England."

"Well, not often . . . and it didn't seem to be so important there."

"Of course it is important everywhere. Always remember that. And you saw the Queen. How fortunate you were . . . more fortunate than your brothers and sisters."

"Oh yes, it was a great adventure."

"Tell me now, what was the nicest thing about it all?"

She did not hesitate. "Coming home to you and Mama and

the children and the Yellow Palace, and Bernstorff and Rumpenheim in the summer."

Prince Christian smiled tenderly. "So it has not made you despise your home? I'm glad of that. What did you think of the Queen of England?"

"Oh . . ." Alix considered. "She is a little lady. You are rather surprised because you would imagine she should be big. She is kind and said she was glad to see me. She was a bit frightening though—as though she wanted to be nice but was too important really."

Prince Christian was silent for a moment. Then he said: "Shall I tell you a secret, Alix?"

"Oh, Papa, yes."

"I might have married the Queen of England."

"Really, Papa. But what of Mama? You are married to her."

"This was before. A lot of letters passed between our governments and she married Prince Albert and I married your mama."

Alix was struck by this awesome statement.

"But if you had married the Queen she would have been our mama."

"The thought seems to disturb you. Don't let it. It can't happen now, you know. Besides, everything would have been different then."

"I might have been Alice or Lenchen."

"Oh, things don't work out that way. Still, I think what happened was really the best for us all, don't you?"

Alix looked at the denuded Christmas tree, at Mama with Dagmar at the piano and Thyra standing by watching; and the boys with their heads together examining each other's presents.

"Oh yes, Papa," she said fervently. "It happened the best way."

They had come back from Rumpenheim to Bernstorff. It had been a wonderful summer, with river trips and picnics and conversation. Cousin Mary had been there and she told Alix what a good impression she had made in England. The royal children had all enjoyed meeting her and the Queen had said she seemed a very pleasant little girl.

Cousin Mary said that one day Alix would have to marry and leave her home. Had she ever thought of that?

Alix looked so alarmed that Mary did not pursue the subject and Alix quickly forgot it; it had to come, she knew, but it was years away, much too far to be worried about now especially at Rumpenheim when they were going for a trip to Frankfurt and to play Lotto that evening.

Mary did say though that she thought Alix ought to work harder with her English. Her German was good, her French was passable, but her English not so good.

"To begin with," said her cousin, "we will speak to each other this holiday in English."

It was a great help, and she was sad as always to say good-bye to her dear cousin.

But it was pleasant to be back in Bernstorff which was almost like being at Rumpenheim, better though because it was so much nearer Copenhagen.

King Frederick called on them and they had the pea-soup and bacon that he always insisted on. He ate large quantities of it and drank lots of Danish beer. The girls had put on their best dresses for the occasion—to be changed for plainer ones as soon as the visitors had left. The Countess Danner who—unfortunately—accompanied him had an appetite almost as large as his, but she was not nearly so friendly.

After the meal the King put on a Turkish fez hat and brought out a huge pipe and then he started to drink *Akvavit* while Louise watched his glass speculatively so that Alix knew she was wondering how much more he was going to drink and whether they would have enough to satisfy him and how they were going to afford to replenish their stocks in anticipation of his next visit.

Uncle Frederick liked to talk about the Schleswig-Holstein war which he had successfully waged and he would call the children round him and while he puffed at his great pipe and sipped his *Akvavit* he would talk of the war and how he had led his men into fantastic adventures.

The more *Akvavit* he drank the more fantastic would the adventures become. The Countess would yawn, drink her brandy, calculate the value of the furnishings of Bernstorff and clearly be waiting for the time when Uncle Frederick would be ready to depart.

The boys would laugh at these strange adventures, but they had been warned not to show that they did not believe them; Uncle Frederick was the King of Denmark and as such must be respected.

Alix was fond of him because in spite of all the wild stories—which were untruths—he was kind and wanted to see them all enjoying themselves. He loved to hear them laugh and of course they owed a great deal to him.

He was always particularly interested in Fredy who would one day be King of Denmark too. Oh, Fredy, Alix thought, don't get fat and wear a fez and tell outrageous stories which no one believes, and marry a woman like Countess Danner whatever you do. As if he would! Fredy was going to be tall and blond like the rest of the family. He would not be a bit like King Frederick.

And soon they would be back in the Yellow Palace and life would go on in this pleasant happy fashion.

Oh, how glad I am that Papa did *not* marry the Queen of England, she thought.

One day Prince Christian summoned the children together and told them that he had invited a very special guest.

Alix at first wondered if it could be the Queen of England of whom she had thought a great deal since her father had told her he might have married her. But it was not the Queen but a man.

"He's a story-teller," said their father, "and you have read and loved some of his stories, I know. His name is Hans Christian Andersen."

The children chattered together. "There was the ugly duckling who turned into a swan and the little mermaid. Yes, they did know his stories. Was he coming to tell them stories?"

"He is coming because we are going to honour him. He is a Dane and people all over the world read his stories. We should be proud of such men. You must not forget that one day I shall be King and Fredy here will follow me. It is necessary to encourage people like Hans Christian Andersen and if we invite him here other people will ask him to their houses and it is a way of saying that we appreciate our men of genius."

The children were overawed and rather silent when the writer was introduced to them, but not for long, because he was quiet and unassuming—and perhaps a little overawed to be in the presence of the future King and his family. But he was soon put at his ease by the simplicity of life in the Yellow Palace. There was something childlike about him which made for immediate understanding between himself and the children; and they were happiest when alone with him.

He became a frequent visitor to the Yellow Palace and he would sit in the schoolroom or out of doors if the weather was good and tell them about the days when he was the son of a poor shoemaker. When he wrote a new story he would bring it along to read to the children first and they would sit in a circle round him listening entranced.

"It's wonderful," said Alix to Dagmar, "that children all over the world are going to have these stories told to them."

Dagmar agreed that it was; and when Hans brought his stories in volume form to show them and inscribe a copy especially for them they were very excited.

Christian and Louise looked on benignly at the friendship which had grown between their children and the story writer.

So the days passed—days made enthralling by the story-telling of Hans, and amusing by the same occupation of King Frederick. And how different were those two story-tellers. The Little Mermaid had nothing in common with Uncle Frederick's wild, military and equally fictitious adventures. Oddly enough, pointed out Alix, while Hans told his stories about people who only lived in his imagination you believed in them, but when Uncle Frederick told stories about himself you did not believe them for one instant.

Such happy days they were. Going for walks along the promenade—the Lange Linie—watching the ships coming in to Copenhagen from all over the world, studying the fashions in the shops, coming home and copying them with just that difference which made them one's very own; all the excitement of choosing material for a new dress and patterns and accessories, being very cautious that one kept within one's allowance, taking care of the new dress, changing into something simpler when one came in. Countess Danner didn't have half as much fun with her elaborate clothes, Alix pointed out to her sisters. And no wonder because they were sometimes very ugly—and it was gratifying that their cheap ones could look so much more elegant. Christmases, birthdays, to look forward to and with two boys and three girls there was always some celebration about to burst upon them. There were gymnasium lessons with Papa, music and languages with Mama; other more mundane subjects with governesses.

The summers at Rumpenheim with the cousins and aunts were becoming more and more interesting as they grew older. There were little dances for the family and the few friends from the neighbourhood who were invited; there were river picnics and trips to Frankfurt, and of course, animated and interesting conversation.

Then Bernstorff—that beautiful castle—which it was thrilling to approach along the avenue of trees; it was a little like Rumpenheim but more comfortable in a way because it was the family home—and it had the advantage of being only ten miles from Copenhagen so one was not really cut off from that beloved city. At Bernstorff there was more of a holiday atmosphere than at the Yellow Palace, though Prince Christian insisted that they all rose very early in the morning—the best time of the day, he was fond of saying. They had coffee and rolls and then were out in the nearby woods walking, riding or playing with the dogs, of which there were many. Their father would come out of the palace when it was time for *dejeuner* and give a piercing whistle and when they heard it they must all leave what they were doing and run into the castle. His only real displeasure was if they were late. Then lessons would begin and after that perhaps a ride.

They must not be late for dinner which was served at four in the afternoon. If it was a fine day they would be out in the garden again where coffee would be served, or if it were cold this would be taken round the fire. Then they would read together. The girls would do needlework or go and gather flowers and arrange them. Louise was very fond of flowers and her arrangements were exquisite. Alix and Dagmar and even little Thyra had to learn to arrange them. The scent of these flowers permeated the castle and as soon as any showed the slightest sign of decay it must be removed. Each of the girls had her own little domain, for which she was responsible, and Louise would inspect their arrangements and the fresh state of the flowers every day. She was determined that her family should be brought up in a manner suited to their state and the fact that they were poor was a challenge to her.

Life was not entirely confined to the home either. There was regular attendance at the Lutheran church at Gjentofte and the villagers would gaze in awe at their future King and Queen with their good-looking family. The young people had to learn how to accept this homage with a gracious diffidence which was neither indifferent nor patronizing. In fact they must accept it as natural without seeming to be aware of it. Louise would drive into the village with gifts for the poor—which the family could ill afford; and then again they must exercise that peculiar royal behaviour which because their father was destined to be King and their mother Queen was necessary.

And then . . . home to the best-loved place of all—though

by no means the grandest—the dear Yellow Palace with its little rooms and winding passages which was Home.

Who would have thought this happy life would not go on for ever.

Louise was waiting impatiently for her husband's return from the barracks. When reading the English papers which she did whenever possible to improve her knowledge of the language she had found something of greatest interest in *The Times*.

The Prince of Wales was nearly seventeen, and as it was the custom of royalty to marry early, there was a great deal of speculation as to whom this very important young gentleman would choose for his bride.

The article went on that the choice was somewhat limited for His Royal Highness. His bride would be the future Queen of England and therefore some qualifications would be demanded of her which might not be easy to supply. She must be young, for her main duty was to give the country heirs; she must be royal; and she must be a Protestant. This narrowed the choice down considerably and the author of the article had, after great consideration, come to the conclusion that there were only seven candidates for the honour.

Six of these were German princesses; the seventh on the list was Princess Alexandra of Denmark.

Louise stared at the letters. Alix, Queen of England! Her common sense immediately rose to the fore. The seventh on the list. What hope had she!

All the same it was something which she must discuss with Christian at once.

When he came in and she was able to show him the article he was startled.

"Our Alix! Why she's only a child."

"She's fourteen. Why in two or three years she'll be ready."

"English Princes always marry Germans."

"A matter which I believe the English people resent."

"The English royal family is half German. Albert was most definitely. And Victoria is half so. Germans always have the first chance."

Christian was thinking of himself and how he had been overlooked for a Prince of Coburg.

"It could change."

"My dear Louise, Alix is seventh on the list."

"Still she's on the list."

"No, it would always be a German."

"Look at the list. These German Princesses . . . who are they? Daughters of small States. Whereas Alix is the daughter of a future King."

"You are prejudiced," said Christian with a laugh.

"I'm also realistic," said Louise. "We are going to be prepared. Our children have not had an education worthy of them so far. All that has to be changed and we are going to change it."

"When?" asked Christian.

"At once," said Louise. "There's no time to be lost."

Life had changed suddenly. It had become more serious. Bernstorff and the Yellow Palace appeared to be invaded by an army of teachers. They must spend more time at their lessons, said Louise. They were no longer children—at least Fredy, Willy and Alix weren't and Dagmar was fast gaining their grown-up status.

Louise always believed in explaining to the children. She herself had taught them music and drawing, but these were the necessary accomplishments of well-brought-up young ladies; they were scarcely lessons. They had had their Swiss governess, Mademoiselle Schwiedland. But now they had to be prepared for whatever role they might be called upon to play in later life.

Pastor Theobold came to teach them German and Professor Petersen history and geography; there was a new music teacher because Louise thought that they should have professional tuition which she feared she did not give them. So Mr Siboni was engaged.

But most important of all was Miss Knudsen, who came to teach English. Mathilde Knudsen was homely, kindly and quiet; she had been born in the West Indies and spoke English as a native of England. Alix's conversations with Cousin Mary had been of great use to her and she found that she progressed rapidly under Miss Knudsen's tuition. Her accent improved and although she occasionally used quaint expressions which made Miss Knudsen smile she was undoubtedly fluent.

This seemed to be of the utmost importance for her parents were constantly asking her how she was progressing with her English and these constant enquiries made her aware that for some reason learning English so that she could write it with ease and speak it with a degree of fluency was more important than any of her other lessons.

Mrs Knudsen's very special favourite was Alix—not the cleverest of the family, but without doubt the most beautiful; Dagmar was much quicker at her lessons and little Thyra was charming, but Alix, in Mrs Knudsen's opinion, was the flower of the family.

They became great friends and Alix enjoyed walking out in Copenhagen or in the gardens of Bernstorff with her governess, chattering away in English all the time.

Listening to her, her parents exchanged significant glances. Louise as usual was right. If by any chance Alix became number one on that important list, owing to the foresight of her mother, she would be prepared.

There was an addition to the family. A little brother was born and they called him Valdemar. There was great excitement about a new baby. The time had come for Fredy's confirmation.

"As there is so little difference between their ages and Alix is almost sixteen they might as well be confirmed together," said Louise.

So it was arranged that this should be so; and preparations began. There had always been an emphasis on religious education in the household; and as Prince Christian liked his children to follow his example and read a chapter from the Bible every night before they went to sleep, Fredy and Alix were ready.

As Fredy was in the line of succession the Confirmation was a public occasion and King Frederick himself was present among the distinguished company which filled the Slots Kirken in Copenhagen on that October day. The dignity and good looks of the young pair excited the admiration of the spectators; and it was a solemn occasion, for in the Lutheran Church the confirmation ceremony meant that this was an end of childhood and that the responsibilities of adult life were now to be taken on.

The King had wished the Countess Danner to attend and there was some consternation about this as she was not accepted as his legal wife; but the King must have his way and a place was provided for the countess, who then declared that she had no wish to attend the ceremony, only to be asked to it; so embarrassment was spared. As soon as the ceremony was over King Frederick presented Fredy with a commission in his army and Alix with a medallion containing his portrait.

When they returned to the Yellow Palace Louise took her daughter to a new room below that which she had shared with Dagmar. This had been prepared for her occupation, for her piano had been put in it and her bed was there.

It was a symbol of growing up. She had a room of her own.

She turned to Louise, who was standing beside her, and embraced her.

"Oh, Mama, it's wonderful."

"It means you are no longer a child, my dear."

Alix's eyes were shining. "It's wonderful . . . growing up," she said.

A faint apprehension came into her mother's eyes.

"It's as well to remember that it also has its responsibilities," she replied; and she was thinking of that list with Alix's name at the bottom.

Then Wally arrived in Denmark. She was in fact the Countess Walburga von Hohenthal; she was beautiful, cosmopolitan, vivacious and therefore very attractive. She had come to Copenhagen to marry the English diplomat, Mr. Augustus Paget, and with the simple friendliness they showed to visitors Christian and Louise invited Walburga to the Yellow Palace.

She told Louise that she had heard of her charming family and hoped that she would be allowed to meet the members of it. This was arranged and the young Countess was enchanted by the good looks and perfect manners of the young people. She was especially attracted to Alix and was very soon invited to Bernstorff where leading the simple country life, it was very easy to become quickly on familiar terms.

Wally was so amusing. She had come from Berlin and the Court of the Crown Princess, who had been the Princess Royal and eldest daughter of the Queen of England.

"Poor Vicky," confided Wally to Alix, "she had a very trying time when she arrived. First she was forced to ride through the streets in the freezing weather in the kind of dress one would wear in a heated ballroom and when she arrived at the schloss she found it gloomy and it was said to be haunted, and I really think her mother-in-law enjoyed putting her next to the haunted chamber."

"How dreadful!"

"Vicky is very self-reliant. She is in fact brilliant. But she needed someone to confide in and she chose me. And when Augustus goes to England I shall go with him. We shall be received at Court of course, and I shall be summoned to Vicky's formidable mama and even more formidable papa and a report demanded of me."

Wally was a little disrespectful but Alix enjoyed that. What fun to be able to laugh and have little jokes with someone as brilliant as Walpurga.

What Walpurga did not divulge to Prince Christian and Princess Louise was that she had been asked to report on Alix. Her mistress, Vicky, was very anxious that a bride should be found for her brother, the Prince of Wales; and the fact was that she had actually made a journey through Germany to inspect the Princesses who appeared on the list above Alix's name. She was very critical and had found something wrong with every one of them.

It was Wally—eager to have a say in affairs—who reminded her of number seven.

"Augustus writes to me from Denmark that Princess Alexandra is a real little beauty," she had said, "very carefully brought up by her clever mama—accomplished, healthy and beautiful . . . in fact everything that your brother Bertie could desire."

Vicky's father, the Prince Consort of England, who had loved his daughter devotedly (and Wally, who collected gossip, had heard that Queen Victoria had resented this affection between her husband and their eldest daughter and was jealous of it) had asked her help in choosing a husband for Bertie. He had the utmost confidence in her judgment and she was eager to justify this.

So she said: "You are going to Denmark to get married. What an opportunity. You can let me know if these reports of Alexandra are correct."

It was a mission after Wally's heart.

She was soon writing back glowing reports of Alix—a lovely girl, unspoilt, very beautiful, not intellectual—which by all accounts would just suit Bertie—but accomplished and well educated. In fact in Wally's opinion, Alix was the perfect wife for the Prince of Wales.

It was time to set out for the annual visit to Rumpenheim. During the journey Alix and Dagmar speculated on who would be there this summer. They were both looking forward to the round of simple pleasures. Although Christian and Louise were well aware that feelers were being put out with regard to Alexandra's virtues both parents were anxious that this should be kept from their daughter.

"So many girls are told of brilliant prospects which don't come to anything," said Christian. "I wouldn't want Alix to be upset."

"It's much better that she should be kept in ignorance of what's afoot," agreed Louise. "But I'm not sure that it wouldn't have been a good idea for you to take her to England."

"I'll not have her paraded like a prize cow," declared Christian in the raised voice it was now necessary to use to Louise, whose deafness had increased in the last years.

"She would make a good impression."

"I've no doubt of it. I just say I won't have her paraded."

Louise smiled at her husband. There was a great charm about him and this was accentuated by a certain innocence. When he came to the throne it could be for her to guide him.

Nor was Alix the only member of the family about whom enquiries were being made. The charm of the girls had been discussed abroad; they were exceptionally good looking and what was more important, healthy. It was due to the outdoor life they had lived; and the constant exercises had made them walk in a graceful fashion. Whenever they went to a theatre in Copenhagen which the King thought they should do now and then, they were always cheered by the people and it was said that the royal box with the Christian family in it was as great an attraction as what was going on on the stage.

Now there was talk of a Russian marriage for Dagmar—the Tsarevitch, no less. With one daughter married to the ruler of England and another to that of Russia, Denmark's position in the world would be far more significant than it was at this time.

But Christian was saddened at the thought of losing his daughters; and the time for doing so was, he could not pretend otherwise, coming very near.

This was proved on their arrival at Rumpenheim.

A trip had been arranged to visit the Cathedral at Speier and Christian and Louise were to take their daughters, Alix and Dagmar. This was typical of the outings they enjoyed when at Rumpenheim, but this was an outing with a difference. The Crown Princess with the Prince and her son little Wilhelm was on a visit to Mecklenburg-Strelitz and she too wished to visit the Cathedral at Speier on the very same day at the very same hour as Christian and Louise would be there with their two eldest daughters.

As the carriage drove along and Alix and Dagmar called each other's attention to the remembered landmarks, Christian was looking a little sadly at his eldest daughter. If she doesn't like him, he thought, she is not going to be forced. I'll not have our Alix made unhappy for all the princes in the world.

Louise, watching him, followed his thoughts. Dear, good, kind Christian! She could not have had a more loving husband and a better father for her children. But he was unambitious. Perhaps that was what made him so lovable.

The Cathedral rose before them.

"It's magnificent," said Dagmar. She was more interested in architecture than Alix was. She wanted to pause and examine the structure but Louise hurried her on.

"You can look at that later," she said. "Let us get inside first."

They entered the Cathedral. Alix knew afterwards that this was one of the important moments of her life for entering at the other door was another little party—quite clearly an important one. The two groups hesitated and then a young woman came forward and Prince Christian went to meet her.

Alix saw her father bow and beside the young woman was a young man—not tall but with a pleasant smile; and now her father was bringing them over.

"My dear," he said, "I have the honour to present to you their Royal Highnesses the Crown Princess of Prussia and the Prince of Wales."

Walpurga's Vicky, thought Alix. And . . . Bertie!

He was smiling at her, rather conspiratorially, and she found this pleasant. He greeted Dagmar but his eyes came back to Alix. She flushed a little. He was very friendly.

Vicky was saying: "My brother is on a visit and we are both staying for a few days with Aunt Augusta at Mecklenburg-Strelitz."

They started to talk about the Cathedral. What a pleasure to meet in this way. They could look at the Cathedral together. And they must of course arrange another meeting.

Alix found herself walking beside Bertie.

"How strange," she said, "that you should have walked in by one door just as we were coming in by another."

"Very strange," he admitted with a smile as though he

didn't think it strange at all. "But do you know," he went on, "I think they planned it."

"Really?"

"Well, as you said, it was too much of a coincidence . . ."

"But why should they?"

"Don't you know?" he asked.

"No. Do you?"

"Oh, I've a hazy idea."

"Do tell me."

He smiled at her in a way she found charming. "Do you know, I don't think I will. I'll leave you to guess. I'm sure it won't take you long."

"It's intriguing."

"I'm finding it so too."

They were laughing together and she saw Mama half turn to look at them and the Crown Princess too. Oh dear, she thought. Am I supposed to be solemn?

She said quietly: "I think we are supposed not to laugh."

"In cathedrals or not at all?"

"Oh, in cathedrals of course. Not at all would be quite out of the question."

"Quite," he agreed.

"We are not looking at the wonderful pillars and the altarpieces."

"Are you very interested in them . . . honestly?"

"Well, not very much."

"Nor am I."

They laughed again and she put her fingers to her lips as though caught in some fault, which amused him.

"To tell the truth," he said, "when I knew we were coming to a cathedral I protested."

"Do you always protest when you are asked to do something you don't want to?"

"To Vicky, yes. At home, no."

"At home. You mean at your mother's court. I was there once. I met you. Do you remember?"

He was going to say that he did but she knew he didn't. "I'll save you telling a lie," she said. "Of course you don't. I was ten and very stupid. I'd never been anywhere and it was all very grand. You came to a party at Cambridge Lodge and I came to one at Buckingham Palace."

"Very solemn affairs," he said, "parties at Buckingham Palace."

"And you don't like being solemn. But then who does?"

"Some people do." His face darkened a little. She thought: He means his father. Oh, how lucky we are with Papa! Still, Bertie himself liked to laugh. So they went on talking and now and then laughing together and they suddenly realized that the tour of the Cathedral was over and the others were outside.

They came into the sunshine. Alix was flushed and happy; so was the Prince of Wales. It had been a very pleasant encounter.

Christian and Louise were making further arrangements with the Crown Princess.

She and her husband were going on an expedition to Heidelberg the next day. Wouldn't it be pleasant if they all went?

So the next day there was a trip to Heidelberg and there Alix extended her acquaintance with the Prince of Wales.

They had so much to talk and laugh about; he described life at Buckingham Palace and Windsor which was certainly solemn. His father thought young men ought to spend their time studying and not succumb to frivolous pleasure. Poor Bertie, she was sorry for him. He did have rather a hard time.

"Still," she told him, "the time will soon come when you will be your own master."

"I can't wait for it," he said, his eyes gleaming.

She described the Yellow Palace to him and the fun they had at Bernstorff and Rumpenheim; he listened attentively, and she knew that he had had a very different childhood.

She felt warmly protective towards him and it was then that she began to fall in love with him.

Before they said good-bye he gave her a photograph of himself which she accepted eagerly.

The Crown Princess was delighted; she found Alexandra all that she had been described as being. She was certain that she was the wife for Bertie. Christian and Louise were happy too. It would be wonderful if this brilliant marriage which any parent would want for a child should also prove to be a love match.

Back at Rumpenheim Louise and Christian lay awake at night talking of the meeting between their daughter and the Prince of Wales.

There was no doubt that the young people had been taken with each other. They were both young and attractive; even so it seemed too much to hope for.

"Of course I can see why the English want the match," said Louise. "They're afraid of Prussia. Prussia is after expansion and has its eyes on Schleswig-Holstein. England wouldn't want a strong Prussia, and Denmark stands as a buffer between the two. I doubt that Belgium would want it either."

"No, King Leopold is in favour of the marriage."

"It is a very desirable state of affairs," said Louise.

"Providing she loves him. I wouldn't have it otherwise."

"She's in love with . . . or half-way there. He's a very attractive young man."

"But not very serious."

"He's young yet. I heard Thyra teasing Alix, asking her why she always blushes when the Prince of Wales is mentioned. There's no doubt in my mind. It's a perfect match."

And so it seemed. Alix carried Bertie's picture with her always, and looked at it frequently. He was such fun, not at all serious; he wanted to laugh and be gay all the time. Poor Bertie, who had really had rather a sad childhood. He had told her how clever Vicky was and how particularly when he was younger he had felt so inadequate in her company.

There was no need for Bertie to feel inadequate. She assured him of this and he liked to be assured.

She had guessed why they had met in the Cathedral. She had understood the speculative glances. They wanted her and Bertie to love each other because they thought Bertie would be a good husband for her.

She talked it over with Dagmar who was very likely going to Russia.

"How far we shall be from each other!" she cried in dismay.

"We must visit often and we must write. Promise, Alix."

Alix promised.

They were going to be rich, both of them. How different it would be from making their own dresses and changing them when they came in for fear they might be spoiled.

"It will be wonderful," said Alix, "but we shall miss each other sadly."

"We'll have husbands and perhaps children."

"Yes," said Alix slowly. "I suppose that would make up for it in a way."

There was no topic as frequently discussed in the household as that of the marriages of the two girls, but each day Alix waited for some news from England and none came.

One day they were all assembled in the music room and Alix knew that something dreadful had happened because of her parents' solemn expressions.

"The Prince Consort is dead," said Christian. "The poor Queen is stricken in her grief."

"Will this make any difference?" Louise anxiously asked Christian.

"I don't know. The Prince was an astute politician. He would understand the importance of Schleswig-Holstein to Europe and the need for a strong Denmark."

"The Queen has able ministers."

Christian nodded. "But, of course, a death like this is certain to delay matters."

"I do think something definite should have been arranged by now. It is a little undignified to keep Alix dangling. We don't know whether she is betrothed or not."

"She is not . . . yet."

"Oh, Christian, I believe you don't want this marriage."

"I want her to be happy," he said. "And I suppose I want to keep the family together as long as possible. When she goes . . . and Dagmar goes . . ."

"Then we shall have to find matches for the others."

"Wha a politician you are."

"I need to be. Don't forget we have our own destinies."

Christian frowned slightly. How much more peaceful if they had been able to go on living at the Yellow Palace and the girls could have married local noblemen. But for Alix to go right away to England and Dagmar to Russia . . . How could he be pleased about that!

Louise had a quiet talk with Alix in the latter's new room at the Yellow Palace.

"You love your room to yourself," said Louise with a smile.

"Oh yes, Mama, I do. It's not as though Dagmar is far away."

"And, my dear, have you thought that soon you may not be needing this room?"

"You mean I shall go away."

"If you go to England and marry."

Alix blushed.

"My dearest child, do you love the Prince of Wales?"

"I . . . I don't know."

"If I were to tell you you were to prepare to leave for England tomorrow how would you feel?"

"If he really loved me . . . I should be happy. I should be miserable though if it were arranged . . . just because it was suitable."

"So if he loved you . . . you could love him."

"Yes, Mama."

That was good enough; Louise could tell Christian that he need have no qualms.

Christian was pleased when he heard this.

"Nothing should stand in their way, I suppose," he said.

But still there was no news from England.

Princess Alice was married to Prince Louis of Hesse-Darmstadt and by all accounts the ceremony had been more like a funeral than a wedding, with the Queen brooding over them all in her widow's weeds.

The Queen of England, deprived of the presence of that Beloved Being, had no heart for anything but mourning.

But there were forces at work. The world must go on even though the Prince Consort was dead. Leopold of the Belgians who was watching events in Europe, and particularly in England and Prussia, with very special interest, was determined that the match between Alix and Bertie should take place.

He wrote to the Queen and told her that it was necessary for the Prince of Wales to marry and the Princess of Denmark seemed the ideal match. He would arrange a meeting between the Queen on one side and Alix and her parents on the other. And this meeting should take place at Leopold's Laeken Palace.

The Queen rather reluctantly agreed.

Alix and her parents were to have a little holiday in Belgium and while they were at Ostend they would go to Brussels and perhaps stay for a day or so as the guests of King Leopold at the Laeken Palace.

Alix was warned by her mother. "The Queen is on a pilgrimage to Coburg where the Prince Consort was born; she will be at Laeken and is anxious to meet you. You will have to be very careful for they say that she is very stricken by the death of the Prince."

Alix was uneasy because it was clear that her parents were too. She had been surprised that a young man whom she had met only twice could have made such a deep impression on her; she had tried not to think too much of him because she had quickly realized that the marriage had not yet been finally decided on; and the more she thought of it, the more inclined she was to think that it might never take place. After all, who was she? The eldest daughter of the heir to the throne of Denmark it was true, but Denmark was a small country and they were poor and had led rather simple lives. She had heard that Bertie was carrying out a tour of the Far East which had been planned before his father had died. "The Queen is anxious that everything the Prince planned before his death should be put into effect," her mother told her. But her mother was uneasy and she wondered why.

They told her so little. For instance, in the first place they had said they were going on a holiday to Belgium, and Uncle Leopold had invited them to Laeken. They did not say that she was to be there on approval as it were, as the Queen was going to inspect her—for that was what it amounted to.

If the Queen did not like her, then everything would be forgotten. That possibility made her unhappy, which showed that she was in love—or ready to be. When one was young and inexperienced it was difficult to understand one's feelings entirely.

They spent a few days in Ostend and all the time they were thinking of the trip to Laeken. Alix was right when she guessed that her parents were uneasy. There had been rumours about a certain affair at the Curragh Camp in which the Prince of Wales had been involved. Christian thought that the Prince was perhaps inclined to be immoral.

Louise tried to excuse him. "He is young. Most young men indulge in these adventures in their youth. As long as he settles down when he is married all will be well."

"Yes, as long as he doesn't make our Alix unhappy," agreed Christian.

"He seemed fond of her."

"Perhaps he is fond of all good-looking girls."

"Which is natural."

"But I fancy she is more fond of him than he of her."

"Well, he appears to be a young man who likes a little gaiety. He may not show his feelings as readily as a young and innocent girl does."

Christian smiled fondly at his wife. "Oh, you are a statesman, Louise. More than I shall ever be. You are determined to make the best of this marriage."

"Make the best of it! Why if it came about Alix would have made the most brilliant marriage in Europe."

"Only if she were happy," reiterated Christian.

And so they talked and the time had come to make the journey to Laeken Palace.

The Queen and Alix

Shrouded in her widow's weeds, the Queen arrived at Laeken.

She threw herself into Leopold's arms and burst into tears.

"My dearest Uncle," she sobbed, "you see the most desolate creature in the world."

"My precious child," soothed Leopold, "I understand. I have suffered myself."

"Darling Aunt Louise," murmured the Queen, but nothing of course could compare with the loss of That Saint. "A year ago he was with us . . . I had no idea . . . Oh, Uncle."

Lenchen whispered: "Bear up, Mama," and she looked at her sister Louise and sighed. Afterwards she said that she wanted to remind Mama—if it could have been possible to make such an observation, which of course it wasn't—that they had come to discuss a wedding not a death.

Leopold led the Queen to the room which had been prepared for her and all the time she was weeping and talking of the perfections of her beloved Albert.

The Queen retired to her room and said that she would take her meals there in solitude.

"The Christians will be here tomorrow for luncheon," Leopold reminded her. "And they are bringing Alexandra with them."

The Queen nodded without much interest. "I find it hard to consider a wedding at such a time," she told Leopold. "What a sad occasion Alice's was! And how different it might have been! As for Bertie . . . I can scarcely bear to think of him. When I think of that angel's going to Cambridge in that bitter weather and catching his death . . ."

The Queen broke down again. But she did brighten up a little when she heard that Walpurga Paget was joining them at Laeken. Walpurga had been loud in her praises of Alexandra and had played quite a large part in bringing Alix to the notice of the British royal family. So it seemed fitting that Walpurga should be present. Moreover the Queen had always liked her. Wally was a born gossip and so at heart was Victoria; it was only because Albert deplored the habit that she had succeeded in hiding her love of it.

The next morning Leopold was eagerly making his preparations. He was very anxious for the marriage to take place and he was delighted that it should be he who had arranged the meeting. He was going to do everything he could to get the betrothal formally settled. It was a little depressing that the Queen made such a show of nursing her grief. A little solemnity yes, a little wiping of the eyes, a very proper expression of grief, all that was permissible, and moreover necessary, but the Queen's attitude was positively morbid.

The Danish family arrived and Leopold chuckled to himself to notice the good looks of Alexandra. There were very few Princesses who could compare with her. That abundant light brown hair, the way she carried herself so that her simple clothes appeared to be the height of elegance, her manner which was neither deprecating nor bold, made her a charming creature. And Victoria had always been attracted by beauty in either sex. Surely she must admire Alexandra.

Leopold welcomed them effusively. He conducted them to the apartments where he had decided that the encounter should take place. He despatched one of his gentlemen to the Queen's apartments to tell her that the guests had arrived and were awaiting her pleasure.

To his dismay the Queen sent a message that she was so overwrought by the memories of the past which her meeting with her uncle had evoked that she felt unable to meet anyone at the moment.

Oh dear, thought Leopold. This is a slight to the royal family of Denmark. And what of the luncheon? He had better set it back an hour to give the Queen time to compose herself.

"Her Majesty is bowed down with grief," he explained to his guests. "Her bereavement is comparatively recent."

But there was a further shock. The Queen discovered that she could not face the luncheon at whatever time it was to take place; she would take hers alone in her room.

This was anticlimax. Leopold inwardly cursed, considering all the elaborate arrangements which had gone into the preparation of that luncheon. And what were Prince and Princess Christian thinking? If they were not so eager for the marriage they might go off in a huff.

How different was the meal from how Leopold had imagined it would be. Conversation was stiff and the poor Princess was obviously nervous. If we are not careful we shall have her making a poor impression on Victoria when Her Majesty does deign to see the poor girl, thought Leopold.

Even Walpurga was uneasy.

The luncheon seemed interminable but at least Victoria could plead delay no longer and Leopold suggested that Walpurga should go to the Queen and beg her to come and meet the assembled company.

"You will know how to handle the matter, my dear," he said.

Walpurga agreed that if anyone could she could and fearlessly went to the Queen's apartment.

The Queen held out her arms to her favourite and embraced her. "My dear *dear* Wally, I am pleased to see you. You are a young wife. And how is Augustus? Oh, you fortunate, *fortunate* people . . . I remember so well when *He* came to Windsor . . . He was so *beautiful*. I never saw anyone as beautiful as that angel . . ."

The Queen held her handkerchief to her eyes and wept bitterly.

Walpurga knelt. "Dearest Majesty," she said, "I understand."

"Do you, my dear? Do you? Does anybody?"

"I try to, Your Majesty, but I suppose nobody can really understand your great sorrow."

The Queen enjoyed this kind of talk and Wally well knew it. If anyone suggested that the Queen had a devoted family and should count her blessings they would be immediately out of favour. Her Majesty was best comforted by pointing out the magnitude of her loss, the saintly qualities of the

Prince Consort, the harmony which had existed between them and was now alas lost—and no mention of course of the occasional squabbles when Victoria had felt it necessary to remind Albert that though he might be the Saint she was the Queen.

"Such a wonderful man, Wally, and never appreciated by the people nor by my ministers."

"By no one really but Your Majesty, but then you were the one who was closest to him. He was your life and you were his."

"How true, my dear. I think *you* have a glimmering of understanding. When I think of the dreadful day . . . His dear face was so white and strained. And the last time I looked on that beloved face he was as beautiful as an angel. It was as though all the cares had been smoothed away."

Wally covered her eyes with her hand.

"*Dear* child," said the Queen. And she went on enumerating the virtues of Albert and continuing at even greater length on her own misery.

"I don't feel I can face the world, Wally. I constantly think if he were here . . . and then it all comes back afresh. He is *not* here."

"And Your Majesty has to go on as he would wish. Oh, I can understand the tragedy of it all."

"Everything he wished, everything he planned shall be carried out."

It was Wally's chance and she seized it. "He thought very highly of this match between the Prince of Wales and the Princess of Denmark. I had the honour to sit next to him when Your Majesty graciously allowed me to join the royal table and he spoke of this match then."

The Queen nodded.

"I believe he would have been pleased with the Princess. I think her quiet manner, her good upbringing . . . all that would have carried weight with him. When Your Majesty has seen for yourself . . ."

The Queen sighed.

"Would Your Majesty care to see the Princess and her family now?"

Victoria nodded. "Give me your arm, my child."

Wally did so with alacrity.

The Queen entered the room in which the guests were assembled. Her flowing black robes and her widow's cap gave a sombre note to the proceedings—but not more so than the

Queen herself. Her lips were turned down; there was no smile on her face at all.

Alix was surprised at herself. She was not afraid of the Queen. She felt sorry for her. Poor Queen of England who was nursing her grief and wanted to go on doing so; who was torturing herself, turning her back on the consolations of life.

Victoria looked at the tall graceful girl with the lovely hair, the graceful carriage and innocent blue eyes.

She is charming, thought the Queen, so simply dressed, such exquisite manners and surely that was compassion in her lovely eyes?

And the Princess's father. This was the man who had once sought her in marriage. He was handsome and his daughter had inherited his charm. What an extraordinary situation! Bertie's bride-to-be, the daughter of the man who might have been the Queen's husband. Yes, she liked Prince Christian and she liked his daughter.

And Princess Christian? The Queen looked at Louise severely. A domineering woman, she had heard; and no woman should domineer over her husband. It was the wife's place to be subservient. Albert had felt that *very* strongly. In the beginning of their life together she had been very foolish and Albert had had to be very patient. She had in time learned the lesson which all women had to learn, but of course it was more difficult for queens.

I believe she paints her cheeks! thought the Queen. How shocked Albert would have been. He hated any form of artificiality.

The Queen's manner was cool as she addressed Alexandra's parents.

"I can make no promises," she said, staring at Louise's painted cheeks. "Everything will depend on whether the Prince of Wales feels sufficiently affectionate towards your daughter to accept her as his wife."

Leopold was on tenterhooks. If only Albert had been here he might have made her understand that Prince and Princess Christian were proud and dignified. They wanted this marriage, true; and so did the Queen's ministers—and so had Albert—but they would not wish Alexandra to marry if she did not wish to, so there was no need to stress this point.

The Queen looked severely at Alix. "You are young," she said, "and ours is a house of mourning. I do not believe it will *ever* be anything else. You never knew him and you cannot therefore understand what we have lost." She turned away to wipe her eyes and Leopold chose the moment to slip his arm through hers and ask if he might lure her away from the company for a while.

She showed her eagerness to be lured. The interview was over, leaving a rather bewildered Prince and Princess of Denmark with their daughter strangely enough slightly less so.

In their apartments Louise declared: "She was quite insulting."

"She didn't mean to be, of course," Christian defended her.

"She may be the Queen of England but you will one day be the King of Denmark. She seems to forget that. Poor Alix!"

"Alix, my dear," said Christian, "if you wish to abandon this marriage you have only to say so."

"Oh no, Papa. I shall not be marrying the Queen."

"She will always be there."

"Bertie is quite different."

"Indeed yes," said Christian uneasily.

"She kept staring at me as though there was something abnormal about me," complained Louise.

"That's because you're my wife," replied Christian. *"She* might have been once but she married the incomparable Albert instead."

"Surely no one is as good as he is made out to be?"

"He was in her eyes," said Alix.

"She doesn't seem to have upset you as she has the rest of us," said her mother.

"No, she didn't upset me. I think I could understand her."

As Louise said to Christian when they were alone, Alix was so eager to take Bertie that she would accept his mother at the same time.

Alix put on a black dress for dinner.

"My dear child," said Louise, "you look as though you're in mourning."

"She is," replied Alix, "so perhaps we should be in sympathy with her."

Louise said: "Well, it is becoming. It shows up your skin and hair to perfection, and simplicity can sometimes be more effective than fuss and feathers—as Countess Danner might learn."

The Queen did not appear at dinner but afterwards she joined them.

Her eyes lighted up with pleasure when she saw Alix in her black dress. She understood the gesture at once.

"My dear child," was all she said, but there were tears in her eyes.

And there was no doubt in the minds of all observers that Alix had come through the trying ordeal very well indeed.

The Queen had shown her approval. She complained that Princess Louise was deaf and therefore difficult to talk to and that she painted her cheeks and she did not care for what she had heard of her; but Alexandra was charming and so was her father, though of course Denmark was not the most important of countries. However, Bertie might go on with his courtship.

The Queen travelled on to Coburg to see Albert's brother Ernest, whose conduct she was beginning to find most unsatisfactory now that Albert was not there to advise and criticize him. She visited once more the haunts of *his* childhood, wept over his relics in the Museum he had founded with his brother, and in fact wallowed afresh in her grief.

Alix with her parents returned to the house they had rented in Ostend, and the very next day Bertie joined them there.

Alix was happy. How different he was from his mother. It seemed so strange that he should be the son of such a mother and such a father. No one could have been more unlike the sainted Albert. Thank heaven! thought Alix with a laugh.

Bertie was amusing and light-hearted. He talked of his adventures in North America and the Far East—but he did not mention marriage. That was of course to be a more ceremonial affair. And almost immediately there was an invitation from Uncle Leopold for them to return to the Laeken Palace and Alix realized that this was going to be the scene for the great occasion.

Uncle Leopold was beaming with pleasure. The Queen's departure had lifted a great cloud from the Palace. Now there would be a magnificent luncheon with all the guests arriving as arranged and a great deal of animated conversation and laughter. Uncle Leopold, as he usually did, talked a great deal about his ailments, but he did it in a manner which suggested they were like a lot of relations whose tiresomeness he found intriguing.

After the luncheon he suggested that his guests might like to see the gardens and they all wandered out in little groups.

Bertie and Alix were alone. She talked to him about the flowers, of which she was very knowledgeable, and finally they found themselves in a secluded grotto where Bertie suggested they sit down for a moment.

"Alix," he said, "I think you know what I'm going to say, Will you marry me?"

Alix was too straightforward to make a pretence of surprise.

"If you are asking me because you want me to with all your heart, the answer is Yes. If it is because the Queen has commanded you to do so, it is No."

Bertie laughed and taking her hands kissed her. There was nothing inexpert about Bertie's methods of kissing, and he could admirably convey his feelings by the act.

"I think the answer is yes," said Alix laughing.

Bertie kissed her again. She was the most beautiful Princess he had ever seen, he told her. When he saw her in the Cathedral he could not believe his good fortune.

"And when I realized what it was all about nor could I."

"Then we are indeed the happy pair."

Bertie told her how he had been aware of her beauty before he had seen her—he was not counting those occasions in their childhood when he had been too obtuse to notice her—because he had seen a picture of her. It must have been one of those photographs of royal people which were sold in shops because a friend of his was telling him about a young woman with whom he had fallen in love and had brought a picture out of his pocket to show him.

"When I saw it," explained Bertie, "I thought it was the loveliest face I had ever seen. I said: 'Why, she's beautiful!' Then he saw what he had done. He had shown me the wrong picture. 'That's not my girl,' he said. 'That's a picture of the Princess Alexandra.'"

It was a very happy quarter of an hour they spent in the grotto, and at the end of that time they had no doubt whatever that they were in love.

They were radiant when they entered the Palace and were immediately sought out by Uncle Leopold who came towards them, limping effectively to call attention to his rheumatism, and embracing them both warmly.

"My dear children," he said, "there's no need to tell me. I know." And he thought: This could mean England will support Denmark if Prussia should stretch out its greedy hands to interfere with Schleswig-Holstein, which would be very much to the advantage of Belgium.

The few days passed idyllically and then there must be separation.

The Queen decided that Bertie and Alix must say goodbye and not meet again until the wedding day. It was most unseemly for them to be too much in each other's company before they were married. Heaven knew what might happen. And she did not trust the Princess Louise, who had a reputation for being master in the house, and was deaf and painted her cheeks.

As she progressed on her journey she grew a little startled because news of the betrothal had seeped out and the Germans were not pleased. Her welcome was lukewarm in spite of her flowing widow's weeds and her sorrow. Ernest was most difficult. He didn't approve of the Danish match at all, and had in fact brought forth a big rebuke from Albert in the last year of his life for attempting to interfere. Vicky was not very popular in Prussia, particularly now that it was known that she had had a hand in helping to arrange the marriage.

Oh dear, the Queen had always wanted friendship with Germany because Albert was a German, she was half German herself, Vicky was married to one, her darling grandson Wilhelm was one. To be on bad terms with Germany was like a rift in the family.

And as she went on her sorrowing way she grew more and more uneasy.

The journey had done little to comfort the Queen. She had gone to the land of his birth, visited places which they had seen together, wept copious tears, talking of him incessantly; she had not expected to be happy, but she had expected sympathy. She would have to watch Ernest, who was ruling Saxe-Coburg in a most unsatisfactory manner. Albert had wanted his second son Alfred to inherit Saxe-Coburg on the death of Ernest and that meant of course that the dear angel looking down on her from his place of honour above would expect her to make sure that Alfred's inheritance was not ruined before it came to him. Ernest had no children—which was not to be wondered at considering the life he had led. How different from his angelic brother! His debts were numerous. She must make sure that when the time came Affie was not burdened with them.

"Oh, Albert, my precious love, why are you not here to manage these matters? What can I do without you? What can England do without you?"

She told her wardrobe maid, Annie MacDonald, that she longed to join him in the mausoleum at Frogmore. But Annie replied in that rather curt way which some of her favoured servants used towards her, "Well, M'am, you've got your duty to do. You've got the country to look after. And going and lying down there in Frogmore is not what the Prince would have wanted. He'd rather you stayed up here and got on with the work."

"Oh, Annie, you are right," she cried weeping.

And she wondered what she could do without people like Annie and John Brown (dear Scots both of them) up at Balmoral who spoke to her in that familiar way which endeared them to her because it showed how *faithful* they were.

She was certainly worried about Bertie. When had she *not* been worried about Bertie? Their eldest son had been an anxiety to them both. But for Bertie's wicked conduct at the Curragh Camp . . . But she should not think of that because it made her so angry and she must try to think of what was best for the country—as Annie so rightly pointed out.

Albert had said that if there was a match with Denmark the Princess Alexandra would have to understand that the Prince of Wales was marrying her and not her relations, which meant of course that whatever happened about Schleswig-Holstein would be no concern of England's—that was no *family* concern. It might well be a political one.

Did Alexandra understand this? The girl seemed docile. But she had that *dreadful* mother. A woman who painted her cheeks. What would Albert have said!

This must be made clear; and she herself must see that Alexandra's position was *absolutely* clear to her *before* she could be allowed to become the Princess of Wales.

The family was back at the Yellow Palace. Alix and Dagmar shut themselves up in Alix's bedroom and Alix told her sister what had happened at the Laeken Palace. It was all very exciting. Bertie was wonderful. He loved her—for herself—and she loved him; and they were going to live happily ever after.

Dagmar listened wide-eyed; she knew that her turn would come very soon. Thyra they decided was too young to share their confidences. She merely knew that Alix was going to be married and everyone was very excited about it.

The gong was sounding for luncheon. Alix had been looking at her dresses and wondering what alterations she could make to some of them. Though of course she would probably have a new trousseau. Her eyes sparkled at the thought. She would choose the colours and consult the dressmaker. What fun that would be. To have exactly the material one wanted—not to have to makeshift.

She realized that it must have been some minutes since the gong had sounded. She would be late again.

She was right: she was, and the family were all at table. Her father looked at her with tender reproach. She was getting a little old now to be denied a second helping, or to stand while drinking her coffee. Prince Christian realized that all his attempts to cure her besetting sin had failed.

So he said nothing and she slid into her seat. Conversation was a little strained, she sensed, though the younger ones were not aware of it, so she was not surprised that when the meal was over she was asked to step into her father's study.

There her parents said that they had something to tell her and it was obvious from their expressions that it was not very pleasant.

"We have had a letter from Queen Victoria," said Prince Christian.

"An ultimatum," retorted his wife.

"Dear Alix," said Christian tenderly, "I'm afraid this is going to be something of an ordeal. The Queen wants you to go to England without us and to spend a month with her."

"Oh?" said Alix.

"Can you imagine it?" cried Louise.

"Yes, Mama. It will give me an opportunity to get to know her."

The parents exchanged glances. Truly Alexandra was a strange girl. She seemed to have no fear of the forbidding Queen and her house of mourning.

"You mean to say that you don't mind?"

"I think we shall be all right together, Mama," said Alexandra.

She couldn't of course realize what it meant, thought her parents. Or was she so besottedly in love with Bertie that she was prepared to face any ordeal for his sake?

"You will have to be punctual in England," her father warned her.

"I shall try hard, Papa, but I daresay I shall slip up now and then," she replied with a smile.

Bertie was horrified. Poor Alix to be submitted to that. Oh God, he thought, I must save her.

He was delighted with the prospects of his marriage. She was a real beauty and she had charm too and poise. He would have found it very difficult to discover a Princess as attractive as Alix. He was in a way in love with her; he could easily fall in love with pretty women; they interested him more than anything else. He liked gambling, jolly company, practical jokes, lots of fun—all the things he had been deprived of by his parents so far, but women came first. All that would be changed once he was married. The Queen could scarcely treat a married man as though he were a child.

Alix—dear, jolly, beautiful Alix—would be the means of giving him his freedom, so naturally he was in love with her.

He really must care about her quite a lot for he was very indignant at the thought of her having to face that ordeal. Imagine being shut up for a month with Mama at dreary Osborne or Windsor—or Balmoral with that tiresome John Brown hovering over the Queen as though she were incapable and he was her keeper, and anywhere was dreary where Mama was nowadays. Poor Alix, she would have to listen to accounts of the perfections of the Prince Consort, his virtues, the lack of appreciation, how he had lived, how he had died. Surely she wouldn't bring up that incident of the Curragh Camp? He'd soon explain that away if she did, and in any case he fancied Alix was not so strait-laced as not to understand that there was no great harm in sowing a few wild oats before marriage.

Poor dear Alix—he had to save her if he could. He appealed to Uncle Leopold, who saw his point.

Oh no, said Leopold, that was too much. Poor Alix would need to be at home to prepare herself for her wedding. She could not be expected to come to England in the winter of all times and share in the Queen's mourning. He promised to write to the Queen, which he did.

Victoria read his letter and threw it aside. Dear Uncle Leopold, she loved him so much, but he did have a tendency to look upon himself as the head of the family, the head of Europe for that matter. Albert had said so. And what had Albert said of Alix? She must be made to understand that Bertie would be marrying her and not her family. There would be no involvement with Danish affairs, unless it was for the good of England that this should be.

She wrote to Prince Christian. She would expect Alix at Osborne on the 7th of November. He might bring her and stay for two days; then he should return to Denmark and come over to take her back in December. The Queen wished to have Alix to herself for a month.

Alix arrived at Osborne on a cold and misty November evening.

The Queen and her daughters were waiting to receive her. Alix, in spite of the weather, managed to look charming and the Queen noted this with pleasure.

"My dear *dear* child," she murmured, embracing her. "You must be perished with cold and worn out with the journey." She acknowledged Prince Christian's greeting and said that Lenchen should show him to his room. She herself took Alix to hers.

"How pretty you look," she said. "I am glad you came. There is so much we shall have to say to each other."

Alix looked at her and thought of her sad loss and how unhappy she would be if Bertie died; and she remembered how important her own father and mother were to each other, and she believed she understood a little of the Queen's grief. Victoria was aware of this and was certain that in Alix she was going to find a new daughter.

When they were all together in the Queen's sitting-room after supper had been served the Queen explained to them all what Osborne had been like before Prince Albert had changed it. "His one idea was to give me a house which he considered worthy of me. Everything he did he did to perfection. There were many roles he could have played in life, but he was taken from me."

The tears began to flow.

Christian took his leave of his daughter.

"My dear child," he said, "if it becomes intolerable you must let me know. I wouldn't have you unhappy for the world."

She flung her arms round his neck. "Dearest Papa, *you* are an angel."

"Oh no, not that!" he said and she smiled with him.

"Poor Queen, how desolate she is. I shall do my best to cheer her."

"Good-bye, my child. Try to be punctual."

"Oh, I will, Papa, I promise you."

Then he was gone.

There were many interviews with the Queen. Alix understood, she hoped, that when a Princess married, her family was that one which was her husband's. A Princess came into a new country. That country's ideals became hers. That country's customs and so on. Alix must understand that.

Yes, said Alix, she did.

"It was different in my case. I was the Queen. Albert was a second son of the house of Saxe-Coburg, as you know. It was his duty to come and live here. I shall never forget the day he arrived. I stood at the top of the staircase at Windsor and I thought an angel had come to me . . ."

Every conversation came back to him. Alix began to expect it. She learned a great deal about the Prince Consort and the more she heard the more it seemed to her what an uncomfortable person he must have been. His many perfections made him formidable and she did think that perhaps he was a little critical of those who were not of his own opinions.

But she listened sympathetically and the Queen enjoyed talking to her and going over the sorrowful events which had led to his death.

Victoria wondered whether she should mention the Curragh Camp incident. If she did not someone might. It would be better, she supposed, if the child heard it from her. She decided to tell her and played it down a little.

There had been an unfortunate incident in Bertie's past. He had been led astray by wicked people. She would know of course that Bertie did not possess his father's saintly qualities.

Thank God! thought Alix.

But then how many people could be expected to? asked the Queen. There was no one in the world to compare with that Incomparable Creature.

Alix would forget Bertie's one lapse, commanded the Queen. It sometimes happened to young men and she had no doubt that Bertie himself would make a full confession before his marriage. She wanted Alix to tell him that she understood and of course when he was married such temptations would not occur. Alix would see to that. She was very happy that Bertie was going to marry and she wanted Alix to know that she believed whole-heartedly that he had chosen the one who would be the best wife in the world for him.

It was not all gloom and the Queen's daughters, who would be her new sisters, could be quite merry when the Queen was not present. Beatrice—known as Baby still—was six and could even make the Queen smile with her quaint sayings. Alix enjoyed playing with her; and there was no doubt that they got on very well together. None of them was as terrifying as Vicky. Alice, the eldest of the girls, now pregnant, was very quiet and sweet-natured. Lenchen, who was herself getting near to marriageable age, was very interested in everything concerning the wedding; so was Louise, who was only two years younger. Arthur and Leopold kept out of the way, but Cousin Mary Cambridge, who had grown very fat, was a constant visitor and clearly delighted to have Alix in the country and was, Alix knew, secretly congratulating herself that she had helped to set the marriage plans in motion.

There was a visit to Windsor Castle—an awe-inspiring place, very gloomy, but it could have been different in other circumstances.

The weeks passed. Cousin Mary wanted to help with the trousseau and she and Alix spent many a happy hour discussing fashions and materials and what would be required.

It was with the Cambridges that Christian stayed when at the end of the month he came to take Alix home. The Queen did not invite him to Windsor nor did she ask to see him. Alix drove to Cambridge Lodge and there found her father.

They embraced warmly and then he held her away from him and looked at her searchingly.

"You are all right?" he asked anxiously.

"But of course, Papa. What did you expect?"

"And you want to marry and live here for the rest of your life?"

"I want to marry Bertie," she said.

"I'm satisfied now," said her father.

Bertie was waiting for them when they arrived at Calais. Gay and debonair, very gallant and attentive, how different from his mother! Alix was enchanted.

"My dearest Alix, how was it?" he asked earnestly.

"Oh, it was . . . quite pleasant."

"I was so worried about you."

Alix felt she could have endured anything that evoked such concern in Bertie.

"I do hope she wasn't too demanding."

"No, we grew quite fond of each other."

Bertie looked at her in wonderment. Beautiful, lively and able to endure the Queen! She was a paragon.

They travelled to Hanover together and then on to Cologne. The few days they were together were delightful and made up for anything she had endured during her stay in England.

Bertie talked a great deal about the things they would do when they were married. Then they would escape from the Queen's surveillance. It was going to be very different for Bertie from what it had ever been before. Parliament would vote him a big allowance; she would have one, too, of course. They would be able to enjoy life. It was all going to be wonderful. But best of all, they would be free to live their own lives.

"Of course the Queen will be there in the background," said Bertie, "but we shall be the leaders of fashion. My parents were never that. But the people will expect it of us. We are young and they'll like us for that alone. They never liked my father."

"Is that really so?"

Bertie laughed. "Oh, you have had a diet of Mama's special brand. Other people didn't dote on him as she did. He didn't believe in enjoying life. And that is something I believe in whole-heartedly. And, Alix, I believe you do too. That is why we are going to be ideally happy."

Alix was thinking of river picnics and visits to Frankfurt and games on the lawns of Bernstorff. That was what she called being ideally happy. Bertie's ideas were rather different. He wanted what he had glimpsed briefly so far—the society of amusing people, beautiful women who flattered him and were eager to be on friendly terms with the Prince of Wales, horse-racing, gambling, gay parties, good food and wine. There was so much waiting for Bertie to enjoy once he had escaped from that yoke which his father had put about him and which his mother was endeavouring to keep tightly padlocked.

It was with great regret that they parted at Hamburg. Alix to return to Copenhagen to prepare for her wedding, Bertie to go back to Windsor.

He groaned when he considered what awaited him there. "The first anniversary of my father's death; can you imagine, Alix, what that will be like?"

Having been there, she could.

"I expect we shall spend the day in the Frogmore Mausoleum. It's going to be unendurably melancholy."

"You'll endure it," said Alix softly.

"Yes, I shall, because I shall be thinking of you, and reminding myself that soon we shall be married. I shall be my own master then. And I'll have you too."

They embraced and Bertie went back to the house of mourning while Alix rode on in high spirits. Everything had gone so well. She was going to marry Bertie, and they loved each other and would be happy ever after.

Bertie hadn't mentioned Curragh Camp. He had put it aside as unimportant. She did not want him to make a confession as the Queen thought he might. That was all over. Bertie would not wish to disturb her with such a thing. It didn't matter in any case. The past was over. It was the future which was important and that lay before them, bright and promising great happiness.

The Wedding at Windsor

Rarely had there been such excitement in Copenhagen, and the heroine of the hour was Princess Alexandra. Ever since King Frederick had led his armies into battle over the Schleswig-Holstein controversy an uneasiness had prevailed with the King and his ministers because they knew that although it appeared that that particular war had been satisfactorily concluded this was not in fact the case. Schleswig-Holstein was like an ulcer in Denmark's side—dormant at the time but ready to break out at any moment.

King Frederick came to the Yellow Palace to congratulate Princess Christian and Louise on this forthcoming marriage.

"But it is wonderful," he cried. "There is nothing that could please me more. Our beautiful Alexandra to become the Princess of Wales. You know how anxious we have been. This will mean that the English are our allies. The Prussians won't dare to strike while we have England behind us."

"You think that Alix will have so much influence?"

"My dear Louise, not Alix herself. Our dear girl is not made for politics. She has been born to charm. But England would come to our aid if the home of the Princess of Wales was attacked. There could not be anything that pleased me more. And now that the Russians are putting out feelers for Dagmar . . . why, Christian, my boy, you have served your country well through your daughters."

To show his pleasure he presented Alix with a necklace composed of pearls and diamonds.

"There, my dear," he said placing it round her neck, "whenever you wear this think of Denmark."

Countess Danner, who had come to the Yellow Palace with Frederick, looked on sourly. She would have loved to possess such jewellery.

Later in her bedroom the family came to admire the necklace. Alix put it on rather gingerly and said that it did not match up with anything she had and she did not know when she would wear it.

"You'll wear it at balls and banquets to which you'll go with your husband," said Thyra. "Oh, Alix, you'll look marvellous. Shall you have a crown? Oh, *do* have a crown. That would be perfect. And think how it would match the necklace."

Alix said that only Kings and Queens had crowns but a tiara would be very nice. But nine-year-old Thyra thought a crown would be best.

"You'll have to wait until the old Queen dies," she said. "Then you'll get your crown."

"Oh, don't talk about her dying," cried Alix.

"Is it unlucky?"

"I don't know but I met her you know and in a way . . . I quite liked her. Besides I should be terrified to be Queen. Princess of Wales will do very nicely for a start."

Dagmar regarded her sister with solemn eyes. Thyra didn't seem to realize that this was going to be the break-up of the family. In future when they went out riding or played their games or packed up for the summer visits to Rumpenheim, Alix would not be with them. Nothing would be the same again; and then very soon she herself might go away . . . perhaps to Russia.

Everyone was so excited and said it was such good fortune, but losing Alix from the family circle seemed just the opposite to Dagmar.

The Queen was sending despotic messages from Windsor. The wedding should take place in January. She saw no reason for delay.

"Good Heavens," cried Louise, "she cannot dictate to us in this way. Imagine poor Alix leaving at that time of the year. The ports would doubtless be frozen up in any case. Besides it is for us to say when the wedding shall be. January is far too soon."

The Queen wrote back. She granted that the weather might prevent Alix's coming in January, but her daughter Alice was due to have her baby in February and as it was Alice's first and the confinement was to take place at Windsor, that made February out of the question.

March was agreed upon.

Uncle Leopold, not to be left out of the excitement, suggested that Alix should stay a few days in Brussels *en route* for England. It would give her a respite which would be much needed. It would also give Leopold an opportunity of grounding her in what he would expect of her when she was Princess of Wales. He would want to remind her that he had played his part in bringing about this brilliant marriage, also that he was the favourite uncle of the Queen and his opinions carried some weight with her.

The arrangements were finally agreed to and the deputations began to arrive at the Yellow Palace. All day long people were calling from the foreign embassies; the tradesmen came too and there were long speeches to be listened to, gifts to be accepted, elaborate and humble. The shoemakers of Copenhagen presented the Princess with a pair of gold embroidered shoes and the villagers of Bernstorff gave her porcelain vases in a wicker basket tied with ribbons in the colours of the flags of Denmark and England. These small gifts touched her more deeply than the diamond and pearl necklace given by the King.

The Queen wrote that she was presenting the bride with a wedding gown of Honiton lace and it was already being made for her. It would be one of her wedding presents to the Princess, to whom she always referred as dear sweet Alix, which confirmed the belief that Alix had made an unusually good impression on her.

The dark February days seemed to grow shorter and shorter. Poor Dagmar was very despondent and Alix knew that she herself was going to feel the separation deeply, but she had Bertie to comfort her while Dagmar had only her hopes—or fears—of the Russian alliance.

Each day the Rev. M. S. Ellis, who was Chaplain to the British Legation in Copenhagen, came to the Yellow Palace to instruct her in the form of Protestantism which was practised in England and was slightly different from the Lutheranism of Denmark.

Then there were the balls and receptions given in her honour. Wally's husband—now Sir Augustus—gave a ball for her at the British Embassy. Wally was more vivacious than ever and obviously delighted that her efforts had borne fruit. She whispered to Alix that she looked beautiful and Bertie was going to be very proud of her. And Wally of course would pay frequent visits to England. "Don't forget I'm married to an Englishman," she said with a grimace towards her handsome husband.

Alix's grandparents gave a party for her and her grandfather was clearly delighted with her.

"Such an ugly little thing you were when you were born," he kept reminding her.

Then of course there was the reception at the Yellow Palace when she must say good-bye to all those who had taught her and served her during her childhood. This was the saddest of them all.

Dear Miss Knudsen, who had taught her English and had become a friend, was very sad. Alix knew that she owed a great deal to her because under her tuition her English had become quite good. She had only the faintest accent which Bertie assured her was adorable and now and then she used expressions which might not have been exactly English but which she realized were quaint and charming.

Then came the last night in the Yellow Palace. Dagmar stayed late in her room and they sat talking of the past. Poor Dagmar, who was going to be lonely and was a little apprehensive. Dagmar was far cleverer than she was. Louise had always said so. Alix was not the clever one in the family, even though she might be the beauty.

"You were always so much quicker at lessons than I," she told Dagmar to cheer her. "When you marry you'll have nothing to fear. You will understand politics and everything. I'm lucky. Bertie told me he was glad I was not one of those clever women. He couldn't abide them. Suppose he had been like his father. I would never have done."

"There aren't many men like him, I suppose."

"According to the Queen, alas—according to Bertie thank heaven—No!"

"Bertie is a little disrespectful towards his dear papa."

"Bertie is honest. And *I* think he is much nicer than his saintly papa."

"I'm sure of that," said Dagmar.

Then they talked of tomorrow and the journey and the wedding. It was all so exciting.

"I'm sure I shall never sleep tonight," said Alix.

But Dagmar said she would and kissing her good night went rather sorrowfully to her own room.

Alix tried to turn her attention to *The Heir of Redcylffe* which Miss Knudsen had lent her and which she said would improve her English. She must finish it because she must give it back to Miss Knudsen before she left for England.

Alix woke in her little room in the Yellow Palace on the 28th of February 1863 and the first thing she thought was: "I shall never sleep in this room again."

She looked about it at the piano, the cabinet and the work table and remembered how when she had returned from her confirmation her mother had brought her up here and told her that now she was grown up she should have a room of her own. How important that had seemed! She had felt then that she had come to the greatest turning point in her life. But what was that compared with this?

Louise came in.

"Well, my dear, this is the day and there is a great deal to do." She smiled wryly. "You must not be late in leaving."

"We are not to leave until this afternoon."

"No, but there is plenty to do before that."

She was right; the morning was gone before she was ready for it, and then the carriages which would take them to the railway station were at the door.

The family were clustered round her. She was thankful that this was not the final farewell for they were all accompanying her to England for the ceremony; even little Valdemar was to come with them. He was only four and although the ceremony would mean little to him, could not be left at home.

The streets of Copenhagen were crowded. The English marriage had been the main topic of conversation throughout the whole of Denmark ever since the Princess had gone to England and won the approval of the Queen. The English match was the best possible thing for Denmark which would be allied to that most powerful country through marriage; and with Prussian threats beginning to menace that was a very comforting thought. So there were cheers for the elegant girl who had given them this comfort; and how proud they were of her, for she looked very elegant in a brown silk dress with white stripes and a little bonnet perched on her head. Flowers were thrown at the carriage as it passed and people crowded round it so that at one time it seemed as though they would be unable to move. This was a loving demonstration and Alexandra was deeply moved by it.

All the same it was a relief to settle into the train. Christian and Louise smiled approvingly at their daughter.

"The first stage is over," said Christian, "and may I say you did very well, my dear."

"Oh, that part was easy," said Alix with a smile

"They are such loyal good people," added Louise.

"Well, they've known me all my life," Alix reminded her. "They will have seen me perhaps walking along the Lange Linie and gazing into the shops and wondering whether I could copy the dresses there."

"It will be different now," said Louise. "Dagmar and Thyra will have to carry on though for a while."

"It won't be the same without Alix," said Dagmar quietly. "She always knows how a dress is going to look before it's made."

"We're going to miss our Alix," said Christian sadly.

"Now, Papa," reproved Louise, "don't let us be morbid."

She called attention to Valdemar who was talking to his new toy donkey and showing him the countryside they were passing through.

"Isn't this a great adventure, Valdy darling?" said Alix.

Valdemar nodded. "Donkey likes trains," he said.

"And you, Valdy dear, what do you like?"

He thought for a while and then he said, "I like Donkey."

And the happy domestic atmosphere seemed to have come back to them.

* * *

There were receptions everywhere they stopped, even in Germany, which was strange because the Germans were somewhat put out by the match. English royalty usually married Germans; English royalty *was* half German. The Germans felt this departure from an old custom and taking in Denmark was to some extent a slight on their princesses. But Alexandra was young and charming and whatever the statesmen thought the people could not resist a beautiful bride.

At the Laeken Palace Uncle Leopold was waiting to welcome them.

He embraced Alix warmly, and called her his dear child. He was so happy about this match. It was the best thing possible for Bertie and for Alix—his dear, dear children. "I'm as happy now as when Victoria married Albert," he told Alix, "my niece and my nephew but to me they were like daughter and son, as you two young people are. I have suffered such pain these last weeks. My doctors told me I should have stayed in bed. 'In bed,' I said, 'when my dearest Alexandra is coming to visit me *en route* for England for her marriage with that other dear child of mine!' Whatever pain I had to suffer I was not going to stay in bed."

He hobbled round effectively now and then giving a little grimace to indicate how bad the pain was but Uncle Leopold so obviously enjoyed his ailments that his calling attention to them added nothing sombre to the occasion, for with his painted cheeks, his built-up shoes to make him look taller and his pleasant wig, he still retained signs of the singularly handsome man he had been in his youth.

He had promised himself many little chats with Alexandra. He knew so much about the English Court and way of life that he wanted to give her the benefit of his knowledge. If she were in any difficulty at any time she would know that all she had to do was to write to him.

Alix listened charmingly. She was sure, she said, that she would never learn anything about politics. They were so complicated.

"You must remember that you will have a certain influence with your husband, my dear child. And he will become more and more important, particularly if the Queen remains in seclusion as she has since the Consort's death. You could have a part to play. Always remember your own country and your own good friends. The stability of Denmark . . . and Belgium . . . is very necessary to European peace. I should not like to see that threatened or it could mean great trouble. Always remember that if you are bewildered about anything, you can always write to me for advice. I will be to you what I was to the Queen in the days when she needed me."

Alix thanked him, but she was determined not to meddle in politics. She was sure Bertie would not like it.

Leopold said that he had a surprise for her. Would she care to see?

She was eager to but when she saw the dress of Brussels lace and realized that it was to be her wedding gown she was dismayed.

The Queen had told her that she was presenting her with a wedding dress of Honiton lace—and how could she have two wedding dresses?

Alix said the dress was beautiful; then she hurried to her parents to explain her dilemma to them.

"The Queen would be furious if you did not wear the wedding dress she is giving you," said Christian.

"Leopold will be if she doesn't wear his," was Louise's answer.

"What can we do?" Christian wondered.

"I must consult the ambassador," said Louise. "This is too important a matter for us to settle."

So the battle of Honiton and Brussels lace began. The Queen was indignant. It was impossible for dear sweet Alix to be married in *foreign* lace. Everybody knew, commented Leopold, that Brussels lace was the best in the world. But the Queen did not think it was to be compared with Honiton lace. Her own wedding dress had been trimmed with Honiton lace. She could not—and what was more would not—give her consent to dear sweet Alix's being married in anything but the wedding dress which she had provided.

Leopold realized that he must back out graciously.

So Honiton won.

The Queen's own yacht, *Victoria and Albert*, was waiting for the party at Antwerp. They sailed to Flushing and prepared to cross the Channel.

The crossing was smooth and when the *Victoria and Albert* came into the Margate Roads the guns roared forth. Boats came out to the yacht carrying loyal messages of greeting; and the welcome was as great at Southend and Sheerness.

As they approached Gravesend, Louise whispered to her daughter that it was time she went to her cabin to change the simple dress she was wearing. Bertie would doubtless come out to meet her and this was one of the occasions when it was imperative that she must be ready on time.

Alexandra put on a mauve Irish poplin dress which had been specially made for this occasion and over it she wore a long cloak of the same colour as her dress but of velvet trimmed with sable; on her head was a poke bonnet in white, decorated with tiny roses.

The effect was charming and when her parents saw her even they were startled by her beauty, which the exhausting journey had done nothing to impair.

Bertie had come out on his private yacht and on the deck of the *Victoria and Albert* they greeted each other. When Bertie kissed her warmly a cheer went up from the spectators and together they prepared to go ashore.

On the pier, some sixty girls dressed in red and white—Danish colours—were waiting to throw down flowers for her to walk on; the pier itself was decorated with orange blossom; what was so charming were the heads of deputations who came to present her with flowers for they had learned Danish phrases to say to her and their quaint pronunciation amused her.

Then began the drive to London where they would take the train for Windsor.

The entry into London was so enthusiastic as to be alarming. Alix had never seen so many people. They had heard accounts of the beauty of the Princess and were determined to see for themselves; and when they discovered that reports had not been exaggerated, they were delighted. The March wind was biting but that deterred no one. There they were in their tens of thousands all come to welcome the new Princess of Wales. Bertie was already very popular. Royal scandals always managed to seep out and it had long been known that Bertie was at variance with his parents. The Prince Consort had tried to cram learning into his son. Bertie had resisted. The Prince had tried to make another such as himself of the Prince of Wales. But the people did not want another. One German saint was enough. In fact they did not accept Albert as saint. To many of the public he was an ambitious man who had tried to rule England and had suppressed all the natural gaiety of the Queen. But Bertie had stood out against that. Bertie was gay; there were rumours of a little affair at the Curragh Camp of which a great deal had been made, and who could blame Bertie, kept down as he was? Bertie was human, something his father was not. "Good old Teddy," said the people. So they wanted to see what sort of bride he was getting. And when they saw her, very pretty, charmingly dressed, elegant and smiling, they were delighted with her.

"Long live the Danish Princess," they cried. "And long live the Prince of Wales."

Moreover there would be a royal wedding and that always meant a good time. The Queen had been in mourning too long. The people were tired of it. They would now have some gaiety.

The journey through London was a nightmare. The people's enthusiasm had got out of control and the farther the procession penetrated into the capital, the more terrifying an ordeal it became. The people were exuberant. They wanted to show their enthusiasm. They crowded round the carriages and brought them to a halt. At the Mansion House Alix's carriage was almost overturned and she clung to the upholstery in dismay. The people, some well dressed, some ragged, pressed about her. There were shrieks in the crowd as some feared they would be trampled to death. When the carriage was brought to a standstill several men pushed forward and tried to unharness the horses shouting their intention to drag the bride's carriage to Paddington.

It was frightening. Alix had never seen so many people, and tempers in the crowd ran high when there were disputes among the spectators. It seemed at one time that the police would be unable to keep order and that there would be a riot.

The Prince's equerry, however, came to the rescue. He appealed to the crowd to let them pass. Alix smiled at those who pressed round and in her quaint English begged them to let her get through. They fell back. She was so gentle and she perhaps made them realize how they were adding to her ordeal. In any case the crowd fell back and the carriages were able to make their slow progress to Paddington.

They were very late arriving at Windsor and then it was raining. Alix was rather pleased about this. The ride through London had been tiring as well as often terrifying and it was a blessing to be able to ride in a closed carriage.

At last they reached Windsor where the Queen and her daughters were waiting to receive them.

The Queen, in her black mourning dress and widow's cap, embraced them warmly.

"Dear sweet Alix is worn out, I am sure," she said. "She must take half an hour's rest before dinner."

This Alix would have been pleased to do, but she was too excited to lie down and since she must wash and change and had only half an hour in which to do it, she must immediately prepare, remembering always of course that she must not be late on this her first evening at the Castle.

Lenchen came to her room when it was time to go to dinner.

"Mama is taking hers in her room," she explained. "Your arrival has reminded her of the day Papa came and she feels too sad and unhappy to join us."

Truly she had come into a house of mourning. But of course dinner was a much more lively meal—and really quite enjoyable—without that sorrowing presence.

Alix could not stop thinking of the Queen, and how sad it was for her at such a time. When her son was about to marry naturally she would be thinking of her own marriage and her desolation would be great. It seemed wrong to feel gay with the others. She asked Lenchen where the Queen would be and Lenchen replied that she was in the Royal Closet where she spent so much time brooding on the past.

Acting on impulse Alix slipped away from the company and went to the Royal Closet. When she knocked on the door, an imperious voice demanded: "Who is there?" Alix opened the door and stood on the threshold of the room for a second; then she went to the humped figure in the flowing black robes and kneeling looked up into that melancholy face.

"I wanted to tell Your Majesty that I kept thinking of you and your sorrow . . . at such a time . . ."

The tears began to fall down the Queen's cheeks. She bent forward and kissed Alix. "Dear sweet child," she murmured. "So graceful, so beautiful and so *feeling*."

It was very soon clear that the Queen had taken Alix to her heart.

It was Sunday, a day when the dead should be remembered even more frequently than during the week. The Queen decided that Alix and her future bridegroom should pay a visit to the mausoleum that afternoon.

The Queen took Alix's arm and showed her round, while she extolled the virtues of the Prince Consort. Bertie yawned in the special way he had, keeping his mouth closed. He had explained to Alix that it was a habit necessary for royalty to master. There were so many occasions when it was impossible to suppress yawns completely, and the oft-repeated enumeration of his father's virtues was high on the list.

Back at the Castle the Queen talked of the wedding, which would be a very sad occasion. She recalled Vicky's wedding. How different! With her father beside her (looking magnificent in uniform) loth to give her away but at the same time steeling himself to do so. Nothing would ever be the same again.

The wedding was to take place in St George's Chapel, Windsor. The Queen, in whose company Alix often found herself, admitted that there was a great deal of complaint about the place chosen.

So many people wished it to take place in London because they didn't want the trouble of coming down to Windsor. "But Windsor it is to be," said the Queen. "How could I *bear* such a ceremony in the Chapel Royal St James's where I was united to my angel? And as for all the fuss and bother of St Paul's, I just could not face that. The people must understand that I must have seclusion in my grief."

Alix was afraid that the Queen was going on to the familiar theme of the Consort's virtues but on this occasion it was avoided by an adroit turn of the conversation which brought it back to the dresses of the bride and the bridesmaids.

Members of the family were arriving at Windsor. Vicky and her husband had come with their four-year-old son Wilhelm, who was a great favourite with the Queen, though Alix could not understand why for she secretly thought him a rather unpleasant little boy. There was her own brother Valdemar, the same age as Wilhelm, whom the latter regarded with animosity; but both the boys were kept in order by young Beatrice, known as Baby to her mother and brothers and sisters, but who with the advent of these slightly younger children had suddenly found herself almost grown up. Ten-year-old Leopold and thirteen-year-old Arthur were aloof from the nursery but they now and then delivered lordly reprimands when the conduct of Wilhelm became violent.

Valdemar declared that he didn't want to go to the wedding unless he could bring his donkey, while Wilhelm cast acquisitive eyes on the animal and decided that since it was such a favourite with Valdemar it ought to be his.

The presents were arriving. The Queen gave the bride an opal and diamond bracelet, and the City Corporation presented her with a diamond necklace worth £10,000; the Royal Nurseries who provided the bouquet, which was made up of orange blossom, orchids, lilies of the valley, rosebuds and myrtle, presented it in a holder of crystal set with diamonds, emeralds and coral. This holder was a gift from the Maharajah Dhuleep Sing. Bertie came to her sitting-room, one hand behind him, and turning her round so that she had her back to him swiftly placed something on her head. She caught a glimpse in the mirror of a tiara of diamonds. She gasped with delight.

"But, Bertie, I am not *used* to such grandeur."

Bertie laughed at her and then gave her a necklace, earrings and a brooch of pearls and diamonds.

While she was gasping out her bewilderment he produced the keeper ring, which was large and set with six stones, and put it on her finger.

"Do you know what they stand for?" he asked. "That's beryl, that's emerald, ruby, turquoise, jacynth and emerald. What does that spell if you take the first letters of each stone . . . except jacynth. There isn't an 'i' in stones."

B.E.R.T.I.E. She spelt and then she began to laugh and threw her arms about his neck and hugged him.

"In a most unroyal fashion," she said.

"And all the better for that," commented Bertie.

"Oh," she said seriously, "I am going to be so happy."

The wedding day dawned bright and clear, though very cold. A special train had brought the guests down from London, complaining bitterly that it was a little inconsiderate to have the marriage of the heir to the throne out of London. "Have we got to go on for ever weeping for Albert?"

It seemed that he was not to be forgotten. The Queen had ordered that there was to be no gay music and that guests should not wear bright colours. Mauve might be worn as it was a mourning shade, with grey of course.

In the Chapel hung with purple velvet the Swedish singer Jenny Lind charmed all those present in the Chorale. In the royal box was a lonely figure draped in black, the only colour in her costume being the Order of the Garter ribbon across her breast. All were conscious of her but she sat mutely there, unsmiling, aloof.

She was remembering that other occasion when Albert had stood beside her at the altar tall and slim in his brilliant uniform, the most handsome being she had ever seen. Poor Bertie! He looked so undistinguished in comparison, though she admitted that she herself had not been as beautiful as dear sweet Alix. How enchanting the child looked in *Honiton* lace, tall, bearing herself so proudly, coming down the aisle with her father. Dear, beautiful creature.

The Princesses looked beautiful in their white gowns, so graceful, like white swans, and there was Baby Beatrice, looking anything but solemn—naughty little creature! Albert would have smiled to see her. So for the first time during the ceremony, the Queen herself smiled.

And there was Princess Mary of Cambridge leading the Princesses and looking quite magnificent with a lilac moiré train and her lace which the Queen was pleased was Honiton. A handsome creature but without a husband and getting fat, which was a family tendency, thought the Queen with a sigh. Even Albert had put on weight a little.

And there were the children, little Wilhelm between his two young uncles, Arthur and Leopold. How cleverly they disguised the little darling's withered arm. What a tragedy that it had been damaged when he was being born. And what little men Arthur and Leopold looked! If only that angel had been down there she would have been there too, brilliantly dressed in diamonds and Honiton lace instead of up here in her dismal clothes.

And now it was almost too much to be borne because they were singing Albert's own hymn, the one he had composed himself and which she had commanded should be a part of the service.

She withdrew farther into the closet and put her hands over her eyes. This was too much to be borne, she said to herself.

The ceremony proceeded and Bertie and Alix were married.

Vicky, Crown Princess of Prussia, wept openly; Alice, Lenchen and Louise caught up in the emotion did the same and Baby Beatrice watching her sisters and feeling this was a part of the ceremony began to sob with them. Lenchen laid a hand on her shoulder to quieten her, which surprised Baby, who audibly demanded to know why if the others cried she must not!

Valdemar was thinking of his donkey and believed that he had been for ever and ever in this funny place where they kept singing then talking and then crying. How much more sensible his donkey was. Wilhelm couldn't understand what it was all about, but he did know that *he* was not being given sufficient attention.

He sat down on the floor and started to pull at Leopold's kilt.

"Stop it," whispered Leopold, at which Wilhelm promptly bit his leg.

Leopold gasped and Arthur looked down to see what was happening.

"Get up!" hissed Arthur; but by this time Wilhelm had discovered it was rather amusing to bite his uncle's legs, so he set his teeth into Arthur's flesh.

Together the youthful uncles endeavoured to pull him up; he opened his mouth to bawl, so they let him go; they made sure though that he should not get his teeth into their legs again. They exchanged glances: Little horror, said their eyes.

How delighted the children were when the ceremony was over and they could leave the Chapel for St George's Hall where the wedding breakfast was to take place. Their fascinated eyes became fixed on the huge wedding cake, six feet high; Valdemar forgot his donkey and Wilhelm was silent with awe. The cake was more wonderful in their eyes than the beautiful floral decorations of orange blossom, myrtle, azaleas, snowdrops and jasmine which had been artistically placed about the room.

Alix left the company to take off her wedding dress and prepare for the journey to Osborne.

On this occasion her new sister Vicky and Cousin Mary of Cambridge helped her.

Alix was delighted that Mary was there—so magnificent, stately, handsome and kind. She was less sure of Vicky, who was half Prussian since her marriage and of course the Prussians were not friends to the Danes. Bertie had told her that he had always been compared to his detriment with his clever sister and for that reason she felt she could never really be close to Vicky.

Mary said it had been a wonderful ceremony and Alix had been admired from all sides. Everyone had commented on her poise, dignity and beauty.

Vicky agreed that this had been so.

"I'm sure there was only one in the chapel who didn't admire you," went on Vicky, "and that was my naughty little son who—I saw him do it—bit both his uncles on the leg."

"I am sure my little brother Valdemar was equally indifferent," added Alix. "He said he would rather play with his donkey than come to my wedding."

They laughed together, but there was an aloofness about Vicky, made more obvious perhaps by the warmth of Cousin Mary's affection. She must remember though that Mary had been her friend since the days when she was three years old and they had met at Rumpenheim.

There she stood in her white silk dress and Mary exclaimed that she looked lovely.

She was glad because it was time for her to go off to Osborne with Bertie.

Adventure in the Highlands

How difficult it was, thought the Queen, to remain in seclusion when one was the Sovereign. Lord Palmerston, her Prime Minister, had never been a favourite of hers, although she had come to realize the need for a strong man at the head of affairs, and she supposed he was that. But Albert had never approved of Palmerston who had scarcely led a good life in his youth, although it was true that when he settled down and married Lord Melbourne's sister they were devoted to each other and lived in harmony. But Palmerston's eyes would always follow a beautiful woman speculatively and Albert had noticed it and disapproved. Every man could not of course be like her Angel, but a Prime Minister she believed should show more decorum than Lord Palmerston was accustomed to. He was referred to as "Pam" by the people, who for some odd reason adored him. How unpredictable the people could be! They had never appreciated Albert. But Pam was better than Cupid, the name by which the Prime Minister had been known in his youth—for obvious reasons.

Now Lord Palmerston was warning her that there was likely to be trouble over Schleswig-Holstein, that matter which had never really been settled; this would mean of course trouble between Prussia and Denmark for Denmark would not willingly give up the provinces because Bismarck told them to.

How tiresome! And if only Albert were here, he would understand and see that something was done.

"There are three people who understand the Schleswig-Holstein controversy," said Lord Palmerston. "The Prince and he's dead and myself . . ."

"The other one?" she had asked.

Lord Palmerston had replied with the utmost irreverence and that rather wicked smile of his. "God, Your Majesty."

She sighed for the tact and sympathy of Lord Melbourne—long since dead and only now occasionally remembered.

She was worried too about Alfred. Bertie had ceased to be such a concern now that he was married to dear sweet Alix who was so good for him. Alfred had had a very unpleasant adventure in Malta. It concerned a woman. Oh dear, she did hope the boys were not going to be tiresome in that respect. First Bertie at the Curragh Camp—and what fearful results that had had! She wondered Bertie could sleep at night for thinking of it; but she was sure he never did—think of it, that was. His sleep would be quite undisturbed. And now Alfred in Malta.

Bertie had said: "Oh Mama, one doesn't want to make too much of these things. Poor old Affie, he had to amuse himself somehow."

She was annoyed. Bertie had too much confidence since his marriage. He was always appearing in public and Alix with him and people cheered them madly wherever they went.

"Very commendable," was Lord Palmerston's comment. "Makes up for your hiding yourself away, M'am, and satisfies the people."

Lord Palmerston had always taken Bertie's side.

But she did realize that Alfred's affair at Malta was not of the same magnitude as his future as Duke of Saxe-Coburg. Albert had always intended Alfred to take over Ernest's dukedom when he died.

Ernest was not in the least like his brother Albert. Oh, the irony of fate that the saint should be taken and the sinner left. One could not probe too deeply into the life Ernest had led. There were women, and debts in plenty, and no children at all, which was why Saxe-Coburg was to go to Alfred. Albert had often talked to her about Ernest. He just could not believe he used to say how that brother of his with whom in his youth he had been inseparable, could have turned out as he did. But Ernest had changed from the innocent youth who had roamed the forests round Rosenau with his brother and hunted for specimens for their museum. She had always declared that when the influence of Albert was removed Ernest had gone to pieces.

The throne of Greece had become vacant and this had been offered to Alfred. This offer had thrown the Queen into a flutter. It was gratifying, of course, but Albert had always talked of Alfred as though he were the future Duke of Saxe-Coburg and she had declined the honour on Alfred's behalf.

Ernest had immediately declared that he would take on the kingdom of Greece, at the same time retaining his Duchy of Saxe-Coburg.

This was something the Queen could not tolerate. Alfred would be expected to go to Saxe-Coburg as heir to that Duchy and govern while Ernest was in Greece. Oh dear, no. That would not do at all. Albert would have disapproved most strongly. Ernest would be the real ruler, Alfred a deputy. The affairs of Saxe-Coburg under the dissolute Ernest were in a sorry state and it was very likely that if Alfred became deputy ruler he could fall into his uncle's ways and— more practically—perhaps be held responsible for their results.

Her Prime Minister came down to Windsor to see her rather reproachfully because she was not in London which would have made communication with her ministers so much easier. She gave him her severe and rather haughty look which seemed to amuse him, a fact of which she was aware and deplored, but of course she could not tell him that she did not like his manner. She never had liked his manner, but she had been forced to admit since that terrible and most unsatisfactory Crimean war that the country could not do without him.

He bowed over her hand. He must be nearly eighty, she thought. Quite clearly he painted his cheeks. How unmanly! And yet how could one accuse Palmerston of effeminacy? He merely wanted to pretend that he was as well as ever. She had heard that he had been seen solemnly climbing over the railing before his house and when he was on the other side, equally solemnly climbing back. A policeman watching him had very naturally thought he was intoxicated and going over to him discovered to his amazement that the climber was not only sober but the Prime Minister.

"I just wanted to see if I still had enough agility to climb those railings and back. And I did, so you see, there's life in the old dog yet," was his comment.

The story was repeated and the people of course had loved him for it and shouted "Good Old Pam, there's life in the old dog yet!" wherever he went. How strange that all Albert's good works had gone unrecognized—or almost so—and this absurd escapade had brought Palmerston even more popularity with the masses.

What was it about him? she wondered. That air of confidence and nonchalance. He knew she didn't like him and he simply didn't care; his attitude reminded her constantly that it was the people who selected their rulers. And they were behind Pam.

She asked after his gout. He said it bothered him from time to time.

"And Lady Palmerston is well?"

"She is and will be honoured when I tell her that Your Majesty enquired."

"You have come over this affair of Greece of course."

"That, M'am, and the even more important question of Schleswig-Holstein."

"There is trouble brewing there."

"There's always trouble brewing there. And with Bismarck in the ascendant the situation is not improved."

"The Prince Consort would never have agreed to Alfred's taking the Greek throne. And I think we should strongly oppose its going to my brother-in-law."

Palmerston seemed to agree with this opinion. He thought it was possible that one of the Danish Princes might be offered the Greek throne. He could see no harm in that.

"You mean one of Alexandra's brothers. Not the eldest. He will be King of Denmark."

"The next one perhaps," said Palmerston.

"He's so *young*."

"Princes have responsibilities thrust early upon them as Your Majesty well knows from personal experience."

She nodded gravely.

But he had not really come to talk to her about the Greek throne. He was concerned with Prussia—deeply concerned.

Bismarck, it seemed, was the real ruler of Prussia and he was out for conquest. He was talking of a united Germany and his slogan was "blood and iron."

"Very descriptive words, Your Majesty," commented Palmerston, "and leaving us in no doubt of their meaning."

"William of Prussia would abdicate in favour of the Crown Prince," he went on, "but I do not think the Crown Prince is eager for it. Nor is Bismarck."

"My daughter and her husband don't like the man."

Old Pam's smile was impish. "Alas, M'am, sometimes monarchs have to accept statesmen they don't like."

She agreed with dignity that this was sometimes a great trial to them. And she secretly thought how often it occurred to her that she would be rather relieved to be rid of those two old men, Palmerston and Russell. The alternative though was Disraeli with greasy curls and painted face or Gladstone with his thundering virtue. Indeed, monarchs did suffer from the statesmen the people gave them.

But Lord Palmerston had come not only to talk of Greece and Prussia but of her own seclusion. He hinted that this had gone on long enough and that the people didn't like it.

"Bertie and Alix I hear are seen very frequently in society."

"And a good thing it is that they are socially inclined," said Lord Palmerston. "It makes the situation less tricky."

Less tricky! What an expression!

"The people like to see their Sovereign now and then you know. They like to see the crown and the sceptre and the purple velvet." His eyes dwelt on what Baby called her "Sad Cap".

"They must be made to understand my tragedy," she said sharply.

Palmerston sighed. "In the meantime, M'am, we will be grateful to the Prince and Princess of Wales for keeping the people happy."

"I don't think there should be so much night life. And I hear that the Prince of Wales is sometimes seen in places less reputable than they should be."

Palmerston smiled. "The people like him for it. So I think we should be grateful to his Highness . . . all of us. A gay Prince of Wales makes up for a Queen in mourning."

It was straight speaking, but what one must expect from Lord Palmerston.

If he was hinting that she should come out from retirement he would have to learn that she had no intention of doing so.

As for Bertie—he was inclined to wildness; but at the moment she supposed she must not reprove him, since he was— so the Prime Minister suggested—taking the burden from her shoulders.

Bertie had seemed all that one could want in a husband. Often Alix asked herself how many princesses achieved what she had—a real love match. Bertie could be passionate lover and tender husband all at once. He was proud of her beauty; he was constantly telling her that she was the most beautiful woman in the assembly. It was fun to be with him; he laughed a great deal; he was amused by her occasional struggles with the English language; he explained jokes to her which she had failed to see; and the honeymoon was the happiest time of her life—and afterwards, too. Bertie loved society; they settled in at Marlborough House and entertained a great deal, but after a few weeks it occurred to Alix that they were rarely alone. She enjoyed company; it was the greatest fun to wear beautiful clothes and be admired. She and Bertie had similar tastes in many ways. They liked gay, light-hearted people. They never wanted to discuss anything that might be called "serious". She had lived very simply in Copenhagen; he had been repressed all his life. She was now being shown a new and glittering world; he was having everything that had been denied to him before. They were both determined to make the best of it.

The first shadow crossed her mind one day when she had thought how pleasant it would be if she and Bertie dined alone in Marlborough House. They had driven in the Park in the morning and received the acclaim of the people; they had gone to a reception in the afternoon where several people had been presented to the Princess of Wales; and she had told Bertie that she had a surprise for him that evening. He was to invite no one to Marlborough House. Then he would wait and see.

They dined alone. "You see," she had said, "there are always so many people around us. I thought it would be much more fun to be alone for once."

Poor Bertie! He did his best; but it seemed difficult to maintain the conversation; he missed his gay friends. It was obvious that that was one of the occasions which was not a success. Alix knew that she must not do that again. But it was rather startling.

There was amazing news from home. Her brother William had been elected to the Greek throne. How strange to think of little Willy as a King. He was to change his name to George as being more suitable for a Greek Monarch, and to leave for Greece immediately.

It seemed incredible. Here she was the Princess of Wales and Willy King of Greece when a year ago they were living humbly in the Yellow Palace.

Sometimes she thought of the family at home. They would be as sorry to lose Willy as they had been to lose her. She had thought that everything was worth while because of the love between herself and Bertie, but when she realized that charming as Bertie was he often glanced at the clock when they were alone together and brightened considerably when some of his gay friends arrived, she began to have some misgivings.

Then she discovered that she was pregnant.

Bertie was delighted. He was very solicitous. She must not tire herself. He thought that perhaps late nights were not doing her any good. She should retire early.

She had said: "Oh, yes, I should like that!" Still being naïve enough to think that he would be with her. She had forgotten the little dinner for two which had not been a success.

He was so tender. He would make her sit down and himself wrap a rug about her legs. He would tell the servants to bring a tray to her room. And then he would kiss her and leave her.

He liked to go out and join his friends at some of the fashionable clubs where he was often incognito. It amused him to take a cab as a private person.

Alix stayed in her room, thinking how comfortable it was to enjoy an early night. But she did wonder what Bertie was doing.

She was often fast asleep when he retired for the night. It wasn't quite what she had imagined in the beginning.

The Queen usually spent autumn in the Highlands which was the best time with the heather on the hills and the beautiful fresh air. Dear Balmoral! Some people said it was more like a German schloss than a Scottish castle. That was because it was Beloved Albert who had planned it. The old Balmoral—which they had become fond of when they had first come to Scotland, was not good enough for her, Albert had said; he had wanted to build something more worthy. She had been reading through her old journals—a habit she had fallen into lately and which she found morbidly fascinating. Often Alice or Lenchen would find her with the tears streaming down her cheeks while she read of past happiness. There was a nice little hall, she had written, and a billiard room with the dining-room next to it. A good broad staircase and the sitting-room above the dining-room. She remembered it so well. "Castle" had been rather a pretentious name for old Balmoral. But what happy days they had had there in the beautiful wooded hills which had reminded dear Albert so poignantly of his homeland and the Thuringian forests.

How different the new Balmoral with its forty-foot-square tower and the oriel windows. Now it was quite magnificent, as Albert had said, a royal residence.

And what a comfort to be there with the dear servants. Annie MacDonald was such a treasure and she was beginning to think that there was no one quite like John Brown.

She smiled at the thought of him. He was very tall and handsome; very strong; so brusque in his manners that he never failed to make her chuckle. And faithful. That was what she looked for now. Albert had said he was the best man on the estate. He and the head gillie, John Grant, were completely trustworthy, Albert had remarked. In fact Albert had often stressed that when he went out on a day's shooting he found the company of these two servants more to his liking than that of some of the noble guests whom duty forced them to entertain. She agreed with Albert on this as on everything else.

She liked as many of her children to be with her as possible. The fact that Alice was still in England meant that she and her husband could join the Scottish party; Bertie and Alix of course had their affairs in London—and very gay they were by all accounts; and as she had said to Vicky she thought that Alix showed the strain and was looking peaky; she was not very strong and rather highly strung she feared. Of course Bertie was not like his father who had always been the most solicitous of husbands and whose great concern had been for his wife's comfort.

Vicky with Fritz and the children Wilhelm, Charlotte and little Henry were having a brief holiday in Scotland too which was very comforting. She could never forget that Vicky had been her father's favourite and although she had been a little jealous of those whom she had—quite wrongly she realized now—imagined had cut her out a little, she now felt drawn towards Vicky who was more like her wonderful father than any of the others.

Dear Vicky, she had her troubles and what a disaster it was that Beloved Papa was not here now to advise her. The King of Prussia was very weak and quite under the influence of that dreadful Bismarck whom Vicky and dear Fritz, quite rightly, could not endure. Not only that but little Wilhelm was a source of anxiety. Such a bright little fellow. Albert had loved him especially and seen great qualities in him. How criminal of those doctors and nurses to be so careless at his birth. Poor Vicky was heartbroken about his deformity. The Queen would never forget how her daughter had described her son's christening when the dear child had been half covered up to hide his arm which was without any feeling and hung helplessly. And now some of the doctors were talking about cutting his neck and in fact the poor child had been submitted to wear a horrible machine; he had to put it on for an hour every day. Vicky had explained that it was a belt about his waist with a rod at the back with something rather like a bridle attached to this. Into this the poor little boy's head was fixed. It was very complicated. But of course the decision to operate was unthinkable unless it was going to be a complete success. The doctors had some notion of strengthening muscles and bringing the arm back into use. Very depressing but now Vicky was in Scotland with the children and little Wilhelm was spared the humiliation of his horrid machine. It seemed much better to accept the fact that his arm would never be right and do the best to disguise it. No wonder the poor child liked to assert himself now and then. He must feel this deeply.

It was very pleasant to have talks with Vicky. Somehow she could talk more freely to her eldest daughter than to the others. Vicky was such a woman of the world. Alice for all her married state still seemed innocent and unworldly. She could discuss having children, female ailments and *feelings* with Vicky. Vicky had a wisdom which the others were not old enough or not experienced enough to share; and although she could discuss with Alice Mr Gilbert Scott's proposals for a magnificent Memorial to be set up in Kensington to dear

Albert, to Vicky she could talk of Affie's affair and his obvious love of the gay life and Bertie's life with Alix, for the Queen was well aware that Bertie was leading a life of his own in some of the gayer clubs while Alix stayed at home.

Trouble seemed to be never far off, both in domestic and foreign affairs; and with such a family as hers, the two were often unhappily combined.

Alice came in to suggest they go for a drive to Clova. "It would do you good, Mama," said Alice.

The Queen sighed. "It was always one of Beloved Papa's favourite spots."

"Grant won't be able to come with us as he is with Vicky in Abergeldie."

"My dear child, we can well do without Grant. Remember we have Brown."

"Oh yes, Mama, I believe you feel safer with him than with any of the others."

"He's a good faithful soul."

"Inclined to forget his place, Mama, at times, don't you think?"

"Brown *never* forgets his place, which is to protect me. I can tell you, Alice, that I would well dispense with the bowing and sycophantic greetings and addresses I get from *some* people. I, as Beloved Papa did, always prefer sincerity."

"Well, Brown will accompany us to Clova. I will go and tell Lenchen that you wish to go. What do you think—about half past twelve?"

"That would be very suitable, my love."

Dear Alice! she thought. She does not look really well. I don't think she is very strong. Such a comfort though. And Louis is rather *helpless*. It's very sad that he can't provide a home for Alice. Poor Alice, she had not been so well since her confinement. A very sad time. Dear little Victoria Alberta—the Queen was very pleased with those names—had been born in Windsor Castle in the same bed which the Queen had used in confinements and Alice had actually worn the same shift which her mother used for all her children. It had been such a trying time because dear Alice looking so wan had resembled Beloved Papa when he was on his deathbed; and when Louis had come in and been so tender and loving and embraced dear Alice she had suddenly seen herself and Albert after the birth of one of the children; and it was all very hard to bear.

She would send for Annie MacDonald and prepare herself

for the drive, although she didn't really need Annie as much as she used to because Brown seemed to have taken charge even of her clothes. Sometimes he would chide her because he considered her cloak too thin. "The mist'll get right through to your bones, woman," he would say in his dear blunt way which showed that he was careless of whether he offended her because his main concern was her health. The dear, good, faithful creature! Albert had always been so amused by his rough ways.

They were ready to depart at twelve, just herself, Alice and Lenchen. The younger ones were doing lessons with Tilla, Miss Hildyard who had been with them for so long and was such a dear good creature.

Lenchen was fussing about luncheon because they were taking some broth with them and some potatoes ready to boil. There was absolutely no need to fuss. Brown would take care of everything. It would be dark when they came back but Albert had always enjoyed night driving and as he had said with Grant and Brown they were perfectly safe.

Smith the coachman was driving and Brown was on the box beside him and Willem, Alice's little Negro boy-servant, was standing up behind.

How she loved the dear hills and glens where she had walked so often with the Beloved Being; there was something to remind her everywhere. She was telling Alice and Lenchen how she used to take out her book and sketch while Papa went shooting and the children used to ride on their ponies.

"We remember, Mama," said Lenchen patiently. "We were there, you know."

Alice looked gently reproving but none of the children had Alice's sympathetic ways.

It was very pleasant to stop at Altnagiuthasach where the efficient Brown warmed the broth and boiled the potatoes. "What a long time they take to boil," said the Queen to which Brown replied: "Ye'll nae be wanting them half cooked, so have a wee bit of patience." At which Alice blenched but the Queen just smiled at another manifestation of Brown's stalwart protection.

How good the broth and potatoes tasted when they were ready. "Worth waiting for," said Brown with reproach in his voice for his impatient mistress.

"Well worth waiting for," agreed the Queen, for in spite of her sorrow she could always enjoy her food. She recalled happy picnics of the past when Dear Papa had been so hungry and declared that nothing tasted as good as John Brown's broth and boiled potatoes eaten on the moors.

With great efficiency Brown had the plates and dishes washed in a burn and stored away and soon they were on their way again. And there were the snow-tipped Clova Hills, breathtakingly beautiful.

"I hope you girls appreciate this wild beauty. Beloved Papa was especially fond of it."

Her daughters assured her that Clova was one of their favourite spots too. But, said Alice, wasn't it time that they started to return? They would be very late as it was and there had been one or two flurries of snow.

The Queen smiled at the kilted figure of her faithful Highlander. All would be well, she assured her daughter.

But this was not quite true. It had grown dark and Brown had lighted the lamps; and as they drove along, the carriage gave a lurch and she realized they were off the road. She could hear Brown's remonstrating with Smith, who had evidently taken a wrong turning. Brown descended and taking a lantern, walked ahead of the carriage holding the light high.

"Whatever has happened to Smith?" cried Alice. "He should be able to see the road very well."

Poor Smith, thought the Queen, he *was* getting old. He had been driving them for thirty years. He really must be persuaded that he was too old for the task. A fine discovery to make at nightfall on one of the roads through the Highlands! She was thankful that Brown was with them.

Suddenly the carriage tilted to one side.

Alice took the Queen's hand and held it firmly. "I think . . . we're upsetting," she cried.

She was right. At that moment the carriage had overturned; the Queen had been tipped out and was lying face down on the ground. The horses were down and Lenchen cried out in terror.

Brown was bending over the Queen.

"The Lord have mercy on us!" he cried. He lifted the Queen in his arms. "Are you all right, woman?" he asked.

"I . . . I think so," said the Queen.

"Lord be praised for that," he said and the sincerity in his voice brought tears to the Queen's eyes.

"See to the Princesses," she said.

"All in good time," replied Brown.

Alice and Lenchen, who were not hurt, very soon were helped to their feet. Alice's clothes were torn and dirty and

Lenchen threw herself at her mother begging to be told that no harm had come to her.

The Queen assured her daughters that she was all right but she could feel that her face was sore, and touching it carefully realized that it was swollen; her right thumb was swelling rapidly and was very painful but as no good purpose could be served at this stage by mentioning it, she said nothing.

Smith seemed very confused and naturally Brown took charge of the situation.

"It's good luck I'm with ye," he muttered and said he wanted someone to hold the lamp while he cut the traces. Poor Smith was distraught and useless so Alice held the lantern and very soon the efficient Brown had the horses up. He was relieved, he said, that they were not hurt and there was only one thing to do. He was going to send Smith off for another carriage and he was staying with them to make sure no harm befell them.

"Dear good Brown," murmured the Queen.

They sat as best they could in the shelter of the overturned carriage and Brown brought a little claret for them. Brown could always be relied upon to produce wine and spirits when they were needed.

"Mama, how long will it take for them to bring another carriage?" asked Lenchen.

"I don't know, my love, but as Beloved Papa always said we must make the best of any situations in which we find ourselves."

Brown drank liberally of the claret which shocked Alice but the Queen thought he thoroughly deserved any reward, for what would have happened without him she could not imagine.

"Smith is too old to drive us," said the Queen. "This is the last time he shall do so. We should have realized it before. These good faithful servants go on and on and we are inclined to forget that they become too old for service."

"I'll not have him drive you again," murmured Brown.

The Queen smiled and began to talk of how the Prince had always enjoyed drives in the Highlands, particularly at night when he said they became even more like the Thuringenwald.

"I suppose because you couldn't see so clearly," said Lenchen, which made the Queen frown.

"Eh, now listen," said Brown suddenly when the Queen

was talking of how Papa had always presented her with the first sprig of heather he picked each year.

"Sound of horses," said Brown. "Someone's coming this way."

To the delight of the party it turned out to be Kennedy, another of the grooms who, fearing that some accident had happened since they were so long in returning to the Castle, had come out with the ponies to look for them.

How very thoughtful! said the Queen. Albert had always said what a good servant Kennedy was and Albert as usual was right.

So they were able to leave at once and only when they arrived at Balmoral did the Queen see how bruised her face was. There was something very wrong with her thumb too.

She was so exhausted that she wished to retire at once to her room and ordered that a little soup and fish be sent to her.

She was soon fast asleep but in the morning realized that she had a rather black eye and her thumb really felt as though it were out of joint.

There was a great deal of fuss about the accident. Vicky and Fritz came over to Balmoral to enquire how the party had survived. The Queen's bruises were greeted with horror and the doctors were attending to her thumb, which they feared had been put out of joint.

The Queen brushed it all aside and when she returned to London Lord Palmerston took her to task for endangering her safety by driving at night through wild country.

"My dear Lord Palmerston," she said, "I have good and trusty servants. I can rely on them absolutely."

"Begging Your Majesty's pardon, I must point out that they did not prevent the overturn of your carriage."

"Accidents will always happen, but there was no alarm whatsoever. John Brown behaved with absolute calm and efficiency. I do assure you, Lord Palmerston, that I feel safer driving through the Highland lanes by night than I have sometimes felt on Constitution Hill in broad daylight."

"There have been most regrettable isolated incidents, Ma'm, and these have happened to other sovereigns because there are certain madmen in the world; but the hazards faced on poor tracks in mountainous country could be avoided, and I, with the backing of your Majesty's ministers, would ask you to desist from placing yourself in danger."

"Nonsense," said the Queen. "The Prince Consort delighted in driving at night. It never occurred to him that there was any danger, and I am sure if there had been he would have been the first to be aware of it. He was always solicitous for my safety."

She was an obstinate woman, thought old Pam; and with the backing of the defunct Prince Consort she was immovable; so there was no point in wasting further time on that subject. They must let her continue with her night drives and be thankful for the Prince of Wales who was taking on far more of the royal duties than the Sovereign herself.

The Prince and Princess of Wales had taken a great fancy to Sandringham. It was Bertie's pleasure to bring with him friends from London to pass a very gay week or so in this royal residence which had never held the same place in the Queen's affections as Osborne or Balmoral. Perhaps, he said with a grimace, this was what he liked so much about it. It seemed at Osborne and Balmoral that his father still lived on; everywhere in those houses his influence was apparent. It was quite different at Sandringham.

Alix loved it too; there she could have been very happy indeed. It could have been a sort of Rumpenheim, but wherever Bertie was, there must be people. He took the utmost pleasure in arranging house parties. His friends would go and shoot and then return for lavish banquets and gay parties with dancing, drinking and gambling which went on far into the night.

Her pregnancy was causing her a certain amount of discomfort, and although Bertie was as kind and tender as she could wish for, she sometimes had the notion that he was rather glad for her to retire early. He himself never seemed to tire; he would stay up half the night and then be out early in the morning in search of some fresh amusement. She hardly ever emerged from her room until eleven o'clock and she was sometimes late for luncheon. Bertie was occasionally faintly reproving and she promised herself that she would overcome her habit of unpunctuality. She often thought of how her father would disapprove.

Then one day she and Bertie were about to ride out to the hunt when a messenger arrived at Sandringham with news. King Frederick of Denmark was dead and Prince Christian, Alexandra's father, had now become King.

Alexandra clapped her hands with excitement. Papa, King

of Denmark. It was wonderful. Then she thought of poor old Uncle Frederick who had always been so kind to them all in his odd way; she wondered briefly what would become of Countess Danner.

But she was the daughter of a king and she could not help being excited about that.

The Queen, still nursing a sore thumb, was hoping that John Brown's knee had improved, for the faithful man when he had jumped out of the carriage had injured it and he had limped for days afterwards. She was very sorry to have been obliged to leave Balmoral and come back to Windsor and all the trials which that entailed. Lord Palmerston, who had called on her, hinted that it would be far more convenient if she were in London; but she had no intention of going to London. Lord Palmerston had something very grave to discuss.

"Schleswig-Holstein again, M'am," he said. "It was inevitable that there should be trouble when Frederick died."

"I'm afraid I haven't a very high opinion of the new Queen of Denmark."

"She can hardly be blamed for what has happened," replied Palmerston. "It's Frederick of Augustenburg who has marched into Holstein."

"But he was exiled years ago."

"His father was beaten when he was, Your Majesty will remember, by King Frederick. But King Frederick is dead and there is a new King and Queen, the parents of our Princess of Wales. This is what the Prussians have been waiting for. They want Augustenburg set up as a puppet of theirs."

"We can't allow that," said the Queen.

"It's a tricky situation. Schleswig-Holstein has always been an uneasy spot."

"And what do you suggest should be done?"

"For the moment," said Lord Palmerston, "wait and see."

This sounded a little like Lord Melbourne.

She was very uneasy, though, for trouble between Denmark and Prussia, which this obviously was, was really trouble in the family.

The Unexpected Birth

Alix was plunged into great unhappiness. She could imagine what was going on at home. Her dear father, a few weeks King of Denmark, to be plunged into war, and such a war. She knew that the Germans were determined to set up Augustenburg in Schleswig-Holstein. She dreamed of Schleswig-Holstein: it had always been a kind of bogey in her life. She remembered as a child hearing those dreadful words at the time when Papa had gone away from home for so long fighting the enemy. But on that occasion they had won the battle; and she had thought it was over; now she realized that all that happened was an uneasy truce.

Everything had seemed so wonderful; herself Princess of Wales, William King of Greece, Fredy the heir to the crown of Denmark and Dagmar courted by the Czarevitch of Russia. So important they had become which was good for Denmark, for it was, after all, only a very small country. And now the mighty Prussians were threatening to crush it.

This had happened at the worst moment. She was feeling the discomforts of pregnancy; she was beginning to understand that the romantic relationship between herself and Bertie was somewhat superficial and that if she were to keep his affection she must never ask too many questions or attempt to discover what his activities were when he was not in her company; and now she had this anxiety about her father. She realized how deeply she loved her parents and because Bertie had told her something of his own childhood she could be grateful for what she had unquestioningly accepted as natural; a happy childhood with parents who had loved her and brought her and her brothers and sisters up with a discipline that had its roots in love. That precious security which children needed more than anything had been hers. Poor Bertie had sadly missed it. Perhaps that was why he now so fervently pursued what he called pleasure.

She knew her father well. Although he had been trained as a soldier he was not meant to fight. One comfort was that her mother would be beside him to help him; and her mother had always believed that she was born to rule.

But it was worrying and her happy world had disintegrated.

Now she could not complain of Bertie's attitude towards her. He joined in her indignation; it was monstrous, he said, that Prussia should support that upstart Augustenburg. England ought to come to the assistance of little Denmark. When she awoke in the night after some dreadful nightmare in which she had seen soldiers storming the Yellow Palace and poor Papa trying in vain to fend them off, it was Bertie who bent over her whispering comforting words.

"Don't fret, Alix," he said. "England will do something. I happen to know old Pam's on our side."

Our side. Oh yes, she had a great deal to be thankful for in Bertie.

But she went on worrying; she couldn't eat and her sleep was often disturbed. Those dreaded words Schleswig-Holstein seemed to hammer continually in her brain.

When the Queen considered the problem she naturally thought of Albert. What would he have thought had he been here now? Albert had always been patriotic towards his own country, so he would have been on the side of Germany and that would be against the Danes.

Albert would be right because he always had been right, and of course she would wish to follow Albert in all things. Lord Palmerston might hint at the dark practices of which he suspected the Prussians might be guilty; Bertie might rave against them, it was typical of the British press to write sentimentally about *Little* Denmark; and poor Alix was naturally broken-hearted; but the Queen felt that Albert would believe that Augustenburg had first claim on Schleswig-Holstein and one could not be sentimental about that sort of thing.

Vicky was writing from Berlin and how could she fail to

support the country to which she now belonged. What was happening in Denmark, she said, was King Christian's own fault; he should not have taken the crown knowing what a flimsy claim he had. Of course he *was* dear Alix's father and she was sorry for Alix, particularly in her present condition. It was most unfortunate; moreover there were rumours on the continent that Bertie was rather fond of the society of ladies whose reputation was not of the best. Another trial for poor Alix! Still, that did not alter the rights of the situation.

If only dear beloved Albert had been here it would all have been so much easier to make everyone understand, and she had no doubt that he would have come up with the right solution and been able to persuade either the Prussians to desist or Christian to give way. But alas for the world, Albert was no more.

The 14th of December had arrived again—the second anniversary of his death. There was nothing else to be thought of on that day but the great emptiness that was left by his departure. She and the children would visit the mausoleum and spend some time there; and afterwards she would shut herself in her room and read her journals and mourn afresh.

Christmas was not a very happy season. Alix was sick and wretched, with the terrible Schleswig-Holstein business hanging over everything like a black cloud. In addition, her pregnancy was not proving an easy one and there were occasions when she felt really ill—a fact which she strove hard to keep from Bertie who liked everyone about him to be carefree.

Vicky was writing rather censoriously from Berlin in definitely anti-Danish terms; the Queen's half-sister, Feodora, whose daughter was married to the Duke of Augustenburg, was vigorously on the side of the rebels; and Alix, remembering other Christmases at the Yellow Palace, longed for the old Scandinavian Jul and those days when the only tragedy in life was being late for meals and having to go without a second helping or take her coffee standing up.

On one occasion she had been unable to contain herself and had burst out in an anti-Prussian tirade before the Queen. Victoria had always been affectionate to Alix but in that moment her expression was cold and her manner regal.

"My dear Alix," she said as though Alix was anything but dear to her, "I see that I must give orders that Schleswig-Holstein is a subject which shall *not* be discussed among the family in my presence."

Alix could have burst into tears. It was all so sad and changed. Only Bertie was comforting and quarrelled with Vicky on his wife's behalf.

But, as the Queen said, it was particularly distressing when political matters became family affairs.

Bertie and Alix stayed at Frogmore which Bertie said was less depressing than Windsor and, being in the Windsor Royal Park, was accessible to the Castle and therefore they would not offend Mama by taking up residence there.

It was bitterly cold that winter and Virginia Water was frozen over. When Alix saw it she thought of skating parties at home and declared her desire to go on the ice.

Bertie looked dubious and the Countess of Macclesfield, Alix's chief lady of the Bedchamber, was horrified at the idea. Alix had come to rely on Lady Macclesfield who was very motherly—she had twelve children of her own—and ever since Alix's arrival in England had been in charge of the household which was very useful from Alix's point of view.

"In your condition," said Lady Macclesfield, "it would be folly." And Alix meekly agreed.

Bertie, however, was planning a party; he was of the opinion that everything should be celebrated by a party and when ice hockey was suggested he was enthusiastic.

"I'll tell you what, Alix," he said, "you come and watch us. The fresh air will do you good."

How gay Bertie was! He had forgotten all about the troubles of Schleswig-Holstein. Alix wished that she could throw off her troubles as easily as he could—although of course Schleswig-Holstein was not exactly his trouble, although she was terribly afraid that all was not going well for Denmark.

Bertie was calling wildly to his friends as he slid across the ice. She longed to join them but she was beginning to feel rather sick.

She did not want to spoil Bertie's game by leaving the scene, so she stood smiling and applauding and suddenly she was in pain.

She turned to one of her women and said: "I think I'll go back to Frogmore now. It's a little cold."

At a break in the game Bertie came to her and composing her features she said that she thought she would return to Frogmore because it was rather cold.

"It's beautifully warm," said Bertie, glowing from the game; and she smiled at him.

"It's colder standing about. I should have been on the ice."

"I'm sorry you couldn't be," said Bertie tenderly, but she could see he was longing to join his friends, so she left promptly and went back to the house.

It was fortunate that she did for no sooner had she entered than she was in great pain.

Lady Macclesfield came running to her.

"Good heavens," she cried. "It can't be. It's two months too soon."

But it was.

It was fortunate that a sensible woman like Lady Macclesfield was in charge. Her first act was to get Alix to bed and send to the town of Windsor for Dr Brown, a doctor who, because his practice was there, had served the royal family on other occasions. He had become well known because of this and had a good reputation.

At the same time she sent an equerry to the Castle to inform the Queen of what was happening and gave orders that a special train should leave for London to tell the Archbishop of Canterbury, Lord Palmerston and the Lord Chamberlain of the baby's imminent arrival.

Then she went back to Alix, who was in great pain. There was no doubt that the child was about to be born and there was nothing ready for it.

Dr Brown arrived immediately and even so he was only just in time, and he and Lady Macclesfield between them delivered the child. A boy.

There were no clothes ready so Lady Macclesfield took off the flannel petticoat she was wearing, because of the intense cold, and wrapped the little boy in it. Alix was exhausted and the seven-months' child was naturally rather feeble and would need special care.

It was fortunate that Lord Granville, a member of the Cabinet, happened to be staying at Frogmore, so that Lady Macclesfield was able to present the new baby—wrapped in her petticoat—to him. He was not the Archbishop of Canterbury nor the Prime Minister nor the Lord Chamberlain, whom custom asked should be present at a royal birth, but the circumstances of a seven-months' child were extenuating and it was decided that Lord Granville would do on this occasion.

The Queen came hurrying over to Frogmore to see her new grandson. Such a feeble little thing, but then she had never liked little babies. And dear sweet Alix, who had had so much anxiety about her parents and that dreadful Schleswig-Holstein affair, was very weak.

Alix began to recover in a few days and holding her baby in her arms she was able to forget for a while the tragic happenings in Denmark.

Vicky wrote from Berlin, very excited by the news. She criticized the parents of the newly born child though and hinted that they had brought on the premature birth by their conduct. Bertie's gay life was talked of freely and it was really rather embarrassing, she pitied poor dear Alix. But Alix herself had not taken proper care; she had kept late nights too and not rested enough. Why on the very occasion of the birth she had been out skating.

The Queen replied she was pleased to have a grandson and it was amazing that the birth had been all over in an hour. *Good* Dr Brown from Windsor had done very well and they must be grateful to Lady Macclesfield who, the dear good soul, had done everything that the nurses were trained to do. It was necessary to take the *utmost* care of the child and keep him in cotton wool. Seven-months' children were naturally more difficult to rear than those who had enjoyed the full period of gestation. She thought this would be a *lesson* to Alix and Bertie to take greater care in future.

Settled in at Frogmore the Queen thought longingly of Osborne. She disliked births but felt it her duty to be present. She told Vicky she would have liked to be with her at the birth of her children. She fancied she could be a little comfort to them and it was pleasant to be of some use in the family now that Dearest Papa was no longer there to need her.

She forgot her annoyance with Alix over Schleswig-Holstein because the dear girl looked so pretty in bed and she could always feel lenient towards people at whom it was pleasant to look.

The question of the child's name arose.

Bertie wanted to call him Victor. It will be a change in the family, he said.

Alix liked it, too.

"It should be Albert Victor," declared the Queen. "His grandfather would have been so proud of him, and the least we can do is to keep green the memory of that Dear Being."

"Albert Victor," said Bertie trying it out.

"It's very good," said the Queen. "And when you are King, Bertie, I wish you to be known as King Albert Edward."

"It's departure from precedent," Bertie pointed out, which was irritating because on so many occasions that was just what *he* was always trying to do.

"All the same," said the Queen, "it is what I wish. I want Papa's name to be perpetuated; and it is a way of reminding people of everything he has done for this country."

Bertie did not pursue the question. It would probably be a matter for the government to decide when the time came.

In the meantime there was the christening of Albert Victor to be performed. This was to take place at St George's Chapel with the necessary ceremony due to one who could one day be the King of England. The Queen planted a small evergreen tree at Frogmore in memory of his birth; and so he was christened Albert Victor Christian Edward.

They should have been happy days for Alix, although she was not allowed to see much of her son who was too fragile to lead the life of an ordinary newly-born baby. He was small and delicate naturally but he was beautifully and perfectly formed; the doctors said it would only be a matter of time before he caught up on those two months by which he had made his premature appearance. The Queen told her that Vicky wanted to know if he had any hair and nails and what ministers were present at the birth.

"I could happily tell her," the Queen confided to Alix, "that he is an adorable little fellow with such beautiful features and pretty ears and hands and that Lord Granville was present."

Alix felt triumphant. She was not very fond of Vicky, whom she regarded as an enemy; her country was fighting against Denmark and Alix was afraid to ask what was happening for fear it should be too depressing. In any case the Queen had given orders that no one was to mention that dreadful war to Alix while she was lying in.

"I don't really care for Mrs Innocent," said the Queen, referring to one of the nurses. "Dear Lady Macclesfield tells me she is becoming a continual nuisance with her high and mighty airs and seems to think that she should run the nursery. If she continues to behave badly she shall be sent away. But Mrs Clark is good, I believe."

Alix surveyed her with tears in her eyes. "You are so good," she told her. "I know that you do not like little babies and everything that concerns their being born. But you are here . . ."

Tears always affected the Queen deeply. They were a sign of *feeling*.

"Dear sweet Alix," she said at once, "how glad I am that you came to us. It was a happy day for Bertie and for me."

Then she bent over and kissed the dear girl who looked so pretty.

When she had gone Alix lay still with her eyes closed thinking about the Queen who still mourned for the husband she had clearly adored. She wondered whether she would ever learn to feel the same way about Bertie. She loved her husband; he was charming and kind; she wondered whether he was faithful to her. There were often suggestions that he was not. Albert would always have been faithful to Victoria of course; but Bertie and his father were as different as two husbands could be.

She had learned quite a lot about the Prince Consort; one could not be long in the Queen's company without doing so; and sometimes she thought he seemed intolerable. On the whole perhaps she was better off with a man like Bertie. In time, she thought, he will change. He just feels that he has so much to make up for after being under the sway of his stern father.

While she was brooding letters were brought to her. How good to hear from home!

There was one from her father. She read it through and let it flutter on to the quilt. Her fingers seemed too limp to hold it.

"For God's sake, Alix," was the message, "England must help us. We are going down before the might of the Prussians. You are English now. Help us, Alix."

What could she do?

When Bertie came to see her he found her sunk deep in depression.

"What's wrong, Alix?" Bertie wanted to know; and she showed him her father's appeal.

"Something will have to be done," said Bertie. "England will go in and stand by the Danes. They're waiting for the right moment. Old Pam loves to sweep in with dramatic effect. Don't worry. We shall be there . . . beside the Danes."

She allowed herself to be convinced.

"Why, Bertie," she said, "if England did not help my poor

country I should be so ashamed. They'd think I had failed them in some way."

"You're not going to fail them," said Bertie, and she thought how kind he was until he started to tell her about the races he had visited that day and she saw then that he didn't really care very much about the great tragedy overhanging her family.

The news grew worse. The Prussians were invading Schleswig-Holstein. Vicky's husband had left Berlin to join the forces which were fighting against Alix's father.

News came that Holstein, the pro-German of the two Duchies, was in the hands of German troops and that the Danish authorities had evacuated it. Bismarck demanded that the position of Schleswig-Holstein and the Danish constitution should be investigated, and when King Christian refused to consider this German troops began to march on Schleswig.

The Prime Minister and Lord Russell came to see the Queen.

"The Austrians and Prussians are power crazy," said Palmerston. "They won't stop at Schleswig-Holstein; they'll march on and crush Denmark. This is what Bismarck means with his blood and iron."

"The fleet should be sent to Copenhagen," said Russell.

The Queen stared at him in dismay. "I should never consent. It would be tantamount to declaring war on Germany."

"Which might do that rather blown-up country some good," said Palmerston.

Oh, how she disliked those old men! Albert had always believed in neutrality.

"Prince Albert would never have agreed to make war on Germans."

"We have to consider what is best for England, M'am," Palmerston reminded her.

"War is never good for any country," retorted the Queen.

The two ministers exchanged glances. When it was considered the moment to act, Palmerston would do so; at the moment it was better perhaps to prevaricate; and the attitude of the Queen gave him an opportunity of doing so.

Alix was growing frantic. Her country was in danger and England was doing nothing to help. She fretted and grew pale and thin. Bertie declared it was a shameful thing that England did not go to the rescue of Denmark. He was far from discreet and at every opportunity declared his contempt for the shilly-shallying government and the wicked Prussians.

Palmerston, while deciding it was better for the Prussians, Austrians and Danes to work this matter out for themselves kept an anxious eye on the Baltic ports. He took on opportunity of warning the Austrian ambassador in London that if their fleet appeared in the Baltic they would find the British Navy there too.

The Queen was horrified; she could visualize the country's being dragged into war. She declared that she would not give her consent, and refused to sign the speech from the throne, which the government had prepared for the opening of Parliament. She herself had not attended an opening since the death of Albert.

Throughout the country sympathy ran high for Denmark. Everywhere they went Alix and Bertie were cheered. The people wanted to go to the aid of "Little" Denmark because the Press had given the impression that if Prussia marched on that country Britain would be Denmark's staunch ally. Moreover, the Danish Princess of Wales had appealed to them; she was young, pretty, and had already given birth to the heir in rather dramatic circumstances. Good old Bertie was a gay dog, often at loggerheads with stern Mama, who in any case had offended the public by shutting herself away.

Alix was cheered by public sympathy, but what good was that while Denmark was being hopelessly beaten by the Prussian and Austrian hordes?

She raved to Bertie. Had not Lord Palmerston promised help to Denmark? Hadn't she said: "I am convinced—we are convinced—that if any violent attempt were made to overthrow the rights and interfere with the independence of Denmark, those who made the attempt would find in the result that it would not be Denmark alone with which they would have to contend."

Alix remembered it word for word; and what was he doing now . . . nothing. Denmark wanted more than sympathy.

Some members of Parliament flung those words in Palmerston's face; but he was too wily for them. His sympathies were with Denmark because he could see the dangers to Europe of a strong Prussia; but he was not going to drag England into a war unless it was going to be very much to England's advantage. He *had* made that remark, he had said, yes, he admitted it. But he had meant that he believed that some European country would come to the aid of Denmark;

he had not meant England. It was more important to countries which were geographically nearer for instance, such as France, to preserve the peace of Europe, but the Emperor was remaining aloof. If the Emperor had intervened . . . but that was another story.

"It's perfidious," cried Alix in despair. "My country relied on England."

Bertie was furious and ashamed, he said. So were the people. But many knew that Palmerston though perhaps not morally right was doing England the greater service by keeping her out of war.

By April the war was over—disastrously for Denmark. They had lost Schleswig-Holstein.

John Brown Comes South

The Queen was scarcely ever in London and the people were getting restive. Surely it was the duty of the Sovereign to show herself now and then? The Queen retorted, when her ministers reproached her, that she worked unceasingly for the good of the country and she could not see how her parading in public did her subjects any good.

But even she was taken aback when several notices were stuck on the walls of Buckingham Palace announcing:

"These premises to be let or sold in consequence of the late occupants declining business."

Lord Palmerston laughed when he heard of it; but the Queen, who was at Osborne, was angry.

If people thought they were going to bring her out of retirement they were very much mistaken. She was a widow, and she was going on mourning for her husband; and during periods of mourning widows did *not* appear in public dressed in elaborate garments and sparkling with jewels.

Lord Palmerston shrugged his shoulders. "We have to continue to be grateful to the Prince and Princess of Wales," he said, "who have taken over so many of Your Majesty's duties."

"Duties!" she snapped. "Racing? Gambling? Mixing in questionable society?"

"Oh, the people don't hold that against the Prince," was Palmerston's comment.

The Queen summoned her physician, Dr Jenner. The people must be made to understand that she was in no fit condition to parade in public. They must be made to have *some* understanding of a widow's grief.

Dr Jenner gently suggested that it was more than two years since the Prince Consort's death. Perhaps if she tried to emerge a little she would feel better for it.

She turned on him furiously. "Do you imagine that I shall ever feel better about my loss?"

Dr Jenner was silent, but he did think that if the Queen would try to get out more, ride more often, perhaps sit out of doors sketching, as she used to, it would be beneficial to her health.

"Everything reminds me too much of him," she said.

A notice appeared in *The Times* to the effect that she would, as she always had done, perform her duty towards the State. More than that the Queen could not do.

But the people were not satisfied. What was the use of a Queen who was never seen? Rumours began to be circulated. Had she gone mad? Wasn't there madness in the family? Was that why it was necessary for her to remain in seclusion?

It is not good, repeated Lord Palmerston warningly, for a Sovereign to hide himself—or herself—from the people.

Uncle Leopold, ageing though he was and finding it very difficult to totter about his palace because his rheumatism, so long imagined, had now become a reality, his cheeks painted to a healthy pink, a wig of luxuriously made curls on his head, could not resist adding his warning.

It seemed to him, he said, that the Prince of Wales was already King. He heard that wherever he and the Princess went they were cheered wildly.

This so incensed the Queen that she did agree to come to London and ride through the streets in an open carriage. It was amazing how many people came out to see her pass. There she sat bowing to them, acknowledging their greetings, which were vociferous, but wearing her black robes and widow's cap to remind them that she was still in mourning for the wonderful man whom they no less than herself had lost.

"I am sure," she said with satisfaction to Lord Palmerston, "that the Prince and Princess of Wales have never had a reception like that."

Palmerston bowed. "Your Majesty will, I have no doubt, give your subjects more opportunities of displaying their loyalty."

But soon she was back at Osborne, reading her diaries and going over every little detail in the house *he* had planned and looking forward to the time when she would go up to dear Balmoral where there were even more memories of him.

Alix was agitating to go to Denmark to see her family. She explained it to Bertie who was wonderfully sympathetic. She wanted to show her parents little Eddy, which was the name by which the new baby was known. Victor seeming strange somehow and he couldn't be Bertie because of his father, and to call him plain Albert might seem like sacrilege; Christian was too foreign for the English and Edward was too solemn for such a scrap, so Eddy was the answer. Not only did she wish them to see the baby but she also wanted to explain to them that she had done her best for them, that it was not her fault that England had been so perfidious and left them to the mercy of the Prussians and the Austrians.

"Go to Denmark!" cried the Queen. "That would be *most* unwise."

Alix could be very stubborn. "She doesn't understand, Bertie. They are my family. And I love them . . . dearly. You can't understand what it was like to have a kind good father and a mother who loved you tenderly. I must see them now. Imagine how they will be suffering."

Bertie understood. He said he would stand firm and insist. After all he was of age. He was not going to allow his mother to treat him as a boy in the nursery even though she was the Queen.

On this occasion Bertie did rouse himself; he was rather worried about Alix, who had grown very thin and was clearly not the carefree girl he had married. He was genuinely fond of her and made up his mind to do his best for her, and so insistent was he that the Queen, with some reluctance, agreed to the trip.

She confided to her acting secretary, General Grey, that Bertie was inclined to be indiscreet and General Knollys, who had been appointed his governor after General Bruce had died, did not always appear to have the necessary control over him. There had been the affair of Garibaldi whom Bertie had met when he had come to England in April. Bertie did not seem to understand his position and the fact that he made a point of meeting the Italian leader could be construed as British approval of his methods. Bertie was indeed very rash and had defended Garibaldi as a patriot who was not in the least like a revolutionary. How foolish Bertie could be! He had to learn the rule of Royalty; they stood together and this was particularly important in a world which had so recently been shaken by revolution.

Now he wanted to go to Denmark at such a difficult time. And of course if it were known that Alix wished to visit her family to introduce her father to his new grandson and that the Queen had refused to allow this, there would be an outcry. People never understood; they confused *family* relationships with those of the State.

She sent for Bertie. She would agree to the visit. But there must be conditions. For instance what would their German relations think if he went to Denmark, the enemy with whom they were so recently at war? He must remember that little Eddy was an heir to the throne and he must therefore not be out of the country for more than three weeks. He must not forget also to visit his German relations; he must make it perfectly clear that he was not only the son-in-law of the King of Denmark but also the son of Albert and Victoria.

"That is something I am not likely to forget, Mama," said Bertie with a twinkle in his eye which was disturbing because he could smile when he mentioned his father's name.

So in September Bertie and Alix set off in the royal yacht *Osborne* with their baby and a very small party which included Lord and Lady Spencer, Sir William Knollys and two doctors, for little Eddy was still very frail.

The Queen had taken the precaution of commanding General Grey to write to Sir Augustus Paget, the British ambassador in Denmark, to keep an eye on the Prince of Wales, lest he be guilty of indiscretion. She wished the ambassador to know that this was the worst possible time for such a visit and she deplored it but she had forced herself to understand the natural desire of a daughter to see her parents, particularly after she had recently given birth to their grandchild.

Bertie was prepared to have a good time in Denmark and it did not occur to him that he might not be welcome. He was soon made to realize that although he was Alix's husband he was also the Prince of Wales, the future King of a country which Denmark considered had deserted it in its hour of need; he was regarded with suspicion and the cheers were all for Alix. But Bertie's greatest gift was his convivial spirit; after his lack of popularity with his parents he had been astonished when he had first discovered public response to his temperament; now he had come to regard it as a matter of course. It did not occur to him that the people should not like him; and very soon they saw his point of view, for it was indeed impossible not to like this young man. He was undistinguished in appearance but seemed the more lovable for that, because really with his rather weak chin and not very tall stature he was charming, and his attention to his wife was gallant and pleasant to behold.

It was not very long before the people of Denmark were cheering the Princess *and* the Prince of Wales.

They had landed at Elsinore where the King and Queen of Denmark were waiting to meet them. Alix flew into her father's arms and for some moments would not look at him. Dearest Papa, who had never wanted to be King of Denmark anyway. How he must have suffered! When at last she looked into his face, she saw how he had changed. Anxiety had marked his handsome face. And Mama? Queen Louise had changed less. What a support she must have been through all the tribulations, but she had grown very deaf and could scarcely hear what was said. And there were Fredy and Dagmar—quite a young woman now and good looking—and Thyra and Valdemar, the whole dear family, except Willy who had become King George of Greece.

"Alix, my love," said her mother, "you've grown thinner."

"I've been so *worried* about you all."

"We needed help . . . badly . . . and it didn't come," said Louise shortly.

"Mama, dearest, you must understand that I did *everything*, just everything I could."

"I know you did, my love."

"And so did Bertie. There were such quarrels but he did all he could . . ."

"We won't talk of it now, Alix."

The Burgomaster welcomed the visitors with a speech which might have been a reproach to the Prince of Wales.

"Abandoned as Denmark is by all the world," he said, "and crushed by overwhelming superiority, I hope that the visit of our Princess and her husband will be the beginning of brighter days for the country."

Bertie applauded imperturbably so all accepted the fact that what had happened was no fault of his.

They drove to the royal Palace of Fredensborg, a beautiful residence on the lake of Esrom, which now that Christian was King had fallen to him.

It was a bitter-sweet experience for Alix to be home with her family. There was so much to remind her of the old days and yet how changed it was—how sadly so in spite of the fact Christian and Louise had become King and Queen.

Alix liked to walk in the gardens with Dagmar and talk of the past. But Dagmar wanted to hear about life in England and Alix found herself talking freely. Staying at Fredensborg was the young Czarevitch Nicholas who was courting Dagmar.

Dagmar liked to hear about Alix's arrival in England and was wondering what hers would be like in Russia. She loved little Eddy and thought it was marvellous that Alix had a baby of her own. So did Alix. She wanted lots of children, she told Dagmar, and to look after them herself so that she had a happy family as theirs used to be in the Yellow Palace.

She was so happy to be there with Bertie. She wished they could stay for ever. Bertie was charming, they all agreed, and the simple life suited Eddy. The countryside was so beautiful and she kept asking Bertie if he didn't admire this and that. Bertie always said he did but she could see the glazed look in his eyes which meant that his thoughts were elsewhere; and she knew that he found the homely Danish Court very different from Marlborough House. The simple country life was not for him. Where were the practical jokes, the lavish banquets, the racing, the gambling, the flirtatious pretty women? They were lacking, and although he was ready to endure a little of this for Alix's sake he was longing to go home.

One day one of the men of his suite said to him, "Surely there is no place in the world as boring as Fredensborg?"

"Oh," replied the Prince of Wales, "haven't you been to Bernstorff?"

Bertie's habit of yawning without opening his mouth was of good service to him. "Never mind," he would say to members of his suite, "we'll soon be home."

At home the Queen eagerly read accounts of how the Prince and Princess of Wales were being received in Denmark; and because she thought they had been there long enough and she was getting reports of Bertie's outspokenness with regard to the Prussians towards whom he displayed a venom which almost matched that of his wife, she ordered them to leave at once for Stockholm. There they were to travel *incognito* and to stay at hotels and afterwards they must on no account omit a visit to their German relations.

Christian and Louise begged to look after little Eddy while they went to Sweden where it was already known that they were to arrive. Therefore the King of Sweden immediately invited them to his palace and treated them as honoured guests. He insisted on taking Bertie on an elk hunt and this was such a grand occasion—after Bertie's own heart—that it was talked of not only in Sweden but beyond.

At home the Queen was fuming with rage. No sooner did she let Bertie out of her sight than he was in trouble. Had she not clearly said *incognito*; and there he was staying with the King of Sweden and attending public functions. As for Eddy, she was horrified that he should have been left behind with King Christian and Queen Louise. It was incredible. That child belonged not only to them but also to the nation and if he was not with his parents his place was at Windsor with the Queen. He should be sent back immediately. Lady Spencer could bring him home to Windsor.

Bertie was beginning to realize that he was entitled to have some say in the way he conducted his affairs. He wrote that it was undignified for the heir to the throne to stay at squalid hotels and they were all squalid in Sweden; as for the child, Alix could not bear to be parted from him and after all she was his mother. Surely the Queen would not wish to make Alix wretched and to slight the King of Sweden.

Bertie was getting impossible, said the Queen. In future she would have his orders made very clear before he was allowed to leave England.

On their return to Copenhagen they found that Dagmar had become officially engaged to Nicholas. There were congratulations and great rejoicing. The occasional banquet seemed to the Prince of Wales very meagre, but then of course the Danish royal family had just fought a losing war but he doubted whether they had ever been accustomed to much else. He was amazed that in spite of the humble manner in which she had been brought up, Alix could look as elegant as any woman he had ever seen in any company.

Nicholas invited them to Russia for the wedding.

"It would be lovely if we could go, Bertie," said Alix.

Bertie said they would. He had always wanted to go to Russia.

The two girls spent a great deal of time together discussing weddings and trousseaux. It was so like the old times and if Dagmar had not been as delighted with her grand marriage as Alix had been with hers it would have been heart-breaking.

One day when Alix and Bertie came in from a ride the King said to them: "I have a visitor here to see you, Alix. I couldn't let you leave Copenhagen without seeing him. He would be so upset."

And there was Hans Christian Andersen bowing and smiling and looking overcome by the honour.

Alix was delighted and began telling Bertie how Hans had come to the Yellow Palace and told them stories and how he used to bring his books to show them when they appeared in foreign editions.

Bertie was gracious as he well knew how to be.

"The Princess will be telling your stories to our son as soon as he is old enough to understand," he said.

With reluctance Alix said good-bye to her family.

The royal yacht sailed away and they came into Kiel harbour into those waters which until this year had been Danish and were now German, and according to nautical custom the Prussian flag was hoisted.

When Alix saw it she turned pale with anger.

"That flag is to be removed at once," she said.

Bertie looked up at it, shrugging his shoulders. It was only courteous to fly the flag of a country when a ship was in its territorial waters, he pointed out.

"These are Danish waters," she retaliated.

"They were," said Bertie sadly.

"They *are*," she insisted.

"There's nothing we can do about it," he said.

He was unprepared for her vehemence.

"There is," she said. "I shall not leave this yacht until that flag is removed."

Bertie sent for the Captain and asked him to explain the custom to the Princess of Wales. He left them together. Trust Bertie, she thought sadly, to escape from an unpleasant situation.

The Captain explained that while they were in Prussian waters the flag must fly.

"It shall not fly," she said. "They are waiting for me on shore but I shall stay on the yacht until that flag is taken down and you know that."

The guns were firing their salutes of welcome and the Captain recognized the determination in Alix's eyes.

He gave orders that the flag should be lowered.

Alix was very uneasy. She thought the Queen should have spared them this. They did not go to Berlin of course. That would have been most unwise, for some of Bertie's criticisms of the Prussians had been repeated there. Vicky and her husband, however, did have a brief meeting with them at Cologne. It took place on the railway station through which they had arranged to pass at the same time. At least they would satisfy the Queen that they had met.

Vicky was cool and restrained, remembering the unwise things Bertie had said about the Prussians. As for Alix she felt so sick at heart when she thought of her father's sufferings that she could scarcely bear to look at them, especially as Fritz had come in uniform, wearing medals he had won in the war. It was fortunate that the meeting was so brief.

November had arrived by the time the *Osborne* brought them back to England. Alix was pregnant again.

While Bertie and Alix were still abroad the Queen had a pleasant surprise.

Her doctor, William Jenner, called on her and asked for her indulgence because after consulting with Sir Charles Phipps, the Keeper of the Privy Purse, he had taken an action which she might well feel he should not have taken.

"Pray be more explicit," said the Queen.

"We have been concerned for Your Majesty's health," said Jenner, "and it is my firm belief that you need more fresh air. When you are at Balmoral you are so much better than you are here and we believe it is because you take more exercise. Now up in Scotland we know that you have a very trusty servant and they are hard to come by. We have taken the liberty of sending for one of your servants whom we trust to take the utmost care of Your Majesty."

The Queen looked from one to the other in astonishment. That her doctor and the Keeper of her Privy Purse should decide on what servants she should have was incredible. Had they gone mad?

Dr Jenner said: "Of course if Your Majesty does not approve, Brown can be sent back without delay."

"Brown!" said the Queen, her voice changing without her realizing it.

"John Brown, M'am, to whom we both feel we can entrust Your Majesty's safety in the Highlands—so why not in the South as well."

The Queen smiled. "Brown," she said, "is a very good and faithful servant."

"Your Majesty should get out more. He could drive you, or ride with you, as Your Majesty wished."

"It is quite a good idea," she admitted.

And when they had gone she felt elated. He really was the perfect servant.

Very soon he arrived and she asked that he be brought to her at once.

"So here you are, Brown," she said. "I hope you're going to like the South. I am sure you will find it very interesting."

"It's nae the Highlands," said Brown.

"Of course it is not the Highlands. But I'm very glad to see you here. I hope you are pleased to come."

"I'll nae be knowing that till I've tried it," said Brown.

How she laughed when she was alone. He was so blunt. Of course he was so faithful, so loyal, no respecter of persons, not even that of the Queen, whom he would guard with his life. Albert had always said that he was the best gillie he had ever had—he and Grant that was, and Grant had been the head gillie.

Albert would be very pleased that she had this good and faithful servant with her at Osborne. After all, Jenner and Phipps were right. Why keep him in Scotland? Why should he not be with her wherever she was.

Everyone was noticing the change in her. She smiled more frequently; those about her were astonished by the calm manner in which she allowed Brown to discard ceremony. She would smile at him, admiring his firm chin. She had always admired firm chins and remembered how she used to study her own in the looking-glass until the Baroness Lehzen reproved her vanity. "It's not vanity," she would say. "It's the opposite. I dislike my chin. It's so weak." It was the family chin, of course. Some of her uncles had had it; some of her children had it; so she could not be surprised that *she* had it. No wonder she admired Brown's chin.

"Brown," she said one day, "one can see you're an obstinate man, by the way in which your chin juts out. It betrays a firmness of purpose."

Brown fingered his chin and gave her that look which so amused her because it was half contemptuous, half protective. It made her feel that she was a woman rather than a Queen—a very pleasant feeling at times.

"Ye manage to be an obstinate woman," was his comment, "with no chin at all."

So very funny! "Really, Brown, you *are* amusing."

She was frequently laughing now. Sometimes she pulled herself up sharply and thought of Albert. Then she would go to her room and read her journals and brood on the past until Brown said that she was looking sickly and he'd saddled Flora and it was time they were riding.

There was no doubt at all—Brown made all the difference.

The End of Pam and the Rise of Dizzy

The Queen was secretly dismayed. For several hours of the day she would not even think of Albert. It had happened since Brown had come to Osborne and she realized how right they had been to send for him. Now of course when she went to Balmoral he would go with her, and if she had to go to London he would be there. The prospect of going to London was not nearly so distasteful when she considered that Brown would be there.

Brown was so reliable, so courageous, so amusing, with his dour Highland ways, such a relief after *ordinary* people. Of course, none of the people who surrounded her appreciated him and they were astonished by what she "put up with" (as they expressed it) from a servant.

"Brown is no ordinary servant," she would say with a laugh. "One does not get devotion like that from ordinary servants, I do assure you."

He looked after the horses and the dogs, but that did take up a great deal of his time and she really needed him to have a more personal post. He was to have a salary of £120 a year—rather large, it was true, but the man needed some compensation for leaving his home. How amusing it was to see his delight when she talked of going to Balmoral. She had arranged that each morning he should come to her room to receive the orders for the day. She looked forward to seeing him and hearing his dry comments on the weather—always *so* amusing. He had a contempt for the South of which he made no secret which showed how loyal he was to his native land.

Bertie and Alix didn't like him. Poor Bertie, he was so superficial he could not see the sterling worth of Brown. She was afraid that he was mixing with the wrong sort of people and Lord Palmerston had hinted to her that Bertie's gambling debts were reaching alarming proportions. She did not believe Parliament would increase Bertie's allowance, and she could understand their being reluctant to do so. What would he spend the money *on*? Horse-racing and fast women.

Poor Alix, the Queen was afraid she had to put up with a great deal, and Alfred was turning out to be almost as bad as his elder brother. Who would have thought that with the example Albert had set them they could behave as they did.

So it was natural that Bertie and Alfred should not appreciate Brown. Alice from Darmstadt had written that she thought it an excellent idea that Brown should have come South. It must mean a great deal to dearest Mama to have a servant about her on whom she could rely.

As for Lenchen she was very much aware of the virtues of Brown. She remarked to her mother that his blue eyes were so penetrating and missed nothing and how well they went with that curly beard. He was so strong too. Lenchen at least appreciated John Brown.

June had come and Alix's confinement was near. She had been quite well and after a reception went to a concert. During it she began to experience mild pains and was eager to get back home. She went to bed immediately and very shortly after another son was born.

The Queen was delighted. Two boys in such a short time was excellent and it seemed as though Alix was going to be as fruitful as she was herself, always a comfort for a Queen—which Alix would one day be, of course. Although one could have too many. She often thought of those seemingly perpetual pregnancies when she remembered she had been a little irritable and rather a trial to poor Albert.

The new baby was of course much stronger than poor fragile little Eddy; and it was so pleasant to see dear sweet Alix sitting up in bed looking so pretty and happy too, because there was no doubt that Alix was born to be a mother.

The baby was to be called George.

"George!" cried the Queen. "Why George?"

Alix explained that the Cambridges had always been great friends of hers in the days when Cousin Mary came to Rumpenheim and Alix was only three years old.

"Poor Mary Cambridge," said the Queen. "So large and still unmarried."

"I thought it would please them to call the baby George after the Duke."

"Poor George!" said the Queen. "There was a question at one time of my marrying him."

"As there was of my father," said Alix with a smile. "There were so many eager to marry the Queen of England."

The Queen admitted this. "And how fortunate I was to have succeeded in marrying the most perfect angel that ever existed. But then his very virtues make me miss him all the more."

Alix hoped the Queen was not going to lapse into one of her monologues on the virtues of Albert, which Bertie had said had become slightly less frequent since the arrival of Brown. At least, he added, that was one good reason for bringing Brown south. Bertie was so irreverent.

Alix talked about the beauties of little George and how it

was easy to see even at this stage that he was remarkably intelligent.

The Queen smiled fondly. Little babies were not a subject she greatly enjoyed. So his names were to be George Frederick Ernest. But she thought that every member of the family should bear Albert's name.

Alix said that Albert could be added, of course.

"A pity Bertie did not think of it," said the Queen severely. "Of course I should have preferred Albert to come first."

"His brother is Albert Victor," Alix reminded her.

"Of course. Well, second perhaps. George Albert and the rest . . . if he must have George."

"Bertie says George is a King's name and that there have been four of them recently in succession."

"But this little fellow won't be King and as Eddy is called Eddy, he might have had Albert first."

But she was not talking with her usual vehemence and Alix sensed this.

"I do believe," Alix said afterwards to Bertie, "she talks of the Prince Consort out of habit now rather than sorrow."

Which, said Bertie, was slightly more bearable.

In spite of the assiduous care of John Brown life was a little trying. There was constant anxiety about Bertie and the life he was leading; she had heard many stories of the scandals surrounding her uncles and their debts and the troubles they had got into with women; she greatly feared that Bertie was following in their footsteps. The people were displeased about her seclusion. There were pieces constantly appearing in the papers. Some of the ill-mannered politicians were not averse to standing up and pronouncing tirades against her. It was to say the least annoying.

Was it not enough that she worked hard for the good of the country? Had she not kept them out of war during that dreadful Schleswig-Holstein affair? If it had not been for her those two dreadful old men, Palmerston and Russell, might have dragged them in on the side of Denmark. It was true that she was very annoyed because Austria and Prussia between them had not given the Duchies to the Duke of Augustenburg which had been the object of the war so everyone had been led to believe but Prussia had annexed Schleswig and Austria Holstein, which was very wrong. All the same England would not have been justified in going to war.

It was all going to be very awkward because very soon she

was going to Coburg to unveil a statue of Albert. All the family would be there and with this *distressing* conflict still in their minds, together with its *disgraceful* conclusion, it was going to be very awkward.

And now here was *Punch* with a most unkind cartoon. Oh, why did royalty have to suffer so much from these *vulgar* people? There she was, as they liked to portray her, most unflatteringly (not that she had ever been vain about her appearance) as the stone statue of Hermione. And Britannia (Paulina) standing before her with the words in a balloon coming from her mouth: " 'Tis time; descend. Be stone no more."

It was really too much to be borne. Not only must she work for their good in secret but she must appear at those worthless ceremonies, those tiresome, tiring public occasions.

Well, she was going to do no such thing; and they must be told so in such a way that there was no doubt about it.

Soon after the birth of little George, Alix and Bertie went to Denmark and stayed at Rumpenheim. How different it was from the old days. Everyone was talking about the war and of course most of the family had suffered very much through it. There was great bitterness and all the family feeling seemed to have disappeared.

Bertie was vehement in his condemnation of the Prussians and he hoped all those who had not stood by Denmark would realize how wrong they were now they saw how the Prussians and Austrians had seized the spoils.

There was speculation that there might well be trouble between those two, and Prussia would be at Austria's throat before long; they could depend on that because Prussia would not be satisfied with Schleswig merely. Bismarck was stretching his greedy hands across Europe.

It was so different; one could not escape from the consequences of the war.

Dagmar's fiancé, Nicholas the Czarevitch, had died of tuberculosis and she was very unhappy; but he had a brother Alexander and everyone was sure that Dagmar would have no difficulty in falling in love with him, so although she had lost her prospective bridegroom there was another waiting for her and his position was just as glittering as that of his brother. In fact it was exactly the same position.

It was all faintly depressing. Poor Dagmar felt that too.

And then they must go to Coburg where the Queen was unveiling the statue.

Victoria was in no mood to enjoy the occasion. She could never be in Coburg without thinking of dearest Albert and the happy holidays they had spent there. All her children were to be present because for any one of them to be absent would be an insult to dearest Papa. Albert's brother Ernest would be there too. How strange that he who had led a somewhat wicked life should still be alive and Albert, who was younger, should have died! She remembered the occasion when she and Albert had witnessed the unveiling of a statue to Beethoven and how they had laughed because when it was unveiled it had its back to them. What good old days—how different from these sad and tragic times!

While in Germany they met Prince Christian of Schleswig-Holstein, Sonderburg-Augustenburg, the younger brother of the man who had aspired to Schleswig-Holstein, and whose family had now been robbed of their estates by the Prussians and Austrians. He and Lenchen became very interested in each other and as Lenchen was the next daughter for whom she must find a husband, the Queen saw no reason for not agreeing to their betrothal. As far as her daughters were concerned she always remembered the sad case of her aunts who had never been allowed to marry. There had been scandals about some of them and some of them had been very bitter. But then of course poor old Grandpapa George III was always very odd.

Lenchen seemed very happy at the prospect of marriage and she could go home and think about it very carefully because the marriage could not take place for a while.

Vicky was of the opinion that it would be a good match. Vicky herself was in a very difficult position. Her husband was the Crown Prince of Prussia but Bismarck was not at all fond of her and she told the Queen that he had said she was pro-English.

"What an unfeeling man," cried the Queen, "to imagine you could ever forget your native land!"

It had been a difficult life in Germany for poor Vicky in that dreadful haunted schloss with her mother-in-law who resented her, and that dreadful Bismarck who was really responsible for the terrible reputation Prussia was getting for being the menace of Europe. And besides that, of course, she was very worried about little Wilhelm with his poor sad arm and all the treatment they were trying to give him.

The Queen was glad when it was time to leave. She was very much looking forward to being at Balmoral. She smiled to think how pleased Brown would be.

Alix was very uneasy. How she hated being in Germany! To have been at Rumpenheim with her sad relations who had lost so much and then to be expected to be friendly with their enemies was unendurable. She was angry when a message arrived for her and Bertie to the effect that the Queen of Prussia would come to Coblenz to greet them as they passed through. It would be a brief meeting fortunately, said Bertie. For form's sake really.

He was unprepared for Alix's stony silence. He tried to change the subject but she burst out: "Do you think I am going to be polite to the Queen of Prussia when the King and Bismarck have done everything possible to ruin my father, my home and my family?"

"I know it's hard to meet them," soothed Bertie. "But it's just to greet them and then pass on. They understand it's a little awkward. That's why it's been arranged like this. It'll be over in an hour."

"It will not," said Alix.

"Oh yes, it will," murmured Bertie.

"It will not be over in an hour," repeated Alix fiercely, "because it is never going to begin."

Bertie stared at her.

"My dear," he said, "do you realize that the Queen of Prussia is coming to Coblenz expressly to see us."

"Yes, I do," said Alix, "and there is one thing you must understand, Bertie, I am not going to see her."

"It would be an insult."

"My parents have been worse than insulted by Prussia."

"Alix, I know this, but we couldn't possibly refuse to see them."

"I could," she said, "and I shall."

Bertie was reminded of the time when she had had the flag hauled down from the mast. This was a new Alix. She had seemed so easy-going; she did not question him when he stayed out all night. He was aware that she knew of his friendships with other women and she accepted this as necessary to his extreme virility. Dear Alix, such a good wife, he had always thought. So pretty and so accommodating.

But this was different. He now recognized that determination, and knew that he could not ignore it.

He tried pleading with her. "What can we do? What excuse can I make?"

"Excuse! Do we have to make excuses? These people have murdered Danes; they have stolen our territory. Do we have to make excuses because we don't fall on their necks and kiss them?"

"We have to remember that this is the Queen of Prussia."

"It is precisely because I remember that that I will not see her."

"Mama will be displeased."

"I am sorry, but if she is that must be so."

"Alix, consider . . ."

But her lips were tightly pressed together and there was a hard glitter in her eyes. She would not leave the train to meet the Queen of Prussia.

Bertie was in a dilemma. He must go alone, which he did.

The Princess of Wales, he explained, was indisposed. Perhaps she had taken the journey too soon after the birth of little George.

The Queen of Prussia coldly agreed that this might be so, but she knew of course that the Princess of Wales had insulted her; she had been fully informed of the incident of the flag.

The little Danish Princess gave herself airs which was extraordinary considering she had never been of great importance and but for the fact that the Prince of Wales had married her would have been even less so after the defeat of the Danes.

She would have to learn that she could not insult Prussia with impunity.

The Queen broke her journey on the way back at Ostend in order that she might see Uncle Leopold.

Poor Uncle Leopold, he was getting very old now. She remembered sadly how beautiful he had seemed when she was a child and she had called him her second father. There was still something very impressive about him. She could see the paint very clearly on his wrinkled cheeks. Poor dear man, striving to look well, and she remembered how when he had been young he had loved to talk of his ailments. He said his rheumatism was crippling him then; it wasn't, of course, but it was just that he enjoyed imagining himself a martyr. She had heard him and old Baron Stockmar talking of their ailments with almost as much excitement as they did politics.

And now he was rather a sad sight, still in his built-up shoes to give him height and his wig which somehow called attention to his ageing face. But he was as warm and affectionate as ever.

She was still his dearest child and he still attempted to advise. Now he was lecturing her on her love of seclusion. "It is not wise, my dearest child. The people want to see you. We can't afford to shut ourselves away. We have to think of the people all the time."

"It's so tiresome that they should want to see me."

"Even more tiresome, my dear child, when they lose interest in us, or worse still turn against us. The Prince and Princess of Wales will take the popularity which should be yours."

"Bertie gives me great cause for alarm."

"He's a very wild young man, I believe. He takes after my father-in-law, George IV."

"Yes, I fear so. *That* sort of thing is in the family . . . like getting fat. I've noticed Bertie is putting on weight."

"Too much rich food and wine, you should tell him."

"Bertie is becoming quite unmanageable."

"All the more reason why you should take your place in society."

She listened patiently. Dear Uncle, he did like to manage everything. He had always been so. She remembered how she had remarked on this to Albert.

"I remember," said Leopold, "when your Cousin Charlotte first became my wife . . ."

The Queen's attention strayed. He was rambling on about how docile Charlotte had been, how she had looked up to him, how she had been a little jealous of him . . .

Victoria had heard it all before. Dear Uncle, he was getting so old.

She would be glad to be back in Balmoral.

Old Pam was beginning to feel his age. He was past eighty, but he was not going to give up. "If it wasn't for the gout," he told his wife Emily, "I'd be as good as I was twenty years ago."

But there was the gout and that spring he had had a particularly bad bout of it. He had gone down to Brocket Hall which Emily had inherited on the death of her brother, Lord

Melbourne, and she had induced him to stay there for a bit.
But as she said, it was hopeless trying to keep Pam quiet. The
despatch boxes came down regularly and he was up half the
night dealing with them, because he liked to ride in the day
and he urged her to continue giving her parties in the evening. There were frequent dinner parties at Brocket Hall and
he liked the guests not all to be old. A sprinkling of young
and pretty women was always desirable and he continued to
have an eye for them which Emily assured him she was
aware of.

"Oh, I've followed the path of virtue since I married you,
Em," he told her. "I never sin outside my thoughts."

She was afraid for him and wondered how he would feel if
he was no longer able to continue in politics; he was afraid of
what would happen to her if he were to die. Theirs was a devotion which was almost incongruous but it was steadfast as
both knew.

With the coming of October he began to feel ill but he
tried to hide it. He would have a day in bed and the next day
he would be up and go out with Emily for a drive.

Lord Russell thought it wise to advise the Queen that he
was anxious about the Prime Minister's health.

What joy to be at Balmoral! Brown was in his element.
This was the place. This was the life. The Queen was planning trips she would take with John Brown.

"Aye," said Brown, "that's a bit of a rough road, woman."

"Nonsense, Brown. We should be perfectly safe with you.
We will go to Loch Oishne. It was always a favourite spot of
the Prince Consort's."

Brown muttered that he was nae going to be responsible if
she got it into her head to travel too far away and come back
by night.

The Queen laughed. "Oh, you'll look after us. You always
do."

She was so delighted to be back among the beloved hills.
But there was this terrible news about Lord Palmerston. She
did hope he was not going to be so ill that she would have to
return to London. She would write to Lady Palmerston and
send her sympathies. How difficult it must be to nurse a man
like Lord Palmerston. She was sure he would never do what
he was told.

In the meantime she would forget her Prime Minister and
enjoy the simple life. What fun it was when Dr Macleod

came in and told them about a most horrible murderer with whom he had talked when he visited the prison. Dr Pritchard had murdered his wife and mother-in-law and had been a dreadful character. It was really very distressing to realize that there were such terrible people in the world. But he of course was no longer in it, having been hanged by the neck last July.

Death, she thought. We all came to it. Dear Albert now lay in the mausoleum at Frogmore and how often during the months following his death had she longed to lie there beside him.

Now . . . She thrust aside the thought, because it was quite a long time since she had wished she were there with him. It was not that she was forgetting, she reminded herself. She was merely reconciled to living out the span allotted to her.

All the same it was very interesting to listen to Dr Macleod and the next day which was Sunday they went to church where prayers were said for the recovery of Lord Palmerston.

Lord Palmerston lay in bed wondering whether he would reach his eighty-first birthday. He had breakfasted off mutton chops and port wine and told Emily that he felt better after such an excellent meal.

Emily came and sat by his bed but refused to allow him to get up. His protests were mild enough for he did not really feel well. But to cheer Emily when the doctor called he told him that he wanted to be up and about and couldn't think why they were keeping him in bed. "You'll die if you go out in this weather," warned the doctor.

"Die!" cried Palmerston with the accustomed wit. "My dear fellow, that's the *last* thing I shall do."

A few days later he was dead.

He was buried in Westminster Abbey and crowds witnessed the ceremony. They were silent crowds and the spirit of genuine mourning was evident. He had been the people's darling with his amorous adventures in his youth which had earned him the name Cupid, becoming on his marriage to Emily the reformed rake, his wit, his unruffled good humour, his refusal to bow to royalty, his ability in foreign affairs—all this was remembered at the passing of good old Pam.

The Queen was saddened because she hated death.

"But," she said, "I never really liked him."

* * *

The Queen hated these ministerial crises and she was really very perturbed to contemplate that Lord Palmerston was no more. Although she had never liked him, she had to admit that she was feeling his loss deeply. He had been a strong man and that was what the country needed, particularly when it no longer had Albert to lead the way. He had been very courageous, anyone must admit that; and he had been calm; of course he had thought that he was infallible and he had been most disrespectful at times, but the country was going to miss him and apart from his vanity he was a great man. Moreover he had been the Prime Minister and there was nothing to do but summon Lord John Russell and ask him to step into Palmerston's shoes.

Poor Lord John, he was getting so old, but what alternative was there?

When she considered her ministers nowadays she thought longingly of Sir Robert Peel, that great good man whom she had failed to appreciate until Albert had revealed his virtues to her. There was hardly one man of stature in her government now because she refused to consider Mr Gladstone whom she could never like. But there was one . . . She smiled tolerantly, thinking of him. Mr Disraeli was such a *feeling* man, and even his enemies—and he had many— would admit that he was clever. In the first place she had thought him rather odd—so was his wife, a very flamboyant woman, a widow too and she had never believed in widows remarrying. But Mr Disraeli had shown himself to be a charming man. While Mr Gladstone had fulminated against the cost of the Albert Memorial, Mr Disraeli had made such a delightful speech. Nothing was too expensive, in his opinion, to honour the great Prince Consort. She had warmed towards him immediately; and when they had spoken together he had talked of Albert as an Ideal and had so understood her grief that there was an immediate rapport between them.

She had shown her approval by seeing that he and his wife had good seats for Bertie's wedding; and she thought it was rather touching how devoted he was to Mrs Disraeli who was thirteen years older than he was; and she of course adored him. They reminded her of herself and Albert and that made her warm all the more to Mr Disraeli. He of course was a Tory as dear Sir Robert had been—but he had not been a great friend of Sir Robert; he had as a matter of fact been one of those responsible for the downfall of the great man. But politics were politics and Mr Disraeli had to defend his principles even if it meant going against his leader, which showed of course how honourable Mr Disraeli was.

However, there was no question of Mr. Disraeli's forming a government at this stage. All she could do was write to Lord John Russell.

The melancholy news of Lord Palmerston's death reached the Queen tonight. This is another link with the past that is broken and the Queen feels deeply in her desolated and isolated condition how, one by one, tried servants and advisers are taken from her. The Queen can turn to no other than Lord Russell, an old and tried friend of hers, to undertake the arduous duties of Prime Minister and carry on the government.

Poor little Johnny Russell—so old and tired. How much better it would have been if she could have sent for the stimulating and exciting personality, Mr. Disraeli.

Only two months after the death of Lord Palmerston another tragedy occurred which touched the Queen far more deeply.

Uncle Leopold died.

She had talked of Lord Palmerston's death as a broken link with the past, how much more so was Leopold's.

She shut herself in her room and wept thinking of her childhood when he had seemed godlike to her, perfect in every way, the father whom she had sadly missed, the adviser and the friend. Of course as time went on he had sought to rule her, but that was his way; and first Lord Melbourne and then Albert had been beside her to teach her that much as she loved this dear uncle he must not be allowed to rule England. Dear Uncle Leopold who had been first Charlotte's husband and then Louise's and had arranged that all his relations should marry throughout Europe most advantageously. He had been a great power in the world and a great influence on her life.

He wished to be buried at Windsor. Of course it should be so. His body should be brought over and there should be a very sad ceremony for this beloved relation.

She was horrified when the Belgian Government refused to

allow his body to be sent to England. He was the King of the Belgians, it was said, and England was not his native land.

The Queen was both furious and tearful.

"You'll be upsetting yourself, woman," said John Brown, "for no good at all."

"You're right, of course, Brown, but this was my beloved uncle, the friend of my childhood, and he is dead."

"We all have to die when our time comes," mumbled Brown.

How right he was.

"It's the Catholic Clergy who are raising objections," went on the Queen.

Brown's lips curled; he didn't think much of any church but that of Scotland.

"Nasty beggars," he said, which made the Queen smile and feel so much better.

It was most unfortunate that with the passing of Lord Palmerston and the premiership of Lord John, Mr Gladstone should have become the Leader of the House while remaining Chancellor of the Exchequer. This meant that the Queen was obliged to see more of him and as she confided to John Brown, she could never take to the man. She would never forgive him for voting against granting the money for the Albert Memorial; he was so different from Mr. Disraeli, whom the more she saw the more she liked. She had forgotten that she had once thought him a mountebank; now he was amusing and exciting. The manner in which he kissed her hand was so reverential and he spoke of Albert in hushed tones as though he were speaking of the Deity.

Mr Disraeli understood the Queen's grief; he never tried to minimize it, he often dwelt on its magnitude; he told her of his devotion to his own dear Mary Anne although it was absurd to compare the strange, quite ugly creature with beautiful Albert; but in Mr Disraeli's eyes his wife was a beauty which was very touching, particularly after all the unkind things which people said about his marrying her for her money.

She had sent him a copy of the Prince's speeches bound in white morocco; he replied by letter containing elegant phrases which exuded gratitude and in person he expressed his delight in the gift with tears in his eyes so that she had no doubt of his sincere appreciation.

But of course he was in Opposition, which was very irritating, because while Johnny Russell's government remained, unfortunately that *tiresome* Mr Gladstone must be often in her company.

Only one thing could she find in his favour. Mrs Gladstone was devoted to him. She often wondered what it must be like to be married to such an *un*attractive man. *Poor* Mrs Gladstone!

She was not sorry when the Russell government was defeated and forced to resign. She had in the past been fond of Little Johnny, but that was in Lord Melbourne's day and now he was seventy-three and seemed older than Lord Palmerston had been at eighty. Gladstone's Reform Bill was the reason for the government's downfall. Clever Mr Disraeli and his leader Lord Derby had put forward more popular measures and as a result Lord John and Mr Gladstone were so badly defeated that they had no recourse but to resign.

Lord Derby came in with his Tories and although he was the Prime Minister the Queen was amused to note that the leading light of the new government was her dear friend Mr Disraeli.

Benjamin Disraeli was jubilant. He could see in the very near future he would achieve the great ambition of his life—to become Prime Minister. And when he did he could be sure of the two women who were most important to him, Mary Anne, his wife, and Victoria the Queen.

Disraeli had always been a favourite with women—particularly those older than himself—but although the Queen was some fifteen years younger than he was, she was a matron, the mother of nine, and since the death of the Prince Consort appeared to be older than her years.

Derby was ailing; there was no doubt of that; Lord John Russell was too old for office; Melbourne was gone, Palmerston was gone. Who was left? The answer was Disraeli, who would tower above them all, his only rival being William Ewart Gladstone whom the Queen disliked more and more as time passed. Poor old Gladstone, he did not know how to treat romantically-minded ladies—for the Queen was one no less than Mary Anne.

Disraeli's great regret was that his sister Sarah was not alive. How she would have enjoyed his triumph. Dear old Sarah who had been so loyal all the years and followed his successes with such glee—how sad that she should die before he had reached the pinnacle.

But it was seven years or so since Sarah had died, and they had buried her in Paddington cemetery. She had never married, although twenty-nine years before her death she had been engaged to William Meredith who had died in Cairo when he and Benjamin were travelling together. Had she married him she would have had a husband and family with whom to concern herself and might not have been so devoted to her brother.

So he had lost Sarah, but he had Mary Anne and nobody could have been more faithful, no one could have lived more for another person than she lived for him.

Returning home late from the House he would always find her waiting up for him; she liked to make sure that there was a snack ready in case he should feel hungry.

On this occasion she would be jubilant he knew for she would be fully aware of the situation and what it meant.

"I'm not clever like you, Dizzy," she would often say. "I'm a regular dunce." But she knew well enough what was good for her Dizzy and she would be fully aware of Lord Derby's failing powers and that her clever husband was poised waiting to spring into the saddle.

True to custom when he arrived home, there was Mary Anne in a brilliantly coloured peignoir waiting up for him, presiding over a table laid with cold chicken and champagne.

"Celebrations tonight," she greeted him. "This is a good day for my dearest Dizzy."

Dizzy replied with that gallantry which had so delighted the Queen that the best part of it was coming home to Mary Anne.

"I'll drink a glass with you," she told him. "To the next Prime Minister."

"A little way to go yet, Mary Anne."

"A step or two," she admitted.

"Gladstone's waiting to spring."

"Sanctimonious old devil," said Mary Anne.

"You sound like the Queen."

"Is that what she calls him?"

"Not quite, but she looks really severe when she mentions his name."

"And she smiles for my Dizzy."

"I know how to treat her. It's always well to flatter people but where royalty are concerned you lay it on with a trowel."

Mary Anne giggled; her eyes grew sentimental. "Is the chicken good, my dearest? And you were hungry!" She raised her glass. "May you be as good a Chancellor of the Exchequer and Leader of the House as you have been a husband to your Mary Anne. And," she added, "very soon I shall substitute for the first two titles that of Prime Minister."

"You go too fast, my dearest wife."

"No one goes as fast as my Dizzy."

"What should I do without you?"

"Is that what you asked yourself when you married me for my money?"

"Not so earnestly as I do now, for you know that if I had to make the choice again I'd marry you for love."

She smiled at him, eyes glazed with affection.

"Do you know, Dizzy," she said. "I believe you mean that."

"With all my heart," said her husband.

A Royal Birth

The Queen was a little worried. She was laughing now and then, usually at some of Brown's quaint sayings. She found that she was enjoying rides in the country, particularly at Balmoral which would always be nearest her heart, although she loved Osborne too.

Was she being unfaithful to Albert because she was not thinking of him every hour of the day?

She wrote to Vicky and told her about her feelings. She would never forget that Beloved Papa was a saint and that there could never be anyone like him, but she did find that her grief was less vehement. Of course there were times when she was sunk in melancholy but she did find some solace in the children of course. Baby Beatrice—not such a baby now—had always been so amusing and it was so pleasant to have the children with her, reading together, but she feared sometimes they would go a very long time without mentioning Papa, and she was very ashamed afterwards; it seemed a slight to his memory.

Vicky wrote back that dearest Papa would be watching over her and perhaps it was his will that she should stop brooding.

"You have your life to lead, Mama, and great duties to perform. I am sure it is Papa's will that you should remember that, although you long to join him, you must await the call."

Vicky was a comfort of course; and so was dear Dean Wellesley to whom she also confessed her waning grief.

She still mourned, replied the Dean, and that showed how deep her affection had been. To spend her days in brooding and weeping was not in fact a sign of great grief for a loss as much as pity for oneself.

She was comforted by this and allowed herself to be amused by *clever* Mr Disraeli and *honest* John Brown.

Whenever she rode out John Brown would be on the box; wherever she was he was never far away; he looked after her clothes and wrapped her cloak about her; he scolded her for not standing still while he fastened it; when she was feeling unwell he would carry her from her sofa to her bed. "Where is Brown?" she would ask if he failed to appear.

One of the most startling facets of the relationship was that the handsome Highlander was more than a little fond of his whisky and there had been occasions when he had been unable to answer the Queen's summons because he had taken rather too much.

When she demanded an explanation he replied nonchalantly: "I was o'er bashful last night, woman."

Bashful! She knew what he meant. He had drunk too much whisky and had been unable to wait on her. What an amusing word! Bashful, meaning slightly intoxicated—or perhaps not exactly slightly.

She would say roguishly when she saw him helping himself to what he called a wee dram, "Now, Brown, pray do not become too bashful!"

"Nae," he would reply, "I'll content myself with a wee dram or two the night."

The Queen laughed. He did her *so* much good.

But of course it was hardly likely that the relationship between them should go unnoticed.

It seemed incredible that this imperious Queen who could subdue any one of her ministers with a cold stare or an icy comment should find it amusing that one of her servants should be too intoxicated for his duties. What could it mean?

There seemed to be one construction to put on this—and it was immediately put.

Eyebrows were raised; titters were heard. What is the relationship, it was asked, between the Queen and her Highland servant?

It was a mystery. He was good looking in his rough way—tall, curly-haired and bearded, with the famous strong chin which she admired; he talked to her as no one had ever talked to her in her life and was allowed to.

Such delicious scandal material could not be allowed to go unrecorded.

The scandal was taken up hilariously not only in England but also on the Continent.

There were cartoons, lampoons, imitation Court Circulars in which the activities of Mr John Brown were recorded. It was inevitable that sooner or later there should be talk of *Mrs* John Brown.

She had married him, said some. It was the only solution. She would never have allowed him the liberties she did if that had not been the case. Why was she always going up to Balmoral? So that they could live in comparative seclusion there? Why had she brought him down from his native Scotland? Why was she never seen out of his company? And all the time she was pretending to be heart-broken about Albert!

The Queen could not be kept in ignorance of rumours. She remembered an occasion long ago, before her marriage to Albert, when Lord Melbourne had been the most important person in her life. She had seen him every day; she had admired him, and in fact she was a little ashamed when she read her old journals and realized how besotted she had been. She had been pulled up with a jerk when someone had shouted Mrs Melbourne at the races. But that had not hurt her friendship with Lord Melbourne; and ill-natured gossip was certainly not going to rob her of John Brown's.

People were wicked and ill-natured. They said unkind things and those dreadful cartoons, with their horrid pictures, were often quite lewd. But then their target was royalty; they had even maligned beloved Albert.

She would ignore them, and their ill nature should certainly do nothing to drive Brown from her favour. She was going to raise his salary to £150 a year. He was worth every penny.

But the Queen's family and her ministers were concerned about the rumours.

She was gradually emerging a little from her seclusion. One of the public gibes had gone home. If the Queen was so overcome by grief that she needed seclusion, it was asked, she would not find it in the company of gillies any more than in that of her own class.

She refused to be ordered, she said. She would not allow anyone to force her into something to which she had no inclination; and appearing in public was something to which she was averse.

She did agree, though, to attend the opening of the new Parliament, but she would have none of the usual ceremony. She would not wear the robes of state but insisted on keeping to her widow's robes and her "sad" cap, and she commanded that the robes of state be laid on a seat beside her; she refused to read the speech from the throne, and the Lord Chancellor had to read it instead. The people were sullen; they had no wish to dispense with the brilliant ceremonies to which they looked forward, but since the Queen had gone into mourning there had been none—even royal weddings were sombre affairs.

She did however go to Aldershot a little later on to grace one or two ceremonies and there was Lenchen's coming wedding to be arranged.

How different it would have been, she mourned, if Albert were here. How interested he would have been in Lenchen's future.

There would soon be two weddings because as well as Lenchen Mary Cambridge had become engaged. And time too! thought the Queen, for it had seemed as though Mary would never get a husband. She was a good-looking woman but getting so large and she was no longer young, so it was a blessing that she had become betrothed to the Duke of Teck for he was her second cousin, his grandmother being the elder sister of Victoria's own mother. Quite a pleasant man—and it was a relief to get Mary married.

It had been a disturbing year, the Queen decided. Prussia was showing itself to be fiercely militant and that man Bismarck was determined to carry out his policy of blood and iron. His great dream to amalgamate the German states with Prussia at their head was becoming a possibility. Prussia had squabbled with Austria over Schleswig-Holstein and war had broken out between them.

The Queen hated the thought of war and such a war was particularly distressing to contemplate because it made dissension in the family. Vicky and her husband must naturally stand with Prussia but other members of her family were on the side of Austria; there was Ernest of Saxe-Coburg, cousin George of Hanover and Alice's husband of Hesse. It was unbearable to contemplate; she could not decide with whom to sympathize. Albert had always been devoted to Germany and a strong Germany was what he had always advocated; but what would his reaction have been if Prussia was at war with Saxe-Coburg, his old home, with Hanover which had always been part of British possessions since the days of George I, and Hesse of course where dear Alice staunchly supported her husband.

The Queen was aroused at last from her lethargy. She felt strongly for poor dear Alice; she commanded that the Hesse children be sent to her at Windsor and she herself despatched first-aid bandages and medicines for the wounded soldiers of Hesse.

Terrible news came from Hanover which the Prussians had seized. Poor Cousin George was driven from his kingdom. This was shocking. England had lost Hanover. She wept bitterly, thinking of poor blind George and how terrible it had been at the time of his accident when his parents—that wicked pair—had been so distressed that everyone had been so sorry for them.

One by one the small principalities and dukedoms fell before the might of Prussia and seven weeks after the conflict began Austria was defeated.

It was very, very sad. Vicky was triumphant in a veiled way; Alice was desolate; and when the Queen thought of poor blind George Cumberland, an exile from his kingdom, she could have wept bitterly.

War was so devastating—particularly when it made such conflict in the family.

It was a great relief to get away from it all and go to Balmoral where faithful Brown was clearly in his element, to take rides to the places which Albert had so loved and to see the celebration of Halloween when the villagers made their bonfires and the gillies were out with their burning torches. So comforting to have Brown wrap the rug about her when she went for a night drive to see the bonfires the better and to be scolded by Brown when she coughed.

"If you would come, woman, you must take the risk of being choked with the smoke."

But he produced a wee drop of spirits for her to sip and demanded to know whether or not she didn't feel the better for it. So pleasant, so good to be away from the terrible conflicts and storms of government.

How different life seemed, thought Alix, from the carefree days of poverty in the Yellow Palace. They were all grown up now. Willy—how strange to think of him as King George of Greece—was finding life very serious in his new kingdom. He wrote to Alix that his new country was engaged in the fearful struggle with Turkey and England could do so much to help.

Alix consulted Bertie who was as blandly sympathetic as ever. He was very fond of pretty Alix and wanted to make up to her for some of the anxieties he caused her. He would do anything for Alix, except of course give up the gay life which was so important to him. He must see his lively friends; he must have that freedom of which he had been starved during his adolescence; he must be surrounded by pretty women who were not too morally scrupulous. He loved the races; he found gambling completely exciting. These things were of the utmost importance to him. If Alix would not interfere in his gay life he would be ready to support her in any way she wished.

She was philosophical. She had been foolish to imagine that the married life of her parents was a usual one. Her dear uncomplicated father and her clever mother had loved each other and their family life had been the most important thing in the world to them. She could only fully appreciate those days at Rumpenheim, Bernstorff and the Yellow Palace now that they were past. She loved Bertie—how could she help it? Bertie was charming; he was kind; he adored little Eddy and Baby George; already they looked for him and shouted with glee when they saw him. He was never unkind; he always insisted that she should be treated with the utmost respect; he was proud of her; continually he told her that she was the most beautiful woman in England. But that was one side of his life; there had to be the other. There were rumours about his friendships with women and she knew it would be unwise to probe too closely into that. She had to accept dear charming Bertie as he was and then they could be happy.

She was learning to do this and only occasionally sighed for the ideal relationship which resembled that enjoyed by her parents in the days before greatness had overtaken them. Not to be royal. What bliss that must be! Sometimes she went to the nursery and put on a big apron and bathed the babies herself. The boys had loved that; they adored her even more than they did Bertie. Young Eddy's great eyes would fill with tears when she told them she must leave them. And sometimes Bertie would come in when she was playing the humble wife and would crawl round the floor with the two boys on his back shrieking with joy.

When she reminded Bertie about her brother's plea for help against Turkey he was so full of sympathy that she wondered whether he was eager to placate his conscience because of some recent misdemeanour of which he was secretly ashamed. He would speak to the Foreign Secretary, he said; and he kept his promise.

The result was a summons for Bertie to come to Windsor to face his enraged mama.

The Queen looked distastefully at her eldest son.

"Really, Bertie," she said, "you have no sense of decorum. Do you imagine for one moment that it is *your* place to advise *my* Foreign Secretary as to the course of action he should take?"

Bertie replied that Alix was anxious about her brother.

"And do you imagine that the State should take notice of these family relationships?"

Bertie found it difficult to stand against her. He realized that he could not interfere and he had only agreed to do so to placate Alix. He had done his best and the Queen and the Foreign Secretary would not help George of Greece. He could do no more. Poor Alix, she felt so deeply for her family.

"You will write to your brother-in-law," said the Queen, "and tell him that we can do nothing to help him. He will have to accept the situation and try to bring about peace in his country."

Alix was sad. First her parents had been refused help by

this powerful country into which she had married; and now her brother. It showed clearly that she had no influence with her new relations.

She had become pregnant again.

There was news from Denmark. Dagmar was soon to leave for Russia and her marriage to the Czarevitch.

Bertie was excited. He and Alix had been invited to the wedding and there was nothing he enjoyed so much as travelling abroad but the doctor, Sir James Paget, was rather uneasy about Alix's condition and said that on no account must she undertake the arduous journey.

Alix was desolate. Not to be at Dagmar's wedding was very disappointing; she and Bertie had so looked forward to going.

"Of course," said Bertie, his eyes gleaming in anticipation, "it would be unthinkable for neither of us to go to Dagmar's wedding." Sometimes Alix fancied that he preferred to be alone on the journeys abroad.

The Queen disapproved of Bertie's travelling out of the country, particularly without Alix. Vicky was always aware of any scandal that was circulating and it seemed that it always did about Bertie. His love of gambling was to be deplored but even more so was the fact that it came only second to his love of fascinating women.

Bertie had no intention of going to Osborne to be lectured by the Queen so he went direct to the Prime Minister, Lord Derby, and asked if he did not think relations with Russia would be improved if he went as a guest to the wedding and at the same time made himself agreeable. Disraeli was inclined to think that the Prince was an excellent ambassador and there could be no harm in his taking the trip and possibly a great deal of good. Disraeli had nicknamed him Prince Hal (because of his love of enjoyment) and this seeped out and the Prince was often referred to in this way.

Armed with ministerial approval Bertie faced the Queen at Windsor and told her that Lord Derby and Mr Disraeli were of the opinion that although Alix was unable to attend the wedding he, in the interest of foreign relations, should do so.

Since Mr Disraeli thought it was a good thing, the Queen supposed it was.

"But you must visit Prussia on your return journey," she told him. "You must be Vicky's guest for a short while."

Bertie inwardly grimaced. Vicky was so censorious and in

his light-hearted way he did deplore recent Prussian activities. However, the Queen was adamant. No Vicky, no Russian wedding, whatever her ministers said.

Bertie went off to Russia in high spirits. There was no doubt that he was a great success. His easy manners, his charm, his delight in the gayest entertainments brought him great popularity. He was constantly seen in the company of beautiful women and there was a certain amount of scandal. Alice was worried about it. It seemed very wrong of Bertie to show such pleasure in the company of women when poor Alix was unable to accompany him and by all accounts her health was giving some cause for anxiety. She felt it her duty to write to Sir William Knollys on the subject and Sir William spoke to Bertie, who was very amused that gentle Alice should follow in Vicky's footsteps. Vicky had always been critical, like an echo of their father, and he expected it from her. Sir William thought that Princess Alice had probably been very disturbed by rumours and that was her reason for writing to him.

Bertie said he must be pleasant to people. It was part of his duties to be so.

"Perhaps Your Highness could try to be impartially gracious."

Bertie thought that it was necessary to do honour more to some people than others and it would of course depend on their qualifications to deserve that honour. There was a twinkle in his eye and Sir William understood that he had no intention of changing his ways; but perhaps he could be induced to be a little more discreet.

Vicky, of course, wrote to the Queen. She did think that Bertie should be a little more thoughtful where poor dear Alix was concerned.

With the new year Alix was alarmed by strange pains which she was feeling in her limbs. In early February these grew worse; by the middle of the month she could only walk with great difficulty and was confined to her room. The doctors diagnosed acute rheumatism.

The fact that the birth of a child was imminent gave cause for alarm, and a few days after she had been confined to her room her daughter was born. Before her pains had started, her temperature had soared and there was no doubt that she was in a fever, yet the baby was safely delivered and appeared to be well.

Sir James Paget was very anxious about her. The fact that she had given birth to a child while in the throes of rheumatic fever could mean that her life was in danger.

In her delirium she talked of the Yellow Palace and kept calling for her parents. He deliberated whether to send a messenger to Windsor where the Queen was at that time or to send immediately for the Prince of Wales, who was out of London. Fearing that the Princess was on the point of death he decided that there was no time and he acted on his own judgment by telegraphing direct to Denmark begging the King and Queen to come at once as he feared for the life of the Princess of Wales.

Within a few days Queen Louise was at Marlborough House. King Christian was following and would arrive two days later. Louise went straight to the sickroom and took her daughter into her arms, speaking to her in the manner she had done as a child. Alix was immediately comforted; the tension seemed to have passed and although she was in great pain the change in her was remarkable.

The Queen, who had now heard of the state of Alix's health, at once came to Marlborough House from Windsor, but by the time she had arrived Louise was already in the sickroom.

The Queen was astonished that Louise should have come to England uninvited. Surely, she fumed to herself, if Alix's parents were needed *I* should have been told so that I could have invited them in the proper manner. "Where is Sir James Paget?" she demanded.

Sir James presented himself, dignified and unrepentant. "The Princess's life was in danger, M'am, and it was my duty to save it."

The Queen of course appreciated that and would not have had Sir James act otherwise, but she wondered whether it was part of his duty to invite *people* to her Court; she had never liked that woman who was so deaf that she could not understand what was said to her, and who painted her cheeks.

The Queen burst into the sickroom and when she saw Alix with her hand in her mother's looking so wan and ill and yet so much at peace because Louise was there, all her anger faded. After all she might be a domineering woman and deaf; she might paint her cheeks; but she was Alix's mother and Alix wanted her at that time more than her relations by marriage.

The Queen kissed Alix and gave a gracious nod to Louise.

"My dear sweet Alix, this is dreadful. You so ill and my not knowing."

"Dr Paget sent for Mama," said Alix. "I felt better as soon as she came."

The Queen's eyes filled with tears. *Dear* sweet Alix, she was not clever but she was such a good child and so pretty; and devoted to that woman who after all was her mother.

"You must get well quickly," said the Queen. "I am pleased that Sir James had the good sense to send for the Queen of Denmark."

The emotions of the people were deeply touched by the plight of the invalid. Alix was the most popular member of the royal family; she was beautiful, gracious and sick. Bertie amused them with his adventures, but they were not amusing doubtless to the Princess; and now she was very ill; crowds clustered about Marlborough House, all sorts of people sent in advice on treatment, embrocations arrived in their thousands; one old lady sent a roll of oil silk; ointments were sent to the palace, all kinds of cures were suggested. A special staff was needed to deal with them and bulletins of the Princess's health were issued regularly while crowds waited to see them.

Alix was without doubt very ill indeed and the pains in her joints continued so it was some months before she was able to walk and then could only do so with the aid of sticks.

The new baby was christened Louise Victoria Alexandra Dagmar three months after her birth, when Alix was carried to the drawing-room and even then could only hobble about on her two sticks.

The Queen was very sympathetic but she blamed Bertie—and indeed both of them—for the rackety life they led. They would have to be a little more careful now—not so many late nights, not so many wild parties. Bertie must try to be the sort of husband to Alix that Albert had been to the Queen.

John Brown in Command

A new paper calling itself Tomahawk *was being published; it* was meant to be satirical and was most libellous; its leading topic was with that subject of which the Press was trying to create the greatest possible scandal—the Queen's relationship with John Brown.

On the paper's birth there had been constant hints about that relationship and in August of that year there appeared a cartoon which could not be ignored.

It was entitled "A Brown Study". It showed John Brown sprawling against the throne with his back to it and a glass in his hand, while the British Lion roared at his feet.

The implication was clear and when Bertie saw it he was secretly amused. He had suffered so much criticism regarding his own conduct, but what was that compared with this?

He was planning a trip to Paris—his favourite city—and he knew that the Queen would put up a certain amount of opposition as she always did at the hint of his travelling abroad. He thought it would be good strategy to get in first, so with *Tomahawk* in his hand he arrived at Osborne.

As he came uninvited the Queen was not waiting to receive him. She was in her apartments and the way was barred by John Brown.

The Prince was furious. No wonder the cartoonists had such a field day with his mother and this crude serving-man. The Prince of Wales would certainly not accept this unbecoming behaviour.

"Ye canna see the Queen now," said John Brown. "The woman's resting."

"I think the Queen will not be pleased to hear that the Prince of Wales has been denied admittance."

"She's nae in a fit condition to be badgered," said Brown firmly.

The Queen, hearing voices, called out: "Brown, who is that?"

"It's your eldest," answered Brown. "I've told him ye'll see him in the morning. Ye're too tired to be bothered the night."

"Thank you, Brown," said the Queen.

And what could Bertie do after that but go away fuming? Brown would have to go. The position in which he put the Queen, the position in which he put them all, was quite ridiculous.

The next morning Bertie triumphantly waved "A Brown Study" before his mother.

"Have you seen this, Mama?"

She glanced at it. "Oh dear, another of those tiresome things. Brown is so imperturbable. He doesn't care a pin about them."

"Mama, this is an attack on *you*, on the Crown."

"Of course any attack on honest John Brown is an attack on me."

"But this is making the throne . . . ridiculous."

"What nonsense, Bertie! This is just malicious people being malicious."

"Brown must go, Mama. He was very rude to me."

"Ah, that is it, is it? You don't like him. It is the first time I have understood that my servants must win *your* approval."

"Mama, they are suggesting he is not just a servant and it is the people who disapprove as well as myself."

"The people know nothing. They cannot understand my grief at Beloved Papa's death and they would like to deny me the comfort my faithful servants give me. I hope you have not come bursting down here just to tell me this. But while you are here there are one or two matters I should like to discuss with *you*. Your debts, mostly incurred by gambling, and I am horrified to learn by presents you have given to *women*, are mounting. You are going the same way as my Uncle George who caused such distress to *his* parents by the trouble he got into with women. I hope you do not write scandalous letters. And what of dear sweet Alix who is *pathetically* ill?

What does she think, I wonder, at these rumours? There is an actress . . . I heard . . . but I sincerely hope *that* is not true. I think it is time I took a close look into your manner of living. Vicky is quite horrified . . . and even Alice has heard. Sometimes I can't help feeling *relieved* that Beloved Papa is not here. He would be so distressed and when we think of how when he was so ill he went to Cambridge . . ."

The Prince turned away in dismay. What was the use of trying to remonstrate with her; she could turn the tables so adroitly because all the time she was reminding him that although he might be the Prince of Wales, she was the Queen.

He left Osborne deflated, a fact which John Brown noted, and his sardonic insolent smile was not lost on the Prince of Wales.

"A Brown Study" had sent the sales of *Tomahawk* soaring and rumours about the Queen's relationship with John Brown magnified. Some said that he was her lover, others that he was her husband; there was one rumour that she had inherited her grandfather's madness, that she was a raving lunatic at times and only John Brown could keep her in order; there was another rumour that John Brown was a medium who could put her in touch with Albert and this was the reason for his influence over her.

Spiritualism was having a vogue in England at the time and the Queen had been heard to express interest in the new cult. What more natural than that she should wish to be in touch with Albert?

But the most usual theory was that the Queen and Brown were lovers; and the fact that the Queen would not appear in public and so deprived her people of the glittering ceremonies they loved, and that John Brown's arrogance and indifference had not endeared him to those who were in contact with him, made both the Queen and her Highland servant become very unpopular.

She had however consented to attend a review in Hyde Park, with Brown of course in attendance as usual on the box of her carriage.

She was astonished therefore when Lord Derby called on her and told her that he thought it very unwise for John Brown to accompany her to the review.

"And why not, pray?" demanded the Queen.

"The people might resort to violence. The mob can easily

be aroused and these distasteful cartoons have been read by thousands."

"And because of unscrupulous scribblers who have tried hard to damage the character of a good honest man, he is not to perform his usual duties?"

Lord Derby tried to imply discreetly that it was not the defamation of John Brown's character which worried him so much as that of the Queen's, but the Queen would not see this.

"I shall not be dictated to," she told Derby coldly. "And I shall certainly not allow my comfort to be spoiled by the interference of wicked people."

That was as far as the Prime Minister could get with her. He went to Disraeli and told him of the Queen's response. Disraeli was grave. "There could be trouble," he said. "John Brown there in the Queen's company with that smug self-satisfaction of his . . . for all the world as though he is the new Consort. Now if the Queen would relegate Mr John Brown to the Highlands where he belongs and take some handsome Prince for her husband—preferably a gay one—nothing would delight the people more."

But it was no use hoping for the impossible. The Queen had made up her mind that John Brown should accompany her at the Hyde Park review and accompany her he should.

Over cold patty from Fortnum and Mason's and champagne fresh from the ice bucket taken together after Dizzy's return from the House he and Mary Anne discussed the situation.

"It'll be a miracle if there's not trouble with the mob over John Brown," said Dizzy.

"There are occasional miracles in public life," Mary Anne reminded him. "Think of my own Dizzy's climb to fame."

"That's not a miracle, that's hard work."

"Geniuses might make miracles happen. Couldn't you bring your dulcet tones to drive home the truth by putting the whole thing in one of your clever little nutshells?"

"My dearest Mary Anne, what a delectable concoction of metaphors. But even I am not capable of mixing them into a tasty little cake to delight Her Majesty's palate."

"Oh come, Dizzy, you're capable of anything and you can't tell me that she doesn't take more notice of you than that crude John Brown."

"We run neck and neck, my dearest, and I couldn't tell you who is the favourite."

"Now who's talking in metaphors and I won't have my Dizzy compared with a horse, even a race-horse. And as for that John Brown he's nothing better than an old carthorse."

Dizzy laughed; but he was very anxious about the review.

Affairs in Mexico provided the miracle. Napoleon III had set up the Archduke Maximilian as ruler of Mexico and given him the title of Emperor; he had married Princess Charlotte, Uncle Leopold's daughter, so was therefore close to the Queen. But the Mexicans would not acknowledge him. The civil war in North America had come to an end and Washington warned Napoleon that the army he had set up there must be withdrawn. This was done but Maximilian remained, hoping to raise an army of his own and retain his position. It was hopeless; the Mexican republic was restored and Maximilian court-martialled, sentenced to death and shot.

In view of such a catastrophe, it was decided that the Hyde Park review must be cancelled.

"God has sent us our miracle," said Dizzy.

But Mary Anne was certain that her clever husband had arranged it.

Although she would have been pleased to, the Queen could find no reason why Bertie should not go to Paris to attend the International Exhibition.

Her ministers seemed impressed by Bertie's popularity abroad and called him a good "ambassador". She feared that meant behaving very frivolously but in her heart she had to accept the fact that Bertie did balance to a certain extent the disfavour into which the family had fallen by her love of seclusion and devotion to John Brown—so off Bertie went to Paris to open the British section of the Exhibition.

Alix, often feeling very ill, unable to walk without the aid of sticks, was a little depressed wondering what Bertie was doing in his favourite city. Paris, he had said, suited him better than any other foreign capital; he felt at home there; he believed he understood the mood of the people; and the Emperor and his wife always made him feel so welcome.

Bertie had always been devoted to Napoleon III. When he had visited Paris as a boy with his parents and had made the acquaintance of the Emperor he had said, rather to the embarrassment of the Emperor and those who heard him, "I wish you were my father." The Emperor remembered this and there was always a special friendship between him and the Prince of Wales.

So Bertie settled down to enjoy his visit which he did to such effect that Vicky, and Alice too, were soon expressing alarm at his behaviour and saying how sorry they felt for poor Alix.

While in Paris he met the Sultan of Turkey and the Khedive of Egypt who intimated that they would like an invitation to come to England. The Queen was disturbed. Bertie knew that she disliked the ceremonies which must take place during the sojourn of visiting potentates, but he considered the visits necessary. Once again the government was on Bertie's side and it was decided that it would be a direct snub to Turkey to refuse to invite the Sultan and the Khedive.

"Very well, then," said the Queen. "But they are Bertie's responsibility. He must take charge of them."

The Queen's ministers thought that in view of the Prince's amiable nature this was a good idea; as for Bertie, he greatly looked forward to doing the honours. Alix would not be able to join in as they could have wished because her limbs were still painful, but her condition was improving and the Queen had agreed that if she maintained progress a visit to Wiesbaden would not be frowned on.

The Sultan was affable in the extreme; he was greatly taken with Alix and eyed her speculatively as though contemplating what a delightful addition she would be to his harem; he compromised by offering her one of his palaces in Constantinople where she could recuperate very happily, he was sure.

Bertie organized entertainments for the Sultan who was delighted with everything he saw. The Queen received him graciously at Osborne and declared that she would bestow the Garter on him.

When he heard what a great honour this was the Sultan was delighted and as the Spithead Review was about to take place Bertie thought it would be a good idea for the presentation to be made on board the Royal Yacht.

Bertie enjoyed making the arrangements; and Alice, who was visiting England with her husband, Prince Louis of Hesse, had to admit that Bertie had a way of enhancing such occasions. Bertie was at his best entertaining and if he was over gallant to the prettiest women and pressed their hands too frequently and whispered to them what might well have been the arrangement of an assignation, this must not be stressed, because the Queen's minister affirmed that when Bertie was a host or a guest, relations with foreign countries were always improved.

So it was with the Sultan. But even Bertie could not command the ocean.

Although it was the month of July the sea suddenly became grey; the wind had risen and the poor Sultan unused to such conditions began to feel queasy. It would be unthinkable to mention such bodily discomfort on such an occasion and he managed to stagger on deck.

Bertie whispered to Louis of Hesse that they had better get the ceremony over as quickly as possible and Louis agreed. But the Queen was unused to being hurried and was quite unaware of her guest's discomfiture.

She came on to the deck with John Brown standing a pace behind her and the ceremony was about to begin.

The Queen said to her equerry: "You have the ribbon?"

The equerry replied that it was the second equerry who had the ribbon.

The Queen held out her hand but the second equerry stammered that he was of the opinion that it was the duty of the first equerry to hand the ribbon to the Queen.

Fortunately the Sultan felt too ill to notice this hitch in the proceedings and that the Queen was glaring at the equerries, and Bertie was clearly nonplussed.

John Brown's raw Scottish accent broke the silence.

"What's all this mithering. Ye've nae brought the ribbon?" He looked about him and seeing Prince Louis wearing the order which the Queen had bestowed on him, he quickly took it off the Prince and handed it to the Queen.

"This one'll do. He'll nae know no difference," he said.

There was a second's silence and then taking Louis's ribbon from John Brown the Queen proceeded to bestow it on the Sultan.

The Queen was amused. She discussed the affair with Bertie and Alice.

"It was so funny. The idea of those stupid men . . . They had forgotten to bring the ribbon . . . and there we all were. Really it was a most unprecedented situation. And then Brown, so resourceful *always*, took Louis's. I shall never forget the astonishment on Louis's face when Brown whipped it off. Tell your husband, Alice my dear, that he shall have his ribbon back. But how very clever of Brown. What we should have done if he had not been there to act so promptly I can't imagine. But then it is not the first time that I have realized how very *much* I rely on him."

"Louis was astounded," began Alice. "Without a by your leave . . ."

"My dear child, there was no time for by your leaves. That is the *virtue* of Brown, he never stops to consider what people will think. He sees the right thing to do and does it. I wish others were more like him."

Bertie said he had told Alix about it and they had nearly died of laughing.

That any member of the family should nearly die of laughing now that the Prince Consort was dead would have been unthinkable if the person responsible for the mirth had not been John Brown.

As it was the Queen permitted herself to smile; and the outcome of that affair was that what might have caused a great storm and possible dismissals had been turned into a joke by what the Queen called the resourceful good sense of honest John Brown.

Shortly after the Sultan's visit Bertie and Alix left for Weisbaden, Alix having to be carried on board the royal yacht in a sedan chair which had been made for this purpose.

Fortunately the waters soon appeared to be having an effect and although it was still necessary to use her two sticks she could walk more easily. Her knee remained very stiff and she limped painfully but there was an improvement.

She was, of course, unable to lead a very social life and it was absolutely necessary for her to retire early. This quiet life was very irksome for Bertie during the first week or so and after that unbearable. He was so kind, so thoughtful, no one could have been more gentle and sympathetic but as soon as she was safely in bed he went off on his adventures.

His neglect of the Princess of Wales could not go unnoticed particularly as he was seen late at night in the company of ladies indulging in the highest of spirits which was hardly seemly when the poor Princess of Wales was an invalid.

Alice, now back in Darmstadt, was shocked by the stories which were filtering through. As was to be expected, Vicky was greatly alarmed. There were such scandalous reports of Bertie's conduct, she wrote to her mother. Bertie was so flirtatious—and perhaps that was a mild way of expressing it;

moreover he was gambling too heavily. He must be persuaded to stay away from the races.

The Queen wrote back firmly. She knew Bertie's weakness. Dear Papa had known it and had done his best to curb it right until the end. It was always the same when Bertie was on the Continent—not that his behaviour was any better at home, but it was easier to keep a rein on him there. She wrote to Bertie. He must stay away from those places where he could not be seen without losing his character.

Bertie wrote back jauntily—he could be flippant when he was away; it was when he was faced by that stern Majesty that he was nonplussed. "It is Vicky who has written to you. One would imagine she thought me ten years old instead of twenty-six."

Bertie ignored the warnings.

Alix, aware of the scandal, was not very happy. She missed the babies—they were her great consolation, she was realizing. It was unpleasant to have to suffer the pains of her limbs and that of humiliation besides, for there was no doubt she was humiliated. She loved Bertie. She had determined to from the beginning and it had not been difficult, for Bertie was always so charming to her. She had now to face the fact that Bertie could never love one person whole-heartedly. Bertie's restricted childhood had resulted in a feverish desire to catch up with the good things of which he had been deprived for so long; and Bertie's idea of the best in life did not agree with Alix's. She liked the occasional ball, the banquet; she liked wearing her beautiful clothes and she enjoyed the admiration which had come her way since she had been Princess of Wales; but in her heart she knew that the really important things in life were not to be found at glittering balls and magnificent banquets and among friends who gushed admiration, respect and homage. Life in the Yellow Palace had taught her that and sometimes she thought sadly of all the simple pleasures of that comparatively humble household and sighed for them. She could find them in some measure in her nursery. The children's growing dependence on her; the delight with which she was received in the nursery—these were the real joys of life. If only Bertie had agreed with her then they could have begun to build up a real happiness.

She was disappointed in her marriage, but she must not be foolish. She must take what she had and be grateful. No one she supposed could attain the complete ideal.

So she tried not to care too much as the scandals about

Bertie's gay life reached her; she never mentioned them to him and for this he was grateful; he loved her—as much as he was capable of loving a wife. She must be content with that.

Often she thought of her family and all the sadness which had come to them in the last few years. How was Dagmar faring in Russia? Was she happy? She knew that Willy had his trials in Greece. And dear Papa and Mama, how they had suffered!

To be young again; to be so poor that they made their own dresses; to change the new merino when one came in for fear of getting it spotted—how desirable that state of affairs sometimes seemed; to be a girl again, very poor, living in the heart of a family of which every member was more important to the others than all the riches and pomp of the world!

One must be content with less than an ideal. She had to keep repeating that to herself. She would try not to think of Bertie's infidelities but one thing she would not do was show friendship to the Prussians who had treated her poor country so badly. When the Queen of Prussia called at Wiesbaden to visit the Prince and Princess of Wales, Alix refused point-blank to see her.

Bertie tried to remonstrate. "It's important, Alix. It's just a matter of being polite to them for a few minutes."

"Polite!" she cried, her usually mild eyes stormy. "But I don't feel polite to the people who have done their best to ruin my parents and my country."

"It's not the monarchs. It's their governments."

"They represent their country and I could never face my parents if I received them as friends."

"Come, Alix, be reasonable."

"No, no, *no!*" declared Alix.

Bertie did not insist. He was always diffident about showing his authority. If there was a violent disagreement between them she might refer to those amatory adventures of which she must have heard hints. They must never be mentioned; while they were not it was as though, when they were together, they had not existed. So Bertie was patient and kind; and he explained to the King and Queen of Prussia that Alix had suddenly become so unwell that she was confined to her bed and unable to see them.

It was hardly likely that such an insult to the King and Queen of Prussia could be allowed to pass. The Queen wrote direct to Queen Victoria and told her that her Danish daughter-in-law had insulted the King of Prussia, for she did not believe that Alix had been too unwell to receive them.

How very tiresome of Alix! thought Queen Victoria. Of course she must not insult the King and Queen of Prussia! What was Bertie thinking of to allow it? Racing and other women, she supposed! Oh dear, if Albert had been alive, none of this would have happened.

She wrote to Vicky and Alice. They were at hand. They must speak to Bertie and impress on him the importance of retaining good relations with Prussia . . . not that she herself secretly felt very friendly towards them after the manner in which they had behaved, but it was not the fault of the King and Queen. It was that *dreadful* Bismarck. And Alix must be made to realize this.

Bertie was in despair. He could not bear to insist that Alix receive the Prussians. Vicky and Alice had both written to him pointing out his duty—Alice did so diffidently but Vicky was very positive. In despair he begged Alix's mother to come and help him with the difficult task as she was with them when the imperative demand came from Vicky. Bertie and Alix must name a date when the King and Queen of Prussia could call on them.

Louise was in a dilemma. Alix could be stubborn; like most easy-going people she would drift along and then suddenly take a stand and when she did there was little hope of moving her. Moreover she had been very ill and was by no means recovered. Louise said that she would meet the Prussian King and Queen in her daughter's place, even though it would be repugnant to her.

This would not do, wrote Vicky authoritatively. Alix must be made to receive the King and Queen of Prussia. It was necessary for Bertie to act. He sent the invitation and then went to Alix.

She regarded him stonily.

"I'm sorry," he said, "but there was nothing else I could do. If I could have spared you this I would have done so. I understand your feelings . . . but the pressure was too great." He kissed her lightly on the top of her head. "It'll soon be over," he comforted.

How like him! He could not really understand and although he was kind, there was just a shadow of impatience. Wasn't she making rather a fuss over something that was not so very important?

She was silent and he went on explaining: "Mama insists, I'm afraid. And there's Vicky and Alice . . ."

"Those two interfering old women," she cried. "What has it to do with them!"

Bertie laughed. "I know Vicky behaves as though she is my governess but she's only a year older than I, and Alice is two years younger."

But Alix could not smile. She felt sick and humiliated.

She knew though that there was no help for it. The King came as arranged and her manner was so correct, although she was seething inwardly, that the King at least was not aware of her resentment.

The Queen had noticed for some time that Lord Derby was not looking well. He was after all a very old man and the tasks imposed on Prime Ministers could hardly be expected to be good for their health.

She was constantly asking him how he was and showering him with sympathy which would have been gratifying if he had not known that she was not so anxious to see him in better health as to see him in retirement.

The reason was that if he gave up office the obvious sequel would be that she must send for the man who had rapidly become her favourite politician.

She was at Osborne that February when Lord Derby came to the conclusion that he would delay no more. He wrote to her telling her of his decision and advising her to send for Benjamin Disraeli.

This she did with the utmost pleasure.

She smiled as he came into her drawing-room and she held out her hand for him to kiss. He bent over it with a flamboyant bow and kissed it with fervour. Then he made a charming speech, for he was very clever with words; he offered her loyalty and devotion. And she felt her spirits lifted as she had on that first day when Lord Melbourne had visited her and she had just become the Queen of England.

It was a moving scene and she felt more at peace, she told herself, than she had since Albert's death.

Her new Prime Minister thereupon began to enchant her in much the same way as Lord Melbourne had. He discussed matters of state with her intermingled with amusing anecdotes about the people they knew, he assumed she would act in such and such a way because such superb intelligence as she possessed would make her realize immediately why such and such must be done.

And while he talked his eyes would admire her in a manner which was unmistakable and she glowed to such admiration because she was sure it was genuine. After all she was young compared with him and everyone knew how he doted on his Mary Anne and thought *her* beautiful when she was older than he was and really quite ugly—so it seemed very plausible that the Queen must in fact seem to him the attractive woman that he could not help implying that she was

She was certain that it was going to be a delightful relationship.

In great spirits Disraeli left Osborne.

Mary Anne was waiting up for him. She was well over seventy but she seemed young in candlelight with her eyes dancing with the delight which only his triumphs could put there.

The champagne was waiting; the little supper laid out and there she sat watching him eat, her wrinkles scarcely perceptible by candlelight, her rather girlish giggle and her adoring inconsequential chatter making a young girl of her.

"Tell me all, Dizzy, tell me all! What did she say? Oh, she was delighted, I am sure. And so she should be. It was time old Derby went. I'll swear that was just what she was waiting for. Did she tell you so, Dizz?"

"Her Majesty was graciously pleased to accept me as her Prime Minister."

Mary Anne giggled afresh.

"And you kissed her hand and bowed wonderfully I know, and now you will make her agree to everything you wish. I know you, Dizzy, I know your methods."

"I have my simple rules," admitted Dizzy. "Never deny, never contradict and sometimes forget."

"And these will be applied to Her Majesty?"

"They are made for her."

"And she will never know about those rules. She will believe just what you want her to. Clever Dizzy. When I think of those days when I was married to Wyndham Lewis and you were a struggling author with political ambitions . . ."

"Encouraged by the wife of the Member for Maidstone."

"Yes, we did encourage you. Not that you needed encouragement. You always knew that you were meant for greatness and so did I . . . which is strange because in many ways I am such a stupid woman."

"Nonsense. You are the cleverest woman in the world. That's why I married you."

"You married me for my money."

"I needed it," he said plaintively.

"And now you don't need my money?"

"I need you more than ever."

She was silent for a second. There was a terrible secret which she must keep from him for as long as possible.

"I almost didn't marry you," said Mary Anne quickly. "You flung out of the house and I called you back and then we told each other not to be silly. Our only difference really was that I thought we ought to have waited a while before marrying and you didn't want to wait. But we made up and married and lived happily ever after. And now you are at the top of the tree."

"Say rather I am at the top of a greasy pole," said Dizzy.

"You'll stay there," she prophesied. "Or even if you do slip down you'll pop up again, because that is where you belong."

Then he talked of his plans for the future and how his real opponent was William Ewart Gladstone; but he, Dizzy, had the Queen on his side and should he tell Mary Anne a secret—the Queen had no liking whatsoever for Mr Gladstone.

Mary Anne urged him to talk and he did and while she listened she was turning over in her mind whether she should tell him.

No, she would not. Let them go on for a while being happy. She would not mention the pains she had had, the fears which might well be realized. How long would she have to live? How long did one live when the malignant cancer had begun its deadly work?

But no matter. She would say nothing tonight; she would sit there in the candlelight, her face averted lest he should notice the strain and she would think of these thirty happy years when she had taught Dizzy to love for herself the woman he had married for her money.

She would always remember the dedication "the perfect wife" which he had made to her in his novel *Sybil*.

Dizzy's Beaconsfield

How pleasant it was to have a Prime Minister on whom she could not only rely but who was able to charm her at the same time. The relationship was ripening fast; she looked forward to his letters, which she answered with pleasure. It was like Lord Melbourne all over again, and yet different in a way because dear Lord M. had treated her as though she had been a beloved daughter; for Disraeli she was not exactly that. He behaved as though she were not only the Queen, possessed of statesmanlike qualities, but a very attractive woman as well. He made her feel as she had when Albert was alive—desirable, charming, feminine, though Albert had never flattered her as her Prime Minister did and it really was rather pleasant—although Albert would not really have approved—to let oneself be persuaded that one was still a woman.

To him she could confide her fears about Bertie. He mixed with such a rackety set, she said. She had never liked some of those University friends of his. There was for example Sir Frederick Johnstone—a very wild young man. When Bertie had run away from Cambridge he had been on the point of joining Sir Frederick and some of his other cronies who were at Oxford. Disraeli was sympathetic. It was a great worry to the Queen in view of all her other responsibilities, he understood; but he believed that she should not concern herself too much over the Prince's high spirits. He would settle down in due course. Young men often believed they had to sow their wild oats. He himself had been no exception.

How very amusing, thought the Queen, and when her Prime Minister called and they had discussed State matters she would enjoy settling down to hear of his early struggles and the great excitement he had felt when his book *Vivian Grey* was published.

He told her how he had met Lord Melbourne at Caroline Norton's house.

"*Dear* Lord Melbourne," said the Queen.

"A very civilized gentleman," commented Disraeli. "He asked me what I wanted to be in life and I said Prime Minister."

"How prophetic!"

Then he told her of his marriage and his devotion to Mary Anne, which touched the Queen deeply. It was wonderful, she said, in this age to find a really happily married couple.

She spoke of Bertie and hoped all was well between him and Alix. Did the Prime Minister think that the Princess of Wales *was* somewhat neglected by her husband and were people noticing that this was so?

The Prime Minister replied that the Prince of Wales always behaved with the utmost consideration to his wife in public.

"Ah, but in private?" insisted the Queen.

"I am sure the Prince would never be anything but charming, in private or public."

"It is possible to neglect charmingly?"

"Absolutely!" said the Prime Minister smiling so that the Queen felt she had been very witty.

"All the same," she went on, "I do not like his friendship with the Mordaunts. The wife I have heard is rather flighty and the Prince is seen with her more than with her husband. And then there is that actress: what's her name? Hortense Schneider."

"The Prince is gregarious by nature."

"His father would be grieved if he were here. At least it is a relief that he doesn't have to suffer that."

"And if he were here how delighted he would be by your book, M'am."

The Queen smiled. She really was rather delighted with her venture into authorship. Arthur Helps, a very clever man and so useful, as his name implied, had edited it for her and Messrs Smith, Elder and Company had just produced her

Leaves from the Journal of Our Life in the Highlands, which was taken of course from what she had written at the time. It was enjoying a success which gave her great pleasure.

"Ah," said Disraeli roguishly. "I know exactly how we authors feel when we see our work in print and the public all agog to read it."

The term "we authors" gave her such pleasure, for after all it was true. She was not of course an author in the sense that Mr Disraeli was, but nevertheless she had produced *Leaves*.

"I found the dedication so poignant," said Disraeli and he quoted in a very moving voice: "To the dear memory of him who made the life of the writer bright and happy, these simple records are lovingly and gratefully inscribed."

"So you remembered it word for word," said the Queen softly.

"M'am, I can never forget it. So much is said in so few words. In that seemingly simple sentence is compressed twenty years of perfect marriage."

"How well you understand! But then you *are* as fortunate as I was."

Disraeli wiped his eyes with perfect composure.

It was so pleasant to have such a man for her friend, thought the Queen.

When she left for Osborne, she asked him to continue to write to her, not only on political matters—just his clever chatty letters which told her so much. A Queen did not want to be left in the dark.

He promised and of course he kept his promise. *Her* letters were a delight, he told her. It was two writers who communicated though a Queen and a Prime Minister.

When the primroses were out at Osborne she gathered a quantity and sent them to him.

"I thought you might like these, *particularly* as I gathered them myself."

He had always delighted in them, he told her, and from now on they would be his favourite flower.

The Irish question which obsessed Mr Gladstone was threatening the first Disraeli ministry. Gladstone wished to dis-establish the Irish Church and there was a great deal of opposition in Ireland. As for Disraeli, he told the Queen that the Irish question had not really been acute since the famine and he was certain that the Fenian uprisings had been aggravated by foreigners and that they would die out of their own accord. His idea was to let the Irish solve their own problems without too much interference from Her Majesty's Government. Mr Gladstone did not agree with him.

It was a very uneasy situation for the new government and none knew better than the Prime Minister how insecure was his position.

He had an idea that if the Prince and Princess of Wales visited Ireland some good might come of it.

The Queen said she was always uneasy when Bertie was out of the country for she could never be sure what he was up to.

"His Highness has been remarkably successful as our ambassador abroad and the Princess is so attractive that no one, not even the Irish, could fail to be charmed by her."

"She is pregnant, you know," said the Queen.

"But the child is not due until July."

The Queen hesitated; she could usually be persuaded by the Prime Minister who made her feel that the suggestion in the first place had been in her mind.

"I am sure a great deal of good will come of it," went on Disraeli. "His Highness's method of living does not appeal to Your Majesty because it's shall we say a little riotous now and then, but I know you are thinking, M'am, with me that it is an excellent plan for the Prince to do something at which he excels and he has proved himself to be a wonderful ambassador."

"The government would have to pay his expenses."

Disraeli wilted a little; than he said: "I am sure this could be agreed upon."

And so on the 15th of April Alix and Bertie boarded the *Victoria and Albert* at Holyhead bound for Kingstown.

The Irish visit was a great success. Bertie was charming as usual and managed to say the right thing at the appropriate time and his gaiety very quickly endeared him to the Irish. His appearances at the races were applauded; so was his natural *bonhomie*. The Prince of Wales was a good fellow and for a time the Irish were ready to forget their grievances. The brilliant banquets and balls which were given in his honour were a long way from the hungry forties and Disraeli calling on the Queen congratulated her on the inspired notion to send the Prince to Ireland.

"Which was your notion," said the Queen with a smile.

"I sensed it was in Your Majesty's mind," replied the Prime Minister, "laying it on with a trowel", as he would have said.

She was far too sensible and honest to believe him but it was gallant and courteous to put it like that.

When the royal pair arrived home the Queen sent for them to come to Windsor and she congratulated them on the success of their tour.

"Mr Disraeli is so pleased," she told them.

She studied Alix anxiously. The dear sweet girl seemed so much better, although she confessed that her knee was still stiff. She walked with a limp which because of her elegance was somehow attractive.

Others thought so too because it became quite a fashion to walk with what began to be called the Alexandra Limp.

Poor Mr Disraeli was going through a very uneasy time and this caused a great deal of worry to the Queen. That irritating Mr Gladstone would interfere in Ireland and he insisted on bringing forward his Bill for the dis-establishment of the Irish Church. Disraeli, who had taken over a weak ministry from Lord Derby, was in no position to resist.

He came to see her at Windsor. He kissed her hand fervently and gazed at her with mournful eyes which warned her that this idyll which had begun to mean so much to them both was threatened.

"Alas, M'am," said Mr Disraeli. "Gladstone has defeated us on the Irish question with a majority of sixty-five."

"This is intolerable."

"It has to be tolerated, I fear."

"What do you propose to do?"

"Offer my resignation."

"Which would mean that That Man would be my Prime Minister."

"I fear so, M'am."

"I should not like that at all."

"Alas, but it is a state of affairs which Your Majesty would be forced to accept. There is only one alternative. Your Majesty could refuse to accept my resignation. Then there would have to be a general election. This could not take place for six months because that time would be needed to arrange the new constituencies which are the result of the new Reform Bill."

"That is the answer," said the Queen. "You have offered me your resignation, which I refuse to accept. You will remain in office until the election in which time perhaps opinions may have changed."

Disraeli bowed.

"Very well, M'am. I shall continue for a little longer to be Your Majesty's Prime Minister."

How much longer would these pleasant *têtes-à-têtes* continue. It reminded her so much of the past when Lord Melbourne had been defeated in the House by Sir Robert Peel. How she had disliked Sir Robert although she had come to respect him. Albert had made her see Sir Robert differently. But she would never feel that respect for Mr Gladstone. There was a man whom she could never like. His wife was a quiet, pleasant creature; she had been Catherine Glynne before the marriage, a member of a very good Whig family who owned Hawarden Castle in Flintshire. It was said that she was devoted to her husband. *Poor* Mrs Gladstone!

John Brown told her that she was foolish to be so drear. He implied of course that as long as *he* was there to see to her needs she would be well looked after. It was true, she knew; but she would miss Mr Disraeli; and the idea of his party replaced by Mr Gladstone's was *most* depressing.

As if she had not enough to worry about without Mr Gladstone's bringing in his Dis-establishment of the Irish Church! It always came back to Bertie. He was becoming just a little truculent. Success went to his head and he had been over congratulated about the Irish tour.

She was really worried about him. She was constantly hearing snippets of gossip, and she did wonder, as was often suggested to her, whether they were a little exaggerated.

The idea of the heir to the throne—*her* throne—dancing attendance on an actress as he apparently did on that Hortense Schneider and prowling round her dressing-room when *The Grand Duchess of Gerolstein*, in which the enchanting actress was appearing, was over. And it was not as though this actress was the only one; Alix should really try to keep a firm hold on him. Alix was a little careless. Her inability to appear anywhere on time was really rather trying. That . . . and Bertie's escapades together with the dissension the terrible wars had caused in the family, and the impending ministerial crises made life very hard to bear.

Now Bertie was writing to her in a very arrogant way, merely because for his own good she had remonstrated with him about attending the Ascot races every day. It was not necessary, she pointed out. Put in an appearance, yes. But to be there every day and gamble as he did was quite unnecessary—more than that it was undesirable.

He pointed out that every year she gave him a lecture on the races and it was a ceremony to which the people looked forward especially when the royal carriages were driven up the course. It would be very uncivil if he stayed at home and would be frowned on.

Was this a reproach to her because she shut herself away so much? Bertie was the last one to understand how she suffered over the loss of Beloved Albert. After all if he had not gone to Cambridge to remonstrate with Bertie he might be here today. He had written:

"I am always most anxious to meet your wishes, dear Mama, in every respect, and I always regret if we are not quite *d'accord*—but as I am past twenty-eight and have some knowledge of the world and society you will, I am sure, at least I trust, allow me to use my own discretion in matters of this kind . . ."

If only Albert were here, how different it would be. She and Bertie would never be *d'accord*, as he put it.

She felt sad and lonely. The children were all growing up and away from her. Louise would be the next to marry. And now Mr Disraeli was going to be replaced by unsympathetic Mr Gladstone whom she could never like.

John Brown came in and found her sitting in the gloom.

He lighted the lamps and said: "It does ye no good mawthering in the dark, woman."

He saw the traces of tears on her cheeks and brought out that which in his opinion was the never-failing remedy—a wee dram of good Scotch whisky.

She found herself smiling. "Now, Brown, you'll be making me bashful."

"Not you," said Brown, "ye've never been near bashful in your life."

He was affectionately contemptuous. Dear honest Brown! He did her so much good.

Prince Alfred whose somewhat gay life had given the Queen many a qualm, returned home from abroad that July and a concert was held at the Crystal Palace in order to celebrate his arrival. Bertie and he went to the concert and rather to the surprise of the audience Alix joined the royal party. This greatly pleased the people for she was heavily pregnant and not expected at such a time. There was a great ovation for her. The leading singers were Patti and Mario and the Princess applauded with great enthusiasm. After the concert there was to be a firework display and as the celebrations were in honour of Alfred, the great moment was to be when a model of the ship *Galatea*, on which he had sailed, was illuminated. Alix stood on the balcony with the rest of the party and although she was feeling rather tired she would not leave until the display was over.

Two days later her child was born a little prematurely, but all seemed to be well. The child was a girl and Alix was delighted. She now had her pleasant little family of four—two boys and two girls—four-year-old Eddy, three-year-old Georgie, one-year-old Louise and now the baby.

As she sat dreaming there, thinking of her own childhood and how excited they had all been at the arrival of a new baby, she felt a wave of nostalgia for the simple life.

Bertie came in, the proud father, and he was delighted with the child. He wanted to bring Eddy and George in to see their new sister. "I promised them," he said.

And so they came and stood wonderingly by the bed, and Bertie lifted them up on to his knee and she was touched by his tenderness towards them. Bertie had suffered in his own childhood and he was going to make certain that he was as different a father from his own as it was possible for a man to be. The boys loved him with a devotion which fear could never have put there and he charmed them in his good-natured way exactly as he did the people whom he met.

But it was their mother who had first place in their hearts and Eddy was apprehensive that the newcomer might take up too much of her time and affection and Georgie was feeling the same.

How she wished that she could have devoted her time entirely to them. However, for a time, she could forget that she was the Princess of Wales and enjoy being a mother.

So she talked of the new baby and showed her to her little

sons and even Louise was carried in from the nursery to join them.

When the children had gone Bertie sat with her for a while and he said that what she needed was a good long holiday away from everything.

Her eyes sparkled. "How I should love to go to Copenhagen and take the children with me. I'm longing to show them Rumpenheim and Bernstorff and I know my parents would love to see the babies."

Bertie grimaced inwardly at the thought of Rumpenheim and Bernstorff; they were so dull and his parents-in-law didn't know how to give the kind of parties he enjoyed, but he pretended to be enthusiastic. While Alix and the children were in Denmark he might slip off somewhere else—perhaps even to his delightful Paris.

"Copenhagen yes," he said. "But I meant a long leisurely tour—say to the Middle East . . . somewhere where you can enjoy the sun and get rid of all those rheumaticky pains."

"It would be very pleasant, Bertie," she said. "Is it possible?"

"I'm sure there'd be no difficulty from the P.M.," said Bertie. "Nor any of his colleagues. Of course, there is Mama." He grimaced openly. "You can imagine the dismay such a suggestion would rouse from *that* quarter. I have already put my foot down about the races. Really, Mama is quite cut off from real life. What can she know about what the people expect shut away with only that odious Brown to talk to?"

"She'll not agree, I'm sure," said Alix.

"Leave it to me," said Bertie. "You're going to show your parents the children, I promise you."

The following month the new baby was christened Victoria Alexandria Olga Mary; her sponsors were headed by Queen Victoria, the Emperor of Russia, and the Queens of Greece and Denmark.

The Queen had moved a little out of seclusion that summer. She had held the first Drawing Room at Buckingham Palace since Albert's death, had given a party in the grounds of the Palace and reviewed twenty-seven thousand volunteers in Windsor Park. This had been achieved by the gentle persuasion of Mr Disraeli. In August following the christening of the new baby she went to Switzerland.

"No fuss," she had said. "Unlike Bertie I like to go about *incognito*." So she travelled as the Countess of Kent, stayed at the Embassy in Paris and was rather pleased when the Empress Eugénie came to see her without any formality; then she went to Lucerne and rented the Villa Pension Wallace which was right on the lake and charming. She spent a very pleasant week or so there with John Brown in attendance driving her when she wished to be driven, taking care of her comfort generally; and when she returned home she went almost immediately to Balmoral.

Some time before she had discussed with Brown the possibility of finding a little house where she could enjoy even greater seclusion than she did at Balmoral, for Balmoral was in fact a castle and there were so many servants and it was impossible to live simply as she so often longed to do.

Brown knew the spot. It had been a favourite one for Prince Albert who had often gone to the Loch Muick; it was isolated and she would be sure of not being worried there. So she built a little cottage there where she could live with just a few servants—those who were old friends like Brown and Annie MacDonald, who could forget that she was the Queen and treat her without that homage which she felt was replaced by loyalty and love.

"This will be somewhere which will not be haunted by *him*," she said. "Somewhere entirely new which he has had no hand in building."

It was a beautiful spot, known as Glassalt Shiel, which meant Darkness and Sorrow, and that, she said, was so appropriate to her mood. She could never look on that scene without experiencing a great excitement. The scenery was almost terrifying in its grandeur and she would stand for hours watching the Glassalt burn falling headlong down the mountainside into the forbidding Loch Muick.

So she had her house—her "Widow's House" she called it and although members of her family tried to dissuade her from living even for a short while in such a lonely spot, she did find to some extent what she sought there—peace.

The Queen was at Glassalt Shiel when she received a note from Bertie suggesting that Alix needed some relaxation and that she wished to take the children to see their grandparents in Denmark. The six months' tour of Europe and the Middle East had been voted desirable by the government but the Queen could not approve of Alix's taking the children out of the country.

She wrote to Bertie: "They are the children of the country, which seems to have been forgotten, and while you and Alix are away they should be left in the care of one person only and that is the Queen."

It was rather selfish of Alix to wish to take them with her. She was going to see her parents. That should be enough for her.

Bertie, always bold when he did not have to come face to face with his stern mama, wrote back in the vein he was beginning to adopt. Alix was certainly not selfish, he replied. She was devoted to her children and he could not understand why obstacles should be put in the way of a proud young mother who wished to take her children to see her parents.

The Queen—always fair—saw the point of this and decided that the three elder children might go; it was of course impossible for such a young baby to travel. At the same time the Queen criticized the way the Wales children were being brought up.

"Papa always believed in discipline," she wrote. "It is an absolute necessity in the bringing up of children. I fear, Bertie, that your children are allowed to run wild, and what the result of that will be I cannot imagine."

Bertie, bold from afar, hinted that it had not always had the desired effect and that neither he nor Alfred who had been submitted to it had turned out very satisfactory from her point of view. He believed that if children were treated severely they grew shy and instead of loving their parents feared them. Of one thing he was determined, his children were not going to be afraid of him. They were not now and they never should be.

The Queen could do nothing. Bertie had always been unmanageable; and she had to admit that Eddy and George were two dear little boys even though there was such a lack of parental control.

Meanwhile Alix and Bertie set off with the three younger children and after a stay in Copenhagen where they had spent Christmas the children were sent home while their parents continued their tour visiting Egypt, Russia and Greece.

The Queen was at Balmoral while the general election was taking place. She would not believe that the country could really pass over Disraeli for the sake of Mr Gladstone although Mr Disraeli had feared this would be the case; and she was very despondent when she heard that Mr Gladstone's government were in power with a majority of one hundred and twenty-eight.

Now she would have to return to London and what was worse send for Mr Gladstone and ask him to form a ministry, at the same time saying good-bye to dear Mr Disraeli.

She would not behave as she had in the past when Lord Melbourne had resigned; she understood that she had been rather foolish then; Albert had taught her that this was something she had to accept. It was none the more palatable for that.

When Mr Disraeli came to see her she almost wept with sorrow and anger.

This was going to be a terrible wrench she feared; she felt such confidence in him; and to think that he was to be replaced by that unsympathetic Mr Gladstone was most upsetting.

Disraeli said that they must accept this trial and hope for better things.

"It is the only thing left to do," said the Queen.

She received Mr Gladstone coolly. He was quite humble and she could not complain that he did not treat her with due respect, but he was so dull and made such boring speeches that she felt as though she were a public meeting. There was a slight compensation for the loss of Mr Disraeli because some of Mr Gladstone's colleagues were good friends of hers. She had always been fond of Lord Clarendon who was now the Foreign Secretary as well as Lord Granville who was the Colonial Secretary; and with the Duke of Argyll who was the Secretary for India she was on terms of affection. As a matter of fact Louise and Argyll's son, the Marquis of Lorne, were *very* friendly, and there was a possibility that they would wish to marry. If they did she would not stand in their way. She was so tired of all the family squabbles and members of it fighting on different sides in these dreadful wars. At least if Louis married Lorne they would be of one nationality; and she had always been especially fond of the Scots.

She sent for Disraeli and told him that she wanted to reward him for his services to her and the country. Would he accept an earldom?

He thanked her in the flowery manner at which he was an adept. He was honoured; he was flattered; he would never forget, etc.; but he declined the earldom.

"Yet I have one thing for which I should be grateful."

"Please tell me what it is," said the Queen.

Then he told her that Mary Anne was ill—very ill. She was dying slowly.

Disraeli wept genuine tears and the Queen, greatly moved, wept with him.

She understood *absolutely*; her heart bled for him; she had suffered it all before him.

"With Your Majesty it was a sharp blow—so much harder to bear," said her tactful ex-Prime Minister. "At least fate is giving me time to prepare myself."

The Queen admitted this and wanted to know what it was that he desired.

"It is for her. I should like her to be made a peeress in her own right."

Oh, how devoted! How unselfish! The Queen could not hide her emotion.

A peerage for Mrs Disraeli—certainly.

"I know," she said, "that you once dedicated a book to the perfect wife. I should like Mrs Disraeli to know that *I* believe her to have a perfect husband."

Mary Anne—now the Countess of Beaconsfield—could not contain her delight. She displayed her coronet whenever possible. She called herself Dizzy's Beaconsfield. What a wonderful husband she had!

She had perhaps two years to live—and not very pleasantly she knew. Each week the pain would grow a little more. Never mind, she would hide it as best she could. She would manage. She remembered that occasion not so long ago when she had been accompanying Dizzy to the House and he was going to make one of the most important speeches of his career. She had planned to drop him at the House and drive home to wait for him there. He had been a little nervous. That fearful Mr Gladstone with his heavy manner—not a bit witty like dear Dizzy—could be very formidable. All the way he had sat murmuring what he was going to say and when he alighted and slammed the door of the carriage he caught her hand in it. She did not cry out because she had known that would have disturbed him and he would have been worrying all the time how badly she was hurt. So while he said good-bye to her she sat with a smile on her face ignoring the agony and let the coachman drive on without telling him that her hand was caught in the door. As soon as Dizzy had disappeared she called the coachman to release her. Well, if she could hide pain then she could hide it now. She did not wish to worry him.

"Poor Dizzy!" she said now. "But you're only out of office temporarily."

"Oh, only temporarily," he assured her.

"What will you do? After all to be Leader of the Opposition will not demand half the time that a Prime Minister has to devote to his duties. There is one blessing though. Your Beaconsfield will be able to see more of you."

"I look forward to it," he told her. "We'll go down to Hughenden. I can finish my book and we can have a very cosy time together."

"Very nice," she said, "for Beaconsfield."

"And for Disraeli," he assured her.

He was reconciled. He wanted to spend time with Mary Anne. There was tragically little left, and he knew in his heart that he would one day take his place on the Government bench of the House—just as surely as he knew that when he did his beloved Beaconsfield would not be at hand to comfort him, to cherish him, to give him that which he had finally learned through her was the best thing that had ever happened to him.

The Mordaunt Case

How tiring was Mr Gladstone! He gave the impression of having too much to do in too short a time. He was too energetic and so sure of himself, backed up by that enormous majority in the House. He was all for reform. In fact he seemed to live for reform. Not only did he want to interfere with the Church but the Army and Navy as well. He would take up the matter of whether sailors should be allowed to have beards with or without moustaches as though it were some war which had to be won. He could not express himself simply; the Queen could not understand the documents he presented to her—nor even his letters. One sentence would last for pages. Oh, tiresome Mr Gladstone! Someone had told her that when he proposed to Mrs Gladstone he had done so in a letter which was so long and involved that the poor woman was quite bewildered and refused him. And at that, commented the Queen, the Queen is not surprised. Although he persuaded her to marry him later. *Poor* Mrs Gladstone!

One grew quite weary trying to keep up with all the papers and to grasp what the man was writing about; how different it had been with dear Lord Melbourne; and with Sir Robert there had been Albert. Mr Gladstone made her realize afresh how much she *needed* Albert. If only *dear* Mr Disraeli could come back. How could people have been so stupid as to give Mr Gladstone that big majority.

She was worried about Bertie whose finances were in a terrible state. He was now in Egypt doing the country so much good, so said Mr Disraeli, and being very popular and visiting the Pyramids and the Sphinx; and the Khedive and the Sultan were being very hospitable. She did hope Bertie was not getting into any trouble there. But Alix was at hand; she should keep a firm hand on him. The children had been sent home and she did enjoy the company of darling Eddy and Georgie and little Louise; her namesake was too young at present to interest her for she never had liked the very young. The two boys were darlings although they were not as respectful as they should be, which of course was due to the way in which Bertie and Alix brought them up; she gathered from little hints they dropped that they were allowed to go into Bertie's study while he was writing letters and climb all over him and that Alix often put on an apron and bathed them herself. There was no discipline and that should be rectified. But Bertie had uttered a dark warning when he had said that the children had grown to love their *Danish* grandparents in a very short time. He hoped they would feel as affectionate towards their very important English grandmama.

They appeared to like her and called her "Gangan", which was amusing. She tried not to think of what Albert would have said to certain naughtiness. After all if the children were so fond of the King and Queen of Denmark they must have some regard for the Queen of England too.

She approached Mr Gladstone about Bertie's allowance. Mr Gladstone answered the summons—*so* unattractive because he was so solemn. He bowed very courteously and she told him that she hoped Parliament would agree to give the Prince of Wales a larger income.

Mr Gladstone addressed her at a public meeting with such long sentences that she was not at all sure what he was talking about.

Finally she demanded, "But, Mr Gladstone, I should be pleased to know what Parliament will decide about the Prince's allowance."

Mr Gladstone was off again but she did gather that Parliament had no intention or disposition to augment the income of the Prince of Wales.

Well, of course, she did deplore Bertie's extravagance; he should not go so often to the races and gamble; he should not entertain fast women. It served him right and was a lesson to him; all the same Mr Gladstone was a very *tiresome* man.

The Prince and Princess of Wales had returned from the East and had reached Paris. The Queen wrote to them there and when Bertie saw the notepaper heavily edged with black, he moaned.

"Oh dear, will Mama never forget?" he wailed.

Alix was excited; she was longing to be home to see the dear children. She was again pregnant and expecting another in November. She couldn't have too many, she told Bertie; she adored them all; but she did wonder how they had fared under the eye of the Queen.

Bertie had further cause for groans when he read his mother's letter:

"I fear you have incurred enormous expenses and I don't think there is a disposition to give you any more money."

"How do they expect me to maintain myself in dignity," he demanded, "when they won't help me pay for it? Imagine the Prince and Princess of Wales travelling abroad like paupers."

"Well, they hardly did that," said Alix with a laugh.

And Bertie laughed with her. "Disraeli would have been far more sympathetic. Gladstone's such an old preacher. And they say too that he prowls about the West End at night look-ing for prostitutes."

"Only so that he can take them home to Mrs Gladstone and together they can persuade the poor girls to lead a re-spectable life."

"Ha, ha," said Bertie.

"You're prejudiced," accused Alix.

The fact that the government would not increase his al-lowance did not worry Bertie greatly. Princes always had debts. It was something governments had to accept.

"She goes on to say that the boys are little dears and Eddy is quite sensible when she has him alone. She thinks they are a little undisciplined. But none of our boys is going to endure what I did from my father."

"The way to bring children up is to make them happy and secure. I know that. I was very fortunate."

"Now, you're not sighing for old Bernstorff and the Yellow Palace, are you? You like Marlborough House? You like San-dringham?"

"Of course I've been doubly lucky."

He was pleased. She looked at him rather wistfully though and thought that she might have been completely happy if Bertie was not sometimes more eager for the company of others than for her own.

There was great delight in the Wales' nursery when the parents arrived. The children ran round them shrieking, Eddy pushing Georgie aside so that he could reach his mother first. Alix picked him up and kissed him fervently. She couldn't help it but Eddy was her favourite, because he was her first-born, she supposed. Then she picked up Georgie and hugged him just in case he had noticed.

"Come and look at my bear," said Georgie.

"No!" cried Eddy. "Come and look at my donkey."

"I can look at them both," said Alix.

"Papa too," demanded Eddy.

"Papa of course," replied Bertie.

One of the footmen had made them each a boat which they could sail in the bath. It was the greatest fun; they could not wait to show their parents.

And Bertie soon had a boy on each knee telling them about his strange adventures at the great Pyramids and how they had looked straight into the face of the Sphinx. They had ridden on camels over the sand and he must draw a camel for them because it really was a very strange beast.

Soon he was drawing camels while the boys watched intently.

They should ask the kind footman who had made the boats whether he could make camels for them, said Alix.

The boys leaped about with excitement, so delighted were they to have their parents back, and because they jostled Louise out of the way a little, Bertie promised her that on her next birthday he would take them all to the circus.

"Will Mama come?" Georgie wanted to know.

"We shall all go, the whole family. Perhaps Victoria is too young, but everyone else shall go."

Then he told them about circuses and gave an example of the various noises animals made. Alix put her fingers to her ears. "I can't think what Grandmama England would say," she commented.

"That's Gangan," said Georgie.

"I hope you were good boys when you were with her."

"Oh yes," Georgie told her. "We had to be because she's the Queen."

That day was devoted to the children and at bedtime Alix herself put on a flannel apron, bathed them and took them to bed.

Eddy put his arms about her neck when she tucked him in.

"I wish you came home from travels every day," he said.

Then it was the turn of George and Louise.

The Queen's birthday dawned. Fifty years old. What a great age! And how different were birthdays now from what they used to be! They were at least a time for remembering and as she lay in bed she thought of waking in Kensington Palace on a birthday morning and wondering what her presents would be and thinking what a great age she was when she was sixteen. So very long ago, in the days when she was so inexperienced and foolish yet aware of a great destiny; and it had taken Albert to teach her good sense, to make her see how she must act. How she missed him! Would she never recover from his loss?

Life would be so much easier if he were here to help her bear it. She needed him to advise her, to stand beside her and support her, to help her with the children too. They were a constant anxiety. Vicky would be Queen of Prussia one day as Albert had always wanted, but could even he have foreseen what conflict there would be in the family? Alice always seemed to be in difficulties and she did not think Louis was a very strong man. They had always known that Bertie was wild—Alfred too. In truth apart from the fact that Bertie was Prince of Wales and therefore more vulnerable, Alfred gave greater cause for alarm. There had been that disgraceful affair in Malta; after that he had declared he was in love with a commoner. Really, there was going to be trouble with Alfred. Lenchen, of course, was married now and how she missed her and it was not very gratifying to remember that her husband, Christian of Schleswig-Holstein—that ill-fated place—was so poor that he found it difficult to support his wife and family. Louise might marry Lorne although it was hardly suitable, the dear young man, whom the Queen liked very much, not being royal. Arthur gave her less cause for anxiety than any of them; he was so like Albert and she was sure that if that Beloved Being could see his son today he would be gratified. No, she did not believe Arthur would cause her anxiety. Leopold was a constant source of it—poor child, he was the only one of her children who was not healthy. It was a pity for if Arthur had inherited his father's angelic nature, Leopold had inherited his brains. He had been so ill recently that she had feared they were going to lose him, but he had recovered and she had begged him to take care. Then there was Baby Beatrice—not such a baby now being twelve years old, but she would always be Baby and, perhaps because Dearest Papa had not been there, was just a little spoiled.

A fiftieth birthday was indeed a time for brooding. They would all come to see her today and she would talk to them about Dearest Papa's virtues and how different it would have been if he had been with them on this day.

Thinking of him she remembered a difference of opinion they had had when he wanted to make their circle more intellectual. He had thought it would be interesting for her, and she had refused. She had feared that "those people" would talk over her head. How foolish she had been and how long it had taken her to learn her lessons under that kind and tender guidance.

But now that she herself had written a book—"Fellow author" Disraeli had called her—she felt that she would like to meet people of literary talents. She had found Disraeli's conversation most enlivening and she believed he had not been bored with hers. Then there was Sir Arthur Helps who had edited her book for her. He was also a very interesting man.

She had already met Lord Tennyson because Albert had said he was a great poet and she had wanted him to know how *In Memoriam* had comforted her.

Sir Arthur talked to her about Thomas Carlyle and when his wife died the Queen sent personal condolences. Later she met Carlyle and the poet Browning.

She told Louise that she was going to read some novels and she read Thackeray and George Eliot; but the books which appealed to her were those of Charles Dickens.

"So *feeling*," she said.

In November a daughter was born to the Prince and Princess of Wales. She was christened Maud Charlotte Mary Victoria.

This was Alix's fifth child. She was delighted with her family and wished that she could become an ordinary housewife so that she could devote herself to them exclusively.

Bertie stared down at the paper in his hand. He could not believe it. This simply could not happen to him! How dared they order him to appear in court! How dared they presume . . . how dared they suggest . . . !

He felt sick. He wanted to shut himself away. He wanted no one to know of this until he had decided what to do. It was true that Lady Mordaunt had been a friend of his; he had called on her when her husband was away; he had enjoyed several delightful meetings when the two of them had been alone; she was very pretty and twenty-one and he had thought her charming.

And what had she done? She must be mad. Yes, that was the answer, she was mad, for she had made some sort of confession to her husband declaring that she had committed adultery with Sir Frederick Johnstone (his great friend from Oxford days) and Lord Cole, another crony and, among other men, the Prince of Wales.

The result was that her husband, Sir Charles Mordaunt, was suing for a divorce and although he did not name the Prince as co-respondent—that was reserved for Sir Frederick and Lord Cole—Bertie's name was mentioned, Lady Mordaunt's counsel was serving a subpoena on him and he must appear as a witness.

The Prince of Wales in the witness box in an unsavoury

divorce case! What would the people say? What would Alix say? What would *the Queen* say?

Bertie was numb with anxiety. This was worse than anything that had happened to him. Curragh Camp was nothing to this. He could not think how to act. He must have advice and the advice he needed was that of a lawyer. He thought immediately of Lord Hatherley, the Lord Chancellor. He shivered at the thought. William Page Wood, Lord Hatherley, was a brilliant lawyer—perhaps the best in the country—but very austere. Bertie knew that for years he had acted as Sunday School teacher in Westminster, the parish where he lived. He would necessarily be unsympathetic but at the same time he would realize what a scandal could mean to the country, and he could be relied on to give the Prince of Wales the best possible advice.

Bertie was right. The Lord Chancellor listened attentively.

"I am innocent," declared Bertie. "The lady must be insane. I am sure this will be proved but in the meantime I have received this subpoena to appear in court."

This was a very grave situation, commented Lord Hatherley. The Prince could plead privilege but that he believed would be most unwise, for he was of the opinion that if any obstruction was placed on his Highness's appearing in court that would be construed as proof of his guilt. He would have to appear in court, and of one thing he must make certain: the Queen must hear of this first through him. That was imperative. And no doubt, added Lord Hatherley, the Prince would wish to be the first to inform the Princess of Wales.

Bertie realized the wisdom of this and went straight to Alix, who was immediately alarmed by his downcast expression.

"Bertie, what on earth has happened?"

"Something terrible."

"The children . . ."

Bertie shook his head. "Oh no." Alix sighed. As long as there was nothing wrong with the children she could feel relieved. "It's . . . Alix, I've got a thing called a subpoena. They're going to take me into court."

"Whatever for?"

"It's Lady Mordaunt. She's gone mad, I think. She's made some sort of confession to her husband and he's trying to divorce her . . ."

"And you . . . ?"

"Oh no. It's Fred Johnstone and Cole. They're cited as corespondents, but she's made some wild statements about me and her lawyers have sent this thing."

"Oh God!" said Alix.

"Well, she must be mad."

"But she has named you."

"She's mentioned me. The woman's insane . . ."

"But you were friendly."

"Oh come, Alix, I'm friendly with so many. It's part of my duties."

He was bland even though very anxious. Alix's voice was trembling a little as she murmured: "And she had no reason . . .?"

"Of course not," said Bertie indignantly.

She felt wretched and miserable. She thought of Lady Mordaunt—young, twenty or not much more, very pretty, very gay. Bertie had called on her frequently, she knew. He must have visited her often when her husband was absent.

"I've spoken to Hatherley," said Bertie. "He said I must tell Mama without delay."

The Queen re-read Bertie's letter. It was his painful duty, he had written, to tell her that he had been subpoenaed to appear as a witness at the court of Lord Penzance . . .

Her son! The Prince of Wales! Ordered to go to court! A divorce case and Bertie's name mentioned! She could feel almost thankful that Albert was not here to suffer this.

Bertie declared that he was innocent. Of course there were malignant people who were ready to make the most cruel accusations against royalty. Unkind things had been said against her and John Brown. Poor Bertie! Strangely enough when she came face to face with real disaster she found she could be very strong. It was only when she contemplated something alarming that her spirits quailed. So Bertie was commanded to appear in court because a loose woman had mentioned his name. Very well, Bertie must appear in court and if he told her that he was innocent she believed him. She sat down at her desk and wrote a tender letter. She believed that he had been maligned; she had the utmost confidence in him; and she wanted him to know that his mother was with him.

Bertie was touchingly grateful and was more frank than he had ever been before. He told her that he feared Sergeant Ballantine, whom Sir Charles Mordaunt had engaged to act for him, would twist everything he said and try to compromise him. He was in a terrible dilemma. To go into the box and to have his words twisted by a brilliant lawyer or to stay out and let people impute his absence to guilt.

The Queen was anxious. She could not explain her fears to Mr Gladstone. How she wished dear Mr Disraeli was her Prime Minister now. Of course Bertie was wrong to have put himself in such a position where this was possible. If he had not moved in "fast" circles no one would have been ready to believe this whatever that mad woman and her clever Sergeant Ballantine said. Whatever happened Bertie had done himself a great deal of harm.

The Lord Chancellor agreed with her. The monarchy was not so firm that it could afford such scandals as this. Mr Gladstone thought that the Queen's love of seclusion had already irritated public opinion; for the Prince of Wales to be connected, however innocently, with such an unsavoury divorce case would not improve it.

"How difficult it is for royalty," said the Queen with some asperity. "I am blamed for living too quietly; my son for living too riotously. People are never satisfied."

There was great excitement when the case opened. It was the first time a Prince of Wales had ever been summoned to the witness box. The majority were certain that he had been Lady Mordaunt's lover. Albert Edward—Teddy as he was beginning to be called by the people—was another such as his great-uncle George IV who had amused the people with his scandalous love affairs.

The Mordaunt story was gradually revealed to an avid public. Lady Mordaunt had given birth to a child and a few days after its birth it had been discovered that there was something wrong with the child's sight and it would almost certainly be blind. This had so upset Lady Mordaunt that she had become hysterical.

When her husband came into her bedroom she cried out: "It is my fault the child is blind. You are not the father. Lord Cole is the father. I have been wicked and done wrong."

"You are distraught," said Sir Charles, trying in vain to soothe her.

"No," cried Lady Mordaunt. "I have been unfaithful to you with Lord Cole, Sir Frederick Johnstone, the Prince of Wales and that's not all . . ."

Sir Charles, very distressed, tried to comfort his wife.

"She has some fever," he told the nurse. "She doesn't know

what she is saying. I believe women suffer in this way sometimes after having a child."

Two of the nurses replied that during her confinement before the birth Lady Mordaunt had told them quite seriously that the child was not her husband's and that she had committed misconduct with the men she had mentioned.

Sir Charles went to his wife's bureau and found bills which showed that she had stayed at hotels with Sir Frederick and Lord Cole, and as there were also letters to her from the Prince of Wales, Sir Charles believed he had a case.

People recalled the trial of Queen Caroline. This was of less importance than that, of course, but very diverting. "Gay old Teddy" was the universal comment. "Well, he was bound to get found out sooner or later."

There was a great drive to prove Lady Mordaunt insane. Her own father stated that he believed this to be so, and that she was suffering, as several doctors affirmed, from puerperal mania.

The mention of letters from the Prince of Wales caused a great deal of excitement but disappointment followed when these were published in *The Times* and proved to be somewhat innocuous, even though they did show that the Prince was on terms of cosy friendliness with Lady Mordaunt although not with Sir Charles, apparently, for the outraged husband told the court that *he* had never invited the Prince to his house in spite of the fact that His Royal Highness was a frequent visitor there in his absence. Teddy's visits, laughed the public, were made when Sir Charles was out of the way naturally.

The excitement reached its climax when Bertie took his stand in the witness box. Calmly and clearly he answered the questions put to him.

Yes, he was acquainted with Lady Mordaunt before her marriage. She had visited Marlborough House. He had seen a great deal of her both before her marriage and after.

At last came the all-important question: "Has there ever been any improper familiarity or criminal act between yourself and Lady Mordaunt?"

The Prince threw back his head and answered firmly: "There has not."

The court broke into applause which the Judge repressed and Bertie left the court with relief. The case was over—dismissed on account of Lady Mordaunt's insanity.

Bertie felt jaunty. He had come through that with honours, he believed. Even Ballantine had not dared to go too far with the Prince of Wales.

"The gross implications which have been wantonly cast on me are now cleared," he wrote to his mother.

The Queen read his letter and sighed. It was not as simple as that. She knew well enough that whatever the outcome of the case people were going to believe Bertie guilty. His conduct was not without reproach. There were all those gambling debts and the rumours of how he was always in the wake of some woman. Vicky had heard it said on the Continent and so had Alice. Bertie was a gambler, he drank too much and was too interested in food; but his besetting weakness was women.

The Lord Chancellor shook his head over the affair and Mr Gladstone was not very happy about it, while *Reynolds' Newspaper* was asking whether a young man who paid visits to a young married woman in her husband's absence was really innocent.

There was the expected spate of cartoons. A paper was being sold in the streets called *The Infidelities of a Prince;* and although this recounted in florid terms the adventures of George IV when Prince of Wales it was bought by many on the understanding that it was an account of the exploits of their own Teddy.

Bertie pretended to shrug it aside. Alix was quiet and rather sad. It was all so different from what she had dreamed in the Yellow Palace.

The Fatal Fourteenth

It was a sad spring. Alix felt depressed and her rheumatic pains increased. There was restraint between her and Bertie and sometimes when he reproved her—very gently—for her unpunctuality, she had to stop her temper from flaring up and demanding the truth about the Mordaunt affair.

She told Bertie that she thought she would like to get away to the country for a while. Sandringham? suggested Bertie. No, she decided; she would like to go on a visit. The Duchess of Manchester had invited her to Kimbolton and she would like to accept. Bertie was almost pathetically eager to meet her wishes. In fact she believed that he was silently imploring her to put the Mordaunt affair from her mind and not ask embarrassing questions.

It was pleasant at Kimbolton, but wherever she went people cheered her and she fancied that their show of friendship was tempered with sympathy because of Bertie's infidelities.

Why, she asked herself, should she be so hurt? She had always known in her heart that Bertie was unfaithful. How different though to know these things oneself than to be aware that they were being publicly discussed. Pride, her mother would say. Wounded dignity.

She had a great desire to see her mother; she felt that at home she could express her true feelings and throw off the pretence which was necessary at such a time.

When she returned to Marlborough House she told Bertie

of her desire to visit Copenhagen to see her family. Bertie, determined to give her what she wanted, said that he would persuade Mama.

The Queen did not need a great deal of persuading. She understood Alix's feelings very well; and she had been telling herself since the Mordaunt affair how fortunate she was in Albert, who had never given her the faintest cause for uneasiness in that respect.

Bertie went with her as far as Calais and when he said good-bye he looked so sad and sorry that she kissed him fervently. Whatever else he was Bertie was the kindest man in the world.

It was wonderful to be back at Bernstorff. Queen Louise, alas grown very deaf now, was a great comfort. They talked of Alix's affairs and she found herself defending Bertie. He was always so kind and good to her. Of course he loved gay society and this could be dangerous, but at heart he was the most indulgent of husbands.

"One must not ask too much of life," said Louise.

But the charm of the old home had necessarily diminished since the family had broken up. There were no cosy chats with Dagmar, and she missed the babies.

The visit was a short one, for war had broken out between France and Prussia and the Queen sent a peremptory message. Alix must return at once.

Bertie was already leaving for Copenhagen in order to escort her home.

The Queen was distressed. She hated war and had always been determined that England must be kept out of any conflict if at all possible. Lord Clarendon, before his death, had told her that trouble was brewing over the Spanish succession and that if the Prussians tried to bring in a German heir to the throne, as they were trying to do, Napoleon would never allow it and would even go as far as war.

How right he was, for now Napoleon had declared war on Prussia.

This would be another split in the family. Vicky and Bertie were at loggerheads now. Vicky must naturally support her adopted country and Bertie was anti-Prussian out of sympathy with Alix who because of the Danish-Prussian war over Schleswig-Holstein and the defeat of her father, hated the Prussians fiercely.

If Bertie were going to Denmark he must be warned not to

be indiscreet. He must remember that everything he said was noted and that he was a representative of his country; he had already angered the Prussians by his sympathy with the Danes and although everyone understood his desire to be loyal to Alix, that was not a very good thing to do.

Bertie promised to be discreet and went off to bring Alix back.

It was most provoking, sighed the Queen. Not only the dreadful war which brought about such unnecessary suffering but the conflict in the family. Both her sons-in-law, Vicky's husband the Crown Prince of Prussia, and Alice's Louis of Hesse Darmstadt, were fighting with the Prussians. Poor Alice, who at her father's death had proved what a good nurse she could be, was working hard at a hospital in Darmstadt and looking after the wounded from both sides of the conflict. The Queen was proud of Alice—the quiet one—who had always been so efficient. Alice wrote that she had founded the Women's Union for nursing the Sick and Wounded in War and that she felt that this was doing so much to alleviate sufferings imposed by this cruel war.

The Queen was terrified that Napoleon would be victorious, although she knew that Bertie and Alix were secretly on his side. Bertie had always been fascinated by Napoleon and it had been reported to her (though Bertie did not know this) that there had been one dreadful occasion when Bertie as a boy had told Napoleon, in the hearing of several people, that he wished he were his father. What terrible sacrilege! Fortunately Albert had never heard of his disloyalty. Oh, the wickedness of Bertie!

In a way she could understand the fascination of Napoleon; she herself had been a little impressed by him; he had such Gallic charm and he had really made her feel that he was a little in love with her. How very foolish, but the man, though far from handsome, was charming. But what had that to do with his wicked act of declaring war on Prussia? The Queen was torn in her emotions; the family was so involved.

Strangely enough the Prussians seemed to be gaining the ascendancy. Of course the Germans had always been magnificent soldiers and so ready to be disciplined, but she would have thought that the might of France must prevail.

Alix showed clearly that she hoped the Prussians would be beaten and Bertie had made some very indiscreet remarks which Vicky strongly resented. Then she became triumphant because it was clear that the French were in difficulties. Paris was threatened.

"What will Bertie and Alix say now?" wrote Vicky maliciously.

Bertie said it was terrible to think of the most beautiful and exciting of cities—Paris—being under bombardment.

Vicky's retort was: "What mischief that court and still more the fascinating Paris has done to English Society!" Which was of course a sly dig at Bertie who had so much enjoyed slipping into Paris for a brief stay where he had hosts of friends—all very elegant, very gay, witty, amusing and far from virtuous.

September came and with it the battle of Sedan and the surrender of the Emperor.

Alix and Bertie had gone with the children to Abergeldie for the autumn holiday and they were there when news reached them that the Empress Eugénie had escaped from France and landed in England.

Bertie was horrified. "To think of that charming lady in flight. It's terrible. We'll have to make her see that we welcome her."

Alix agreed. She was very sad because once more the Prussians had been victorious.

At first they had had no idea where the Empress Eugénie was and they were being entertained at Dunrobin Castle when the news came that she and her son, the Prince Imperial, were in Chislehurst.

Bertie immediately wrote to her and told her that his house in Chiswick was at their disposal.

Lord Granville, who had taken over Lord Clarendon's post at the Foreign Office, was worried. The Prince and Princess of Wales were too impetuous; their sentiments did them credit but they did not seem to realize that they were out of their element when they dabbled in politics. The Prussians were victorious; the Emperor was deposed; and here were they, representatives of a foreign power, showing sympathy with the fallen enemy.

The Queen had been very uneasy when she heard that Eugénie was in England. They had entertained each other and professed friendship, but she, unlike Bertie, realized the political implications.

Lord Granville came to see her, accompanied by Mr Gladstone. It was most unfortunate, they declared.

The Queen replied that she considered it presumptuous of the Prince and Princess to have acted as they had; and while they were wondering how the impulsive couple could be extricated from the difficulty in which they had placed the government, Eugénie replied to the Prince thanking him for his gesture but telling him that she had already been presented with Camden House at Chislehurst, so she had no need to avail herself of their generous offer.

While the Queen was sighing with relief more news came to her from Germany that her old governess, the Baroness Lehzen, had died. Deeply moved, she took out her journals and read of those long ago days when Lehzen had meant so much to her and had in fact been the most important person in her life. She thought of the early days and the dolls Lehzen had dressed for her. How they had loved those dolls! At that time she had thought that she would need Lehzen for ever and ever and that she would always be the most important person in her life. And then Albert had come—and he and Lehzen had disliked each other and Albert had shown her that Lehzen must go and now she believed that that had broken poor Lehzen's heart.

I owed her so much, she thought, and however misguided she was, she adored me.

So the Queen wept and thought of the past and how sad it was that poor Lehzen was no more.

Mr Gladstone was disturbed by what he referred to as the royalty question.

There was now a Republic in France and Germany was united as one great Empire under Prussian hierarchy. This had been proclaimed in the Hall of Mirrors at Versailles—the more to stress the defeat of France.

"The point is," said Mr Gladstone to his Foreign Secretary, Lord Granville, "it is always dangerous for Royalty in general when a royal crown is lost. This would not have been so important a few years ago when the monarchy in this country commanded great respect. There were complaints against Albert as the German who wanted to rule this country, but there was no doubt in any mind that he was a sober-minded religious man, determined to do all in his power for what he believed to be right. He might have been called a dull man but everyone knew he was a good one."

Lord Granville grasped the point.

"Yet if we have lost one Emperor we have gained another."

"Power-crazy Germans," said Mr Gladstone. "And in place of a monarchy across the Channel we have a republic. Republics are catching. As I said, a few years ago the monarchy had a certain popularity. That has been lost over the last few years. The Queen's insistence on remaining in seclusion is in a large part responsible. The scandal about her relations with John Brown another. She is defying the people. They want her to appear in public. They want a Queen to be a Queen. The Prince of Wales compensated in some respect, but since this disastrous Mordaunt affair, his popularity has waned a great deal. He is often hissed at when once he was cheered. Pity is expressed for the Princess because of the way in which her husband treats her. The Queen is never seen and the people have no respect for the Prince of Wales. That is the sad state of affairs and so we have a royalty question."

Lord Granville could only agree with everything the Prime Minister said. If the Queen would rouse herself a great deal of good could be done.

But the Queen refused to rouse herself. She could only find consolation in the Highlands with John Brown in attendance. She arrived at Balmoral for the autumn holiday and while she was there a very interesting event took place.

The hills were looking particularly beautiful and there was so much to remind her of the old days when she and Albert had loved to walk across this very grass. The Lord Chancellor, Lord Hatherley, was with them; he was very solemn and she did wish he would not reproach her about her seclusion, though very mildly of course which was as much as he dared to: but Beatrice was there and she was always pleasant company. On this occasion Louise had gone for a walk with the Marquis of Lorne and some other friends so there were two parties.

The Queen talked to Lord Hatherley about the manner in which Albert had described the countryside and how he had revelled in it, seeing a resemblance to his native forests and mountains. It was such a pity they had cut down so many of the trees. Why did people have to spoil everything? she demanded.

Lord Hatherley murmured that the timber would no doubt be put to very good use. The Queen said that she would like to call at the little inn Brown talked so much about. He had worked there once for a while before coming into the royal service.

They called at the inn in which the Queen was very interested and kept smiling to herself, imagining Brown in such a place.

It was when they returned to Glassalt Shiel that the significance of the day became apparent. Louise came to her room and before the dear child spoke she knew.

"My dear child, you look very happy," she said.

"Oh, Mama, I am. Lorne has proposed and I have accepted him." Louise looked anxiously at her mother. "I knew you would approve."

"I shall pray that you will be happy, my child."

"I told Lorne that you would not withhold your consent."

The Queen sighed. "I would never wish my dear children anything but their happiness. Of course *I* am going to miss you. I am losing all my children, one by one."

"We are not lost, Mama."

"But it seems that you grow away after marriage. Think! Beatrice is the only daughter I have left now and I suppose she will soon be thinking of leaving me."

"At least, Mama, I shall not leave the country."

"That is a great comfort to me, my dearest child. And I am fond of Lorne. He is a good young man. This will be the first time that a Sovereign of this country gives consent for a royal Princess to marry outside royalty since the days of Henry VIII when he allowed his sister Mary to marry the Duke of Suffolk."

"I know, Mama, and so does Lorne. We appreciate your goodness and we shall endeavour to show our gratitude all through our lives."

"My dearest, all I shall want is to be shown that you are happy."

They embraced fondly and the Queen said how sad it was that Dearest Papa was not here to see his daughter's happiness.

There was no point in delaying the marriage and six months later Louise and the Marquis of Lorne, heir to the Duke of Argyll, were married in St George's Chapel, Windsor. Giving way a little to pressure the Queen allowed the marriage to be celebrated with a certain amount of pomp and although she would not wear a dress of any other colour than black she did make a concession by ornamenting it with glittering jet and wearing diamonds and rubies.

So Louise became the future Duchess of Argyll.

Napoleon had now escaped to England and had joined the Empress and his son at Chislehurst. The Queen at once visited them there and wept with them for the loss of their position and assured them that as long as they needed a refuge it was theirs in England.

Almost immediately after Louise's marriage Alix gave birth to another child. This time things did not go well. The child was weak and it was thought wise hastily to christen him. He was given the names Alexander John Charles Albert and the next day he died.

Alix was heart-broken. Life seemed to be going wrong for her. She had not yet recovered from the shock the Mordaunt case had given her, though often she asked herself why she should have been so distressed because something she had always known existed was brought out into the open.

Bertie was as kind and charming as he knew well how to be. They had lost little Alexander, he reminded her, but they had their two boys and three little girls and no one could say that was not a fine family. She tried to be comforted. After all, she *had* a fine family; and whatever his faults Bertie was always kind to her.

She planned a memorial window to the child to be placed in Sandringham church depicting Christ blessing the children.

The people, however, were determined to be dissatisfied. So the Princess had lost her baby. It was small wonder, was the verdict, when it was considered what anxieties she must suffer. Nobody was going to believe in the Prince's innocence over the Mordaunt case. Why was he only cross-examined by the defending counsel? If Sergeant Ballantine had got at him it would have been a very different story. There was a special law of course for royalty.

Parliament were asking for an annuity for Prince Arthur and the radical party had so agitated against it that in the division fifty-four votes were cast against it.

It was quite obvious, said Mr Gladstone, that the royalty question was assuming alarming proportions. There was a wave of feeling against the monarchy and the fact that a Republic had so recently replaced a monarchy across the Channel was a pointer.

The Queen must emerge from her seclusion for this was at the root of the matter.

It was said that when she was in Scotland she took long drives; she walked; she even climbed hills; she visited the local people when they were sick and took great interest in the life of the neighbourhood; she even danced reels with her Highland servants; but continually she complained of ill health which prevented her from doing her duties in London.

"She *must* return," said Mr Gladstone.

Was she to have no peace? she demanded. Overwork and anxieties killed that Noble Being, the Prince Consort. She was sure some of her ministers and her subjects would like to see her worn out in the same way.

Dr Jenner—that good faithful man—supported her. He assured Mr Gladstone that the Queen was in no position to take on a strenuous public life. At that time she was badly stung by a wasp and this seemed to set off a train of ailments. She was distracted by her neuralgia; and an abscess had developed in her arm. It was years since she had felt so ill—not since long ago before her accession to the throne when she had had typhoid fever.

The trouble was that having pleaded her inability to face the public because of her weak physical condition, now she was really ill people did not believe it. *Reynolds' Newspaper* took up the attack with fervour. After commenting on the gambling habits of the Prince of Wales with reference to his amorous adventures, it turned on the Queen. A pamphlet was produced called *What Does She Do With It?* which referred to the Queen's income. What *did* she do with all the money that was bestowed on her? How did she spend it, cooped up in Balmoral or Osborne, living her cosy quiet life with Mr John Brown in attendance?

Everyone was reading *What Does She Do With It?* and again Mr Gladstone stressed the danger of the situation. Vicky wrote that dear Mama must see what was happening and take the lesson of France to heart.

"Do none of them understand that I am ill?" cried the Queen. If only Mr Disraeli had been Prime Minister instead of that difficult Mr Gladstone! As it was there was no one who could comfort her but John Brown who told her to stop bothering her head about them and come for a nice little drive up to the Spital of Glenshee and he'd take some cold chicken and boil some potatoes and they'd have a drop of whisky with it, or claret if she preferred.

There were days when she was so ill that she could not walk without pain; then John Brown would lift her as easily as though she were a baby and carry her from her bed to her couch.

"How strong you are, Brown!" she would murmur.

"Aye," he replied. "I manage. Ye're still an armful, woman, but not what ye was."

Indeed she had lost nearly two stone in weight. When those *unfeeling* people saw her they would realize how ill she had been and that this was no pretence.

But at least she had Brown to comfort her.

Alfred came up to Balmoral to see her. What a trial Alfred was! He was just as wild as Bertie but lacked Bertie's charm. He began to make trouble as soon as he arrived and he and Brown were soon on bad terms. Brown's habit of acting as a sort of guardian of her apartments irritated her family. Bertie had felt the same. They resented the fact that they, the Queen's sons, had more or less to ask Brown's permission to see the Queen.

"Mama," Alfred said, "do you think it wise to allow Brown so many liberties?"

"My dear Alfred," she replied, "pray do not presume to tell me how to manage my household. If you would only turn your attention to your own affairs they might be managed a good deal more satisfactorily than they are at present."

This was a reference to one or two scrapes Alfred had got into with women. Alfred thought that was beside the point. Dalliance with women was a noble enough occupation; treating servants as friends closer than one's own flesh and blood was not. But although it was easy to grumble about these matters in the Queen's absence, it was not possible to do so in her formidable presence.

Vicky arrived with her children and she too was horrified by the ascendancy of John Brown.

Trouble came to a head when a band of musicians who had been playing for the servants to dance Highland reels irritated Alfred who ordered the music to stop. Brown wanted to know why the musicians had stopped playing and was told by the servants that the Duke of Edinburgh had ordered it.

"It's nae his place," declared Brown and commanded the musicians to start up again.

Alfred, discovering that his order had been countermanded by Brown, was furious. He demanded an apology from Brown who refused to give it.

Alfred stormed into his mother's apartments. This was intolerable, he told her. He had been insulted by a servant.

The Queen listened and said: "Brown was in charge of the servants' dancing. You should not have interfered."

"This is monstrous," cried Alfred.

"Are you telling me that I don't know how to manage my household?"

"Certainly not, Mama, but this man Brown gives himself such airs. I think he's drunk . . . with either spirits or power. His position here is invidious."

"What are you talking about, Alfred? Brown suits me very well and brings more comfort into my life than a number of other people."

"No man on board my ship would be allowed to behave as he does."

"Pray remember," said the Queen, "that this is not a ship but a royal residence and you are not the captain of it, but I happen to be the Queen."

Alfred went off grumbling.

Young Wilhelm behaved very badly, making a scene because he was expected to sit in a back seat in the pony carriage bowing to all the people as he passed as though he were their sovereign. He really was becoming very arrogant and he had been extremely rude to Brown who made no effort to hide his dislike of the boy.

One day Vicky's daughter Charlotte was with the Queen when Brown came in and the Queen told the child to say good morning to him.

"Good morning," said Charlotte with a curt nod.

"That won't do," said the Queen. "Brown expects you to shake hands with him."

"I can't do that, Grandmama."

"What do you mean, child? You *can't* do that!"

"Mama says I must not be too familiar with the servants."

The Queen grew pale with anger.

"Dinna fash yersel', woman," said Brown. "And don't blame the wee lass. It's the way they've brought her up."

The Queen sent for her daughter.

"I am astounded," she told her. "Charlotte has just behaved in a shameful manner."

"But what on earth has the child done, Mama?" asked Vicky.

"I have rarely been so ashamed . . . that a granddaughter of mine could have behaved in such an arrogant, ill-mannered way. She should be whipped and sent to her room and I should insist on this being done if I did not know that *she* is not to blame. I cannot understand how you young people can expect your children to behave like ladies and gentlemen when I consider the way in which they are brought up. If Dearest Papa were alive he would be so distressed."

"But, Mama, I cannot understand what she has done to make you so angry."

"She refused to shake hands with Brown . . . to his face. She said you had forbidden her to be too familiar with *servants*."

"But, Mama, I *have* forbidden her and Brown *is* a servant, and she was absolutely right to refuse."

"Papa and I brought up you children to show tact and charm to *everyone* . . . the highest and the lowest. And I would have you know that *I* told her to shake hands and she disobeyed *me*. Did you bring her up to disobey her grandmother and the Queen?"

"Of course not, Mama."

"Well, that is what she did."

"The children have always been made aware of your position, Mama, but I and Fritz have been very anxious to instil in them not to be familiar with servants. That can be very dangerous."

"Brown is not an ordinary servant."

"We know that well, Mama."

"And I will not have him treated as such. During my illness he has been my great comfort. I get precious little from some of you children."

"Poor Charlotte," went on Vicky. "It is a little difficult for her, you know. You would not have her mixing with the servants I'm sure; and yet she is supposed to treat Brown as though he is . . . the Prime Minister at least."

"That is a ridiculous statement. Brown has never been treated as the Prime Minister. Brown is a very good friend. Papa noticed him and singled him out for special service."

"For service, yes," said Vicky.

"And very good service he gives."

"We none of us have doubted that, Mama, but you must be aware that there is a good deal of comment concerning Brown's position in your household and surely in view of the present unrest everywhere even you must be aware that this is not a good thing."

"Even I? Are you suggesting that I am less aware of what is going on than others!"

"You do shut yourself away, Mama, and you must admit the people are getting very restive and there is a certain uneasiness. Mr Gladstone . . ."

"Pray don't talk to me about that man."

"He is your Prime Minister, Mama."

"It was never my wish that he should be."

"But it is the people's wish."

The Queen was angry. How dared her daughter presume to dictate to her! This was intolerable. She began to speak; she talked of the lack of sympathy she received from her children. Alfred and Vicky should have been a comfort to her and what happened? They came down and tried to disturb her household. Since Dearest Papa had died where could she turn for comfort? Because she had a good servant they would like to take him away from her. She had had a sympathetic Prime Minister and in a few months time he was replaced by Mr Gladstone. She felt ill and lonely. Her grandchildren disobeyed her; her children conspired to disrupt her household. She would be rather glad to be lying in the mausoleum at Frogmore beside the only one who had ever really cared for her.

Vicky said: "Mama, pray do not distress yourself so . . ."

"Pray refrain from giving me your unwanted advice. I wish to be alone."

"Mama . . ."

The Queen regarded her daughter stonily. "Surely you heard me express my wish?"

"Yes, Mama," said Vicky with resignation.

"And send Brown. I will take a little whisky. And then I shall rest."

There was no way of warning Mama, thought Vicky. This absurd situation with Brown was growing worse rather than improving. He seemed now to be more important than the Queen's own family.

But there was nothing to be done. That was the way the Queen wanted it and the Queen's words were law, at least in the family.

Was there no end to trouble? *What Does She Do With It?* was being circulated all over the place. Royal popularity was at its lowest when one of the more radical members of parliament, Sir Charles Dilke, made a speech which was a direct attack on the Queen. She failed in her duty, he pointed out; she lived in seclusion at Windsor, Balmoral or Osborne; she only appeared in public at times when she wanted Parliament to vote money for her family; she had a vast income and on what did she spend it? Was she hoarding it? Wasn't it meant to be spent on ceremonies and State occasions? What was the point of having a Queen who never appeared in public? It would be much less expensive and more to the point to replace royalty by a republic.

The Queen was fuming with rage when she read the report of the speech.

Who was this man Dilke? He should be ostracized. She hoped she would never be asked to meet him. He was obviously a scoundrel.

Mr Gladstone was upset. He was soon on with the old theme. If she would only come out of retirement . . . if she would be seen in London . . . it would make all the difference. It was true that she was in communication with her ministers, that she worked on state papers, but a Queen must not only do her duty, she must be seen to do it.

"I shall do as I wish," she said. "Those who think that I shall be frightened by this man Dilke have made a very grave mistake."

She refused to brood on it. It was getting near the end of the year and there was one day which she dreaded more than any other, the 14th of December, the day when Albert had died. Ever since that day ten years ago his memory had been kept fresh; every year when the 14th came round she stayed alone in her room and thought of him and then went to the mausoleum and meditated on his virtues and the great loss his going had brought her.

She was brooding on this when a letter arrived from Alice who was staying with her children at Sandringham with Bertie and Alix.

Sandringham, thought the Queen. Bertie and Alix were too often there, and by all accounts giving very gay parties. Bertie liked to entertain and the entertainments there were said to be lavish. She was concerned by his love of the gay life and Alix could not like it either. She believed, though, that Bertie had a little to vex him in Alix's way of never being at a place on time. Bertie had ordered that all clocks at Sandringham should be half an hour fast so that Alix should be helped to keep her appointments. How ridiculous! Alix would soon discover that the clocks were fast and be as late as ever.

The Queen disliked clocks to be fast. "After all," she said, "it is a lie."

She was glad that Alice was at Sandringham. There was something very gentle about Alice and she and Alix had become such good friends.

"It's the first time in eleven years that I have spent Bertie's birthday with him," wrote Alice. "Bertie and Alix are so kind and give us such a warm welcome showing how they like having us . . ."

Oh yes, it was good for the children to be together and although the girls had married abroad they could come home fairly frequently. It must be very pleasant for Alice to be in England for that poor Louis of hers was not so comfortably off as one would have liked.

I hope I was right to agree to the marriage. What would Albert have done? This was the Albert season and she sat brooding on that terrible time when he had gone to Cambridge in dreadful weather and come home to her so ill.

There was no one like him. There never would be, Blessed Angel that he was. How fortunate she had been to have twenty years of her life with him—but having known such perfection it was harder to bear his loss.

She heard that Bertie had gone up to Scarborough to Lord Londesborough's place accompanied by Lord Chesterfield. Alix had stayed behind. The Queen could imagine what gay parties there would be up there. Oh dear, how different he was from Dearest Albert!

A week or so later there was disturbing news. The Prince of Wales had left Scarborough and was at Marlborough House and Lord Chesterfield had been taken very ill. A few days later the Prince was ill.

Bertie left London because he had desired to be at Sandringham and when he arrived there his illness had been diagnosed as typhoid fever.

The Queen could not believe it. Bertie stricken with typhoid fever, the disease which had killed his father ten years ago and at precisely the same time!

It was like a horrible pattern—a judgment.

She felt that the train would never arrive; it was snowing; she sat brooding, thinking of that terrible time ten years ago.

Brown was beside her. "We're there," he said gruffly. He fastened the cloak about her. "Can't you stand still, woman?"

he demanded, and she smiled faintly; poor Brown, he was upset because he knew she was.

The carriage was waiting. Brown helped her in and off they went to Sandringham.

The place looked gloomy. She glanced up at it; she did not like it—fast clocks and fast parties. But he was ill now—her eldest son, sick as his father had been.

Lady Macclesfield, that good faithful woman on whom Alix relied, came forward to curtsey.

"My dear," said the Queen, "what is the news?"

"Very bad, I fear, Your Majesty."

"And the Princess?"

"She is with the Prince."

The Queen nodded.

"It cannot be typhoid."

"I fear so, Your Majesty. And Blegge the groom who accompanied His Highness to Scarborough is suffering from the same disease. They must have caught it there."

"You had better take me straight to him."

Lady Macclesfield inclined her head.

"And the Princess, how is she taking it?" asked the Queen.

"The Princess is wonderful," said Lady Macclesfield fervently.

Alix had come to the door of the sickroom with Alice.

"My dearest children," said the Queen with tears in her eyes, "what a blessing that you are together at this time."

She kissed them both and they took her in to see Bertie. He looked unlike himself with the strange glazed look in his eyes and the unnatural flush on his cheeks.

Oh dear God, she thought, it is so like that other nightmare. And it is soon to be the 14th of December.

The very best doctors were attending him—not only the Queen's favourite William Jenner but Dr William Gull, Dr Clayton and Dr Lowe. The whole country waited for news as the fever soared. Bertie's failing were forgotten; he had become "Good Old Teddy". He was a jolly good fellow; he liked women; he had a mistress or two, that only showed how human he was. He was a good sport; he was the sort of man they wanted to be King—and he was sick with the typhoid fever.

Forgotten were the grudges against the royal family. The Queen was with her son who was dying of the dreaded fever which had killed his father, and in the streets crowds waited eagerly for bulletins of his progress to be issued. The question on everyone's lips was "How is he?" He was better; then he was worse; there was some hope; there was no hope. Everything was forgotten but the dramatic illness of the Prince of Wales. The fact that the 14th of December was fast approaching seemed significant. It was more than that—it was uncanny.

During one of the more hopeful periods Alix went to St Mary Magdalene's Church at Sandringham, having first sent a note to the vicar to tell him she would be there. She wanted him to pray for the Prince that she might join in but she would not be able to wait until the service was over for she must get back to his bedside.

The church was crowded and there was a hushed silence when the Princess, wan with sleepless nights and anxiety, appeared. All joined fervently in the prayers. But, commented the Press, Death played with the Prince of Wales like a panther with its victim. But while the Prince lived there was still hope. Alfred Austin, the poet, wrote the lines by which he was afterwards to be remembered:

"Flashed from his bed, the electric tidings came,
He is not better; he is much the same."

Alix, with Alice and the Queen, were constantly in the sickroom but Alix did not forget poor Blegge and made sure that he had every care and attention. Alice was a great help; quiet and efficient and having had some practice in nursing during the wars, she devoted herself to her brother and gave that little more than even a professional nurse could have given. Alix thought she would never forget what she owed her sister-in-law. The Queen, in times of real adversity was always at her best. She would sit quietly behind a screen in Bertie's bedroom, not attempting to interfere, only to be there in case she could be of use.

It was the 13th of December—the day before the dreaded 14th—and Bertie had taken a turn for the worse. It was a repetition so close that it was eerie.

The doctors were despondent; it was clear that they thought there was no hope. Bertie often lay as though in a coma; at other times he would throw himself about and utter incoherent ravings.

Alix said: "Dear Mama, you must get some sleep."

"Not yet," said the Queen. "After . . . tomorrow."

"Mama, it is all over," said Alix.

"Oh no, my dear child," replied the Queen firmly. "When my dearest Albert was so ill I never gave up hope."

"But it was no use, Mama. He died. Blegge has died, Lord Chesterfield has died. And now . . ."

"My dear Alix, you must be brave. He is still with us."

She tried to comfort Alix. The poor child was almost at breaking point. It was the 13th—and everyone seemed certain that Bertie was going to die on the anniversary of his father's death.

"Oh God, spare my beloved child," prayed the Queen.

Through the night of the 13th she waited and when the 14th dawned she was filled with a terrible apprehension.

Everywhere the tension was felt; it was as though the whole nation held its breath.

The 14th. Ten years to the day. There she had sat by his bedside and he had said: *"Es ist das kleine Frauchen"* and she had asked him to kiss her. She remembered how his lips had moved so that she knew he had heard what she said.

She had sat there while everything that was worth while in life had slipped away from her; and she had plunged then into such utter desolation that she had not before known existed.

And now their son was dying. Poor wayward Bertie whom she had never loved as she should have. He had been a backward child and a disappointment to Albert who had so wanted a clever son. Albert used to worry so much about Bertie's coming to the throne and not being fit for the heavy responsibilities. Had they always been fair, always kind to Bertie?

It was too late for such thoughts now. In any case Bertie was a man and he had grown far from his mother; the way of life he chose was alien to her, as hers was to him.

But she remembered that there had been moments in his childhood when she had loved him; and he had been so popular with his brothers and sisters, and usually good-tempered. She thought of his pushing his little wheelbarrow in the gardens at Buckingham Palace and Windsor; playing with his bucket and spade at Osborne, or riding his pony at Balmoral.

Alix loved him; his children adored him; there would be many to grieve for poor Bertie.

Dr Gull came to her; there was complete despair in his face. She could not bear to ask how Bertie was; she could not bear to go to his bedside, for there she could not help but see that other face; she could not shut out the echo of his words, *"Gutes Frauchen."*

Oh, beloved Albert, dead for ten years. Am I to lose our son on the anniversary of the darkest day in my life?

A miracle had happened. On the fatal 14th Bertie had come as close to death as it was possible for anyone to do and live. All day long he had seemed to be sinking fast and even the doctors had lost hope.

The Queen implored Dr Gull to tell her the worst but he only shook his head because he could not bring himself to say, "The Prince is dying," which was what he believed to be the truth.

He left the sickroom and paced up and down the terrace. Only a short while now, he thought; and even he felt himself caught up in that fatalism which had been accepted by almost everyone else. The Prince was going to die on the 14th.

One of the nurses came running out on to the terrace.

"Doctor," she cried, "please come at once. I think he is dying."

The doctor hurried into the sickroom. He looked down at the patient who was lying very still; he was pale and as the doctor took his wrist to feel his pulse he realized at once that the fever had passed.

He turned to the nurse. "I believe there is hope," he said. "The crisis has passed."

Alix came to the bedside. "There is hope . . ." she began.

Dr Gull answered: "The fever is passed. I think a miracle has happened."

The Queen embraced Alix; then she turned to Alice. "It's a miracle, no less. He was on the verge of the grave," she cried. "Very few people have been known to recover who have been as ill as he has been."

Dr Gull, who had been keeping visitors from the sickroom during the last day, said that the Queen might go and sit at her son's bedside for a short while, though not to tire him.

Bertie looked at her and the sweetness of the smile on that pathetically pale face touched her deeply.

"Dear Mama," he said, "I am so glad to see you. Have you been here all the time?"

She could have wept. "I have been watching over you, my darling child," she told him.

He smiled faintly and said: "Where is Alix?"

Alix came to the bed and she took his hand.

"No one could have shown you greater love and care," said the Queen brökenly. "Such tenderness!"

Alix knelt by the bed and her tears fell on to the coverlet.

Dear sweet Alix, thought the Prince. When he was well he would try to make amends. He would live more quietly, the sort of life that she wanted. He would spend more time with her and the children.

The children? His spirits lifted at the thought of them. He longed to be with them, play the old games with them.

There was so much to live for.

The Would-be Assassin

It was a happy Christmas after all. Although for the Queen it was the mourning season she could not but rejoice at Bertie's recovery. He was still very ill, and although he was on the road to recovery he must not be allowed to overstrain himself.

Alix wanted to show her gratitude for his recovery so she presented a brass lectern to the parish church on which was inscribed:

To the glory of God
A Thanksgiving-offering for his mercy,
14th December 1871
Alexandra

It was a miracle, said the Queen. On the anniversary of the very day on which Albert had died Bertie had come face to face with death and been allowed to return to life. The Queen believed that Albert had been caring for her son and that it was a sign from him. She was sure that the spirit of Albert was not far away. In fact, as she said to Alice, it was this knowledge which enabled her to go on.

Careful nursing was still necessary and Alix was determined that no one but herself should look after her husband. This was the happiest time of her marriage for Bertie relied on her. He had no wish now to be with those brilliant witty friends; he was quite happy to sit and talk with Alix and have the children to see him and talk to him, being as quiet as they could be, for they had been warned not to tire Papa. Never had Alix felt so close to her little family. This intimacy was what she had always longed for; and the fact that Bertie enjoyed it made her very happy.

The Queen was pleased. "They are hardly out of each other's sight," she wrote to Vicky. "They are like a pair of young lovers."

She was pleased. Alix was a good sweet girl, though her unpunctuality was tiresome. As for Bertie, he had always had a sweet nature and now that he was not racketing about with a lot of fast friends, he was really very charming. As for the children, although not disciplined as much as the Queen would have liked them to be, they were so devoted to their parents that they obeyed without being forced to do so. They referred to Alix always as "Mother dear", which was rather charming. She would hear young Georgie saying "Where is Mother dear?" Or "Mother dear told me this or that." And to see those two boys vying for her favour . . . well, it was quite touching.

Of course Alix was not clever—she hardly ever read a book, nor did Bertie for that matter—and she could never understand politics as a Queen should and she was apt to become over-emotional when these matters touched her family (as she had been over the Danish-Prussian war) and that was not a good thing, but she was a good homely woman, an excellent wife and mother; and after all that was important.

The Queen decided that William Jenner and Dr Gull should be rewarded for their services and Mr Gladstone agreed. It would please the people and Mr Gladstone was relieved because the people had changed their attitude towards the royal family since Bertie's illness. Royalty had become popular and to see the crowds waiting for the bulletins even in January was astonishing when such a short time before people like Dilke had appeared to have quite a following.

The Prince had come close to death and there was nothing like death for enhancing popularity and as Mr Disraeli commented: "To have come closer to death and lived was an even greater achievement than to have died."

The royalty question had become much less acute.

So it would be very pleasing to the people if William Jenner was gazetted at K.C.B. and Dr Gull was made a baronet.

That was not all. There must be a thanksgiving service, said her ministers.

Bertie had recovered and by the end of February the ceremony was to take place. The people lined the streets to cheer and cry "God Save the Queen" and "God Bless the Prince of Wales." It was very affecting, said the Queen and most fitting and it showed that however much the people were led astray by *wicked* people who wrote *scurrilous* pamphlets and *disgraceful* scoundrels like Sir Charles Dilke who called for a Republic to replace the Monarchy, the people themselves were ready to show their loyalty.

Seated next to Bertie, who still looked pale, and considerably thinner which moved the people deeply, they came through Temple Bar. Behind her on the box was John Brown, looking very handsome and very efficient, keeping a watchful eye on the crowds. "I dinna trust these southerners," he had told her.

"Good old Teddy," roared the crowd.

And on impulse, her eyes full of tears of gratitude for his survival, she lifted his hand to her lips and kissed it. It was the right gesture. The crowd roared its approval. The Queen was human. She was a mother rejoicing that her son who had come to the grave was with her once more.

It was very dark in the Cathedral but the service was moving and when it was over they drove once more through the streets.

Mr Gladstone was pleased. This was the sort of ceremony that the people loved and moreover expected from its royalty.

The next day the Queen was riding in her carriage with Prince Arthur, and Brown as usual on the box, when a young man stepped off the pavement and pointed a pistol at her.

It was not a new experience for the Queen although it was some time since the last attempt had been made on her life.

Arthur cried: "My God!" and tried to leap from the carriage; but someone was there before him. The ever-watchful Brown had seen the young man raise his arm and with one bound he was off the box and he had the offender in his grasp.

The Queen could not take her eyes from that stalwart figure on whom she believed she could rely as she could on no one else. What should I do without him? she asked herself. And now he had saved her life.

The Queen lay on her bed, trembling slightly. It could so easily have happened. This was the sixth time an attempt had been made on her life. Could she go on hoping that they would continue to be unsuccessful? How alert Brown was where her safety was concerned! Of course Arthur had tried to seize the man but Brown was there before him. Who knew, if Brown had not been there, Arthur's efforts might have been too late.

The Prime Minister called. She did not ask him to sit down in her presence. That was a very special favour reserved for a minister who was also a friend. It had never been offered to Mr Gladstone, although Lord Melbourne had arrived at the stage when he took the familiarity as a matter of course and did not always ask her permission. Even on an occasion like this when she had narrowly escaped from death Mr Gladstone put on his speaker-at-a-public-meeting attitude and although he expressed concern at what had happened he was not moved as Mr Disraeli or Lord Melbourne would have been.

The pistol, he told her, had been unloaded and the young man who had pointed it at her was mentally deficient. When questioned he had babbled about frightening the Queen into freeing Fenian prisoners. He was, of course, Irish, and his name was Arthur O'Connor.

"Those Irish!" cried the Queen. "What trouble they make."

Later when she heard that O'Connor had been sentenced to a year's imprisonment she was alarmed. "What when he comes out?" she demanded. "Has it occurred to people that he might make another attempt and this time be successful? Could he not be transported?"

As it was the understandably fervent desire of the Queen that O'Connor should be transported, the government offered him the opportunity of leaving the country and paid his passage money so the Queen had nothing more to fear from the dull-witted O'Connor.

There was one who had come out of the affair with honours. This, she said in secret glee, is a vindication. What did Bertie, Vicky and Alfred think now of the man of whom they had been so critical? They had to admit that John Brown had saved their mother's life and they should be eternally grateful to that good and faithful man.

If they weren't, she was.

Bertie, however, when she discussed the matter with him, replied that Brown did his duty, he would agree to that; but that was what he was employed for.

"My dear Bertie," cried the Queen, "you should have seen the manner in which he leapt from the box and tackled that wicked young man."

"Arthur did the same."

"Arthur tried to protect me, yes. But Brown was there before him. Why, had the pistol been loaded it could have been fired before Arthur grasped the would-be assassin's arm."

"Before Brown did too, had it been loaded," added Bertie. "But, Mama, do not let us consider such a terrible possibility."

"It is a possibility ever present where royalty is concerned," replied the Queen. "It has happened to me before and I feel some small consolation in the fact that all those who have had the desire to kill me have been mad."

"Pray do not talk of such a thing, Mama," said Bertie with real feeling which was touching, particularly as he looked so pale and so much thinner after his illness.

"My dearest child," she said tenderly, "I believe you are glad that I have been spared."

Bertie kissed her hand and the tears came to her eyes. Bertie was really good in many ways.

"I am going to give good faithful Brown a gold medal commemorating the occasion and twenty-five pounds a year shall be added to his salary."

"A very excellent reward for doing his duty," said Bertie. "And you will let Arthur know how much you appreciate his efforts."

"I am having a gold pin made for him."

The Prince of Wales raised his eyebrows. A gold pin was

not very much when set beside a gold medal, the Queen's effusive thanks and praises, plus twenty-five pounds a year.

As the Prince said to Alix: "This affair has made Mama even more besotted over that man Brown."

Death, a Betrothal and the Return of Dizzy

The Queen had grave news from her stepsister Feodora, whose health was far from good.

"Dearest sister," wrote Feodora, "how I long to see you. Sometimes I feel that there may not be many more opportunities."

Such sentiments touched the Queen deeply.

Mr Gladstone thought it was not the time to leave the country. Royalty was enjoying a wave of popularity occasioned by the Prince's recent illness and the action of Arthur O'Connor.

Both Queen and Prince could have been lost to the nation and since they had not been, they were appreciated. Now was the time to enhance that popularity.

How unsympathetically expressed! How unfeeling! *Poor* Mrs Gladstone, how could she cope with marriage to such a man! How different was dear Mr Disraeli, who was looking so forlorn these days! She knew the reason. His dear wife was growing more and more ill every day and he knew it.

He told the Queen of Mary Anne's sufferings and how she tried to hide them from him. "I know, M'am, with your great heart, you will understand why I wish to spend so much time at Hughenden."

"I understand *perfectly*," replied the Queen. "Oh, I wish there was something I could *do*. Please tell her how much I think of her and of you."

"That will cheer her very much," said Mr Disraeli.

She could sympathize. Had she not suffered it all when her Dear Saint had been so ill. She knew how poor Mr Disraeli felt for *his*. And now her sister was ill, dying she feared, and Mr Gladstone thought that she should ignore the dear soul's wishes and not make the journey to Baden Baden.

"It would be an action quite contrary to your Majesty's nature," said Mr Disraeli.

Oh, why were the people so foolish as to deny her the services of such a man as her Prime Minister and give her Mr Gladstone instead?

The Queen left for Baden Baden where she found Feodora wan and very ill.

They embraced tearfully and Feodora said: "I knew you'd come. I knew I shouldn't ask in vain."

The Queen tried to cheer her sister by talking of the past. "How beautiful you were!" she said. "I was so proud of you for I knew I could never be so pretty."

"My dear modest little sister. You had a charm and dignity with which I could not compete. You always behaved like a little Queen."

"Do you remember Uncle King and how he cast his eyes on you and I am sure wanted to marry you?"

Feodora remembered.

"I always loved Uncle King," went on Victoria. "He was my favourite uncle. But of course he was too old for you. That was why you were hustled out of his sight. Oh, I remember your wedding day and now Uncle George was going to give you away and didn't come and Uncle William had to do it."

"How it brings it all back," said Feodora. "I could almost feel young again talking to you."

They talked often, for Feodora was not able to go out much. Sometimes though they took a little carriage drive together but she tired easily and Victoria was very careful of her.

They took a tender farewell and the Queen was so pleased that she had made the visit. Particularly as later that year Feodora died.

At the same time the Queen heard that the Countess of Beaconsfield had passed away. Poor, poor Mr Disraeli! How sad and wan he looked. The Queen hastily sent her condolences.

"But," she said to Brown, "he will have the satisfaction of knowing that he did everything for her."

At Hughenden Disraeli brooded on his loss. Mary Anne had been eighty-one—a great age, but bright and devoted to the end. He himself was sixty-eight—an old man, but with Mary Anne he had felt young. He had always known what an emptiness her going would leave, but even so he had not believed it could be so great. There was nothing very much to life for him now, he supposed. Whatever ambitions were realized, there would be no one to share them with him. He knew that his triumphs had been doubled because he could come home and talk of them to Mary Anne over iced champagne and cold chicken; he knew that adversity would be greater without her to share it.

Life had certainly lost its savour.

He forced himself to sort out her papers and among them he found a letter addressed to himself.

She wanted them to be buried in the same grave, she wrote. She told him that he had been the perfect husband.

"Do not live alone, dearest. Someone I earnestly hope you may find as attached to you as your own devoted Mary Anne."

Never! thought Disraeli. Did she not know that for him, though he searched the whole world, there could never be another like Mary Anne, whom he had made his Countess of Beaconsfield.

It was a tragic year. Shortly before the death of Feodora and the Countess of Beaconsfield there had been terrible news from Hesse Darmstadt. Alice had seven children. Really she had had too many far too quickly following on one another. The Queen was always deploring what women were expected to suffer in what she called the "shadow side" of marriage. Her daughters did not seem to regard it as such and thought that the inconvenience and humiliation of birth was compensated for a thousand times by the children they produced. What Vicky had suffered over Wilhelm was amazing. She was constantly trying to find cures for his poor arm and the Queen believed that one of the reasons for his arrogance was that he was not disciplined enough.

And now poor Alice wrote in such distress. She had been in the courtyard of the Palace and little Frederick William, aged three, had suddenly appeared at the window. He had shouted to his mother and before Alice could call to the nurse he had leaned too far out of the window and fallen on to the cobbles.

"My heart seemed to stop beating," wrote Alice. "Poor child! What a dreadful calamity!"

And now the child had died from his injuries.

How sad that one's children had to grow out of their happy childhoods and live tragic lives of their own.

The Queen wrote long loving letters to Alice and was relieved that Dearest Albert was at least spared this terrible tragedy.

There was no end to family troubles. Bertie was growing plump and well; and as he lost his wan looks so he did his feelings of repentance. He was with his old companions again and there was scandal about the wild parties which were once more taking place at Sandringham. Stories reached her which she would rather not have heard. For instance, it was whispered that Bertie and Alfred were looking for a house where they could entertain their actress friends. They were too fond of the company of actresses. Bertie's friends were men of questionable morals. In spite of that unsavoury Mordaunt affair Sir Frederick Johnstone was still constantly in his company; his greatest friend was Lord Hartington—Devonshire's heir—known among his acquaintances as Harty-Tarty. Not without some importance in the political world, Harty-Tarty was a very unusual man; he pretended to be rather stupid, which might have been to call attention to the fact that he was really rather clever. One of the richest men in the country, he liked to go about looking like a tramp. Worst of all, of course, was his liaison with the Duchess of Manchester, a young German of great personality who had married the Duke of Manchester. Manchester was hardly a suitable husband for any young woman and Countess Louise von Alten, as the Duchess had been before her marriage, was not the woman to make the best of such a union. She had immediately selected Hartington as a more congenial companion; his political aptitude and his eccentricity appealed to her. They had been together for many years so that their *affaire* was almost a marriage; but of course it was rather shocking and the Queen had often warned Alix about being too friendly with the Duchess of Manchester. Poor Alix, as though she had any say in the matter!

Bertie had taken a long holiday convalescing after his illness but the better he grew the more he invited scandal. He was as at home in Paris as he was in London and he had a wide circle of friends there—aristocratic, elegant, extravagant and, the Queen feared, immoral.

There was no controlling Bertie—and Alfred was as bad without having half his brother's charm and good nature.

Children *were* a trial; and not only children! Poor Napoleon had died at Chislehurst and many of his adherents had come over to attend his funeral. They had tried to work up enthusiasm for a protest against the new Republic and Bertie behaved tactlessly in his good-hearted generous way by inviting several of the agitators to Sandringham, because he said they were friends of his. Mr Gladstone was most put out and very critical. The Prince's sense of political decorum was sadly lacking, he said.

So life was becoming as difficult as it had been before Bertie's typhoid attack. And now Alfred was set on marrying the Grand Duchess Marie Alexandrovna, the daughter of the Czar of Russia. The Queen did not like the idea of a match with Russia. She knew that Bertie and Alix were in favour of it because Alix's sister Dagmar was married to the Czarevitch and Marie Alexandrovna was consequently connected to them by marriage.

It was all so distressing and what sort of a husband would Alfred make the young woman after the kind of life he had led? At least if Bertie was gay that had come mainly after marriage—so she believed. Of course there had been that disgraceful affair at the Curragh Camp.

Alfred, however, was set on the marriage, and negotiations with the Russians were by now well ahead so she supposed she had better see the girl. In accordance with her custom she would invite her to Balmoral that she might inspect her and make sure that she would be a suitable wife for Alfred.

The Czar's reply was that he had no intention of sending his daughter on approval; and the Queen must meet them somewhere midway between Russia and England. The Queen was indignant. Was she—the Queen of England—expected to run after these Russians! Alice, who had been taken so tenderly into the maternal embrace since the death of her little son, wrote that as Alfred was so eager for the match, couldn't Mama make the journey, say, to Cologne? That would be such a help and a kindly gesture in a way.

Really, her daughters could be very arrogant at times. How dared little Alice, who lived somewhat humbly, one must admit, in Hesse Darmstadt, attempt to dictate to the Queen of England. She wrote one of her vehement letters scattered with italics. Did the dear child think *she* should tell her mother, the *Queen* of England, what *she* should do. She would remind Alice that she had been twenty years longer on the throne than the Emperor of Russia, and was, she believed, the *Doyenne* of Sovereigns and a *reigning* Sovereign which the Empress at least was *not*.

Bertie invited the Czarevitch and his wife Dagmar to come to England with their children, who were quite charming, particularly the eldest boy, so that the Queen forgot her animosity to the Russians and found them quite pleasant which paved the way to her acceptance of Marie Alexandrovna.

Soon she was telling herself that alliance with Russia was a good thing because it might have the excellent effect of increasing friendship between England and Russia.

She had a serious talk with Alfred.

"I hope you will lead a different life now you are about to be married," she told him. "It would never do to be on such terms with fast women as I know you have been."

Alfred was rather sullenly silent, refusing to discuss past misdemeanours, which boded little good for his marriage, for it seemed hardly likely that his attitude would have been such if he had decided to turn over a new leaf.

Mr Gladstone was being his difficult self. He had made one of the longest speeches of his career—it lasted three hours—on his Irish University Bill. Many Irish families would not allow their sons to attend the Protestant Dublin University and Gladstone wanted to form a new centre of learning for Catholics. The expense would have been great and as the Bill was not even supported entirely by Irish Catholics, Mr Gladstone found himself unable to carry it through. It was rejected by 287 votes to 284 and to the Queen's great delight Gladstone had no alternative but to resign.

Gleefully she sent for Mr Disraeli, but he was too clever to take office in the circumstances; he knew full well that he must wait for that triumph. Gladstone must battle on. Disraeli wanted office after a general election when he felt sure he would be in with a big majority.

Bravely Gladstone continued in office. He reduced income tax from sixpence to threepence in the pound and held out hope that he would be able to abolish it altogether.

The Queen laughed. A bait, she said, to catch electors, which she was certain would fail.

She was right. At the general election the Conservative party was returned with a majority of 46.

With what joy did the Queen await the arrival of her new Prime Minister. He bowed over her hand; he kissed it lingeringly; tears filled the Queen's eyes and she was happy to note they glinted in those of her new Prime Minister.

"This is a very happy day," she told him.

"M'am," he replied, "I feel alive again."

It was a reference of course to the death of Mary Anne. He had come back to serve the Queen in the highest capacity and that was to be his great consolation. How well she understood!

"Mr Disraeli," she said, "pray sit down." It was the great honour. Gladstone had always been obliged to stand, but that had not made him cut short his long addresses. Now she could savour the joy of pleasant human contact and no longer be treated as a public meeting; she would have that sweet sympathy and understanding which was so important to her.

"This is a day, Mr Disraeli, that I always regard as a very special one in my life."

Of course Mr Disraeli knew to what she referred. He would never be found wanting in such a point.

"I remember the date well, M'am. His Royal Highness looking so splendid in his uniform, inspiring us all with hope for the future by his very nobility of countenance. And Your Majesty so young yet so dedicated."

Of course Mr Disraeli would remember that it was the anniversary of her wedding day.

And how typical of him on such an occasion to shelve tiresome politics and talk of personal things—the last days of Mary Anne's life and most of all her own sufferings, the virtues of her dear dead Saint and the noble manner in which she had continued to serve her country though in seclusion.

With Mr Disraeli she could view the future in a much happier frame of mind.

The Aylesford Affair

Disraeli was not exaggerating when he said he had found a new zest for life, a zest of which the death of Mary Anne had robbed him. The Queen had become the centre of his existence; she sensed this and was comforted and delighted by his feelings towards her. Disraeli could never be the father figure that Lord Melbourne had been; but a mother herself, she did not need a father now. Disraeli enchanted her. He flattered her in a manner which to many might have seemed outrageous but to the Queen it was all very natural. Disraeli adored her; and she in turn was ready to give him a very special affection.

She found herself waiting for his visits, looking for the light of admiration which leapt into his eyes as he bent over and kissed her hand. He made her feel as though she were a very attractive woman as well as a Queen and she could never quite resist such admiration, perhaps because it had never been apparent in Albert's feelings towards her. Albert had been the most faithful of husbands and love between them had been great; but never had Albert flattered her. She was his good wife, his dear adoring Victoria but never had he shown this ecstatic admiration which she found in the attitude of Mr Disraeli.

She knew that before his marriage to Mary Anne he had had mistresses and he now had many women friends. Like so many clever men, he found the society of women so much more to his taste than that of men—in every way. Lord Melbourne had been the same; so had Uncle King George IV and, going back much further, Charles II.

Mr Disraeli had that very pleasant gift for gossiping which she had so enjoyed in Lord Melbourne's time for he had been a past-master at it. Albert had never gossiped and had never approved of the practice; but a Queen should know a great deal about the people around her—personal things, the sort of items which gossip brought out so admirably.

The new Prime Minister was so amusing. His wit delighted her as Lord Melbourne's had done; in fact it was almost as though history were repeating itself. There she was looking forward to her Prime Minister's visits, settling down to a little gossip and like Melbourne he would bring in State matters and discuss them in such an easy, light-hearted manner that it all became a pleasure.

India was a topic which absorbed him. He was going to make her Empress of India, he cried, looking at her with great admiration. He called her the Faery Queen very often, and to his friends rather irreverently "The Faery"; when she disagreed with him he had a rather arch way of putting his head on one side and saying with a kind of tender reproach: "*Dear* Madam." This amused her and carried her on the way to making her see his point of view.

How very different from Mr Gladstone! She liked to discuss the last Prime Minister with the man who had replaced him. What did Mr Disraeli think of those rumours about Mr Gladstone? Was it really true that he prowled about the streets inviting *loose* women to accost him? The story as she had heard it was that he was so concerned for these women that when they approached him he tried to reform them and instead of going home with *them* as they asked, he invited them home with *him*, where, if they accepted his invitation they would find Mrs Gladstone waiting with hot soup and a warm bed that they might spend the night in comfort and the next morning be persuaded to mend their ways.

"What an odd manner for a Prime Minister to behave!" said the Queen.

Mr Disraeli agreed that it was indeed very odd.

"It lays him open to all kinds of suspicion," went on the Queen. "Does he not realize that?"

"Oh perfectly, Madam. But he is such a figure of virtue that he believes none could seriously suspect him of having other motives than those of reform towards his protégées."

"He is a strange man. Many people might think he is immoral."

His friends have warned him about these nocturnal prowlings, M'am," said Disraeli, "but he is a man of purpose."

"I wonder," said the Queen, her lips pursed; then she remembered that Albert would have said it was unchristian to suspect vice where it was not proved and Albert would probably have thought Gladstone an admirable man. She dismissed the thought, hastily remembering that Albert had not liked Mr Disraeli at all and had thought of him as a flamboyant upstart—but then of course Albert had not really known him.

She went on: "Sometimes I wonder whether he is a secret Papist. He seems to concern himself so much with religion and this Irish question."

"It is hard to imagine Mr Gladstone either a papist or a libertine," said Disraeli wryly. "The two have been known to go together—but not in a Mr Gladstone."

"*Poor* Mrs Gladstone," said the Queen.

And they shelved gossip to discuss the position with India.

Bertie was deeply interested in India. In view of the situation he believed that he, who had proved himself such an excellent ambassador, should visit that country.

He visualized a glorious and splendid tour, with wonderful Arabian Nights type of entertainments put on for his benefit. The government should put up the money for the expenses of such a tour for it was clear that the heir to Crown and the Empire should not travel like a pauper.

He said nothing to Alix. She did not come into his plans. He certainly did not wish to have her with him on the journey. He wanted to be free to enjoy it.

He raised the matter with Disraeli and other ministers who responded cautiously. Bertie, however, wilfully misconstrued their attitude as enthusiasm and went to Windsor to see the Queen.

"Mama," he said eagerly, "you know that your ministers believe that it would do great good if I toured India, and this is just the time to do it."

The Queen was always uneasy when Bertie was out of England; she was never sure what mischief he would get into. Often though Disraeli had mentioned the ambassadorial qualities of the Prince of Wales and that, although he was apt to be a little indiscreet at times, his journeys had on the whole done immense good for the country's relations with foreign powers.

The Queen listened. If Mr Disraeli believed it would be good for the Prince of Wales to travel in India perhaps he was right.

"What of the money to provide for the cost of all this?"

"Oh, Mama, that's a small point."

"I should have thought it was a very big one," said the Queen. "I can give nothing and I know you are in debt. But if the government is willing to meet your expenses I see no reason why the trip should not be arranged."

Bertie was jubilant. "Of course the government will pay, Mama," he said. "It is such an excellent project."

"Alix must not go," said the Queen sharply.

Bertie smiled. That was just what he thought.

"It will be a wrench to part from Alix," he said, "but I'm sure she'll realize that she can't leave the children and come with me."

He was pleased. It was going better than he had dared hope.

Alix was distressed.

"Bertie," she cried, "is it true that there is a project afoot for a trip to India?"

"Oh, nothing definite," said Bertie airily. "Dizzy's been turning over the idea in his mind. Seems to think I rate as a good ambassador."

"When would they want us to go?" asked Alix.

Bertie was silent for a few seconds and then plunged: "I don't think they want you to go, Alix."

She turned pale; he saw her clench and unclench her hands.

"So you are planning to go alone?" she demanded.

"Everything is quite unsettled so far."

"But not so unsettled that it has not been decided that I am to stay behind."

"There are the children," said Bertie. "You would hate to leave them."

"They would be in good hands. And a wife's first place is with her husband. I want to come with you."

"Well, of course, it's what we both want," said Bertie evasively.

But she knew he didn't. She wanted to turn away and weep. She knew that he wanted to go off alone; that he would not miss her at all, that he was already planning the pleasures that would be his.

Bertie had his way; the journey to India was arranged and Alix stayed at home, although she did accompany him to Calais.

Knowing that a very glittering, exciting and novel adventure lay before him, and that poor Alix was hurt to be left behind, Bertie was suitably sad on saying good-bye to her.

"You have the children to comfort you for this parting," he said. "I haven't that consolation."

No, thought Alix, half angry, half exasperated, but you'll find ample to make you forget your family!

Everyone noticed how melancholy she was and felt sorry for the poor Princess of Wales who put on such a brave face although the whole nation gossiped about Bertie's infidelities.

Alix went back to her nurseries and told the children about Papa's journey and soon their father was sending home accounts of his journey; at least he never forgot to write to them, telling them about his reception in India and the wonderful places he saw. He had shot an elephant and would bring a baby elephant home for the boys to see; he had also killed a tiger. Perhaps he would bring home some tiger cubs for them to play with. They were such lovely little creatures—like big cats and very playful when young.

George would read the letters to Eddy because Eddy could read only slowly and, although the elder, was far behind George in his studies. George had to look after Eddy always and explain things to him when he could not understand them.

So George read and re-read their father's letters and every day they looked for them.

Disraeli told the Queen that he was really delighted with the work the Prince was doing in India.

"None could have done it better save yourself, M'am," he said. "And we should not wish to see our gracious Queen indulging in pig sticking and tiger shooting at which by all accounts His Royal Highness excels."

Bombay, Calcutta, Poona and Baroda. Everywhere the Prince went he made an excellent impression. Even at Lucknow, where in view of past events there was a hint of hostility, he managed to charm the inhabitants. There was no doubt that Bertie had the right manner to grace such occasions and win the superficial affection of multitudes; everywhere he went he was greeted with enthusiasm. He was given such gifts; he was cheered everywhere. He was called the Future Emperor. No one could have denied that it was not an eminently successful and well-timed exercise.

But Bertie's way of life must mean that he was always on the edge of scandal. Sometimes he managed to skirt skilfully across it; but this he could not always expect to do.

One of Bertie's greatest friends was Lord Aylesford, who devoted so much time and energy to sport that he was known as Sporting Joe. He had been a prominent member of the Marlborough House set and Bertie had often been his guest. Sporting Joe had a remarkably pretty and rather flighty young wife who had been on terms of great friendship with the Prince of Wales—even greater than her husband was aware. It had not been possible to take her on the Indian tour but, against the wishes of the Queen, Bertie had included Aylesford in the party.

Lady Aylesford was not of a nature to remain faithful to her husband or to the Prince of Wales during such a long absence and no sooner had they left than she struck up a friendship with another member of their circle, Lord Blandford, heir to the Duke of Marlborough. So serious did this friendship become that Blandford decided to leave his wife and set up house with Lady Aylesford.

When Lord Aylesford heard of this he was very distressed and explained the position to the Prince. Bertie was uneasy. The Mordaunt case was still fresh in his mind. He had been very friendly with Lady Aylesford—as he had with Lady Mordaunt; if Aylesford was going to make trouble and there was a public scandal he might well be drawn into it.

"Blandford is a scoundrel," he cried. "I'll never speak to the fellow again."

But Aylesford wanted greater satisfaction than the Prince's disapproval. He must go home, he said. He must know exactly what was happening. Reluctantly the Prince agreed and Aylesford left for England.

With the departure of Aylesford and one or two others—including Lady Aylesford's brother who had been a member of the party—a great deal of the fun departed. Sporting Joe had a genius for arranging amusing pastimes. The Prince missed him very much and the more he missed him the more he raged against Blandford, the cause of the trouble. His anger was tinged with a certain anxiety which made it the greater, since he himself had perhaps been a little indiscreet with the fascinating wife of Sporting Joe.

He had left India and was in Egypt on the way home when news reached him that Lord Aylesford was planning to divorce his wife and of course he would cite Lord Blandford as co-respondent. In the heat of the affair Aylesford made known the Prince's criticism of Blandford.

Lord Randolph Churchill, the fiery-tempered younger brother of Lord Blandford, decided to defend the family honour. This defamation of his brother's character coming from someone like the Prince of Wales was ridiculous, he said. The Prince had known of the affair between Lady Aylesford and Blandford before he left England yet he had insisted on Lord Aylesford's accompanying him. The family were eager to prevent a greater scandal and tried to persuade Aylesford to drop the idea of divorce.

Lord Randolph, a man of immense vitality, a certain impulsiveness, great ambition, a love of the limelight and a complete lack of discretion, determined to do everything in his power to stop the divorce and stated that the Prince of Wales was the chief instigator of the trouble and that he would never forgive him for calling Blandford a scoundrel. He went on to declare in his club and to acquaintances who, he must have known, would not keep the information to themselves, that if the divorce were proceeded with, evidence could be produced which could ruin the Prince of Wales.

In his impetuous way he turned his indefatigable energies into an effort to stop the divorce. The Prince could stop it, he was sure; and as His Highness had influence with Aylesford, it seemed that if he were to forbid Aylesford to proceed the outraged husband would comply with his commands.

Meanwhile Churchill asked for an audience with the Princess of Wales.

Alix, who had heard rumours of the scandal, was feeling sick at heart. How different everything might have been if only Bertie had been a faithful husband, or if she could have been indifferent to his infidelities. She had tried not to attempt to discover with which women he was friendly; she had tried to laugh at rumours and to tell herself that a virile man like Bertie needed outlets for his energies which marriage could not supply. He was not the only unfaithful husband. He was so charming, and especially tender and generous when he was indulging in his adventures. He was so good to the children; so eager that she herself should be treated with respect; and she was never allowed to suffer any indignity in public. He would have been angry, even with his mistress of the moment, if she had dared to show a lack of respect towards the Princess of Wales. He was tolerant about her besetting sin of unpunctuality; he tried not to show his exasperation when she was as much as half an hour late, which she knew she often was. It was impossible not to love Bertie deeply. If she could have loved him a little less how much easier it would have been.

She looked at the little man with the burning purpose in his eyes, feigning respect but in fact threatening.

"A most painful business, Your Highness."

"Then it is a pity everything is not done to stop it," she answered.

"I am in complete agreement. That is why I have come to Your Highness. The Prince could have great influence here. This case must not come before the public."

"And you think I can prevent that?"

"I think Your Highness might persuade the Prince to prevent it."

"I have no say in these matters."

"You have influence with the Prince and I believe that if you could make known to him what bringing this matter into the public eye would entail it would be an end to it. I must explain to Your Highness that if Aylesford takes this to court, the Prince will be subpoenaed and this will be a repetition of the Mordaunt case. Although this time it will not go so easily for the Prince."

"I don't understand you, Lord Randolph."

"Lady Aylesford, Your Highness, received letters from the Prince of Wales. When this trouble arose and divorce was threatened, she gave those letters to my brother, Lord Blandford. If Lord Aylesford went on with the divorce, these letters would be published."

Alix put her hand to her brow. Letters! It was always letters in these scandals. Oh, Bertie, how could you be so indiscreet as to write letters to these women! There had been letters in the Mordaunt case—fortunately they had not been too revealing. She trusted these were not either.

Lord Randolph tried to dispel her hopes. "Your Highness," he said, "if the contents of these letters were revealed I fear the Prince of Wales would never sit on the throne."

He left Alix in a state of great anxiety.

When the Prince heard what was happening he was furious. What angered him most was not the fact that the letters might be published but that Churchill had dared to go to Alix and inflict such agonies upon her. He knew how she would feel and he hated himself for having become involved with Lady Aylesford. The last thing he wanted to do was hurt Alix.

He raved to his friend Lord Charles Beresford.

"I'll never speak to Churchill again. I'll see him hounded out of society. I'll challenge him to a duel."

"Your Highness couldn't do that," put in Beresford.

"What do you mean I couldn't do it? I will do it. I'll have his blood for this."

"It would be treason, Your Highness."

"Treason. I'd like to see him in the Tower. I'd like to have him before a firing squad. And if I decide to challenge him to a duel I'll do so, Beresford, remember that."

The Prince, usually mild-mannered and good-tempered, had inherited a spark of the Queen's hot temper; and when it was aroused—though it rarely was—it could be alarming.

Lord Charles knew that he had no alternative but to carry the challenge to Churchill.

When he received it Lord Randolph replied that it was absurd. He could not of course accept the challenge. At the same time he had no intention of changing his course of action. If there were divorce proceedings the letters the Prince of Wales had written to Lady Aylesford would be published.

The Queen of course had been informed. As usual when the family was in real trouble she stood firmly behind it. Bertie was the victim of unscrupulous people, she said.

Mr Disraeli was naturally her great comfort.

"Bertie assures me," she told him, "that the letters are innocent."

"I am sure they are, M'am, but the wrong construction can be put on innocent matters, and people are inclined to believe the worst. His Highness is quite right not to attempt to interfere in Lord Aylesford's private affairs."

"I shall let the Prince know that *I* believe he has acted rightly, by not allowing this man Churchill to blackmail him—for that's what it is."

"That's what it is, M'am," agreed Disraeli.

"Perhaps he should delay his return until the unfortunate affair has blown over."

Disraeli thought that if Aylesford decided to divorce his wife it might be a long time before it blew over; and although it was not right for the Prince to persuade Lord Aylesford not to take divorce proceedings, it might be suitable for someone to do so other than the Prince.

The Queen waited for Disraeli to suggest a name.

"The Earl of Hardwicke could I think be very persuasive."

The Queen smiled. She could trust her Prime Minister to do everything that was possible.

When Disraeli explained to Lord Hardwicke how important the Aylesford affair was to the Prince of Wales, Hardwicke promised to do his utmost to persuade Aylesford that to continue with the divorce would mean the loss of the Prince's favour.

The Queen wrote to Bertie that dear Mr Disraeli was dealing with the matter so that he could be assured that the affair was in the best possible hands.

Bertie, however, did not like Disraeli. The Prime Minister was one of those clever fellows, erudite as Bertie could never be, of a literary turn of mind, making constant allusions to classics of which Bertie—who rarely opened a book—was ignorant. Bertie felt he had more in common, oddly enough, with Mr Gladstone.

And now, he supposed, Disraeli was smiling to himself at the thought of the Prince in another scrape.

On his journey home he had heard that the Queen had been proclaimed Empress of India and he considered it a great slight that he had had to discover this through newspapers when he would have thought it would have been the duty of the Cabinet to inform the Prince of Wales before making the news public.

Disraeli had need of all his clever diplomacy to placate the Prince on this issue; and he worked persistently on the Earl of Hardwicke.

Bertie's feelings on nearing home were apprehensive. He had to face his wife and his mother; strangely enough it was meeting with Alix which alarmed him most.

He wrote to her that he wanted to see her before he saw anyone else and he wanted to see her alone. He *must* talk to her.

Several members of the royal family had gone to Portsmouth to meet him and Alix arranged that they should all stay behind while she went out and boarded the yacht as it lay off the Needles.

She was greeted fervently by Bertie. He had forgotten how beautiful she was, he told her; he wanted her to know how he had missed her; it was wonderful to be home.

He embraced her almost furtively while he wondered how much she knew about the Aylesford affair.

Alix was so delighted to see him that she could not hide her joy.

"Bertie, it has been so long! The children are almost wild with joy. They wanted to come out with me but you said come alone."

"Yes, Alix. It's this fellow Churchill. I'll swear I'll never speak to him again. I challenged him to a duel, I was so angry. Making insinuations about me. All the time I was thinking of you. I am accustomed to having lies told about me. It's the effect it has on *you* that bothers me. That scoundrel came to see you . . . talking the most ridiculous nonsense."

Alix sighed, then she was smiling happily. It was so comforting to believe it was nonsense. So she did not ask Bertie the questions he so clearly did not wish to be asked. She could not have this reunion spoiled for anything in the world.

The children were so excited when they went ashore. They jumped all round him, demanding stories about tigers and elephants.

"Later, later!" cried Bertie, beaming *bonhomie* and happiness. How could anyone have wanted to make him anxious when there was so much in life that he enjoyed!

Shortly after his return the Earl of Hardwicke was able to report to the Prime Minister that Lord Aylesford had decided not to divorce his wife. Everyone was relieved—the Prince of Wales more than anyone else. But he refused to receive Randolph Churchill; and as the latter could not be invited to any gathering which the Prince honoured with his presence, and as only such gatherings were considered worth attending, Randolph and his beautiful wife were outcasts.

She was an American so they decided to travel in America for a while; but the Queen did not think this was enough and because the affair had to some extent become public knowledge, it seemed necessary that Churchill should offer a formal apology to the Prince of Wales.

Although the Prince accepted the apology he made it clear, when the Churchills returned to England, that he had no desire for their company.

"The Kiss of Death"

Mr Gladstone was making himself a nuisance to the government. But then didn't opposition leaders always criticize those who were in power? The Queen would have thought Mr Gladstone would have had more *principle*; it would have been *some* compensation for his lack of charm. Mr Disraeli, on whom she was relying more and more, and who never failed to amuse and please her however awkward the matter with which they had to deal, cared passionately for the prestige of England and was determined not only to maintain but increase it. How proud he had been when he had had her proclaimed Empress of India. "Victoria Regina et Imperatrix," he had announced, making her a sweeping bow; and she could not have been more delighted than he was.

"How my Mary Anne would have rejoiced in this day," he told her lugubriously; and they both shed tears for their dear departed.

She stood firmly beside Mr Disraeli in all his endeavours. She had told him that she was worried about him.

"You are no longer a young man," she told him severely, "and I am *very* concerned about your health."

"Dear Madam," he cried, "you are not going to suggest that I retire?"

"That is the very thing which I am anxious to avoid. But

leading the House of Commons is too much for you and I am sure Mary Anne would have agreed with me when I say that I do not wish you to do so any longer. So I am offering you a peerage. I am sure the Earl of Beaconsfield will continue to serve me for many more years from the House of Lords than would have been possible in the Commons."

He was elated yet melancholy. Here he was at the very pinnacle of success. Not even in his wildest dreams could he have visualized a greater glory. He was the Queen's dearest friend and although he referred to her now and then to his intimates as "The Faery" in a rather mocking mood, he loved her. Not in the romantic, tender way in which Melbourne had loved the young girl; but with a great affection tinged with irony; he stood back and laughed at himself—a very old man with dyed hair and touched-up complexion pretending to be a gallant admirer of a plump though still graceful mother of nine, never beautiful, now very plain, scorning as she did all adjuncts to beauty, in her widow's garb to which she persistently clung. She was the only person in the world who was important to him. He came home to the house where Mary Anne used to wait for him and he thought of recounting to her his conversation with the Queen; how delighted she would have been. "But with Mary Anne gone," he said to one friend, "I am dead . . . dead though in the Elysian fields."

What a prop Lord Beaconsfield was in the troubles that followed! thought the Queen. He reminded her of Lord Palmerston in his political outlook—*not* in any other way, of course; she had never liked Lord Palmerston. There was trouble between Turkey and Russia as there had been in the days of that most unsatisfactory Crimean War when Palmerston had acted so promptly. Lord Beaconsfield wanted to protect Turkey from Russia; Mr Gladstone was against English help to Turkey and indeed he did all he could to embarrass Lord Beaconsfield and the government. There was a point when the country was on the brink of war with Russia for Lord Beaconsfield had assured her that on no account must Russia get a hold on the Baltic ports; how magnificently he had extricated the country from that affair and brought about, as he said so succinctly, "Peace with honour."

She was so relieved. She hated war; she could never forget the suffering endured by the poor soldiers and in the end it almost always turned out to have been so unnecessary. In addition, there was also the family conflict—Alix's sister Dagmar being Russian now through her marriage. How very awkward it would have been for the two sisters if there had been war between the countries into which they had married. And Alix was so fiercely loyal to her family—which was right of course, but when one married one's family was one's husband's. People who were not royal were fortunate never to have to face problems like that.

The family brought her constant anxiety, but she was beginning to think that her children had not turned out so badly. She was growing a little fonder of Bertie who had such a good nature and was so eager to please; he was frivolous and she supposed in his pursuit of women rather wicked but now that memories of Albert were fading a little—although she did not care to admit this and now and then tried to convince herself that this was not so—she had begun to take rather a lenient view of Bertie's peccadilloes. Alfred she would not easily forgive for behaving so rudely to faithful Brown and calling him a servant to his face; poor Alice was not well; the dear child seemed to have troubles and Louis was rather a weak man. Leopold was a constant anxiety because of his weakness through that disease which she was discovering was in the family. Some of the boys seemed to have it although the girls eluded it. She was terrified that Leopold would one day bleed to death. Arthur was a very good young man—more like Albert than any of them; he did not seem to get into those scrapes which her other sons seemed to find irresistible—strange as it was in the sons of Albert. She trusted Louise was happy with Lorne, but she was not sure; however they all had their own lives to lead and she herself was very busy with her own. Fortunately she had her dear Lord Beaconsfield to assist her in public life and faithful Brown in private; so she was really quite fortunate.

And when Vicky wrote to her about the behaviour of her eldest son Wilhelm, she realized that she was indeed lucky. Wilhelm was turning out to be a very arrogant young man. She had always suspected that arrogance was his besetting sin; she remembered how he had wanted the place of honour in the pony carriage and how he had driven about at Balmoral and Osborne as though he were the Sovereign.

He always signed himself in family letters as Wilhelm Prince of Prussia, which since his father never signed himself Prince, seemed strange. Willhelm was more like his grandfather and of course he had been brought up in the shadow of Bismarck.

What hurt Vicky more than anything was that he seemed to have taken a dislike to her and the reason was that she was English. Wilhelm hated the English; he could not bear that England was of more importance in the world than the new German Empire; he dreamed grand dreams fostered by Bismarck. Vicky wrote to her mother that he would allow people to talk in a disrespectful manner about her and instead of reproving them sniggered with them.

"That is quite shocking," replied the Queen. "I cannot imagine what Dearest Papa would say if he could know of it. And to think that Wilhelm was his first and favourite grandchild. I suppose it is due to that arm of his. What a tragedy."

Then Arthur became engaged to Princess Louise Margaret of Prussia. This was rather a shock because the Queen had never thought of Arthur's marrying. There had seemed to be no need for him to hurry into marriage or indeed to marry at all. He was so good that it was clear he could live quite happily without women—unlike his brothers. So why marry? and if he must, why not wait until a more suitable bride could be chosen? But when she saw the bride she was enchanted by her looks, and susceptible as she was to beauty she immediately forgot her misgivings.

Alice was the one who caused her the greatest concern. The Queen imperiously told Alice that she, with Louis and the children, must take a holiday and there could be nowhere more beneficial than a seaside holiday in England. They should all go to Eastbourne for a few weeks and the sea air and sunshine would do them a world of good. She remembered how much good it had always done to her.

So Alice and her family went to Eastbourne and when they visited the Queen she was still concerned about Alice's health. Alice was so devoted to her family; she was always engaged in good works. Alice and Arthur were the two who took most after their father.

The Queen lectured Alice on taking greater care of her health and spoke sternly to Louis. Alice had always taken her duties seriously. She was the one who had nursed her dearest Papa and later Bertie; and had worked so hard during the dreadful Franco-Prussian war. She was so clever; she had translated into German some of Octavia Hill's essays about the London poor; and her reason for doing so was that she hoped the German authorities might take some notice of what had been done in London to alleviate suffering and follow the example in Germany.

Dear Alice! Yes, she and Arthur were the good ones, and apt to be overlooked when compared with the more forceful Vicky and gay and fascinating Bertie.

The sad season was approaching. December must always be a month of mourning, when she shut herself away with her journals and went over her past life, reading what she had written at the time and trying to recapture some of that rapture which she assured herself living with Albert had been. It was so long ago. Seventeen years ago since that dreadful December day when she had sat by his bed and known that he had left her for ever.

November came and with it a telegram from Alice to say that her daughter Victoria had caught diphtheria and was very ill.

The Queen was disturbed; she immediately wrote pages of advice to Alice. She must *not* wear herself out with nursing. She knew her daughter and she, the Queen, was not pleased with the wan looks which she had noticed during the summer. The Queen implored, no commanded, Alice to take great care and as diphtheria was catching, she must not expose herself to infection.

After the tragic death of the child who had fallen from the window, Alice had only six children left—five daughters and one son. There was Victoria, who had diphtheria; Alice known as Alicky, Irene, Ella and baby May; Ernie was now the only son.

Every day the Queen waited impatiently for news; she found it difficult to concentrate on anything else. How she wished the family were still in England for she was certain that with dear Jenner at hand they would have been much safer.

The telegrams came and the news was not good. Alice's husband, Duke Louis, had caught it; Alicky had it; in a very short time all of the family with the exception of Alice had succumbed to the terrible disease.

What could she do? Did Mama think that she would stand by and see her family ill? She was certainly going to nurse them.

"The doctors have told me that I must be careful and of course I will. I must on no account kiss them or embrace them."

"My dearest child," wrote the Queen, "I beg of you take the greatest care of yourself."

Poor Alice! She was doomed to be a martyr. It had always

been the same in the nursery. Vicky had bullied her; even Bertie who had championed her had occasionally teased her, but she had always taken it stoically and without protest, never telling tales.

Five-year-old May, the baby and pet of the household, was now dangerously ill.

"How I wish that I could be there with her," said the Queen.

It was terrible when little May had died. But there was worse to come. They were a devoted family and the death of baby May shocked them all and filled them with grief. They were all sick, with the exception of Alice, who had miraculously kept free of the dreaded disease.

When she had looked at that small beloved face and known that her youngest child was dead she had stared speechlessly before her. How could she tell them what had happened, they who were so sick themselves?

But the truth could not be kept from them. "Baby is dead." The news seeped out, a terrible melancholy fell upon the palace.

Ernie, who had loved his baby sister dearly and was himself very ill with the disease which had killed her, was nearly demented with grief.

"It is not true, Mama," he said. "Tell me it is not true."

Alice could say nothing. She could only gaze sorrowfully at her son.

"She is dead . . . ? Baby May dead . . . ?" he cried.

"She is suffering no more, Ernie, my darling."

"Dead!" said Ernie blankly. Then he looked up at his mother. "Am I going to die, Mama? Are we all going to die?"

He had flung himself into her arms and what could she do, but hold him against her. She kissed him; she tried to comfort him.

"I am here, my son, Mama is here to nurse you, so you will get well."

He held up his face to hers. How could she refuse to kiss her own son at such a moment?

Alice had caught the infection. When the Queen heard this news she was alarmed.

She sent for Bertie and Alix. "She looked so frail when she was here in the summer. I warned her. I should have commanded her to come here. That house of sickness was no place for her."

"She wouldn't have come, Mama," pointed out Alix.

"I trust my daughter would have obeyed me."

Alix shook her head. "She would never have left her family."

The Queen was silent; then she said suddenly: "Do you know what the date is?" And she began to shiver.

"Why, Mama," said Bertie, "it is the twelfth of December."

"In two days' time," she said, "it. will be the fourteenth—the anniversary of your father's death. It was on the fourteenth of December that we feared so for you, Bertie. Your crisis came then when we had all but given you up. And in two days' time it will be the fourteenth again and Alice lies close to death."

"Mama, it can't be. How could it be?" said Bertie.

But the Queen was sure. There was something malignant for her about the 14th of December. That day had been the most wretched of her life; on it she had lost the Beloved Being; life had ended for her on that day, she had often said. And wasn't it true that on the 14th she had nearly lost her eldest son? A miracle had happened then. And now . . . Alice!

"Mama," said Bertie, very tender as he knew how to be on such occasions, "a miracle will happen again."

The Queen sat in her room, praying, waiting for the miracle. She read her journals of that dreadful day seventeen years ago—the first hateful 14th of December. She had sat by his bedside, refusing to believe it; turning away from the blank misery which opened at her feet like a deep yawning pit.

"Please, God," she prayed, "please, *Albert*, you saved Bertie. Leave me Alice."

On the 13th there was no news from Hesse Darmstadt. The Queen went to the Blue Room in which Albert had died and she lived it all again and instead of that dearly beloved face on the pillows she saw that of Alice.

She had looked so ill even in the summer after the good air of Eastbourne. How would she have the strength to get through the illness? Only a miracle could save her. There *must* be a miracle.

She could not sleep that night. She kept saying: "Tomorrow will be the fourteenth." She could not stay in bed. She knelt by the bed in the Blue Room and prayed.

She must make a pretence of eating breakfast. Brown would scold her if she did not.

Brown came to her holding a telegram.

She snatched it.

"I see by your face it's nae good news," he grumbled and even at such a time she noticed the deep concern on his good honest face.

"Ye'll be ill yerself, woman," he said, "if you don't give over grieving. Let me get you a cup of tea."

And he got her what he called his special tea and in spite of everything she remembered how she had once complimented him on the best tea she had ever tasted. It was during one of their trips when they had boiled the water by the wayside. "It should be good," he had said with a grin, "it's laced wi' good Scotch whisky."

And that was the sort of tea that Brown always made for her.

He made it now and she drank and felt a little comforted. But not for long.

There was another telegram.

At half past seven on the 14th of December, the seventeenth anniversary of her father's passing, Alice had died.

The Queen called the family together and told them the terrible news. Leopold sobbed unashamedly, so did Alix, who could never bear tragedy in the family. Poor Bertie was heartbroken; Alice had always been a special favourite of his.

The story of how she had caught the infection was told and the Queen said how typical it was of her. Alice had always sacrificed herself.

How comforting was Lord Beaconsfield who lost no time in hurrying to the Queen to offer his condolences. They wept together and she told him of the virtues of Alice, so very much her father's daughter. They had shared that quality of saintliness, so rare in human beings. And they had both died young.

"Alas, it is often so," said Lord Beaconsfield.

"But fortunately not always," she assured him, gazing up into his wrinkled old face.

The speech he made in the House of Lords was so touching that she had a copy of it sent to her that she might read it again and again.

"My lords, there is something wonderfully piteous in the immediate cause of her death. The physicians who permitted her to watch over her suffering family enjoined her under no circumstances to be tempted into an embrace. Her admirable self-constraint guarded her through the crisis of this terrible complaint into safety . . . She remembered and observed the injunctions of her physicians. But it became her lot to break to her son, quite a youth, the death of his youngest sister, to whom he was devotedly attached. The boy was so overcome with misery that the agitated mother clasped him in her arms, and thus she received the kiss of death."

"How beautiful," said the Queen. "Only Lord Beaconsfield could write so movingly."

She thanked him and they talked at great length about the strangeness of the date. Lord Beaconsfield felt that there was some hand of fate in it. The Prince Consort, he was sure, was watching over her.

"I like to believe that," she told him.

"You may be assured of it, Madam."

"As Mary Anne is watching over you."

He nodded solemnly. "He left you the Prince of Wales," he went on. "He escaped the fateful day; but for some reason the Princess Alice was taken from you."

"She is so young to die," protested the Queen.

"As that beloved saint her father was."

"And on the same day," said the Queen in an awed whisper.

"The fourteenth of December," murmured Lord Beaconsfield.

The Queen held out her hand to him; he took it and kissed it.

"You are a great comfort to me, Lord Beaconsfield," she told him.

"Life will only be important to me," he said earnestly, "while I can be so."

Dear Lord Beaconsfield! When the time came she would send a very special message with the primroses which always went to him from Osborne—the first of the season, picked by her own hands.

She would never forget that beautiful speech of his about the kiss of death.

"His Favourite Flower"

The Queen tried not to brood on the death of Alice. She died as she would have wished, she said, serving her family. It was what one would have expected of Alice.

Lord Beaconsfield suggested that Lord Lorne would be a good Governor-General of Canada which would mean that he and Louise would leave the country. She was a little dubious. She had just lost one daughter to death and she did not like to think of another being so far away; but that was the fate of royal children. Daughters were always taken from their parents.

There was a great deal in the country's affairs to cause her anxiety. A war had broken out with the Zulu rising; and the Prince Imperial, son of the widowed Empress Eugénie, was slain in a very distressing way—he was hacked to pieces by the knives of savages. She hated war but Lord Beaconsfield pointed out that it was impossible to maintain a position as the leading world power possessed of an Indian Empire and colonies without being continually engaged in minor wars of this nature.

She saw the point of that and Lord Beaconsfield had made her fully aware of the growing Empire. Victoria Regina et Imperatrix was not mistress of a small state, she must remember; she was the mighty Queen and Empress who ruled a large proportion of the world. Lord Beaconsfield would like to see those boundaries grow wider and of course he was right.

"I plan to see you at the head of the European community," he told her. "It is absolutely necessary to the peace and well-being of the world that you should be."

Unfortunately Mr Gladstone was of the opposite view. He went about the country preaching peace. "Peace at any price," said the Queen. "Really, men like Mr Gladstone are *dangerous*."

What she did not realize was that Mr Gladstone's policies were winning approval and that since Mr Disraeli had become Lord Beaconsfield, his ministry had been considerably weakened.

No one was more aware of this than Lord Beaconsfield. He was old and tired and far from well, and decided that he could only carry on with an increased majority. He decided therefore to go to the polls.

The Queen felt that she must visit Alice's stricken family and left for Hesse Darmstadt. Two of her granddaughters, Victoria and Ella, miraculously recovered from diphtheria, were to be confirmed and she wished to attend the ceremony.

How very sad it was to be greeted by the children in their deep mourning and the sadness in their faces. Poor motherless children! They only had Louis now, and he had never been a strong man.

She wanted to hear in detail an account of Alice's passing and the children took her to the room in which their mother had died.

"It is exactly the same as when she occupied it, Grandmama," said Ella. "We are going to keep it thus."

"I am glad," said the Queen. "Your dear grandpapa's room is just as it was when he died in it although that is a very long time ago—it will soon be twenty years since he left me desolate and you children without the guidance of the best man in the world. Why, your mama and papa were married after his death . . . very shortly after. It was the saddest wedding I ever attended."

The children looked suitably solemn and many tears were shed talking of their mother.

She continued to indulge in memories of the past and talked constantly of the saintly grandfather the children had never known. They could understand now that they had personal experience of the loss of a dear one.

When the results of the election were telegraphed to her she received a great shock. It could not be. This was a mighty defeat. The government had been trounced at the polls and the Liberal and Home Rule party had a majority of 166 over the Tories.

"It is absolutely incredible," cried the Queen. "Has the country gone mad!"

She realized what this would mean—the loss of her Prime Minister. Her dear friend and comforter would be taken from her, because the new Prime Minister would never allow her to be constantly in the company of the Leader of the Opposition.

"*My* government defeated," she mourned, "and what will replace it?" She set her lips obstinately together. "One thing I shall not accept. I would abdicate rather than accept Mr Gladstone as my Prime Minister."

Her secretary, Sir Henry Ponsonby, tried to put the case as tactfully as he could. It seemed almost inevitable that Gladstone would be the next Prime Minister. It was unfortunate that the Queen should so dislike him; but she had learned before that the will of the people would have to be obeyed.

Abdication, said the Queen, seemed the only answer. How could she possibly work with that man?

There were other possibilities, Sir Henry suggested. There was Hartington; there was Lord Granville.

"I don't like either of them," she said. "Granville has worked against my wishes. As for Hartington, he has been far too friendly with the Prince of Wales—one of the Prince's friends whom I would rather he did not see so frequently. The whole world knows of his liaison with the Duchess of Manchester and do you think that is a pleasant way for a Prime Minister to behave? There have been other rumours about him too. Wasn't he at one time enamoured of a creature called Skittles?"

Sir Henry remarked that quite a number of gentlemen had been enamoured of that lady.

She knew that he was referring to Bertie, who had been one of the woman's admirers. A very good-looking creature by all accounts, and Hartington had left the Duchess of Manchester for her but had returned to the Duchess when he had tired of the Skittles person. It really was rather disreputable.

There was nothing to be done but to return home immediately where at least she could see Lord Beaconsfield. He looked so pale and melancholy that she felt the need to comfort him. "*Dear* Lord Beaconsfield, this is my tragedy as well as yours," she told him.

He kissed her hand; there was sad longing in his eyes. He knew this was farewell to The Faery.

She talked of Mr Gladstone. "I would rather abdicate than accept him," she declared.

"*Dear* Madam," said Lord Beaconsfield, tenderly reproachful. Then he advised her to send for Hartington. After all Gladstone had resigned the party leadership some time ago so she need not send for him. If she could reconcile herself to Harty Tarty she might give him a trial.

"Such a ridiculous name! How could any man be serious with a name like that? He is a most immoral man too with his Skittles and his irregular union with the Manchester woman!"

To cheer her Lord Beaconsfield told her how Skittles had acquired her name; she had quarrelled with some soldiers and had threatened to knock them down like a row of skittles. "Only, of course, her language was such that I would not care to repeat to Your Majesty."

"And this is a woman with whom our would-be Prime Minister's name has been linked!"

"His Highness the Prince of Wales once carried out a practical joke on Hartington. I am sure Your Majesty would be amused to hear of it. The Prince and Princess were visiting Coventry (Hartington was in his suite) and the Prince had asked that when they toured the town they should be taken to a bowling alley. When they reached the alley the Mayor invited Hartington to show his skill. Hartington said he had no idea what had to be done at which the Mayor exclaimed: 'But His Royal Highness was insistent that you should be brought here as a tribute to your Lordship's love of skittles.' The joke has been repeated up and down the country."

The Queen could not repress a smile. She and Albert had been very fond of practical jokes, and Bertie had inherited their love of them. It was rather funny—though not the sort of joke that should be played out on a future Prime Minister.

Then she was melancholy thinking how pleasant it was chatting with dear Lord Beaconsfield and how he reminded her of long ago when Lord Melbourne had been her Prime Minister—and what was more important, her friend.

How could she ever feel friendship towards the ridiculous Harty Tarty, Granville (who had been given the equally ridiculous name of Puss) or worst of all Mr Gladstone, to whom no one could give a frivolous name but Gladdy—which was meant of course to be ironical.

* * *

She sent for Hartington; she sent for Granville. They could not take office, they explained. There was one man the people wanted. They called him The People's William. They referred to Mr Gladstone.

She dismissed them; she brooded. Oh, if only Albert were here to guide her! She remembered the Bedchamber Affair before her marriage when she was a very young and inexperienced Queen.

She knew what was coming. A Queen must bow to the will of the people and the people wanted Gladstone.

She must do her duty. She could, of course, abdicate, she had threatened it often, but in her heart she knew she never would, so she sent for Mr Gladstone.

He took her hand and kissed it; she turned away that she might not look at him while this act, so necessary to etiquette, so repulsive to her personal feelings, was performed.

She noticed that he looked haggard. She was certainly not going to ask him to sit down. She addressed him coldly; there was a distant look in her eyes, when he talked, as though she were not listening; and all the time she was thinking: He defeated *my* government. They have taken Lord Beaconsfield from me and given me this man.

How she missed Lord Beaconsfield! She was anxious about him too because she knew that he was not well. She talked to John Brown about the excellence of that man and how different he was from the People's William.

"Aye," said Brown, "it's been a fight between the Queen's Benny and the People's Willy."

How quaintly he expressed himself; she could not help smiling; so he said he would make her a cup of tea with a dash of whisky in it to keep up her spirits.

That spring she picked primroses at Osborne and sent them to Lord Beaconsfield. What charming letters he wrote to her. He expressed his sentiments so graciously. Again how different from Mr Gladstone!

It was rather a shock to discover that Sir Charles Dilke had been given a post in the government—that radical who had thundered away declaring that a Republic would be better for the country than a Monarchy, and had tried to make enquiries into the manner in which her income was spent.

It was quite humiliating. Strangest of all Dilke had struck

up a friendship with Bertie. Didn't Bertie realize that the man was an enemy of Royalty? She remonstrated with Bertie.

"He is an extremely clever man, Mama. He's very witty and has a wonderful flow of language when expressing himself that it's quite a joy to listen to him."

"This man," she said, "has insulted *me*!"

"He's Under-Secretary for Foreign Affairs in Your Majesty's government."

"What can one expect with Mr Gladstone in charge?"

"Well, Mama, if he is a radical it is as well for me to find out what he is thinking."

"I do not care to see him entertained too frequently at Marlborough House," said the Queen.

"Not really frequently," said Bertie, "only now and then; and since you live so aloof, it is necessary for me to meet these people."

Bertie was right in a way; and of course he had a way with him which Lord Beaconsfield had admired.

All the same, she implied that she did not like this friendship with Sir Charles Dilke.

"Ah, Mama," said Bertie, sadly, "I fear there are several of my friends whom you do not like."

"A fact which a dutiful son should surely try to rectify."

"Indeed yes, Mama, but I wish to take unpleasant burdens from your shoulders and entertain those who are offensive to you."

She bowed her head. There was a good deal in what Bertie said.

The winter had been more than usually cold, and Lord Beaconsfield felt far from well. He went down to Hughenden and tried the quiet life to see if his health would improve; but everywhere were reminders of happy days spent there with Mary Anne and his melancholy increased. He was not meant to lead the quiet country life. He was lonely and bored and even his books could not hold his attention; his thoughts kept straying into the past.

He came back to London. It was March and the winds were icy; he caught a bad chill and took to his bed.

He felt old and feeble and since the death of Mary Anne the zest of life had gone. As he lay in his bed in the house in Curzon Street his mind drifted back to the past and he thought of those nights when he had come home from the House of Commons to find Mary Anne waiting for him with cold chicken and champagne. He could see himself leaning towards her talking earnestly about the success or the failure of the day; and he could see her eyes eternally young while they glowed with love for him.

A messenger came to the house bringing primroses from Osborne. The Queen had heard that he was indisposed and was anxious.

He wrote thanking her for her concern. He drew great pleasure from the primroses.

She wired every day from Windsor asking how he was.

"Dear Lord Beaconsfield," she said to Brown, "I fear his end is near."

And she shut herself away in the Blue Room where Albert had breathed his last; she thought of the terrible day which would live for ever in her mind; and she wept bitterly for she knew that she was about to lose a very dear friend.

April had come. He knew he was dying. It was time, he told himself. He had no more use for life. He had climbed to the very highest pinnacle. No one would have believed that the young Jew who had struggled so hard to make a living from his writing would have become Prime Minister, a peer, and the beloved friend of the Queen.

He had not left the house in Curzon Street for three weeks now, and he knew he never would again. It was gratifying to learn that in the streets people spoke his name in hushed whispers and asked each other how he was today.

"Getting so close to the grave," he murmured. "Soon I shall be lying beside Mary Anne."

His secretary came to his bedside.

"Her Majesty would be pleased to come to see you if you were to ask," he was told.

He shook his head. "I am in no shape to receive Her Majesty. Besides," he added wryly, "she would ask me to take a message to Albert." He sighed. "I'd rather live," he said, "but I'm not afraid to die."

Then he lay back, closed his eyes and did so.

The Queen wept. It was so sad. She could not imagine what it would be like without dear Lord Beaconsfield to come and talk to her. He was always so witty, so amusing and so respectful and affectionate. How she missed this in her present ministers.

"His devotion to me, his wise counsels, his gentleness combined with firmness, his one thought of the honour and glory of the country make the death of my dear Lord Beaconsfield a national calamity," she said.

Mr Gladstone suggested that Lord Beaconsfield should be given a public funeral and be buried in Westminster Abbey. The Queen said this would please her and she thought it right and fitting. But she learned later that Beaconsfield had asked to be buried in the little church at Hughenden beside his wife, Mary Anne.

"How characteristic," said the Queen with tears in her eyes.

So Lord Beaconsfield was buried in Hughenden churchyard. The Prince of Wales, representing the Queen, attended the funeral and a wreath of primroses was laid on his coffin and on this was attached a message written in the Queen's hand: "His favourite flower."

The Jersey Lily

Prince Leopold was in love. He had met the most enchant-ing creature. He had never seen anyone quite so beautiful and a number of other people agreed with him; in fact he was only one of her admirers. She was the daughter of the Dean of Jersey and in her teens she had fascinated a widower, Mr. Langtry, who came to the island in his yacht. He had urged her to marry him which she did and thus she came to London.

Mr Langtry was comfortably situated but not rich and

when he brought his bride to London they lived quietly and did not move into society until one day at a museum they encountered a nobleman whom they had met when he had been in Jersey. He was so struck by the girl's beauty that he asked her to a party at his London house. That was all that was needed.

Lillie Langtry's beauty was so outstanding that no one could fail to notice her. People were soon talking of her, inviting her to their houses, calling her the Jersey Lily; she was photographed everywhere; artists sketched her; when she walked in the park she was recognized; everyone seemed to be talking about Lillie Langtry.

She had hosts of admirers, among them Prince Leopold. Leopold was different from his brothers. In the first place he was a victim of that dreaded disease which dogged certain male members of the royal family. All his life Leopold had been watched carefully; he must never be allowed to fall or cut himself lest he should begin to bleed. This could be fatal or at best mean a serious illness with a spell in bed and the doctors in attendance. Unable to play games, Leopold was more intellectually inclined than his brothers. He was a great reader, well acquainted with the works of Shakespeare and Sir Walter Scott. At Oxford he had attended lectures on history, poetry and music; he had also studied modern languages.

He was inclined to be more rebellious and less afraid of the Queen than his brothers for as the invalid of the family he had been treated more gently. The Queen always questioned him in detail as to his health and did not like him to over-exert himself. It had been a very anxious time when he had almost died of the typhoid fever which had been responsible for his father's death. He was a very good speaker; took an interest in social matters and had been elected President of the Royal Society of Arts.

"Leopold," the Queen was fond of saying, "has inherited his father's brains." But ever present in her mind was the memory of the time when he had one haemorrhage after another and they had all thought he would die. Ever since, the Queen had wanted him sheltered; she would have preferred to keep him near her. Bertie, however, said that it wasn't good for him to be over-protected and Leopold agreed with Bertie. He wanted to live even if it meant doing so for a shorter period than he could expect shut up like a prize orchid in a hothouse.

So the Queen had given way; in fact Leopold was not one to have it otherwise; he had always been wilful; and one did not wish to upset him for if he grew over-excited he could bring on one of those dreaded haemorrhages.

So Leopold led a normal life and so it was that he met Lillie Langtry.

"What a fantastic creature!" he cried. He was sure he had never seen any beauty to compare with hers. Her figure was perfect; her bone structure was divine; her golden hair was abundant and curled delightfully about her enchanting Grecian-type face.

Leopold joined her suitors. Mr Langtry, a somewhat ineffective man whose great interest was sailing, suddenly realized what a treasure he had married and was naturally a little bewildered by all the fuss which was made of his wife. As for Lillie, accustomed to the quiet island life, she was dazzled by the invitations and offers which poured in. Every day she was at some social function. If she had not the adequate clothes what did it matter? She could attend as someone poetically put it, clothed in her beauty with which no court dressmaker could hope to compete. In a simple black dress she was overwhelmingly lovely; her golden hair and sparkling eyes outdid all the diamonds and emeralds and rubies.

Leopold acquired a sketch of her and hung it over his bed and the Prince of Wales returning from Sandringham, called on his brother, saw the picture, and wanted to know who the beauty was.

"Lillie Langtry," said Leopold. "The most beautiful woman in London . . . I'd venture to say in the world."

Bertie's practised eye regarded the sketch. "The sketch makes her charming."

"A poor reflection on the reality," said Leopold.

"I must meet your paragon."

Leopold groaned. "That's the end of my hopes," he said.

The Queen visiting Leopold saw the picture of Lillie over his bed.

"And whom does that represent?" she wanted to know.

"That's the famous Jersey Lily, Mama."

"And why have you hung it over your bed?"

"Well, it is rather charming, don't you think?"

"Leopold, you know how anxious I get about you. I think it would be most dangerous for you to be . . . er . . . become friendly with women."

"Well, Mama, I do have a certain number of female friends."

The Queen frowned. "You have to consider your health, Leopold. It was always a great anxiety to me and to your dearest papa. I should not like you to hazard it in any way."

With that she drew up a chair, stood on it and removed the picture. Leopold watched her with a smile. It was too charming a face depicted there for the Queen to destroy. She was always so susceptible to beauty.

She rose, taking the sketch with her. "You must take care of your health, Leopold, and you will not do so if you squander it dallying with women."

Leopold tried to hide his smile. Really, Mama was a little old-fashioned and life with sainted Papa had made her very prim.

She need not have worried about him and Lillie. Bertie had come into the field and no one could really succeed when Bertie was there.

Now Lillie's name was being universally coupled with that of the Prince of Wales. Bertie was enchanted by the delightful creature and people who wished to please the Prince must invite Lillie to their houses.

Alix was hurt but as usual hid her feelings; she appeared in public with Bertie, smiling and gracious, and he, as ever, made sure that she was accorded due homage. In Alix's presence Bertie always made sure that he behaved as a faithful husband; if the lady he was pursuing were present at such times she would be ignored.

At least, thought Alix, I can be grateful for that. There was one rule from which Bertie was never diverted, however infatuated he might be. This was the almost divine right of royalty. He liked to be on familiar terms with his chosen companions and to play practical jokes on them. When they were told the soup was cold and took a mouthful of almost boiling liquid and burned their mouths, he thought that great fun; when soap was mixed with cheese and someone ate it, that was very amusing. What was not fun was when the Prince of Wales was expected to be the victim of the kind of so-called jokes he liked to see worked out on others. He never forgot his royal dignity—nor that of any member of his family.

Dignity must be preserved at all times. Now that he was putting on weight—and this was to be deplored because he was not tall and the effect was to give him a square look—some of his friends referred to him as "Tum Tum"—but never to his face except on one occasion. Late one night his great crony, Sir Frederick Johnstone, who had been cited as co-respondent in the Mordaunt case, was playing billiards with the Prince at Sandringham. As Johnstone was drunk and over hilarious, Bertie said to him kindly: "Freddy, you are very drunk." Johnstone, too intoxicated for tact, pointed to Bertie's paunch and retorted: "Tum Tum, you're very fat."

Bertie's notorious temper flared up. It was exactly like the Queen's; fortunately it burnt itself out very quickly but before it did he told one of his attendants to see that Sir Frederick left Sandringham early next morning.

On another occasion, in the excitement of a game of billiards when he had made a bad shot, one of his friends cried out: "Pull yourself together, Wales." Bertie had stared at the speaker and the gleam in his blue eyes was icy.

"Your carriage is at the door," he said; and turned his back.

So wise people quickly learned that, while they must amuse the Prince and be on friendly terms with him, it was for him to set the pace. They must never forget that he was royal, and Alix as his wife was also royal. Royalty must never be slighted even by the most favoured mistress.

Bertie's temper was to be feared, but he was not often vindictive and forgave easily. The longest time he had kept up a grudge was in the case of Lord Randolph over the Aylesford affair; and it was agreed that Lord Randolph had acted in an amazingly impulsive manner then.

Once a waiter serving spinach splashed a little on Bertie's shirt front. Bertie looked down at the mark and the rage in his face was terrible; the waiter trembled while Bertie plunged his hands into the dish saying: "Now I shall ruin it completely!" and rubbed the spinach all over his shirt front. He stamped away to change; but when he came back his good temper was restored and he even had a smile for the waiter. That incident was often repeated; it was so typical of Bertie.

Now he had one object in mind—the pursuit of Lillie Langtry. The fact that he had entered the field meant that all Lillie's other admirers must leave the way clear for him. The Prince of Wales and Lillie were seen riding together in the Row; hostesses sat them side by side at dinner parties; if they wanted the Prince to honour them with his presence, they must invite Lillie too; it was necessary to do homage to Lillie to win the Prince's favour; so they did.

There were photographs of Lillie everywhere; they were sold in the shops and a new set was created which became known as The Professional Beauties. Everything that Lillie wore was copied. If she wore a certain type of hat it became known as the Langtry Hat; the manner in which she did her hair was the Langtry style; the most talked-of person in London was Lillie Langtry.

The Queen, who thought it very unbecoming for women to allow themselves to be photographed and known as Professional Beauties, was nevertheless eager to see this woman who captivated society. That she had won Bertie's admiration was nothing—many had done that—but she had never before known such talk as there was about Mrs Langtry.

She invited her to one of her Drawing Rooms; and when the moment came for Lillie to be presented to her, the Queen held out her hand and appeared not to look at her, but that was a gift of hers; she had seen what she wanted to see. There was an undeniable charm about the woman and one had to admit that she was exceedingly beautiful.

A pity, thought the Queen, that she did not remain faithful to her husband. Mr Langtry thought the same; he remonstrated with his wife; she must give up this social life in London and go with him to Ireland; or they might sail on his yacht back to Jersey. Her extravagance was ruining him and the scandal she created must surely be ruining her.

At this the Jersey Lily wept and stormed. She had no intention of going back. For one thing the Prince of Wales would never allow it.

Mr Langtry did point out that as he was her husband he thought he might have more say in the matter than the Prince of Wales. It was the beginning of the end of the marriage, but Lillie continued to dazzle the Prince.

Unencumbered by a husband whom she ignored more than ever, she found life very agreeable. As for Bertie he was deeply enamoured—far more so than he had been over any of his previous conquests.

Alix suffered in silence while the Jersey Lily flourished, and everywhere Bertie was, she was sure to be.

Leopold, shrugging aside his loss of Lillie to his brother, decided to travel on the Continent for a while. In Frankfurt he met Princess Helen Frederica Augusta, daughter of the

Prince of Waldeck-Pyrmont. She had a strong and interesting personality and Leopold had wanted to marry for a long time, if only to show that he was well enough to indulge in normal activities.

"Leopold marry!" said the Queen when she heard. "But he is not strong enough."

Bertie thought he should be allowed to see if he were strong enough and Leopold was determined not to be wrapped in cotton wool.

"If he could lead an ordinary married life so much the better," said the Queen.

"Give him a chance to try," retorted Bertie.

Leopold was created Duke of Albany and betrothed.

Lillie was for a time like a moth dancing madly about a candle, but when she became pregnant it was necessary to retire from society for a while. Whose was the child? Perhaps the Prince of Wales was the father? Who could be sure?

Everything went wrong at once. Mr Langtry became bankrupt and left Lillie who had ruined him, he declared; there was rumour that Lillie was to be cited in a divorce case; many hostesses who had eagerly welcomed her to their houses no longer did so; and when she walked in the Park they looked the other way.

The Prince of Wales was not in London; and everyone was sure that when he did return Lillie Langtry would have become a distant memory to him—that was if he ever thought of her at all.

Lillie took a small room and stared disaster in the face. Many would say it was the just reward of sin. She had danced in the sun for a while; and now the sun had disappeared, and she was left to face the consequences.

She still had her astounding beauty and if it was impaired, for she was heavily pregnant, once the child was born she would regain it. She would start again. She had always wanted to act; and she was sure that if she could make a name for herself on the stage she would win back all the adulation she had had before even if in not such high places.

She wept a little for Teddy, as she had called him, who had been such a kind and chivalrous lover. It was not only the dignity of his title that appealed; Teddy was a very charming man; she would never have another such lover.

She must live through the next months; she must have her child and then when she was completely recovered see what could be done. She had enough money to carry her through until then.

Her landlady was knocking at the door. There was a visitor to see her. A gentleman.

Lillie stood up hastily and looked at her reflection in the glass.

"You look lovely, my dear," said the landlady; and in fact it was difficult for Lillie in any circumstances to appear otherwise.

"What is his name?"

"He wouldn't give it. He said a friend of yours."

"All right," said Lillie. "Bring him up."

She could scarcely believe it. He stood in the doorway—square, a little squat, the beard hiding the rather weak receding chin.

"Teddy!" she breathed. And then, "Your Highness."

Teddy smiled delightedly, and looking around the room grimaced.

"It's the best I could afford," she told him; "and the landlady is kind."

"My poor Jersey Lily," cried Bertie. "But you're as beautiful as ever."

He drew up a chair to the table and regarded her.

"You should have let me know," he said.

"I'm being cut in society."

"You wouldn't have been if I'd been there." Bertie's blue eyes were quite beautiful when he smiled.

"You know Edward Langtry is bankrupt . . . and everyone blames me. I am to have a child. Hostesses don't want me at their parties now."

"You'll change that," said Bertie.

She was unsure of his attitude; he was not the same passionate lover as he had been; but he was still the staunch friend. Lillie was adventuress enough to adjust her mood to his.

She said quickly: "I'd like to go on the stage. I think I might have a chance. If I could only get a start . . ."

Bertie clapped his hand to his thigh enthusiastically. "Why, Lillie, it's just the thing. You'd be irresistible."

Bertie was excited.

"The difficulty is getting a start," she told him.

"That should not present insurmountable difficulties," beamed Bertie. "You leave this to me."

Bertie left her considerably heartened; and very soon he

was back to see her. He brought with him a friend of his, an actor-manager named Squire Bancroft.

"This fellow controls the Prince of Wales's and the Haymarket theatres," he said. "You two should have a talk."

Bertie had proved himself to be a loyal friend. Of all the people she had known he was the one who had come to her aid; and the manner in which he did it made his help so easy to accept. Bertie was delighted to be of assistance; not only was he giving her an opportunity, he was going to do all in his power to see that she was a success.

An astute businessman such as Squire Bancroft was fully aware that a play featuring Lillie Langtry, the well-known beauty and friend of the Prince of Wales, could not fail to be a success; particularly if the Prince gave his continued support. At a suitable time after the birth of her daughter Lillie went into rehearsal and the following February she appeared in *Ours* which had as its setting the Crimean War. It was a comedy and if Lillie was not a great actress she was a great beauty and London flocked to see her. Moreover the Prince of Wales was in the audience, and it seemed that the play would go on running for a very long time. Offers came from America, and as she became more experienced Lillie began to show a certain talent.

Lilly was happy, going from success to success; and Bertie was extremely gratified. They had ceased to be lovers, but as in the case of many of his mistresses he remained one of her most staunch and loyal friends.

The Queen Left Lonely Once More

The Queen had arrived from London and left the train and stepped into the waiting carriage which was to take her to Windsor Castle. As she sat there waiting for the horses to start up, John Brown suddenly leaped down from the box and putting a white, worried face through the window, said: "A man's just fired at Your Majesty's carriage."

The Queen sat back against the upholstery feeling slightly faint. This was the seventh attempt at assassination. The last time she had been saved by good faithful John Brown. She wondered what had happened this time to avert the hand of death.

She was soon to learn. Two boys from Eton who had watched her arrival had seen the man lift his pistol; one of them had knocked it out of his hand with his umbrella before he could fire it; the other had hit him with his umbrella, clinging to him and holding him until he could be arrested.

The carriage took her off to Windsor where her faithful servants, under the command of John Brown, fussed over her and made her comfortable and insisted on her resting—which made her smile since she was the Queen, yet comforted her to realize what faithful servants she had.

It was all very distressing for the pistol which had been aimed at her had this time been loaded; but the public indignation was so great and there were so many demonstrations of loyalty that it seemed the Queen had never been so popular.

She was touched by all this concern; and when it was proved that the man—a certain Roderick McLean—was mad, she felt that it was worth while being shot at to realize how much her people loved her.

Mr Gladstone arrived, all concern and displaying the humility he never failed to show in her presence but which for some odd reason irritated her, to congratulate her on her escape and to, as she told Brown afterwards, address her as a public meeting as usual.

"It is a great consolation to realize, M'am," said Mr Gladstone, "that whereas rulers of other countries are attacked for political motives, in the case of Your Majesty those who have raised their hands against you have all been lunatics."

Yes, there was some comfort in that. There would always be lunatics and sovereigns would often be the targets of their lunacy, she supposed.

"I should like to show my appreciation to those two brave boys."

"An excellent idea, Your Majesty." "The Grand Old Man" as the people ridiculously called him, was rubbing his hands with glee, she noted. His great aim seemed to be to get her before the public through any reason whatsoever. As if she did not see through him! How different from dear Lord Beaconsfield!

"I could send for the boys," she said.

"Excellent, Your Majesty. It would be even better to honour the school for the bravery of these two. Perhaps if Your Majesty could have the entire school assembled in the quadrangle and address them yourself, telling them of your gratitude and then personally speak to the two brave boys, that would give great pleasure to so many people and public acclaim for such an action would be great."

The idea appealed to her, even though it was Mr Gladstone's; and she decided this was what she would do.

So nine hundred Eton scholars visited Windsor and the two boys received the Queen's personal thanks for their actions.

As for Roderick McLean, he was sent for trial on a charge of High Treason. He was judged not guilty but insane and sent to an asylum "during her Majesty's pleasure."

When the Queen heard the verdict she was indignant.

"Not guilty!" she cried. "A man holds a loaded pistol at his Queen and would have fired if a brave boy had not knocked it out of his hand with his umbrella, and he is not guilty!"

Mr Gladstone explained that this was the law.

"Then," said the Queen with asperity, "it is time the law was altered."

Mr Gladstone pointed out that no alteration in the law could change the future of McLean. He was only fit to be in a lunatic asylum.

"Not Guilty!" cried the Queen. "That is what I object to. Any man can raise his hand against me and plead not guilty even though he has been *seen* to shoot."

Mr Gladstone promised to look into the matter. The Queen felt very strongly that anyone who had attempted to kill her should not get off lightly for fear others would be led to follow the example.

The Queen's ministers saw the reason for the Queen's anxiety; and soon afterwards an Act was passed introducing a new form of verdict for cases like those of Roderick McLean.

The Queen would not allow the assassination attempt to interfere with Leopold's marriage which was due to take place the following month. Mr Gladstone had, she must admit, worked hard to get Parliament to raise Leopold's allowance to £25,000 a year, though there had been the usual dissenters which was so humiliating. Forty-two members had, in a most uncouth manner, voted against it but fortunately it was passed with a majority of 345.

So Leopold was married to Princess Helen, that rather forceful young woman whom the Queen had regarded at first with some horror because she dared to disagree with her formidable mama-in-law, but she was surprised that she found this attitude refreshing and very soon she became fond of the young woman, particularly as she was quite good-looking and she believed that she would be good for Leopold—who was a bit of a rebel himself.

She decided to buy Claremont outright. It had been left her for the duration of her life on the death of her Uncle Leopold, who had lived there with his wife, Princess Charlotte; but she wished it to be entirely hers so that she could give it as a wedding gift to Leopold and his wife.

So on that April day she even went so far as to put on the white wedding veil and the lace she had worn at her own wedding over her black dress to attend the ceremony in St George's Chapel.

There she prayed fervently that marriage would not prove too much for delicate Leopold; but she felt confident that the forthright Helen would know how to look after him.

* * *

Nobody was more delighted than Bertie at the success Lillie Langtry was having. *Ours* had been a triumph; and although at first its leading actress had clearly been an amateur she proved herself to be highly intelligent and above all ambitious. Those who had believed she had nothing but her outstanding beauty were amazed; Lillie had talent and what was most extraordinary, business ability. Not only was she interested in the stage but acquaintance with Bertie had given her some knowledge of the Turf. She now began to display a most extraordinary ability and she used all her business acumen to put this to advantage. She had been aware of what it was like to be obscure and poor and she determined that never again should that happen to her.

The famous actress had become a considerable figure in racing circles. Bertie could not restrain his delight.

He became very friendly with people in the theatrical profession because he was pleased with them for giving Lillie her chance.

With the coming of that winter Lillie left England for America and there her great success continued.

In the space of a very short time she had become a rich woman and she would be the first to admit that this had been made possible for her by the staunch friendship of the Prince of Wales.

Princess Helen was almost immediately pregnant.

"The idea of Leopold as a father is *very* amusing," said the Queen.

"Why, Mama?" demanded Bertie. "Leopold's a man after all."

"Poor Leopold. He did inherit dearest Papa's brains but his health has been a constant source of anxiety."

"You worry too much about him, Mama."

The Queen shivered, remembering those ominous illnesses, the fear of haemorrhages and the dreadful knowledge that the disease had been passed on through several of her daughters. Alice's little "Frittie" who had fallen from the window had suffered from haemophilia, and so had one of Vicky's boys. It was terrifying not knowing when the fearful thing was going to show itself.

And now Leopold was to be a father!

It was a pleasure to be at Windsor; here she felt a certain

seclusion—not the same as she enjoyed at Balmoral or even Osborne, but it was so pleasant here. She often thought of how Albert had loved Windsor. Here she felt closer to Albert than anywhere else because she could go frequently to the mausoleum; she would often sit in the Blue Room and brood on the past. She could even go for drives and rides in the Park and remember so much.

One day after she had been in the Blue Room she was thinking of the past when going upstairs she missed a stair and fell.

The consternation there was! Brown was called to pick her up. He scolded her: "And what did ye think ye were doing, woman!"

She could smile and be grateful for his care.

"It's nothing," she said.

"I'll get ye a wee drop of the right medicine," he told her.

She drank the whisky while he sat drinking too; she watched him tenderly. Dear honest Brown.

The fall had brought on her old rheumaticky pain and the next morning she was bruised and suffered considerable pain, unable to move.

Jenner was worried. He thought Her Majesty should try to walk a little. She tried but the effort was too painful.

"Rest is what you need," said Jenner. "Let us see how Your Majesty feels after a day or so of complete rest."

Each day Brown carried her from her bed to her sofa. He thought that it wasn't good for her to spend so much time indoors; he would get out the wee pony chair that she could drive round in that but he wasn't going to trust her by herself. He thought he—and only he—should drive her.

The Queen listened to the masterful Brown and gave way to his suggestions. "His one thought," she told Jenner, "is for my comfort."

One morning she had a shock when a servant came in to take her orders for the day.

"But where is Brown?" she demanded.

"Brown, Your Majesty, is unable to attend you this morning. His face is swollen."

"Brown's face swollen." The Queen smiled. Oh dear, did this mean that Brown was "bashful" again? Perhaps the previous night there had been a celebration of some sort in the servants' quarters. And if there had been *he* would have to be there. No celebration would be complete without Brown.

The Queen said nothing. At midday she sent for news of

Brown. Brown's face was still swollen; it was red and inflamed and he appeared to be quite sick.

The Queen sent for Jenner. "Pray go at once and see what ails John Brown," she said.

When the doctor came back she was alarmed. "Brown has caught a chill. I'm afraid that he is suffering from erysipelas."

"Is that a very serious illness, Sir William?"

"It need not be fatal," was the reply.

Need not be fatal! Big strong John Brown seriously ill. It was unthinkable.

"Sir William you must attend him yourself and get Dr Reid."

Sir William was a little surprised. After all he and Dr Reid were the royal physicians and although everyone knew of the Queen's regard for Brown, he was only her Highland servant.

But this was not the time to argue about such a matter.

Sir William called in Dr Reid and they both set about the task of bringing John Brown to health and the Queen's service.

In the midst of this Princess Helen's daughter was born.

Leopold with a child! This was wonderful.

"I must go and see the child," she said.

It was very sad that John Brown was unable to take her and carry her in as she was still unable to put her foot to the ground.

She tried not to worry too much about Brown. After all he was not old and he was vital and full of health. He would scorn this erysipelas as he did everything else he didn't like. John Brown would soon be well again.

She was carried into the bedchamber. Leopold had had one of his bouts and the doctors would not allow him to move, so he had to receive her lying on a sofa; the birth of the child was so recent that Helen was on a sofa also; and when the Queen was carried in she found that a sofa had been prepared for her.

She could not help laughing. "Really," she said, "it is quite ludicrous. Here are we all unable to stand on our feet!"

Helen said she was delighted that the Queen had come and the baby was proudly shown. A lovely little girl, commented the Queen; but the real significance of the occasion was of course that Leopold had been able to beget a child.

How pleased Albert would have been.

At Windsor she was growing really anxious. Brown's condition was not improving.

Each day she sent for Sir William and Dr Reid and demanded that she be given a full account.

"It has somehow taken a hold of him, Your Majesty."

"But Brown is not old. He's so strong."

"That's true," said Sir William. "But it is often people who have never been ill who are suddenly stricken down. Illness bewilders them. They have never had it before. It seems to take them by surprise."

"I don't think anything would take Brown by surprise."

She herself was getting better. The rest had done her good and the pain and stiffness of her joints was disappearing.

And then on that dreadful March day the news was brought to her. John Brown was dead.

She was prostrate with grief. She could not believe it.

"I have lost my best and truest friend," she protested. How could life be so cruel? It seemed that she only had to love and the loved one was taken from her. Perhaps love was the wrong word to use when speaking of a servant, but Brown was no ordinary servant. Dearest Albert, her great love, her reason for living, had been snatched from her at a comparatively early age; Lord Beaconsfield had been taken, true he was a very old man; and now John Brown . . . It was senseless. It was cruel.

She was desolate. It was no use the family's trying to console her, for she was inconsolable.

"He was part of my life," she said. "Now I have to start again. This is the second time. It is asking too much."

She was oblivious to the comments her attitude set in motion.

The question was being asked everywhere. What had been the relationship between the Queen and John Brown? Had he been her lover? Had she been secretly married to him? Had he some peculiar psychic power over her? Was he the medium through whom she was in touch with Albert?

Nobody understood the Queen. She was a lonely woman; her children—though she loved them—could never mean to her what the strong figure of a man beside her could mean. She was essentially feminine; she needed a man to care for her, to look after her, to lean on; and although as Queen she would never give up one tiny bit of her sovereignty, even to Albert, as the woman she wished to exploit her frail femininity. Albert had supplied the perfect prop; and afterwards there had been Lord Beaconsfield to give her what she needed in her public life. But it was her private life that was most important and in that she had good faithful honest John Brown.

And now he had been taken from her.

What could she do? She must start again. It was almost as it had been in that dreadful desolate December more than twenty years ago.

Once more she was alone.

What could she do to show her sorrow? Of one thing she was certain, she would make no secret of it. The whole of England must mourn for the death of good faithful Brown.

She herself wrote an account of his virtues for the *Court Circular*. Her secretary, Sir Henry Ponsonby, trembled for what he called her indiscretions concerning John Brown. He was horrified when she decided that there should be a life of him. She had discovered that he had kept diaries. Sir Theodore Martin had, under her guidance, written what she called an excellent life of the Prince Consort which meant that Albert had been presented to the public as almost a saint. Now she would like him to do the same for that other man in her life. Sir Theodore was a little horrified as to what effect this would have and tactfully replied that because of his wife's physical condition he feared that he must spend too much time with her to be able to do justice to the work, so the Queen decided she would find another biographer. Those about her trembled at what revelations this would bring forth, but the Queen gave herself up to considering memorials. There should be a statue which should be placed at Balmoral; and at Osborne she would have a granite seat set up in memory of him.

She became a little irritable with those about her.

"How I miss John Brown's strong arm!" she was often heard to say.

She talked about him a great deal; his "bashfulness"; his quaint sayings; everything that he had been to her. Often she would lie on her sofa and think of those days when he had carried her to her room.

Then she would weep silently and think of the past and would be so lost in it that she would wake startled and think she heard a voice thick with bashfulness and yet lilting with his Highland accent demanding to know "Why ye're sitting in the dark greeting, woman?"

Once more, she said to herself, I am left lonely.

The Dilke Divorce

In order to overcome her melancholy the Queen decided to prepare for publication another edition of her journal. She would call it *More Leaves from a Journal of a Life in the Highlands*; and it would cover the years 1862–1882. She would dedicate it: "To my loyal Highlanders and especially to the memory of my devoted personal attendant and faithful friend John Brown."

It pleased her very much to go carefully through her accounts of those long ago days and recall them so clearly. She wept quietly because the early part brought back so vividly the utter desolation of the years following Albert's death and how threatening and dour the mountains had seemed when he was no longer there to compare them with his beloved Thuringian forests.

She sent Bertie an advance copy of the Journal which brought him hurriedly to Windsor.

"Mama," he cried, "I do beg of you not to have this generally circulated."

"What do you mean?" she cried indignantly.

"It is too personal."

"My dear Bertie, I know I am not an author of the standing of Mr Dickens or Mr Thackeray or Scott and Tennyson, but I venture to think that my account of my life in the Highlands will give pleasure to a great many people."

"I am sure it will, Mama, but it is exposing your private life to the world."

"*My* private life, Bertie, contains nothing of which I am ashamed."

That shaft went home and Bertie had the grace to blush.

"I am sorry, Mama, but I do feel strongly about it."

"Well, Bertie, I am prepared to admit that it would *not* be good for the family if every member of it exposed—as you say—his or her actions to the world. I can assure you that when dear Papa's *Life* was published—and it was so beautifully and *feelingly* done by Sir Theodore Martin, I read it with the greatest pleasure and felt better than I had done since he had died. And I am sure my first *Leaves* did no harm and did *me* a great deal of good. I might tell you, Bertie, that Lord Beaconsfield complimented me on it and used to refer to us as fellow authors and I venture to think that Lord Beaconsfield's assessment of literary merit must have been far greater than yours for I have heard it said that you rarely open a book."

Bertie said he wasn't thinking of literary merit, but the effect of making her private life known to the world.

"Nonsense," said the Queen.

"I seem not to be mentioned in it."

"Which shows how carefully you have read the book. You are mentioned five times."

"That does not seem much for your eldest son."

"My dear Bertie, had you come more often to Balmoral your name would naturally have appeared more frequently in the Journal. Now, let me hear no more of this matter."

Bertie left Windsor as some described it "with his tail between his legs" as he so often did after his encounters with his mama; but at least the Life of John Brown was not published, although the Queen had gone so far as to have his journals edited.

First there were delays—unavoidable, so the Queen was told; and it might have been that she too began to realize the lack of wisdom in publishing them. The matter was allowed to drop; but that did not mean she did not continue to mourn her faithful Highland servant.

Leopold's married life was progressing favourably. Princess Helen was again pregnant which was remarkable, for his little daughter Alexandra was a healthy little creature. "Yet another grandchild!" sighed the Queen. "So many, that I have to think hard to count them up."

Then Leopold had another of his bouts and the doctors thought a spell at Cannes would be good for him. As the spring had come, the South of France would be delightful so he and his family took up residence at the Villa Nevada and letters reached the Queen, much to her gratification, that Leopold's health had greatly improved.

A year had passed since the death of John Brown and the Queen, who always kept anniversaries, had a superstitious feeling about them. Because she had suffered acutely on such and such a day she would feel that there was some malevolent purpose at work and she would come to dread that day. She remembered that her beloved husband and daughter Alice had both died on the 14th of December and it was on that very date that Bertie had come right up to the gates of death and by a miracle been brought back to life.

Now it was the 27th of March; a year to that day when they had come to tell her that her dear faithful John Brown was dead. She had written in her Journal that she mourned him still. She supposed she would never cease to do that.

She awoke with a feeling of apprehension for she had been reading her Journal before she slept; and when a telegram arrived from Cannes she expected disaster.

It was only faintly alarming; Helen had just sent word to say that Leopold had slipped and damaged his knee. A trifling matter with most people, but the slightest injury in Leopold's case could bring on the dreaded bleeding.

The Queen felt depressed. She wondered whether she should go out to Cannes. Helen understood the care that had to be taken and so did Leopold's servants; but Helen was expecting her second child. The Queen was uncertain what to do. Mr Gladstone was always so *peevish* when she suggested leaving the country. Oh, how she missed the kind understanding of Lord Beaconsfield!

And the next day came the terrible news. Leopold was dead. He had had a kind of epileptic fit which had been brought on by a haemorrhage of the brain.

So she had lost another child.

"He was the dearest of my sons," she said; but she knew that this was what they had been forced to expect ever since they had discovered his weakness. She should be thankful that he had been spared to her for so long.

His body was brought home and he was buried in St George's Chapel at Windsor.

Three months later his posthumous son was born.

An anxious time followed Leopold's death and the Queen's mind was taken from family concerns to State matters.

She was very dissatisfied with her government; there was anxiety about Egypt, the affairs of which country were now almost completely under British domination. A fanatical leader known as the Mahdi had arisen in the Sudan which was under Egyptian rule and therefore a concern of Britain. The government, to the Queen's dismay, decided that it would be better to abandon the Sudan and leave it in the control of the Mahdi, agreeing however to rescue the Egyptian forces which still remained there. Their efforts to do this were so dilatory that there was, as the Queen described it, unnecessary massacre; but finally the government agreed to send out General Gordon to Khartoum.

Mr Gladstone's conception of Empire was, alas, not that of Lord Beaconsfield; and the Queen considered it the height of disaster to the country that that clever, far-sighted man had died to leave matters in the hands of the People's William.

There was also much with which to concern herself at home. Bertie had been elected as a member of the Royal Commission on the Housing of the Working Classes. Mr Gladstone was constantly deploring the fact that Bertie had too little with which to occupy himself and to give Bertie his due he did enjoy having some task presented to him; it might well have been that had he been given some post he would not have got into such mischief as he did.

Bertie had become far too friendly with Sir Charles Dilke, that dreadful radical, and now the Prince himself was becoming something of a radical.

He was taken round London to see how the poor lived and declared himself to be horrified. First of all a typical working man's dress had to be found for him and he went *incognito* in company with others. He came back to her—and told her what he had seen.

Poor Bertie, with all his faults he was very kind-hearted; there were tears in his eyes as he kept reiterating: "Something must be done."

"There was a room without any furniture, Mama," he went on. "A heap of rags and a poor skeleton of a woman lying on it, too weak to move; her children had no clothes whatsoever

. . . I wanted to empty my pockets of everything I had but I was told that if I showed so much . . . *so much*, Mama, there would be a riot. These people would not believe there was so much money in the world! Something must be done."

She herself agreed to this. Something must be done. General Booth and his Salvation Army were making people aware of conditions in the poor districts like those of St Giles'.

She read *The Bitter Cry of Outcast London* and wept.

She discussed it with the Prime Minister and she wondered why men who were so concerned with religion and the vote seemed to think that the distressing housing conditions and starvation of the poor was of less moment. She even felt a little drawn towards Sir Charles Dilke.

"I begin now," she said, "to understand his concern for poor people."

There was worse to follow. General Gordon had reached Khartoum where he was besieged by the Mahdi and his men.

"He must be relieved at once," insisted the Queen.

Mr Gladstone's Ministry was as usual dilatory; his government, he said, had no desire to be involved in a war in Egypt.

The people were with the Queen and they deplored the government's neglect of those men fighting the Empire's battles far away. Then before the relief arrived General Gordon was killed at the storming of Khartoum; she was furious with her government and at the same time very sad. She could not honour his family enough and fell back to her usual method of showing respect by having a bust made and placing it in Windsor Castle.

But in spite of the fact that relieving forces eventually arrived the Sudanese expedition was far from an unqualified success and she brooded on the fact that had Lord Beaconsfield been in command it would have been very different.

Of all her children the Queen had perhaps relied most on Beatrice since Albert's death. Beatrice had then been "Baby" and her quaint doings and sayings had diverted the Queen in her misery. As the youngest, Beatrice—still sometimes known as Baby—had been more constantly with her mother than any of the others. She was now the only one left; she was twenty-seven and the Queen had told herself that Beatrice would never marry. For one thing she was very shy; she disliked going to dinner-parties unless she was certain who her neighbours at the table would be and they were old friends.

So naturally the Queen had imagined that she would always have Beatrice with her.

Her dismay was great when Beatrice came to her and said: "Mama, I have fallen in love and want to get married."

The Queen almost fell off her chair. "In love!" she said. "What nonsense, dearest child. How could *you* fall in love?"

"It was not very difficult, Mama, and I am sure you will agree with me, when you know it is Henry."

"Henry. What Henry is this?"

"Prince Henry of Battenberg."

"It's quite impossible."

"Oh no, Mama, quite possible . . . if you give your consent."

"I should never allow you to be so foolish. My dearest child, you were so desolate when darling Leopold died. And this . . . Henry came along and you imagined you wished to marry him. Everything will settle down in time. Don't worry."

Poor Beatrice! Gone were the days of childhood when her quaintness had made it permissible to disagree with Mama.

She grew pale, wan and listless. She was obedient, but her conversation was dull and confined to "Yes, Mama" and "No, Mama" which was quite boring.

"What *is* the matter with you, child?" demanded the Queen. "And don't talk to me about this foolish matter of Henry of Battenberg."

He came; he was charming; he was devoted to Beatrice

Of course the Queen could not stand by and see poor Baby growing pale and thin. She supposed she would have to give way.

At length she said, "I had better see this Henry of Battenberg."

He came; he was charming; he was devoted to Beatrice and to see the change in that dear child made the Queen weep.

Henry said he did understand her reluctance to part with such a treasure and they would reside in England so that their marriage would make little difference to the Queen.

She embraced them both and wished them well; and referred to herself in a letter to Vicky as "Poor shattered me."

Of course it was not a grand marriage and Vicky would not approve of that; but the Queen wondered whether Vicky's, which had been grand, had brought her much happiness. Beatrice was radiant; and the Queen reproached herself for ever trying to keep such joy from her dearest child.

She embraced her warmly but when Prince Henry and his new wife left for their honeymoon she shivered a little. She hoped poor Beatrice would not suffer *too* much from the "shadow side" of marriage.

A great scandal had broken on London. A Mr Donald Crawford M.P. was suing for divorce and whom should he name as co-respondent but Sir Charles Dilke.

The Queen was very interested when she heard. "Oh, these radicals!" she said to Beatrice. "They are so concerned for the rights of this and that, so anxious to look into the purses of other people, when all the time they themselves are not beyond reproach."

But almost immediately she was anxious on account of Bertie. He did seem to have a habit of being mixed up in public scandals. She would never forget that dreadful Mordaunt case; and then there was that horrible Aylesford affair. And he *was* a friend of Sir Charles Dilke.

Happily Bertie was not involved in this one; and it was a great relief that he was not for it was the most shocking of them all.

The Dilke case was the great *cause célèbre* of the 1880s. It seemed that everyone from the Queen to her humblest subject was following the details as they emerged. The situation was one which could not fail to appeal. The dignified celebrated politician caught up in a very sordid affair and shown in the worst possible light. It appeared that Mr Crawford had received an anonymous letter advising him to "Beware of the Member for Chelsea!"—the Member for Chelsea being Sir Charles Dilke. He had been inclined to think that this was the work of a practical joker until he received a second unsigned letter:

"The first person who ruined your wife was Sir Charles Dilke. She has passed nights in his house and is well known to his servants."

Such a letter could not be ignored and when Crawford confronted his wife with it she said that it was her mother who had sent it.

The Crawfords and Dilkes were connected by marriage and had been on visiting terms for years so the fact that Sir

Charles called now and then at the Crawford house was not a matter to arouse comment. Mrs Crawford, however, was a somewhat frivolous woman and she had been rather friendly with a Captain Forster of whom her husband had been mildly jealous. If the Captain had been accused of being her lover he would not have been surprised, but this accusation levelled at Sir Charles seemed to him incongruous and when his wife admitted that Sir Charles had in fact been her lover, he was astounded.

Furious, he began divorce proceedings and it was then that incredible codes of conduct were revealed which put Sir Charles in the worst possible light.

There were suggestions that Mrs Crawford's mother had been Sir Charles's mistress; and Mrs Crawford claimed that when Dilke had taken her to a house in Tottenham Court Road, a young woman, who had once been a servant in Dilke's house, joined in their sexual activities.

Sir Charles was not called to the witness box but since Mrs Crawford had confessed, her husband obtained his divorce. However, the case against Sir Charles was dismissed because it could not be proved. The mysterious servant who had joined the Tottenham Court Road frolics could not be found, and there was only Mrs Crawford's word to go on; but the fact that the divorce had been granted meant that Dilke, although not proved guilty because no one had been found to come forward to testify against him, was not proved innocent.

The Queen avidly read the newspapers and argued with Bertie, who was eager to protect his friend. Bertie would have done that even if he had believed Dilke to be guilty, the Queen was aware, for he was always loyal to his friends. But *what* friends he chose!

"I cannot help being amused," said the Queen. "When these virtuous people who stump about doing good are proved to be libertines in private it is very revealing."

"I believe that woman is mad," said Bertie.

"She has certainly not put herself in a very good light."

"Some people are ready to harm themselves for the sake of revenge on others."

"A foolish policy," commented the Queen.

"But, Mama, people are foolish."

"Well, *I* do not believe *your* Sir Charles D⸺ out of this affair very well and I am sure this ⸺ to his career."

Be⸺

"That's the wicked part about it," said Bertie. "Dilke's a dedicated politician. He might have become Prime Minister."

"God forbid!" said the Queen—though she thought she might just have preferred him to Mr Gladstone.

Mr Gladstone, however, gravely indicated to Sir Charles that he could not include him in his government and Sir Charles, rising fast, had suddenly found himself sliding downhill.

Sir Charles was frantic. He was ready to try anything to clear himself; and when his friend, Joseph Chamberlain, suggested that the Queen's Proctor should intervene in the granting of the divorce because nothing had been proved against the man who had been accused of being Mrs Crawford's lover, the case was reopened. It was the worst action that could have been taken.

The suggestion that Sir Charles had been the lover of Mrs Crawford's mother was raised and Sir Charles refused either to agree that this was so or to deny it. Two housemaids known as Fanny and Sarah whom Mrs Crawford declared had joined in the sexual revels could not be found to come forward and declare Sir Charles innocent. The fact which went more against Sir Charles than anything was that the house in Tottenham Court Road which Mrs Crawford identified was actually run by a woman who had once been a housekeeper of Sir Charles.

The jury of this second hearing decided that Sir Charles had not told the truth and that he was guilty of the assertions brought against him by Mrs Crawford.

Bertie was sympathetic. He had experience of courts and he knew how damaging they could be. He understood perfectly Sir Charles's predicament. It seemed to him terrible that such a brilliant man should be denied the opportunity of serving his country because his sexual habits might or might not be a little irregular.

He wrote to Sir Charles affirming his friendship. It was great comfort to the stricken man whose political career was of course in ruins, to know that he had the sympathy of the future King of England.

The Queen could not hide her delight. She enjoyed discussing the case in all its details. She regretted that Lord Melbourne was no longer with her. What a wealth of gossip he uld have had to bring to her! So would dear Lord consfield. Those men were so interested in people, which was more than could be said for Mr Gladstone; and who could be absolutely sure that his efforts to rescue fallen women of the streets were all he would like them to be believed? As the Queen said, when these reformers were shown up in a new light it was not only interesting but revealing and, when one considered it, good for the community at large.

While the Dilke case was in progress the Queen had reason to rejoice.

Mr Gladstone's government had become very unpopular over its Egyptian policy and was defeated on its budget proposals. What a pleasure when Mr Gladstone was forced to resign!

Magnanimously the Queen offered him an earldom which he declined.

She welcomed Lord Salisbury to form a new government. This he did but of what use was it for him to be in office when there was a Liberal majority? Salisbury could only dissolve Parliament, and go to the country; the Liberals were still in favour. They held 334 seats against 250 Conservatives; Parnell's Irish Nationalists holding 86. To the Queen's disgust Gladstone was once more her Prime Minister.

But it was not easy. His party was split on his Home Rule Bill. Gladstone was convinced that Ireland must have Home Rule; the Queen firmly believed that to give them this was to encourage rebels. Gladstone was defeated on the Bill and back came Salisbury.

Gladstone was now seventy-seven.

"Poor old man," said the Queen. "It is time he took a rest." But he seemed to be in no mood to do so and he was as prominent as ever as Leader of the Opposition.

But at least she had a Prime Minister whom she liked.

Golden Jubilee

The Queen's Ministers reminded her that in this year of 1887 she would have reigned for fifty years. There must be a celebration. The people would expect it; besides it was a glorious occasion. How many other monarchs had reigned for so long? The Queen must waive her objections to pageants. This was an occasion. She sighed and gave way.

There had been a secret anxiety in the family for some months. Vicky's husband Fritz had developed a throat infection and Vicky was very worried about his health. She feared the worst. The doctors were extremely grave and there was a suggestion that Fritz had a malignant tumour of the throat. Vicky could not bear to contemplate this. Her position in Germany was not a happy one. Bismarck had always disliked her; her father-in-law and his wife had resented her; and worst of all her eldest son, Wilhelm, now married, treated her very badly. Her one friend had been the gentle Fritz, her husband, and as he was the Crown Prince, in spite of his mild nature he had been a powerful one until his illness.

Wilhelm was a cruel young man. His arrogance had grown as he became older; Vicky wondered whether they had made too many excuses for his deformed arm which he cleverly disguised by his uniforms; but he had certainly turned out a very undutiful son. He despised his father for being weak and his mother for being English. He had an obsessional hatred for the English which Uncle Bertie with his *bonhomie* and his extravagance when travelling abroad seemed to have intensified. Uncle Bertie received the full force of his venom. He was the opposite of Wilhelm. Bertie could at times be arrogant when his royalty was assailed, but his good nature, desire for friendship towards all kinds of people, his generosity, his love of gaiety, his amorous adventures, everything endeared him to the people. Wilhelm's haughty arrogance, his obsession with the greatness of the German Empire and his manner towards those about him made him very unpopular. He was in awe of his grandmother, Queen Victoria. She was one of the few persons he respected; and the fact that Uncle Bertie was her eldest son and heir to a vast and growing Empire filled him with rage. He longed to rule that Empire. He had been influenced by Bismarck whose doctrines he had eagerly absorbed; his grandparents had fostered his desires for the aggrandizement of the German Empire; and Wilhelm now saw his great and mighty rival as the British Empire. His grandmother seemed a fitting ruler; on the occasions when he visited her she could by a look make him feel that he was a boy in the nursery again. Yet she never failed to show him affection and had often told him that her husband the Prince Consort had had great hopes for him, his first grandchild. Yes, Wilhelm could accept Grandmama Victoria as the mighty ruler; but to think of all that glory passing into the hands of frivolous Uncle Bertie drove him into such a fury that he felt he would do anything to prevent its doing so. And his mother was Uncle Bertie's sister! He hated the English—and it was galling that he was half English himself, though the English half, he consoled himself, was strongly flavoured with German.

With such a son, and a husband whom she feared to be dying, poor Vicky was in great distress.

She wrote to her mother and begged her to send her an English doctor who was known throughout the world to be an authority on cancer. This was Dr Morell Mackenzie. The German doctors wished to operate. Vicky felt this would be fatal and she hoped Dr Mackenzie would disagree with their verdict.

The Queen immediately send Dr Mackenzie to Germany. To Vicky's delight he said that Fritz was not suffering from cancer and he thought he might be cured with the right treatment.

"Oh, Mama, it is *such* a relief," wrote Vicky.

Poor child, thought the Queen; and she was glad that Fritz would be able to attend the Jubilee.

* * *

The 20th of June 1887. She awoke early. She read through her Journal and remembered that long-ago day—one of the most important in her life, some would say *the* most important, but her wedding day would always be first with her. Mama had come into her bedroom carrying a candlestick to awaken her and she had known immediately. How young she had been—how inexperienced! Eighteen years old and to be a Queen. Lehzen had been there with smelling salts, she remembered; and even then she had scorned the idea. She had meant to be a Queen.

Dear Lord Melbourne had been there to sustain her; she shed a tear for Lord Melbourne. So godlike he had seemed until Albert came along and showed her how weak, how ineffectual all men were compared with Albert.

And now she had been fifty years a Queen.

She thought: And I am alone to celebrate it, for although I have my children I have always been alone since the loss of that dear beloved one.

As she rose, the sun shone brilliantly and she breakfasted out of doors and afterwards drove to the station. Crowds cheered her all the way. The royal train was waiting to take her to Paddington Station; and once more loyal crowds shouted their approval as she rode through the Park to Buckingham Palace.

The streets were already decorated for the great tomorrow. That day she received the visiting royalty and there was a grand dinner-party for the crowned heads of Europe, most of whom had close family ties with the Queen.

She retired early in readiness for the great day.

How magnificent it was! Tears filled her eyes because Albert was not there to share it with her. The thousands who lined the streets shouted their loyal greetings as she came into sight in her open carriage drawn by six magnificent cream-coloured horses; she had especially wanted to be escorted by Indian cavalry, not only as a compliment to her new subjects but also to remind people of the greatness of her Empire.

Behind her rode Bertie, Alfred and Arthur. Alas, there was one son missing, dear Leopold. One thought of these sad losses at such a time. All her sons-in-law were there. It was a great joy that dear Fritz had not been absent as she had feared he might. It was true he could scarcely speak; that fearful affliction of the throat prevented that; but he looked magnificent. How proud Albert would have been to see Germany represented in such a manner and to know the little German States were now one mighty Empire and Vicky would one day be Empress. The German Eagle on Fritz's helmet brought a frenzy of cheering from the crowd. For the Germans! thought the Queen when she heard it and knew for whom it was intended. They knew how to show their might. All her grandsons were there, including of course Wilhelm, of whom Vicky had complained so bitterly. He would be feeling gratified at the cheers for his father.

What an impressive moment it was when she walked into the Abbey to the sound of a march by Handel! And of course Albert's own composition must be included in the ceremony; on that she had insisted. He could not be with her in the flesh but his music should be there; the choir sang the anthem which he had written and her eyes were glazed with tears as she listened.

My dearest Albert, how different everything would have been had you been spared to me! she thought. Everything else I could have borne if you had been with me.

But he had been taken and she had her children. Then she thought of Alice and Leopold, the lost ones, and how sad it was that they so young should be gone and she an old woman still here. Then all the grandchildren. How proud Albert would have been of them!

Her bonnet—made of lace and glittering with diamonds—shook a little. She had insisted on bonnets for all the women including herself, although many were shocked at the idea and thought she should have worn the crown. But she had said it should be a bonnet and she was the Queen and if she could not always have her way in State matters, she would over a matter of bonnets.

She felt tired but elated when they returned to the Palace; but of course this was not the end. The great entertainment was about to begin.

She was helped into her dress embroidered with jewels, representing England, Scotland and Ireland, roses, thistles and shamrocks—and then to the great banqueting hall to receive all the visiting royalties and the many guests who had come from all over the world to celebrate her fifty years as Queen.

At last the long day was over and she sank gratefully into bed; but not to sleep, to brood on the past fifty years and through her mind paraded the significant figures of the past—the Uncle Kings, George and William; dear kind Aunt

Adelaide; Mama with whom there had been such storms; the well-beloved Lord Melbourne; the at first hated and afterwards deeply respected Sir Robert Peel; dear exciting Mr Disraeli; the heartily disliked Mr Gladstone—still not escaped from, she feared; good faithful John Brown; all her living children—and those dear dead ones; the grandchildren; the family by marriage. So many of them dominated always by the one great figure: Albert.

Oh, Albert, if you had lived to see this day, she kept telling herself, how different everything would have been!

Her Golden Jubilee—fifty years since that long ago June day when they awakened her from her bed; and nearly twenty-seven years since she had lost her love, and therefore her zest for living. And she still mourned him. His was the face that came to her whenever she thought of the past.

"Albert," she cried on this great night, as she had cried so often during the last twenty-six years, "why were you taken from me?"

The Arrogant Emperor

A few months later there was grave news from Berlin. Dr Mackenzie now agreed with the German doctors that the Crown Prince was suffering from cancer of the throat. He was in great pain; his voice had disappeared completely, and death was imminent.

Vicky was heartbroken. Fritz had been the bulwark between herself and her German family and the German people. They had never liked her; her mother-in-law had given her the room in the Schloss next to the haunted chamber and had tried to unnerve her with grisly accounts of spectres; when she arrived she had been obliged to ride in an icy wind through the streets of Berlin wearing only a flimsy evening dress; there had been hostile shouts in the streets; and she had never been allowed to forget that she was a foreigner. This had been galling to proud and clever Vicky. There had been wars which had brought about conflict in the family. Alix—and she carried Bertie with her—had hated the Prussians since the Schleswig-Holstein war. Life had been very difficult; but never so as now with her kind, easy-going husband dying and Wilhelm, the heir, strutting, haughty, hardly deigning to notice his mother. And without the protection of Fritz she would be exposed to her enemies.

There was a further development. The old Emperor clearly could not live long; and there were rumours that he might die before Fritz; both were doomed men. There was one who viewed this situation with the utmost complacence: Wilhelm, who on the death of his grandfather and father would be the Emperor of Germany.

The Queen discussed the matter with Bertie and told him how sad she felt for Vicky, who was cleary distraught. Bertie said that the idea of that arrogant young coxcomb, his nephew Wilhelm, becoming an Emperor was more than he could stand; he hoped he never again had to see the arrogant young puppy.

"He was a great favourite of dearest Papa and that is something I can never forget," said the Queen.

"Dearest Papa did not live long enough to know what a grandson he had. Otherwise he might not have been quite so fond of Wilhelm."

"There was his poor arm," said the Queen tolerantly. "I am sure that has been very difficult to contend with."

"Vicky did everything she could for him. He could at least be grateful, but he treats her abominably. And do you know, Mama, I believe he has designs on England."

"Designs on England! Good gracious, Bertie, whatever do you mean?"

"I mean he would like to oust me . . . us . . . from the throne."

"Oust us from the throne." All the Queen's majesty descended upon her. Bertie thought: She may think she likes to live in seclusion; she may imply that she would gladly relinquish her crown; but just try suggesting it! "Why, Bertie, I never *heard* such nonsense."

"But, Mama, Wilhelm has become so arrogant that he is capable of thinking such nonsense. I sent him a kilt and everything that goes with it in Royal Stuart tartan. He asked for it because he said he wanted to wear it at a fancy-dress ball. And do you know, Mama, he had the temerity to have a photograph taken in it and wrote underneath it: 'I bide my time.' This he had distributed widely."

"Little Willie will have to be taught a lesson or two," said the Queen grimly. "And when I next see him I will undertake to explain to him that this will not do. I am sorry for poor Vicky. You children have given me many causes for anxiety but I must say that I have never had to complain of your lack of respect to me as your mother and your Queen."

"Thank you, Mama. It would in any case be impossible to show disrespect to you even if one wanted to—which is equally impossible."

The Queen smiled. Bertie had a very gracious way of paying a compliment. She had certain things to be thankful for in Bertie and she was really quite fond of him. Of course he was frivolous and not really a good husband to dear sweet Alix because of this obsession of his with women; but he had charm.

"*Dear* Bertie," she said. "And young Willy may be left to me."

There came news that the old Emperor had died; Fritz was now Emperor of Germany and Vicky its Empress.

"How proud dearest Papa would have been," said the Queen.

But Vicky was growing more and more uneasy. Poor Fritz was failing fast; he suffered agony and could not speak at all. He was Emperor for a hundred days and then the sad news came that he was dead.

Wilhelm was so triumphant that he made no secret of his elation. Delighted as he was, yet he blamed his mother for his father's death. He kept her virtually a prisoner and would not allow her access to any of his father's papers.

Bertie, attending his brother-in-law's funeral, was horrified at the new young Emperor's manner and the way in which his sister was treated.

Bertie returned to England and reported to the Queen; she was furious and when Wilhelm's envoy was sent to her to announce formally his master's accession she received him with the utmost coldness.

Wilhelm was resentful. Did his grandmother forget that now he was an Emperor he was of equal importance with her as she was an Empress?

Victoria replied that she had certainly received coldly an envoy who came to announce a death in *triumph* and without a word of sorrow. The announcement was to her most callous and unseemly. Such conduct would always be received with coldness by her.

Uncle Bertie, complained Wilhelm, had not treated him as an Emperor.

The Queen was incensed. Is the Prince of Wales to treat his nephew as his Imperial Majesty every minute of the day? How absurd. They were all members of a family and they should be treated as such; that was with affection and kindness . . . if they deserved it! She was a Queen and an Empress but she did not expect members of her family to address her as Your Majesty instead of Mama or Grandmama as the case might be. If Wilhelm felt he was going to flaunt the German Eagle in her private drawing-room he had better keep it where it belonged—in Germany.

Bertie and Wilhelm would never like each other, although Bertie would have forgiven past arrogance if Wilhelm had shown signs of mending his ways. But he did not. The fact that he was the German Emperor had gone to his head and he wanted everyone to remember it every minute of the day.

The Queen agreed with Lord Salisbury that the relations of the two countries should not be affected by ridiculous quarrels like this. They would have to be very careful, though, with such a conceited young man sitting on one of the most powerful thrones in Europe.

Scandal at Tranby Croft

Bertie was once more in trouble. It had all come about in
the strangest manner. He was at this time deeply enamoured
of Lady Brooke, a very forceful, cool beauty in her twenties,
and was so taken with her that he had scarcely any time for
other women. It was like the Langtry affair over again.
Frances Brooke—"Daisy" to her friends—was of an unusual
character and the Prince was completely intrigued by everything about her. It was the usual pattern; if hostesses wished
him to grace their parties invitations must be sent to Lord
and Lady Brooke. The former should be there for the sake of
convention, of course.

Racing was his second greatest interest. He enjoyed gambling in any form, and his favourite form of gambling, off
the racecourse, was the game of baccarat.

Bertie usually attended the most important race meetings
so it was natural that he should go north for those at Doncas-
ter. Things went wrong from the start. Normally he would
have stayed at the mansion of one of his greatest friends,
Christopher Sykes, but Sykes informed him that he was in fi-
nancial difficulties and not in a position to entertain royalty.
Bertie was alarmed and helped his friend out of his immediate difficulty, but understood at once that he could not pay
the usual visit. Sykes had friends near by—a wealthy ship-
owner named Wilson, who could well afford to entertain the
Prince of Wales and would be delighted to do so at his home,
Tranby Croft.

"It would be a great honour for him," went on Sykes. The Prince, who liked to honour people and had a great respect for rich people who had made their money out of their wisdom and their own efforts, was delighted.

"Make sure," he said, "that Daisy gets an invitation."

It was all arranged and the Prince looked forward to a pleasant stay. The Wilsons might not be of his circle but they were determined that he should lack nothing during his stay with them.

He arrived at the house expecting to find Daisy there. There was a message for him. Her uncle had died suddenly and she would therefore be unable to join the party.

Bertie was bitterly disappointed but after a few moments he managed to hide his annoyance. They would get some good baccarat, he decided, unaffected by Daisy's disturbing presence.

Among the players, with the Prince taking charge of the bank, were Mr Wilson and his twenty-two-year-old son, Lieutenant-Colonel Sir William Gordon-Cumming of the Scots Guards, Lord Edward Somerset and Berkeley Levett, a friend of young Wilson. They played with Bertie's counters which he always carried with him on such visits and which were decorated with the Prince of Wales' feathers. The stakes were high and when the play was in progress, to his horror young Wilson was sure that he saw Sir William Gordon-Cumming cheating. Sir William sat with his hands clasped over a £5 counter. He leaned forward to see what cards Lord Edward Somerset had and—so young Wilson thought—dropped three more counters on to the paper in front of him which meant that, after he had seen Lord Edward's cards, he had made £20.

Young Wilson was fascinated. He could not believe that he had seen correctly. For the rest of the evening he watched Sir William and was convinced that he was concealing counters in his hands and adding to them or taking them back according to the exposed cards of his friends.

He was so overwrought that he whispered to his friend Levett to watch. Levett did; and he was of the same opinion as Wilson. Sir William Gordon-Cumming was cheating.

When the household had retired Wilson went to Levett's room and they talked of the matter. Levett said he was sure that Sir William was cheating; but what could he, a very junior officer in Sir William's regiment, do about it? It was a terrible state of affairs.

Wilson said he would tell his mother and ask her what should be done.

"For heaven's sake be careful," said Mrs Wilson when she heard. "We don't want a scandal. This is the first time we have entertained the Prince of Wales. Not a word to anybody. They will all have gone in a few days, so let it rest."

But the young man could not get it out of his mind and he told his brother-in-law, Mr Lycett Green, who was horrified and immediately confided the story to his wife.

There was a conference with Berkeley, Levett and of those members of the family who knew, and the Wilsons decided that cheating had been easy because the table they had used had in fact been three whist tables put together. Now if they had a real baccarat table with the proper lines drawn on it, cheating would not be easy.

This seemed the solution. A baccarat table was produced for it was certain that the following night the Prince would want to play his favourite game.

They were right, he did; and much to the dismay of all the people concerned it appeared that Sir William repeated his tricks of the night before. They then decided that this could not be allowed to pass; they were uncertain what should be done, but there were at the house party sophisticated members of high society who could know and they must be told at once. Among them was General Owen Williams, a friend of Gordon-Cumming; and another was Lord Coventry.

"Good God!" said the General when he heard. "I don't believe, I won't believe . . . But we'll have to tell William."

The attitude of Sir William when confronted by the accusation was strange. He did not ask who had seen him cheat though he denied doing so and asked to see the Prince of Wales.

Bertie was his usual bland good-natured self. He couldn't believe that Sir William had cheated and was ready to believe him. "But," he pointed out, "five people say they have seen you. Five is quite a large number."

"I shall leave this house," said Sir William. "I shall cut those five people dead when I see them."

"Well, there are five of them," said the Prince, "and it won't do you much good if they let this out."

Sir William left them, and the Prince had to admit when talking over the matter with Coventry, Somerset and Owen Williams that it was very strange that Gordon-Cumming had not asked who his accusers were.

"We'd better see them all separately," said Bertie, "and we'll decide whether we believe them or Sir William."

This was done and when the cross-examination was over and the three of them attempted to sum up they had to admit that the evidence was very convincing.

"What can we do?" asked Somerset.

"There's only one thing to be done," replied Bertie. "Sir William must never play baccarat again."

"How can we stop him?"

"We can make him sign a pledge to the effect that he won't."

"Do you think he'd keep it, Your Highness?"

"If we all signed as witnesses he would."

"Would Your Highness be prepared . . . ?"

"Certainly," said Bertie. "We cannot allow Sir William to play again a game at which he has been seen cheating."

Sir William when confronted with the findings of the amateur court was indignant.

"But if I signed such a thing, it's as good as saying that I'm guilty. I refuse," he said.

It was a difficult situation. The General went to his room and reasoned with him.

"My dear William," he said, "you *have* to sign this pledge. You have to give up baccarat for ever. If you don't there'd be such a scandal that you'll be suspected of being guilty in any case. This is a most unfortunate matter and the best way of dealing with it is to hush it up. Think of all the people who know of this. Do you think they're going to keep quiet? Why, they'll be discussing it on the racecourse tomorrow if you don't sign this paper. You've got to."

"It will be talked of in any case. No, I won't sign."

"We will swear everyone to secrecy. The matter will be closed. No one outside the people in this house will know. You've got to do it."

At length Sir William agreed; the Prince of Wales witnessed his signature and nine other members of the ill-fated house-party added their names.

Then they left Tranby Croft.

"What an unfortunate visit," said Bertie. "I hope never to see the place again. How different it used to be at Sykes' place. A disastrous time. No Daisy and this unsavoury affair."

How was it such matters leaked out? They had all sworn

secrecy; and yet within a few weeks Tranby Croft was on everybody's lips. What had happened at Tranby Croft? Something about someone caught cheating at cards? The stakes were enormous. The Prince of Wales was there. It was one of those wild parties he enjoyed with his racing friends.

Sir William found that he was shut out of society. His acquaintances ignored him; when he did meet them face to face they looked straight through him as though he did not exist. He knew that the story was becoming public knowledge.

How could he continue in his career when it was known that he had been suspected of cheating?

He had one alternative. He must go to see his solicitors. Their advice was that he bring an action for slander against the five people who had declared they had seen him cheating.

When Bertie heard this, he was horrified. He had had enough of public courts and he might well be forced to give evidence which would result—as it had in the Mordaunt case—in a great deal of unwelcome publicity.

Before the case could be tried in a civil court—for the accusation was one of casting a slur on Sir William's honour as a gentleman and a soldier—he would have to resign from the army; this he attempted to do. But Bertie forestalled him. If the case were tried in a military court it would be a secret enquiry and that was naturally what he wished.

But Sir William's solicitors would not have this. They wanted a civil case with heavy damages and reinstatement of Sir William as a man of honour. They appealed to the Army pointing out that everyone should have his chance to clear himself before he was proved guilty in a court of law. That was British justice. The Army agreed. Sir William resigned so that the case was to be brought into a civil court.

Bertie was now very anxious. He had foolishly put his name to that paper and since it would have to be brought forward it seemed very likely that he would be called once more to give evidence in court.

He fretted; being older and wiser now than he had been at the time of the Mordaunt affair, he saw how momentous this was. For the second time he, the future King, was being drawn into an unsavoury case. He did what he did before: told Alix the story before she should get full details from another source.

Alix was firm in his defense. Loyal Alix. But she was quiet and there was a sadness in her demeanour. It was beastly of that horrible man who had cheated at cards, to drag Bertie into all this unwelcome publicity just because he had been good-natured enough to try to help. She had always disliked Gordon-Cumming. Not that she had met him often but on the occasions when she had she thought him most unpleasant. But all the same she did deplore the life Bertie lived.

The Queen was less sympathetic.

"Baccarat!" she cried to Sir Henry Ponsonby. "What a manner in which to spend his time! And I dare say he gambled for enormous sums. What are the people going to say?"

The people had plenty to say, for when the case was tried the Prince of Wales received his subpoena and was obliged for the second time to give evidence in a court. The case went overwhelmingly against Gordon-Cumming. He was finished both militarily and socially. The Army turned him out and no club would receive him; he could only retire in disgrace.

But the chief actor in the drama seemed to have been the Prince of Wales. Few people mentioned Gordon-Cumming while Bertie's name was on all lips. His extravagance was discussed. Only a short while ago he had been moved by the state of the London poor. What a pity he did not spend some of his income on alleviating their condition instead of throwing it away on horses and baccarat. He was dissolute, the Press implied. It was such conduct as this which had brought about the downfall of the French Monarchy at the end of the previous century. Monarchy should beware.

The Queen was horrified. "Bertie's conduct has brought us all into disrepute," she wrote to Vicky. "It was very distressing." She summoned Bertie; she spoke to him very severely.

"This dreadful gambling must stop. What dearest Papa would have said I cannot imagine. It is very wrong of you, Bertie, to go to such houses . . . the houses of worthy middle-class people who have made their money by hard work. I gather Mr Wilson built ships which is a very laudable thing to do. You go there; you corrupt such hard-working people. Naturally they are delighted to have you because of the prestige Royalty always gives. But how much longer will it if we all behave as you do? It will not be for long I fear. I could almost be glad that dearest Papa is not here. This would have made him despair of you."

Poor Bertie! He was indeed in disgrace.

Nephew Wilhelm made sure that the very most was made of the scandal.

The Prince of Wales had a new motto, said one German paper: *"Ich Deal."*

Wilhelm even went farther. He wrote to dear Grandmama telling her how shocked he was by the scandal of Tranby Croft. He was very concerned because he had bestowed on his uncle the honorary rank of Colonel in the Prussian Guard. He did not care that his Colonels should be concerned in scandals of this nature, particularly with people who were of an age to be their sons.

Bertie spluttered with rage. "The insolent young puppy!" he cried.

"He is no puppy," said the Queen. "He is the Emperor of Germany and I may tell you that the Queen of England shares his disgust."

The Times joined in the general condemnation of the Prince of Wales.

The gambling gentlemen had made Gordon-Cumming sign a pledge that he would play no more baccarat. Would it not be a good thing if someone could persuade the Prince of Wales to sign such a pledge?

To be treated like a naughty boy at his age was most humiliating. Bertie turned for comfort to Alix as he always did at such times, only to find that she had become aloof. He was deeply wounded and he kept remembering the insolence of that young puppy, his nephew, the Emperor of Germany.

Eddy and George

Alix was deeply wounded. It was not so much the Tranby Croft affair although it was very humiliating to read what was said of her husband in the papers; what hurt most was this persistent pursuit of women. When Bertie was a young man it was forgivable, but now that he was nearly fifty, there was something rather ridiculous in a squat fat man behaving like a young Casanova.

She decided to go to Copenhagen for a visit and take her two youngest daughters, Victoria and Maud, with her. It was pleasant to be in the old home but the health of her parents worried her, that of her mother particularly. Queen Louise was very feeble and now completely deaf. All the same it was pleasant showing her daughters the old haunts and telling them about her own happy childhood.

When the time came to leave Copenhagen Alix was in no mood to return to Sandringham. She wanted Bertie to understand that while he could be very happy without her, so could she be without him. He very much enjoyed the company of other women; she enjoyed that of her family; and as she had had a very pressing invitation from Dagmar she had decided to take her daughters to see their aunt at her villa Livadia on the Black Sea.

Poor Bertie was nonplussed. Sandringham seemed empty although he had filled it with his noisy friends.

He no longer enjoyed the shooting; there was no point in having the clocks half an hour fast and that small matter seemed to change Sandringham completely. When he saw George and Eddy they kept talking about Mother dear and asking when she was coming home and what had possessed her to go straight to Russia after staying in Copenhagen. Why didn't she come home to them?

Even Daisy couldn't restore the Prince's good humour. Daisy was beautiful, witty, astringent, but nothing seemed the same without Alix's tolerant good-humour. And, he kept remembering, she had been a little aloof over the Tranby Croft affair.

He started to fret about the family. Eddy had always given him some concern because he could never learn anything. It was not that Bertie wished his son to be a scholar, he himself had never been that; but Eddy simply could not absorb anything; he could scarcely read and he was quite slow-witted. It was alarming to contemplate that he could be King one day. George was the bright one. He had always outshone Eddy; and he was a good boy, conscientious and humble too. Louise was now married to the Duke of Fife and the Prince wondered whether he was too old for her. She was twenty-two; he was forty. The Duke was a friend of Bertie's; he was rich, had been a Member of Parliament and was a good man of business. The Queen had approved of the match and had in fact bestowed his Dukedom on him at the time of his marriage—although she had to be persuaded to do so. The two other girls, Victoria and Maud, were with their mother. Did they know of her disappointment in him and would it affect their feelings towards him?

He was discovering that he was very much a family man. It was true he loved wild parties, and passionate friendships with women were essential to him; but he wanted Alix there in the background of his life, and he knew now how much he loved his family. He had always been kind and tolerant to them; making sure that they should never feel towards him as he had towards his own father, but he had not realized before how necessary they were to him. Sandringham had become lonely; the flowers didn't look the same. Alix loved them and had done quite a lot of the arranging herself. Her dogs were moping; there was in fact a melancholy air about the place. Bertie wanted Alix to come home. It seemed as if the whole place was crying out for her.

One day a fire broke out in the house and there was a possibility that it would be completely destroyed. That seemed fitting, he thought. Everything had changed. If Sandringham went it would seem like a part of his married life being wiped out. It was symbolic. The house was saved although quite a number of their valuable possessions were lost. Nothing went right without Alix.

George was not well. Bertie worried a great deal about the boys and more so now that Alix was away. During a house party at Sandringham at which George was present, Bertie noticed that the young man was unduly flushed and seemed a little vague, which was unlike George.

Bertie was afraid that his son had a fever and since his own attack and those which Leopold had suffered, and of course the death of their father, Bertie was always alarmed when one of the children showed signs of a high temperature.

He told his friends that the house party was over. He thought George needed quiet and he certainly could not have that with a house full of guests. He was going to take George to London.

No sooner were they installed in Marlborough House than the doctors diagnosed enteric fever.

Bertie was distraught; but at least it gave him the chance to send for Alix.

The thought of her beloved son in danger brought Alix with the girls in great haste back to London. By this time George was beginning to recover and there was great rejoicing. Bertie, delighted to have Alix back, had no desire to see Lady Brooke—in fact he had no desire to be anywhere but in the heart of his family.

Alix was happy; but experience had taught her that it was a state of affairs which would not last. Bertie would continue to be the kind, tender and considerate husband; but nothing could wean him from his pursuit of beautiful women.

At the end of that year Alix had a surprise which made her very happy. Eddy had been spending a few days at Luton Hoo where the Danish ambassador and his wife were having a house party. Alix's old friend Princess Mary of Teck was there with her daughter May. May was a forthright girl, quite attractive and of course royal. She had naturally been a friend of Alix's children all her life for Alix and Mary had never forgotten those early days at Rumpenheim, and often talked of them.

So what a pleasure it was when Eddy wrote that he had asked May to marry him and she had agreed.

Bertie was all for celebrating the occasion, when Alix reminded him that it would first be necessary to get the Queen's consent.

"She'll give it. She's fond of May," said Bertie.

"Yes, but no one must be told before she has given it. You know how she hates to be left out of these matters."

So Bertie went to see the Queen at Windsor.

Memories of Tranby Croft still rankled and the Queen's greeting was cool, but when he told her that Eddy wished to marry May of Teck she smiled.

"An excellent arrangement," she said. "Dear Eddy needs a *strong* wife and he'll get one in May. She's well educated and of good character. I believe she helps her mother who is devoted to good works. A good steadying influence."

The engagement was announced and there was a house party at Sandringham to celebrate it.

How different, thought Bertie, from what it had been like recently! All the damage occasioned by the fire had been put right and it was just like the old Sandringham, with the clocks half an hour fast and Alix still not being punctual. Bertie chided her affectionately and they laughed about her inability to overcome it.

"I'm glad you have it," said Bertie. "It's just a little something to set against all my sins."

Alix was happier than she had been since the early days of her marriage. Her darling Eddy—whom she could not help loving more than any of her other children, perhaps because he was her first-born, perhaps because he was a little simple and not as clever as his brother and sisters and therefore seemed to need her care—now had dear capable May to look after him; and it was wonderful to think that Mary's daughter and her son should be united. It brought those early days at Rumpenheim into greater significance. And in the far distant future Eddy would be King of England and May Queen.

It was a bitterly cold winter and one or two people at the house party developed influenza. This was a particularly virulent type and quite a number of the guests were smitten with it. Princess May had a bad cold and her mother insisted that she remain in the house. It was not long before Eddy caught it.

Alix was an excellent nurse and she did not realize at once that this was any more than an ordinary attack but in a day or so the doctors began to show some alarm and it was clear that Eddy had something more than ordinary influenza. They were soon talking about the approach of the crisis; and then it became widely known that the Duke of Clarence was very ill indeed.

Alix was frantic. Her best-loved first-born was in danger. Eddy lay listlessly in bed; he had never had a great deal of mental or physical energy and now it all seemed to have deserted him.

The crisis came; Eddy did not rally. It was incredible. He could not be dying. He was a young man who had just become engaged to be married.

She stood by his bed and saw life slowly ebb away. She felt numb with misery. Eddy . . . gone.

The nation was stunned. He was so young. He had not been sickly. It had seeped out that he was no intellectual giant and that his inability to learn had worried his family and tutors. But death was the last thing that had been expected.

She knew that some zest had gone out of her; nothing would ever be quite the same again. She had lost her beloved son; her husband was not what she had dreamed romantically that a husband should be; she could not view the future with any great joy. She loved the simple life; her happiest days had been spent at Sandringham with her family, without the crowds of noisy smart people with whom Bertie so liked to surround himself; that life was not for her. The Queen was growing old. Surely even she could not live much longer and when she died great responsibilities would descend upon her and Bertie.

There was another one whose life would be changed; her son George. Dear George, who had always been such a devoted son and had longed so much to have the place in her heart which she had given to Eddy! George had always been so much more worthy—a good boy, hard-working, not really clever—only seeming so in comparison with Eddy—and now he had taken a step towards the throne.

She asked George to come to her and when he did she embraced him tenderly.

"Darling George," she said, "you know what this means? We have lost dearest Eddy and you are now the eldest son."

"I know, Mother dear. I shall have to work hard. I shall have to try to be worthy."

She smiled at him. "My dear, good, quiet George, you will be worthy. That is one thing of which I have no doubt whatsoever."

How she wished that the funeral could be quiet. She told Bertie that it would be a comfort if their dear boy could be buried in Sandringham churchyard. He had loved Sandringham, as they all had.

Bertie shook his head. "There'll have to be a grand funeral in St George's Chapel. Don't forget Eddy was in line for the throne. But we'll have a memorial service in Sandringham and that will be the family occasion."

The Queen was horrified. Eddy dead. How tragic! Poor dear sweet Alix! The Queen embraced her when she came in answer to a summons.

"My dearest child, my heart bleeds for you."

Dear sweet Alix! How lovely she looked in black! The colour suited her. She was a beautiful woman and seemed to look elegant on every occasion.

"Dear Mama," said Alix, "you must not go to the funeral."

"I should be there, my dear child."

"No, no, Mama. These bitter winds are dangerous. It is standing about in the cold at funerals which causes many people to be ill."

The Queen allowed herself to be persuaded. She disliked those occasions in any case and to tell the truth Eddy had not been a great favourite of hers. She preferred George; and she had felt some anxieties about Eddy's being King when she and his father were gone. She did not think he had the stamina nor the sharp mind to be a good ruler. When she considered the manner in which one was beset on all sides by politicians she realized fully the special qualities required by a monarch. Eddy definitely lacked these; Bertie had a certain dignity which would carry him through; besides he was going to be very mature before the Crown came to him. George could be moulded; George was very much aware of his duty. He was brighter than poor Eddy had been. She mourned for the poor boy but mostly for dear sweet Alix who was clearly so stricken.

She tried to comfort her with accounts of her own grief when she had lost her dear Saint. She had also lost two children—Alice her dear dear daughter, and Leopold whom she had come to believe had been her favourite son.

"We all have to suffer, dear Alix. And you have darling George to comfort you."

The Queen faced fresh trials. Lord Salisbury's government

was defeated and she had no alternative but to invite Mr Gladstone to form a new government. How very trying! Mr Gladstone hobbled in on a stick and, as she herself found she was unable to walk without a stick, a faint smile touched her lips.

"You and I, Mr Gladstone, are lamer than we used to be," she said.

Mr Gladstone, respectful as ever, smiled ruefully. But she had no intention of letting him think that she felt any more friendly towards him. The fact that he was old did not endear him to her. He was still that dreadful Mr Gladstone. He was so pale and shrunken that he looked as though he should be in his grave already. At his age he should know better than to cling to office. She was highly suspicious of him expressing his noble sentiments and so anxious all the time to be Prime Minister—though clearly unfit. G.O.M. Grand old man! Gom. It sounded wicked said like that. And with his dreadful Home Rule ideas and his preoccupation with prostitutes . . . he made her very wary.

Still there was nothing she could do but accept him and hope that the people would soon come back to their senses. She could never hope for another Lord Melbourne dear Disraeli or clever Sir Robert Peel; but Lord Salisbury had been quite effective and she hoped it would not be long before he returned.

She was convinced that Mr Gladstone was quite mad. He now wanted to bring into the Cabinet a man with an evil reputation. This was Henry Labouchere who owned the newspaper *Truth* which had made a practice of lampooning and criticizing the royal family. Labouchere was a most immoral man; it was rumoured that he had lived with Mrs Labouchere for some years before he had married her, which, said the Queen, made him quite unfit for her Cabinet. She would not accept him and she could not understand how Mr Gladstone could expect her to. She would have thought *Mrs* Gladstone would have explained if he did not understand himself; but then she doubted Mrs Gladstone had much say in affairs. Poor Mrs Gladstone!

She insisted that if this man—ridiculously known as Labby—wished to be in *her* Cabinet he must give up his paper *Truth*; she knew very well he would never do this.

So in a way she had scored a victory over Mr Gladstone and his strange friends. Although as she pointed out to her secretary, good faithful Ponsonby, that was not the relationship a monarch looked for in her Ministers.

Her seventy-fourth birthday arrived. How old I am! she thought. There could not be much longer left to her. She was tired in any case and her rheumatism was so bad that there were often days when she could not walk. She had a cataract on her eyes which was making it increasingly difficult to read. She thought of waltzing with Albert, although he had never really liked dancing. But to her that had been sheer bliss. She thought of Brown's strong arms carrying her from couch to bed.

Life had lost its savour.

The Queen had created Prince George Duke of York. It was necessary now that his position had changed. Dear George, he had much preferred to be the second son; but now he was taking his duties very seriously.

His sister the Duchess of Fife invited him to Sheen Lodge to a house party and who should be there but Princess May, now seeming to have recovered from the loss of her fiancé.

George asked her to marry him and to the delight of everyone she accepted.

"How very convenient," said the Queen. "Dear George, he is clearly aware of his duty."

They were very soon married in the Chapel Royal at St James's in the presence of the Queen.

The Diamond Jubilee

The Queen had been on the throne for sixty years. This was a cause for great celebration. There must be a glittering Diamond Jubilee.

She was seventy-eight; she was old and tired; and life, she was fond of saying, had not been easy. But this was an occasion which even she could not evade.

The last few years had been a trial to her. Gladstone's government had been defeated and replaced by that of Lord Rosebery; and now Lord Salisbury was back in office again.

A very sad event had happened. Beatrice's husband Prince Henry of Battenberg had volunteered for active service in Ashanti. She would never forget poor Beatrice's sorrow when he left; and the fact that they had lived with the Queen made this all the harder to bear. Poor darling Baby, how very sad for her! Henry had been sent home with a fever—how that dreaded fever in some form or other took its toll of her family!—and he had died on the way. But Baby had her dear children to support her. It was ironical. Poor Beatrice and Henry had been happy whereas Louise and Argyll were far from that and there had been a great deal of talk because Louise had refused to stay with him in Canada.

The Czar of Russia had become very ill and Dagmar, Alix's sister, who had always dominated him since the assassination of his father, was very anxious. Her son Nicholas had married Alicky, Alice's daughter—a beautiful girl, so intelligent and self-sufficient, as she had had to be, poor darling, since she had been so young when her mother had died. Alicky was one of the Queen's favourite grandchildren and she was pleased to see her so well married, although she did doubt whether great crowns were always a blessing.

So life went on—the grandchildren became parents in their turn and had their grandchildren; and she seemed to go on living. Sometimes she wondered whether she was indestructible; and yet how sadly she felt her age at times. But she could still enjoy having the family round her; she liked the children as long as they were not little babies who always reminded her of frogs and had tiresome habits such as dribbling and even more unpleasant ones; but as they began to grow up they were sometimes delightful. It had been a joy to have a visit from Alicky with Nicky her husband and their baby girl; it was very pleasant to see George and May together. What a blessing they so fortuitously had fallen in love after the death of poor Eddy, and had two sweet little boys already.

And now she had reigned longer than any English monarch—even longer than her mad grandfather King George III. There must be a celebration such as the people had never seen before. This was one of the occasions when she must agree that there must be no concession to age, fatigue or dislike of ceremonies. This was to be the Diamond Jubilee.

She had been feeling very dejected during the last days because Annie MacDonald, who had served her as wardrobe maid for more than thirty years, had been taken very ill and she knew her to be dying. Annie was the one with whom, as with John Brown, she had felt herself to be so much at home. Like John Brown, Annie had never flattered her but always spoken the truth even if it was critical. She trusted Annie and now she knew that when she returned to Windsor Annie would not be there.

She went to see her before she left.

"So you're going to London?" rasped Annie.

The Queen said: "It's my jubilee, Annie."

"Mind you wrap up well. Those bitter winds . . ."

"It's June, Annie. It's the heat I fear."

But Annie's eyes were glazed. She was far away in the days when she and John Brown used to scold their mistress for not taking great care of herself.

Another faithful creature lost!

She travelled from Balmoral to Windsor for a service at St

George's Chapel on the 20th of June, which was the actual date sixty years before when she had acceded to the throne.

The next day she took the train to London.

The Jubilee celebration took place on the 22nd of June. The sun shone brilliantly as the Queen left Buckingham Palace and began the circular tour of her city. She had been determined that the pageantry should stress the significance of Empire. Prime Ministers of the colonies; armed forces culled from all over the world where the British flag flew; delegates from all the dependencies. The troops which formed part of the colourful procession were from Australia, South Africa and Canada; there were Indians who looked magnificent in their brilliant uniforms; soldiers from Africa, Hongkong, Borneo and Cyprus. All the world must know that she was indeed an Empress.

From the Palace the cavalcade went to St Paul's where a service was conducted; and after that began the great tour.

In the Park the guns boomed; in the streets the people cheered. London had gone wild with enthusiasm for the longest reign. The Queen, always easily moved, was in tears as she read the loyal greetings on banners stretched across even the poorest streets. "She wrought her people's lasting good," said one. What a glorious epitaph! Albert would have been proud. "Our Hearts Thy Throne," said another. What loyal loving messages! It had been a wonderful reign. She could rejoice. But she had had such wonderful support during her long reign. Lord Melbourne, dearest *dearest* Albert, Sir Robert Peel, clever Disraeli and now Lord Salisbury who was very adequate; and she must not forget—nor would she ever—those who worked behind the scenes, her dear good Annie MacDonald who had been unselfish in her service and dear kind faithful John Brown whose strong arm she so sadly missed even now.

Dear people! Happy day! It was a wonderful thing to have lived so long; to have been a Queen and at the end—for she knew she was very close to that—to hear her people say "Our Hearts Thy Throne."

There had been great progress during the time she had been on the throne. The electric light and the telephone had been introduced. What wonderful inventions! And before setting out on her historic journey round her capital she had pressed an electric button which had telegraphed her message to all parts of the Empire.

"From my heart I thank my beloved people. May God bless them."

Bertie sat beside her—squat, square and comforting. Bertie was always at his best on such occasions. The people cheered him too. "Good old Teddy!" His sins were very easily forgiven. Who but Bertie could have sailed triumphantly through the Mordaunt and Baccarat cases and all the rumors of profligacy and extravagance to be the people's "Good old Teddy"? How strange people were. They had never shouted like that—with genuine affection—for Albert who had been so good and devoted himself to their service; and, although they had the deepest respect for their Queen and an affection for her in a remote kind of way, it was Bertie who was their Good Old Teddy, Bertie who had their warm-hearted love.

That was good because Bertie would soon be their King. King Edward VII—and she had once so wanted it to be King Albert; now that did not seem so important. What did matter was that the people loved Bertie; they would accept Bertie; and they had a great affection for their Queen.

It was the most tiring and most gratifying day of her life.

The End of an Era

This was the dawn of a new century—the twentieth. She would not have believed she could have lived to see the end of the 1800s. More than eighty years had passed since she had been born in Kensington Palace and there had been that momentous christening in the cupola room when Uncle King had refused to allow her to be called Elizabeth or Georgiana.

"Victoria," he had said. And they had been angry because Victoria was not a Queen's name. So they had said then; they could not have said that now, for there had never been a more queenly name and she had made it so.

How tired she was and old now, how old! So stiff with the rheumatic pains that she could not move without her stick and often had to be wheeled about the Palace. She smiled to think of her Diamond Jubilee when she had been wheeled on to the balcony because the loyal crowds would not be satisfied without a glimpse of her.

"Go it, old Girl!" someone had shouted. So blunt, yet so loving. It reminded her of faithful John Brown.

Now she was the head of a large family. She had lost three children—Alice, Leopold and so recently Alfred. Dear Vicky she feared was very ill and some of the doctors had hinted at the dreaded cancer, in this instance of the spine. Such sorrow for a mother of over eighty to have to endure! There were so many grandchildren all with their own problems, all with their own complicated lives to be lived.

Dear Mary of Teck, May's mother, had died soon after the Jubilee, a sad blow; she had always loved big Mary with her rather careless attitude to life and her kind heart. Poor Alix felt her loss deeply for they had always been such friends and now the marriage of George and May had made that bond even closer.

And the next year had seen the passing of Mr Gladstone. It was about time, of course, for he was a very old man.

"I cannot say that I think he was a great Englishman," she had said. "Clever he was, talented, but he had no notion of the honour and prestige of the Empire. I shall never forget that he gave up the Transvaal and the way in which he abandoned that great patriot General Gordon of Khartum. He started a kind of class war. I fear he did a great deal of harm. I am always sorry for *poor* Mrs Gladstone!"

All the same she was rather glad she had shaken hands with him just before his life ended. It was the first time he had ever received such a favour from her.

Then of course there had been that terrible conflict with the Jameson Raid when Wilhelm had behaved so disgracefully and sent a telegram to President Kruger congratulating him on keeping his independence in spite of the British Imperialists. How angry they had been with Wilhelm whose hatred of the British Empire and in particular of Bertie was intense. Had she felt stronger she would have liked to summon this recalcitrant grandson to tell him how his arrogance displeased her and how hurt and angry his beloved dead sainted Grandpapa Prince Albert would have been had he been alive, and that she could be almost glad that he was not since thus he was spared the grief he would have been made to suffer by such an ungrateful grandson. The Jameson Raid was one of the causes she was sure of that terrible Boer War when everything seemed to go against them and in favour of those horrid, cruel, over-bearing Boers. It was said that the whole world was on their side; and a dreadful thing had happened to Bertie and Alix who after visiting Alix's father were in the train at Brussels when a mad youth tried to shoot them. It was true the crowd on the platform would have torn the boy to pieces had not Bertie stepped out of the train and begged them not to harm him. A court of law was where he should be taken, said Bertie; and such was his presence and his way with the people that although they were foreigners and he a representative of the most hated country in the world (at that time) they obeyed him. Of course the boy turned out to be an anarchist and in the service of the Boer supporters, but it was a horrible incident and did show how very unpopular Britain had grown.

The fatal 14th of December had come and she had visited the mausoleum at Frogmore and thought as she always did on the occasion of her wedding day and in contrast that dreadful 14th when she had sat at his bedside and been too stunned to realize the truth.

Then she travelled down to Osborne, the house he had loved and designed; and she thought of his pride when they had gone there for the first time and he had shown her how his ideas had been carried out; and how the whole household had gathered together and he had sung the German hymn about blessing the house.

She was not ill, but tired. Her rheumatism had grown worse and she could scarcely see to read—which was most trying of all. She had had at last to agree to wear spectacles for reading, but they were tiresome and not much good.

On the 15th of January she took a drive. She felt happier about the situation in South Africa where Lord Roberts had done so well and Lord Kitchener was proving so effective; but when she returned from her drive she felt so weak that she decided to go to bed.

Her doctors thought that the family should be sent for; they came, the sons, the daughters, the grandchildren. Bertie was in tears; he could not believe that his mother, who had dominated his life, was about to die. There had been so many differences between them but the family bond had grown strong with the years. They had at last learned to understand each other.

Wilhelm arrived, even his arrogance subdued; he waited humbly in corridors hoping for a chance of seeing his grandmother before she died.

In the streets bulletins were issued; a solemn hush had fallen over everything.

"The Queen is dying," said the people.

It could not be; she was the great figure-head, the symbol. The Queen had always been on the throne as long as they could remember. More than sixty years she had reigned over them. She could not be going now.

She lay in her bed. She could not remember exactly where she was. Sometimes she thought she was walking in the gardens of Kensington Palace with Lehzen, a bright, plump little girl who had just discovered that she might one day be Queen. "I will be good," she had said. Good Queen Victoria! "Victoria is not a Queen's name," her mother had said. It was now. The great Queen's name—as great as Elizabeth. But that Queen had not always been good. Perhaps Victoria had not been but she had always tried to be.

She thought of storms with Mama whom she had later learned to love and understand; and Albert, dearest beloved Albert, who had guided her and made her what she was before he left her desolate. She hoped no one would mourn her as long and bitterly as she had mourned Albert.

All the figures of the past filed slowly through her mind— gay, solemn, good and bad. Mama, Lehzen, dear Lord Melbourne, Flora Hastings (Oh, the nightmares that woman had given her!), Sir Robert Peel, Disraeli, Mr Gladstone, honest John Brown, Annie MacDonald so recently lost, Alice, Leopold, Alfred, those babies whom she had nursed and her darling Albert whom she had never ceased to mourn.

He would be waiting for her. She knew he would. He would take her hand as he had on their wedding day and he would smile at her. *"Gutes Frauchen,"* he would say.

"It is the end," whispered Bertie and he covered his face with his hands and wept.

Her favourite doctor, Dr Reid, supported her on one side, Wilhelm on the other.

Her children and her grandchildren waited to be summoned to say farewell, but she was past knowing them. She lay half conscious, her eyes glazed, far far away in the past, waiting to step into the future.

Slowly life left her. A faint smile touched her lips; she was calm and her face seemed suddenly to grow young again.

At half past six in the evening she died.

A pall had settled over the nation. "The Queen is dead," the cry went up. The nation had suffered a great disaster. The indomitable little figure, the great Queen and Empress, was dead; and with her, it was believed, she had taken something of great value.

All had been well while she remained at the helm—the legendary figure who could subdue the country's enemies, who could castigate the tiresome Russians, who could call her mischief-making German grandson to order, who could reduce Bertie to the state of a naughty boy in the nursery. But now the great Queen was no more.

"We have lost our beloved Mother," was the cry. "The Queen is dead. Nothing will ever be the same again."

Bibliography

V.R.I. Queen Victoria, Her life and Empire
The Duke of Argyle

History of England
William Hickman Smith Aubrey

Edward VII and his Circle
Virginia Cowles

Victoria in the Highlands
The Personal Journal of Her Majesty Queen Victoria, with Notes and Introductions and a Description of the Acquisition and Rebuilding of Balmoral Castle
David Duff

The Tragedy of Edward VII
A Psychological Study
W. H. Edwards, translated from the German

Dearest Mama
Letters between Queen Victoria and Crown Princess of Prussia, 1861–1864
Edited by Roger Fulford

Edward the Seventh
Catherine Gavin

The Greville Memoirs
A Journal of the Reign of Queen Victoria
Charles C. H. Greville (Edited by Henry Reeve)

The Greville Diary
(Edited by Philip Whitwell Wilson)

King Edward in his True Colours
Edward Legge

Victoria R.I.
Elizabeth Longford

The Private Life of Queen Alexandra — Hans Roger Madol

King Edward the Seventh — Philip Magnus

Queen Victoria, a Personal Sketch — Mrs Oliphant

Britain's Prime Ministers — E. Royston Pike

Victoria of England — Edith Sitwell

Life of Her Majesty Queen Victoria — G. Barnett Smith

The Prime Ministers of Queen Victoria — G. Barnett Smith

Queen Victoria — Lytton Strachey

Dictionary of National Biography — Edited by Sir Leslie Stephen and Sir Sidney Lee

Unpredictable Queen
The Intimate Life of Queen Alexandra — E. E. P. Tisdall

The Personal Life of Queen Victoria — Sarah A. Tooley

The Life of Queen Alexandra — Sarah A. Tooley

More Leaves from the Journal of a Life in the Highlands from 1862 to 1882 — Queen Victoria

Queen Alexandra, The Well-Beloved — Elizabeth Villiers

The People's King
A Short Life of Edward VII — W. Holt-White

Edward the Peacemaker
The Life of Edward VII and his Queen — W. H. Wilkins

H.R.H. The Prince of Wales — Anonymous